C000215775

THE SEEDS OF POWER

Book One of The Russian Quartet

Further Titles by Christopher Nicole from Severn House

Black Majesty Series

BOOK ONE: BLACK MAJESTY
BOOK TWO: WILD HARVEST

The Dawson Family Saga

BOOK ONE: DAYS OF WINE AND ROSES?
BOOK TWO: THE TITANS
BOOK THREE: RESUMPTION
BOOK FOUR: THE LAST BATTLE

The McGann Family Saga

BOOK ONE: OLD GLORY
BOOK TWO: THE SEA AND THE SAND
BOOK THREE: IRON SHIPS, IRON MEN
BOOK FOUR: WIND OF DESTINY
BOOK FIVE: RAGING SUN, SEARING SKY
BOOK SIX: THE PASSION AND THE GLORY

BLOODY SUNRISE
BLOODY SUNSET
CARIBEE
THE FRIDAY SPY
HEROES
QUEEN OF PARIS
SHIP WITH NO NAME
THE SUN AND THE DRAGON
THE SUN ON FIRE

The Russian Quartet

BOOK ONE: THE SEEDS OF POWER

THE SEEDS
OF POWER

Book One of The Russian Quartet

Christopher Nicole

523187

MORAY DISTRICT COUNCIL
DEPARTMENT OF
LEISURE AND LIBRARIES

This first world edition published in Great Britain 1994 by
SEVERN HOUSE PUBLISHERS LTD of
9–15 High Street, Sutton, Surrey SM1 1DF.
First published in the USA 1995 by
SEVERN HOUSE PUBLISHERS INC, of
425 Park Avenue, New York, NY 10022.

Copyright © 1994 by Christopher Nicole

All rights reserved.
The moral rights of the author have been asserted.

British Library Cataloguing in Publication Data

A full CIP record for this title is held at the British Library

  ISBN 0-7278-4691-4

All situations in this publication are fictitious and
any resemblance to living persons is purely coincidental.

Typeset by Hewer Text Composition Services, Edinburgh.
Printed and bound in Great Britain by
Hartnolls Ltd, Bodmin, Cornwall.

AUTHOR'S NOTE

THE SEEDS OF POWER is the first of a four-book
fictional history of a Russian family, covering the
century from 1853–1953.

"The will is free;
Strong is the soul, and wise, and beautiful;
The seeds of godlike power are in us still;
Gods are we, bards, saints, heroes, if we will!"

Sir Edwin Arnold
Written in a copy of Emerson's
Essays.

CONTENTS

PROLOGUE

The trumpet blared, and the horses trotted out of the drive of Blaistone Manor, following the pack of dogs, already yelping with excitement. The riders made a vast splash of colour against the green of the meadows, blue and red, tall hat and cap, hallooing to each other. Behind them, the servants streamed out of the yard, making across the broken ground for various vantage points; the villagers would already be in position, to oversee the hunt.

Colin MacLain's sympathies were entirely on the side of the fox – but as a cornet in the 11th Hussars, the famed Cherry-Pickers, as well as the nephew-in-law of Lord Blaistone, he was expected to take part, and indeed to lead the cavalry charge like the horseman he was. Today he wore civilian clothes, red jacket and white breeches. But Colin MacLain wore any clothes well. Six feet tall, dark-haired and well-shouldered, he had slim hips and long legs. His face was a trifle long and inclined to be serious, but he waved and smiled at his companions. The hounds began to bay as the hunt charged downhill towards a distant copse. One of the riders pulled aside from the group, and rode to the left, seeking the shorter, steeper route. "It's that damned Russkie!" Lord Blaistone shouted. "He'll be in Three-mile Bottom before he knows it. Colin, fetch him back!"

Colin pulled his horse aside and directed it to the left of the hunt-track. It was a matter of clearing several low hedgerows as well as scattering through muddy patches, before he reached the bottom of the slope. In front of him was the deep bog which was avoided by any rider who knew the surrounding countryside.

But the Russian visitor did not know this country, and he and his horse had galloped straight into the mire. Colin took in the situation at a glance as he pulled on his reins. The horse, already half submerged in the oozing black mud, had broken its neck going over. Its rider had been pitched some twelve feet from the bank, and had regained his feet, his hat gone and his head and shoulders covered in mud; he was already waist deep, and with every attempt he made to gain the bank he sank deeper. "Keep still, for God's sake!" Colin shouted.

The Russian seemed to notice him for the first time. "Then get me out!" he bawled in good English.

Colin dismounted, and looked to the left and right. There were no trees close by, and he had no rope. He was considering his alternatives when he heard feet behind him. "Took a fair old tumble, he did, Mr MacLain," the girl panted; she had been running.

Colin looked down at her. He recalled that she was one of the scullery maids at the Manor. She was not an easy young woman to forget, for with her curling red-brown hair and her full body went an extremely attractive, finely-chiselled but strong face. "He's going down," she said.

"Help me!" shouted the Russian, who was now embedded almost to his chest.

Colin unsaddled his horse, and took off his jacket to tie it to the harness. "That'll not reach him," the girl said.

"No, it won't," he agreed, and sat down to pull off his boots before dropping his breeches. The girl hastily looked away. Colin tied one leg of his breeches to a sleeve of his jacket, held on to the other leg, and swung the improvised rope round his head. The Russian grabbed at it, but it

2

fell a good four feet short, and now he had sunk to his shoulders.

Colin pulled the clothes back in. He could use his belt as well, but he knew that wasn't going to reach either. That left him with his shirt, which was not of very strong material, or . . . "I'll need your gown."

The girl gazed at him, carefully keeping her eyes from drooping to his drawers and exposed legs, her cheeks pink. "Or the man will die," Colin said.

"I've nothing else," she protested.

"Would you stand here and watch it happen?"

The girl drew a deep breath and scooped her gown from around her thighs and lifted it over her head. Hastily Colin turned away from her, and tied the top of the gown on to the other trouser leg. Then he tied his belt, which was of leather with a heavy buckle, on to the hem of the gown, reversing his previous arrangement as the harness was slippery with mud. "Catch the belt!" he shouted, wrapping his hands in the rein and again swirling the improvised rope round his head. "Hold on!" Without the bridle Colin could not control his horse. "You'll have to help me," he told the girl.

She stood beside him, bare shoulder against his shirt, as they heaved on the makeshift rope. Sweat streamed down their faces, as the man began to move. "It's going to rip," the girl gasped.

"He's coming."

The Russian had emerged to his thighs, and was being drawn across the surface of the mire. He had travelled only a few feet when there was a tearing sound, and both Colin and the girl fell, the remnants of her gown settling on the bank.

The Russian was almost within reach. He scrambled up, grasped the gown, and threw the other end, together with the bridle and reins, across the mud. "Got it," he grunted, grasping the reins.

"Come on," Colin said. "Heave!"

3

The girl put her arms round his waist to lend her weight to his, and with a great squelching sound the Russian gained the bank, bringing with him the rest of Colin's clothes and the remnants of the girl's gown. He crawled up the bank, and fell on his face, panting. Colin sat down, equally exhausted, leaning against the girl, who had also fallen down. For several seconds the only sound was of their breathing, and the nervous stamping of Colin's horse.

"I'll buy you a new gown," Colin said when he had got his breath back. "What's your name?"

"Jennie, sir. Jennie Cromb."

"Your father works for his lordship?"

"My father is dead, Mr MacLain. But my mother is one of the laundrywomen at the manor, yes."

Colin nodded. "I'll speak with her. She can't whip you for saving a man's life."

"You don't know my Ma," Jennie Cromb muttered.

The Russian raised his head, and wiped some mud from his face. He was a young man, not greatly older than Colin himself, and was quite personable in a stocky, barrel-chested, big-featured manner. Now he grinned. "*I* will buy the young lady a new gown," he said. "As it was my life she saved."

"You're very kind, I'm sure, sir," Jennie said, and for the first time seemed to realise that she was sitting between two men, naked. "I must hurry." She untied the remnants of her gown.

"Take my jacket," Colin suggested, untying the mud-stained garment in turn and handing it to her.

She stroked the material. "Oh, sir, I couldn't."

He smiled at her. "You must, or you'll have them hunting you instead of the fox."

She put the jacket on, thrusting her arms into the sleeves and pulling the whole across her chest. "I am grateful, sir." She hurried up the slope.

"Wait!" the Russian shouted. "You can't just run off. You do not even know my name."

4

"But you know mine, sir," Jennie reminded him, and went up the hill.

The Russian remained kneeling, gazing after her; her legs were as white as her breasts, and the hunting tunic uncovered her buttocks as she moved. "By God, what a beauty!" He glanced at Colin. "You are Lieutenant MacLain. We met last night."

"That is correct, sir," Nicholas said, pulling on his breeches. "And you are Count Georgei Bolugayevski."

"Spoken like a Russian." Bolugayevski rose to his feet and held out his hand. "I owe you my life."

Colin squeezed the offered fingers. "And his lordship one good horse."

"He has others," Bolugayevski said carelessly. "Will your mount seat two?"

"Not to follow the hunt, I think, Count. Besides, you should have a hot bath." He replaced the bridle, mounted, and gave the Russian his arm to get him up behind, then turned his horse to walk back towards the manor.

"That bog came upon me suddenly," Bolugayevski remarked. "But you must have known it was there."

"I was sent after you by his lordship," Colin said.

"Ah! Then I owe everyone my life, it appears. That girl seemed to know you?"

"Well, I suppose she does, in a manner of speaking. I have stayed here before. His lordship is my uncle."

"Ah!" Bolugayevski said again. "Does that girl belong to him? I mean, is she his serf?"

"Well, no, I wouldn't say that. We don't have serfs in England."

Bolugayevski appeared to consider this. "I would like her," he said.

"Whatever for? She's a scullery maid."

"I am not the least interested in her employment, Lieutenant. I would like her for my bed. She is a fine looking woman."

"She is that, but not really in your class, Count."

5

"I was not considering marrying the girl, Lieutenant. Do you suppose his lordship would sell her to me?"

Colin turned his head. "Sell her? She's not a slave. I told you, we don't have serfs in this country."

"Then how does one get hold of a woman?"

"Good lord! I don't know. I mean, if it was someone you intended to marry . . . but a scullery maid. You'd have to ask her, I suppose."

"And would she say yes, do you suppose?"

Colin grinned. "I think that one would very likely slap your face, Count."

"By God, sir, you are lucky to be alive," Lord Blaistone said in his habitual shout. He sat at the head of his dinner table and looked down to his wife at the far end. In between, their guests sparkled with starched white shirt-fronts, bare shoulders, and jewels. Wine flowed and the conversation was animated. The Count's adventure had added an extra event to an eventful day.

"But Colin was there," declared Lady Joanna Brewster. "Weren't you, Colin? You are a hero."

"Will you reward the girl, my lord?" the Count asked. He was seated on Blaistone's right, and could speak in a lower tone than the others.

"I'll give her a tip," Blaistone agreed. "And a new gown, by God! Ha ha!"

"Do you not think I should also do this? I must replace her gown, at the least. As you know, sir, I depart England two days from now. I should be distressed to do so without seeing her again, to give her my thanks.

"Permit me to visit her."

Blaistone raised his eyebrows. "You wish to go to one of my tenant's cottages? I doubt you'll find it very edifying."

"My lord, my father also has tenants. A vast number of them."

Blaistone gave him an old-fashioned look. "Tenants, or serfs?"

6

Bolugayevski shrugged. "It is all a point of view."

"Harrumph," Blaistone commented. "Yes, by all means visit Mrs Cromb, Count. You may learn something of interest," he added under his breath.

Colin MacLain threw his cards into the centre of the baize-topped table. "I am afraid I am not doing very well."

"You're not concentrating," Lady Joanna told him, severely. "You're brooding on that Russian fellow."

"Oh, really, I am not," Colin protested. If he was not concentrating, it was because he kept remembering Jennie Cromb's body, the length of her legs, the splendour of her hair, the entrancing stain of the vee at her crotch, the swell of her quite magnificent breasts . . . he had never seen a more compelling sight.

"Well," Joanna said, "whether you were thinking of him or not, he is clearly thinking of you." She nodded to the doorway of the card room.

Colin turned his head and saw the Russian standing there. "Deal me out of this hand," he told Lord Tapham, and got up. "You look as if you are going somewhere," he said, turning to the Count.

"I have decided to leave tonight," Bolugayevski said, leading him into the drawing room. "Do not worry, I have said goodbye to Lord and Lady Blaistone."

"Yes, but are you sure you should go any distance tonight, Count?" Colin asked. "You're probably more shaken up than you realise."

"I must be in London tomorrow, and as you say, I am all shaken up. Thus I shall not sleep." Bolugayevski held out his hand. "It has been a great pleasure meeting you, Lieutenant. And I can never forget that I owe you my life. If I can ever repay you, be sure that I will do so. Again, goodbye. You will always be my friend. Oh, by the way . . ." he picked up a mudstained pink hunting jacket from where it was lying in the chair beside him. "This is yours, is it not?"

7

Colin took the garment. "Where the devil did you get it?"

"You loaned it to the girl Jennie, do you not remember? To protect her modesty. She asked me to return it to you, with many thanks. Again, goodbye."

Colin watched him walk towards the doorway.

The rest of the party broke up after breakfast the following morning. Colin was dressed and ready to mount up, when he was beckoned by his uncle. "A word before you go, Colin." Lord Blaistone led the way into his study, and sat behind his desk. "That confounded Russian fellow," he remarked.

"He left last night," Colin said. "He was determined on it."

"Yes, and do you know why? He took Annie Cromb's daughter with him."

Colin sat down. "Jennie? You mean he abducted her?"

"Now, there's the point. He went to their cottage last night to thank her again for her part in saving his life. Having got there, he invited her to come outside to speak with him privately. Ten minutes later Jennie returns, packs her belongings, and says she's going up to London with the gentleman. She gives her mother twenty sovereigns not to object. Would you believe it?"

"By God," Colin said. "You mean Mrs Cromb let her daughter go?"

"My dear fellow, look at it from her point of view. Twenty pounds is a year's income for her. And she has two other daughters. The girl promised there'd be another pound a month as long as she was away."

"Jennie Cromb told you this?"

"No, one of the other daughters. She seemed upset by the way it happened."

"I should think so too," Colin said.

"Your innocence is showing, Colin. This sort of thing happens every day. Actually, I was warned about this

8

by Prince Wotichevski. Seems these Bolugayevskis have some scandal in their recent background. In fact, he's being sent home so soon because of some unpleasantness over cards in London. Yet I liked the fellow. Strange."

"And now he's made off with one of your servants. Do you wish me to do something about it?"

Blaistone grinned. "No, no, she's made her bed and she must lie on it. As for doing anything about it, you'd likely find yourself on the wrong end of a duel if you attempted to interfere. Not to mention an international incident, and we don't really want to have any incidents with the Russians right now; things are tense enough as it is. I just thought you might like to know the sort of fellow you dragged from the bog."

"The bog is where he belongs," Colin muttered.

"I must remember to strike Bolugayevski off my guest list," Blaistone said. "Hopefully, we'll never see the lout again."

Part One

THE SERF

"Here, lady, lo! that servant stands
You picked from passing men."

Robert Louis Stevenson
Songs of Travel.

Chapter 1

THE SIX HUNDRED

The horses pawed the ground restlessly. They formed six ranks, nearly seven hundred of them, each a splendid, carefully selected creature. Their riders were no less magnificent, at least in appearance. In the first rank were the red jackets and blue breeches of the Thirteenth Light Dragoons and the blue uniforms with the six-sided Polish helmets of the 17th Lancers. In the second the men of the Eleventh Hussars, striking in their crimson breeches with the double yellow stripe, blue tunics smothered in gold braid, and their black busbys with the scarlet flash. In the third were the Fourth and Eighth Hussars.

Colin had been as pleased as anyone in the regiment when war had been declared against Russia. Perhaps more than anyone else, because ever since the Jennie Cromb episode he had felt a personal animosity against everything Russian. Nothing had ever been heard of the girl again. She had vanished off the face of the earth.
    Even after a year Colin could not get the image of her out of his mind. He had wanted her himself, then, but as a gentleman had known it was impossible. And thus he had let her go to a lecher, and death. Thus he had sailed for the Crimea in a mood of angry vengeance.

The trouble with fighting Russia, was finding somewhere to fight. The Russians had invaded the Balkans, but, as both Prussia and Austria-Hungary had opted for neutrality, they could not be got at anywhere, except by sea, and navies cannot win wars, they can only prevent other people from doing so. Thus a British squadron had been sent to the Baltic, and another had been sent to the Black Sea. This had been followed by an army, in the first instance only to Rumania. But the army had rapidly been assailed by cholera, and the generals had decided to try more healthy campaigning country. Thus the decision had been taken to invade Russia itself. By sea.

They had opted for the only part of southern Russia practical for a seaborne assault: the Crimean Peninsular. It was felt that if the port of Sevastopol were to fall, Russia would be brought to her knees. Colin, being somewhat better read than most of his fellow junior officers, had reckoned that the fall of Sevastopol would bear the same relation to Russian strength as the capture of say Plymouth would to the British. But he could not deny that *were* an enemy to land in England and take Plymouth it would probably mean the fall of the government, so perhaps there was some argument for the strategy.

Certainly, in the beginning, things had gone well enough. The Russians had been taken by surprise. They must have known a British troop-carrying fleet had left Varna, but presumed it was withdrawing to Turkey. The landing, in mid-September, at a place aptly called Calamita Bay, had been unopposed. But as the terrain had not been reconnoitred in any way, this landing had taken place on an open beach some thirty miles north-west of Sevastopol.

No sooner had the fifty thousand-odd French and British troops been safely ashore than a gale had blown up, and it had been realised that the ships could no longer lie off the exposed coast. Now at last a reconnaissance was made, and it was found that there were two protected ports, Kamiesch and Balaclava, lying south-east of Sevastopol. Another reconnaissance had discovered that, however surprised they had been by the attack,

14

the Russians had managed to put the city into a state of defence, with sunken ships blocking the harbour and formidable earthworks facing inland. The only solution had seemed to be a siege, and a siege required secure bases. As re-embarkation in the bad weather was impossible, the two armies had been forced to march around from the north of Sevastopol to seize the two inferior ports and regain contact with their ships. This march had necessitated crossing the River Alma, and here the Russians had been brushed aside, with heavy casualties in both armies. The ports had been reached by the end of September. Now at last the siege could begin.

The cavalry, few in numbers and thus too precious to be risked, had nothing to do at the Alma. Nor did they have anything to do with the siege. Morale had suffered, even if few of the officers seemed to have any concern over the total lack of generalship being revealed by their commanders. Colin was an exception. He was appalled by the initial landings, the slipshod way in which every manoeuvre was carried out, the confidence apparently enjoyed by all the staff that the Russian defences would crumble at the first attack. Well, that had been proved wrong. Sevastopol was discovered to be an enormously strong fortress, defended by the most determined of men. It was going to be a long siege, and now cholera had returned.

The Russians were not interested in standing on the defensive. This morning, 25 October, 1854, the bugles had blown summoning the entire British army to stand to. Scouts had reported that General Menshikov, the Russian commander, had brought his field army out of Sevastopol and was advancing to throw himself between the besieging part of the British lines, and Balaclava. His idea was to destroy the British base. Obviously he could not be allowed to do that, and every man in the British army had begun to look forward to a real fight at

15

last. The battle had commenced at dawn, and there had already been some severe clashes. But the field, a series of valleys between low hills, could not be overlooked save from the various heights which had been appropriated by the generals, and it was impossible for any private soldier or junior officer to tell what was going on. The Light Brigade had been sent into one of the valleys and told to keep out of trouble, which had left the men muttering more angrily than ever. They had heard the gunfire from the very next valley, and had learned from a messenger that the Russians had made a general assault there, and had been driven back by the 93rd Highlanders.

The Light Brigade Commander, Brigadier-General James Brudenell, Lord Cardigan, red-faced and belligerent, was furious. "Those damned fellows have all the fun," he complained to the Divisional Commander, Major-General Lord Lucan. They were walking their horses to and fro in front of their equally agitated subordinates, the animals' tails swishing with an impatience as great as their riders'. "What the devil are we, on a confounded parade?"

But now a galloper came down the hillside waving a piece of paper. The staff officer's name was Captain Nolan, and he handed the paper to Lucan. "From Lord Raglan, my lord."

General Lord Raglan was the Commander-in-Chief.

The Major-General studied it, then raised his head. "Guns? I see no guns, Nolan."

"They are Turkish guns, captured in the recent attack, and being carried off by the enemy, my lord. Lord Raglan is determined they shall not have them." Nolan pointed. "They are in the next valley. He wishes you to advance and cut them off."

Lucan walked his horse forward. The valley made a slight dog-leg, and then divided into two, separated by a low hill. Lucan studied the situation, then returned to his command. "There are guns on those hills."

16

"The guns we want are in the valley, my lord."

"I see those also," Lucan said. "There are a devil of a lot of them. My people will be subject to cross fire from the hills."

"My lord," Nolan said. "I have given you an order from the Commander-in-Chief. Those guns must be retaken. Will you carry out the order, or not?"

Lucan cleared his throat, very loudly. "Of course I will carry out the order, Mr Nolan." He turned to Cardigan. "Lord Cardigan, you will advance your brigade and seize those guns."

Cardigan had also been studying the valley in front of him. Now he said, "May I point out that it is against the rules of warfare for cavalry, unsupported, to attack guns."

"I know it," Lucan said. "But Lord Raglan will have it. We have no choice but to obey."

Cardigan glared at him for a moment, then turned to his men. "The Light Brigade will advance." And then added, loud enough to be heard by those in the front rank, "Here goes the last of the Brudenells."

The trumpeter sounded the call, and the six hundred and seventy-three horses walked forward, Cardigan well out in front. Colin rode at Captain Wharton's elbow, in front of their squadron, and could see nothing save the green-brown slopes to either side, the sweep of the valley in front of them. Then they began to round the dog-leg, and he caught his breath. There were certainly guns on the slopes to either side, but these were very obviously Russian guns; the gunners for the moment were too surprised at the sight of the English brigade to think of firing.

Of Turkish guns being driven away there was no sign.

The bugle called for a trot, and speed was increased. Now the gunners on the hillsides woke up, and black explosions marked the slopes, followed by explosions from in front of the cavalry, at the end of the valley. There was no longer any time for thought, as the call

17

rang out to charge. It was at this moment that Nolan, who had accompanied the cavalry and was riding at Cardigan's shoulder, suddenly let out a yell. "The wrong valley," he shouted. "You are attacking the wrong valley."

It was doubtful if anyone heard him. He urged his horse past Cardigan's, and received a sharp rebuke from the Brigadier-General. A moment later he was dead, hit by a flying shell fragment, the first casualty of the charge.

Now the valley was filled with the sound of thundering hooves as the horses moved into the gallop. But above the rumble was the roar of the guns, and Colin could hear the shrieks from behind him. Whole rows of men and horses being mown down by grapeshot.

Colin lost all sense of reality. He counted himself certainly dead, for the shot was flying all around him. Yet he was unhurt when he reached the enemy ranks. The Russian gunners abandoned their weapons in consternation, but a squadron of green-coated horsemen galloped forward. Colin swung his sword as the first horse reached him, and sent the man tumbling from the saddle, but his mount cannoned into Colin's, and unseated him. He landed on his feet, and realised he had lost his sword. Then he was surrounded by dust and hooves as the rest of the brigade caught him up; he was astonished at how many had so far survived. He looked left and right for his horse, but could not see it, stumbled forward, and a Russian cavalryman loomed above him. He drew his revolver and shot the man, then reached for the bridle, and received a tremendous shock in his back. For a moment he thought another horse had kicked him, and continued reaching for the rein, but then his legs lost their strength and he fell to his knees and then on to his face.

Boots thudded beside him, and someone turned him over with a thrust of the toe. The revolver was levelled again and then was suddenly lowered. Colin gasped, aware of a quite startling pain where up to a moment ago he had felt nothing. The man knelt beside him. "Colin?" he asked. "Colin MacLain?"

Colin blinked. "Bolugayevski, by God," he muttered. "You bastard."

"My God, I have killed you," Bolugayevski said, and began shouting in Russian.

Colin lost consciousness.

Light filtered very slowly through a cloud of sweeping darkness. Colin did not like the light, for it brought pain, surging through his body. He had tried to escape it and the agony that accompanied it, and retreat into the world of darkness.

This time the light and the pain would not go away. He moaned, and tried to move, and the pain increased. Then he heard voices, speaking some unintelligible language. Russian! He was in the hands of the Russians! He tried to concentrate, to focus, to understand where he was and what was happening, and the voices came closer. Then he saw a face, bending over him. A woman's face, vaguely familiar, yet it was no woman he had ever seen before.

It was a handsome face. Too strong for true beauty, and yet reassuring in its straight lines, chin and nose and forehead. He couldn't make out the colour of her eyes, and her hair was invisible, tied back on her head in some kind of bandanna. Without warning it smiled, and became beautiful.

Now he was surrounded by faces, male and female, peering at him, clapping their hands. They made the pain increase, and made him aware, too, of how thirsty he was. "Water!" he whispered.

A cup appeared before him, and a few drops were poured on to his lips. He sucked at them anxiously, but the cup had been taken away, and in its place there was a man's face, bending over him. This face was very like the woman's save that it was much older. "You are fortunate, Lieutenant MacLain," the man said,

19

in English. "You are going to live. Georgei will be very relieved."

Now the pain was constant, but so was the nursing. Colin gathered that the nursing had been continuous from the moment he had been brought into Sevastopol, when he had been unconscious, as he had stayed unconscious, for several days. Sevastopol!

He was too weak, and in too much pain, to do more than grasp at life, or to be embarrassed as the Russian women bed-bathed him and changed his soiled linen – even by the presence of the handsome woman on these occasions.

"You are in our house." Georgei Bolugayevski sat beside his bed, his face serious. "I insisted upon it. You are much better off here than in the hospital. In the hospital, men die like flies."

Colin licked his lips, and Georgei held a cup to them; the water was mixed with brandy, and sent his mind reeling. "Were there many prisoners?" he whispered.

"Not many," Georgei told him. "Now you must rest, and try not to think about what happened."

Colin watched the woman moving about the room, straightening flowers. "What are you called?" he asked.

She turned, and immediately held the cup to his lips. He was grateful for the water, but his brain was active. "Name," he said. And when she continued to stare at him, uncomprehendingly, tried to point at himself. To his horror he could not move his hand.

The woman understood, and herself held his wrist to lift his arm. He looked at wasted flesh and muscles. The woman smiled, and spoke, then raised her eyebrows. "Colin," he said.

She nodded. Her brother would have told her that. "Dagmar," she said.

*   *   *

20

"Dagmar is my eldest sister," Georgei explained that evening. "She is the oldest of us all."

"Is she not Russian?"

"Well, of course she is Russian. But Papa married a Danish lady. I am half Danish."

Colin considered this. But it did not seem relevant: they were still his enemies. "Are we still at war?"

Georgei grinned. "Very much so. Your people, and the French, will not go away."

"What happened in the battle?"

"Which battle?"

"There has been another one?"

"Oh, yes, only a few days ago. At Inkermann, just outside the city. But you are speaking of Balaclava. We gave . . . how do you British put it? We gave you a bloody nose. But we could not reach Balaclava. So you could call it a draw."

"The cavalry . . ."

"Your cavalry is virtually destroyed. Well, it destroyed itself. Do you know who gave the order for that senseless charge?"

"It came from the Commander-in-Chief."

"Then he should be at least cashiered, if not shot."

Colin tried to remember. "There were some Turkish guns you had captured . . ."

"Ah!" Georgei said. "I think I understand. Then perhaps it is merely your brigade commander who should be shot. We did capture some Turkish guns. But you did not go after them. They were in the next valley. Instead you charged several emplaced batteries of our field artillery. None of us had ever seen anything like it before. I should hope we will never seen anything like it again, either. It was mass suicide."

"Were they all killed?"

"Except you, you mean? No, no. But the casualties were very severe. I don't think many got back."

"What of Lord Cardigan?"

21

"Oh, *he* got back. We were under orders to let him do so. Now you must rest."

"That is all anyone ever tells me," Colin complained. "What is going to become of me?"

"You are our guest. My guest. My God, when I think that I shot the man who saved my life. My business is to have my people nurse you back to health. Yours is to get well."

"As a prisoner," Colin said bitterly.

Georgei grinned. "You are better off here than out there with your comrades. Soon winter will be upon us."

Georgei came to see him less often, suggesting that the siege was continuing, and perhaps intensifying. Now his most regular visitor was Georgei's father, Prince Alexander Bolugayevski. Apart from Dagmar, of course, who came every day. But they could not communicate. She spoke no English, and he spoke no Russian. Even if he had not felt it impolite to ask any of the servants about her, he could not communicate with them either.

Yet he was on terms of the most complete intimacy with the women who served him, whether it was changing his dressing or attending to his necessaries, as he could not get out of bed, or washing him. There again Dagmar was often present. In the beginning he was too weak to feel embarrassed by her presence but as he regained his strength she seemed so much a fixture that it was difficult to think of her as anything other than a most attractive nurse.

Prince Bolugayevski was not a soldier. He had been caught in Sevastopol by the suddenness of the Allied descent. Despite the inconvenience of being besieged he appeared to be a good-humoured man who did not seem the least bothered by what was going on around him. "You are making excellent progress," he said. "When I first saw your wound, why, I thought, this man has no chance at

22

all. But you are a very strong young fellow. All you need is patience, and you will make a full recovery."

"Can you tell me where I was hit?"

"The bullet entered halfway down your right side, in the back; Georgei was mounted when he fired, and you were on foot. Thus the bullet had a downwards trajectory, and this was very fortunate for you. It split three ribs, tore away part of your kidney and exited just above your groin. But it missed your lungs, your heart, and your bladder. Any of those would have been fatal. And . . ." he smiled, "you have two kidneys. But as I said, I despaired of your life when I first saw you. Is not modern medicine capable of miracles?" Bolugayevski was smiling. "But now that you are recovering, you are bored. You need something to occupy your mind. You shall learn Russian."

Colin turned his head, sharply. "It would be a good idea," the Prince said. "You may be with us some time." He smiled. "Sevastopol can hold out forever."

Colin had to accept that it was no idle boast. The city was not even properly besieged, and there remained always a road open to the north, through which the Russian wounded could be evacuated, and replacements, both of men and munitions, brought in. The French and British were incapable of closing this route; they lacked the men and winter had now arrived with a severity unexpected so far south. He spent every morning with a local schoolmaster who spoke English, and who began to teach him Russian, but he was constantly distracted by the howling wind and the snow clouding down outside his window.

"Your comrades are in a bad way," said Mr Yevrentko. "They are still in tents. Those of them who are not in hospital. In the hospital they are dying like flies. But do you know, some English gentlewomen have come, to nurse them? That is truly remarkable."

"Mademoiselle Dagmar nurses me," Colin pointed out.

"You mean Countess Bolugayevska," Yevrentko said severely. "And it is here in the safety and comfort of her own home. To send a gentlewoman into a hospital full of men and disease . . . it is unheard of."

"Countess Bolugayevska?"

"Of course. Is she not the Prince's eldest daughter?"

"They are saying thirty British transports sank last night," Yevrentko told Colin the next day. "I think, when the spring comes, your people will sail away again, eh?"

Colin found himself disliking the fellow, but he was learning Russian, and he was regaining his health and strength. Dagmar Bolugayevska spent less time in his room, as he changed from an invalid into a guest. By early December he was able to leave his bed, and move about the room, although only when supported by two of the Bolugayevski male servants. "You will soon be fully recovered," Georgei told him. "Now, I have arranged for my tailor to come in and measure you up for some clothes. I am afraid your uniform is destroyed beyond repair."

"When will I be transferred to a prison camp?" Colin asked.

Georgei gazed at him in astonishment. "Do you wish to be transferred? They are not very nice places."

"Am I not a prisoner?"

"You are my father's guest. However, one of the reasons I suggest you wear civilian clothes is so that you do not attract attention when you go out."

"You mean you will let me go out?"

"As soon as you are strong enough. And when the weather improves. It would not do for you to catch a chill while in your weakened condition."

"And suppose I told you that as soon as I am strong enough I intend to escape back to my comrades?"

"I would say you are mad. You seriously wish to go out into the ice and the snow, the starvation and the disease, which is the British encampment? Our spies tell

24

us they are dying at the rate of a hundred a day out there."

"And do you seriously think I would remain here, in the lap of luxury, while my comrades are dying?"

"*Your* comrades are all dead, or sent back to England," Georgei said. "Thanks to the incompetence of your generals. Why do you not practice a little Russian pragmatism, my friend? You are, as you say, a prisoner of war. It would be very easy for us to send you to that prison camp, where men, sadly, are also dying at a great rate, and from where there is no possibility of escape. They must sit it out to the end of the war. Now, we are inviting you to do the same, only here with us. The end result will be the same: you will be sent home when the war ends. You cannot affect that with odd notions of honour. What you *can* affect, by a simple act of will, is whether you return to England a strong and healthy man, able to resume your place in your regiment and in your society, or whether you return as a half-starved and shattered wreck, unable to do more that eke out a miserable existence on a small pension for the rest of your days."

"You put things with admirable succinctness," Colin remarked.

"In Russia, it is necessary always to understand the realities of any situation," Georgei said, seriously. "We are having a bad winter, down here. But we are also having a bad winter further north. Have you any idea what it is like, to have a bad winter, in Central Russia? You do not. I have read a lot of English literature. It is my hobby. I remember reading, not so long ago, the memoirs of an English parson, named Woodforde. He recalled the coldest winter he had ever known, so cold that his piss froze in the pot beneath his bed. Colin, in Russia, in winter, if he cannot warm his surroundings, a man's piss gets frozen in his bladder. Now consider, you are a small landowner, in central Russia, and winter closes in. You have made every preparation for it, but

25

yet it is a more severe winter than you expected, and it lasts longer. So it is that by March you are running out of wood to burn and food to eat, and there is as yet no sign of a thaw. Then you must think, we can only survive to see the spring if I can reduce the number of mouths to be fed, bodies to be warmed. Now, I know you English. Your initial reaction would be, you must do the gallant thing. You must walk out into the snow, and perish. But is that not a sign of total weakness? You are the one on whom the family will depend, when spring arrives. It is the weakest of the family that must be put out to die, however painful it may be to sacrifice a well-loved servant, or even a child. Can you understand that?"

"I can understand why Russians have large families," Colin said. "And I can also understand how fortunate I am to be British."

Georgei grinned good-naturedly. "And perhaps you can also understand why we drink vodka instead of beer, eh? Now, no more serious talk. Do you know what you need, now you are stronger? You need a woman. It has been a long time, eh? What sort of woman would you like?"

"You mean, I tell you, you snap your fingers, and she appears?"

"Well, as long as you do not seek the moon, it will be something like that, yes."

"Suppose I asked for Jennie Cromb?"

Georgei frowned. "Jennie Cromb?"

"My God! You do not even remember her. You abducted her from Blaistone, remember? What did you do with her? Throw her out on to the street?"

"Jennie!" Georgei slapped his thigh. "I just did not connect her name with Cromb. I have never called her that. I did not abduct her, Colin. She came with me of her own free will. I agree, she had to be . . . persuaded to come with me to Russia. But I am very fond of her, and I insisted."

"You mean she is alive, and in Russia?"

26

"Oh, indeed. Very much so. In fact, she is a mother. My son."

"My God," Colin said again.

"You are welcome to have her, if you wish. She is at Bolugayen, with the rest of my family. I will take you there. In the spring."

Chapter 2

THE SISTER

The Russians had no doubt that Sevastopol would still be holding out in the spring. In the spring! Colin felt inexpressibly guilty, yet Georgei's words were insidiously sensible. What purpose *would* he serve by insisting upon being transferred to prison? He stood a much better chance of escaping from here. But even that was not possible until he was fully fit again.

Meanwhile, Russian, and clothes. He was amazed at the variety of garments the tailor provided for him. "A dinner suit? Where on earth am I going to wear a dinner suit?" he asked Yevrentko.

"At Christmas, Mr MacLain. You must be properly dressed at Christmas."

Which by Colin's reckoning had occurred several days before, uncelebrated. Now he recalled that the Russians followed a different calendar to the West. Was he to eat with the family? Although he had continued to be served his meals in his room, he had the run of the house. He was not yet strong enough to try leaving it, and did not know what would happen if he did try. All around him was hustle and bustle as silver was polished and floors washed and vast quantities of food disappeared into the palace kitchens. The French and British might be starving at Balaclava and Kamiesch, but there was no shortage of food and warmth within the Bolugayevski Palace.

The whole was overseen by Dagmar Bolugayevska. She

28

made a splendid figure, in her white gowns and her hair, which was a tawny yellow, piled on top of her head, her rope of pearls, and her quick, incisive movements. Colin was fascinated. After so long, he did, indeed, want a woman, and the woman he wanted was Dagmar.

For the time being, he could look, and dream, and be curious. "Is the Princess on the estate?" he asked Yevrentko.

"The Princess is dead," the schoolmaster replied. "She died some years ago. Since then, the Dowager Princess has been mistress of Bolugayen. But Countess Dagmar has also managed her father's house."

"Why has she never married? How old is she?"

"It is impolite to inquire a lady's age," Yevrentko said severely. "But if you must know, the Countess is twenty-six years old. That she has not married is because she regards it as her duty to stay with her father, until perhaps *he* marries again. There was talk of it before the war, but it cannot now happen until after your people go away."

Oddly, Colin got the impression that the schoolmaster was lying, although in what respect he couldn't decide. He's in love with her, he thought. "Are there other children apart from Dagmar and Georgei?" he asked.

"There are the two younger daughters, Anna and Alexandra. But they are on the estate."

"No brothers?"

"The Prince has been unfortunate in that respect. There is only Count Georgei."

"And are the two younger daughters as handsome as their sister?"

"They are beautiful," Yevrentko said reverently. "Their mother was a beautiful woman."

He's in love with all of them, Colin thought. And they are as far above him as are the stars. But not so far above himself.

Next morning he deliberately put himself in Dagmar's

way. "I only learned yesterday about your mother," he said. "I am very sorry."

"It was a few years ago," she said. "Your Russian is coming along very well."

"Thank you. May I ask what she died of? She cannot have been very old."

She had been making lists. Now she checked, her writing block in her hand, raising her head to look at him. "Mother died in childbirth, Mr MacLain."

"Oh, I . . ." He was totally embarrassed.

"So did the babe," she said. "He would have been another brother. It was very sad."

"I did not mean to distress you."

"But you are curious. I do not blame you for that." She placed her writing block on the table. "Are you sorry to be here for Christmas? Do you have brothers and sisters, a mother and father?"

"I have a mother and a father, and a sister."

"Who will be worrying about you. But as we informed your general that you had been taken prisoner, and again, that you had recovered from your wound, they will at least know you are safe."

"Does General Raglan know I am in this house?"

"I imagine so. Does the fact that he knows you are here concern you?" she asked.

"Well, of course it does, mademoiselle . . . ah, Countess. Is that how I should address you?"

"No," she said. "You *should* address me as Your Excellency. But I think in all the circumstances we could settle for Dagmar. Why are you unhappy to be here?"

"I have no business being here."

"You are afraid you will be cashiered?" she suggested.

"I will certainly be severely reprimanded."

"For not dying in prison? It is a senseless world, is it not? Honour! All men think about is honour, when it is the most absurd thing in the world. Perhaps you should stay here in Russia," she suggested.

"Don't you have notions of honour in Russia?"

"More than in England, I suspect. But they are only important in places like Moscow or St Petersburg. Not on Bolugayen."

"You mean your father might offer me a job?"

He was being facetious, but she appeared to take him seriously. "Why, yes, I think he might very well do that."

"I know only soldiering."

"Then we will have to teach you something else." She tapped his hand with her fan. "You are distracting me from my work. The party is only two days off."

"Are you really going to have a big party, in the middle of a war?"

"But of course. The Bolugayevskis' Christmas Ball is a famous event. Should we be stopped by a few British shells?"

He presumed she had indicated that he was to keep out of her way for the next few days, but to his surprise, she sought him out only two days later, the Russian Christmas Eve. He was in the cellars with Yevrentko, making a few tentative passes with a sword. "You will exhaust yourself," she commented.

They had not heard her come in, and both turned in surprise.

Yevrentko bowed. "Mr MacLain wished to practice, Your Excellency."

"Actually, I am trying to get fit," Colin explained.

"Of course. Are you a good swordsman, Mr MacLain?"

Colin looked at Yevrentko.

"Mr MacLain is an excellent swordsman, Your Excellency."

"I thought he would be. You may leave us, Yevrentko."

The schoolmaster hesitated, then bowed again. Colin tossed him his sword, and he carried both weapons from

31

the room. There was a single chair, and Dagmar sat down. "You have been avoiding me."

Colin wiped sweat from his forehead and neck. "I was under the impression that you were busy."

"I was. But it is all done now. I like your suit."

Colin put on his jacket. "You should congratulate your brother. Or his tailor."

"Is that the sort of suit they wear in England?"

"The cut is not quite the same, no. But it is very well cut. As usual, I am most grateful."

"Tell me about England," she invited. "I mean, Georgei has told me about it, but his is an outsider's view. I would like yours."

"Well, actually, I'm a Scot."

"You mean, you're the English equivalent of a Cossack?"

He had never thought of it that way, but he supposed in a manner of speaking he was. "You could say that."

"Is it true there are no serfs in England?" Dagmar asked.

"Quite true."

"But my brother brought one of your women back with him."

"You know of this? I mean, you approve of it?"

She shrugged. "Whether I approve of it or not is hardly relevant. Georgei does what he pleases."

He stood beside her. "Is Jennie well? Georgei said she is a mother."

"Why, yes, I believe she is. Yes, she is well." She raised her head, a faint frown between her eyes. "You mean you knew the girl?"

"It was she and I who dragged your brother from the bog."

"Of course. I had forgotten. I wish I had been there."

He was, as always, angered by these people's casual references to Jennie Cromb, as if she had no meaning

32

outside of their own requirements. "Would you have stripped naked before a strange man?" he asked.

To his surprise she did not look the slightest put out. "Why, yes, to save my brother, certainly. And would you, then, have carried me off, Mr MacLain?"

He gulped in embarrassment. Dagmar smiled, and stood up, tapping him on the shoulder with her fan. "I should hope you would have, Mr MacLain, otherwise I should have been very angry with you." She walked to the door, and turned back to look at him. "There has not been serfdom in England for many hundreds of years, I believe. But would you like there to be?"

"Good God, no. I think it is a despicable custom. With respect, mademoiselle."

"There is no need to apologise, Mr MacLain," she said, and she swept from the room.

The Bolugayevskis' Christmas Ball was the biggest affair Colin had ever attended. He was able to lose himself in the kaleidoscope of uniforms and swords, exposed shoulders and *décolletage* dresses, unswept hair, glittering jewels and orders. Georgei, resplendent in his dark blue uniform as an officer in the Actirski Hussars – the tunic was entirely obscured by the masses of gold braid – introduced him to various people, but they did not seem interested in him. Despite Dagmar's compliment his Russian was not yet good enough to appreciate all the idioms of conversation.

To his surprise all of the guests were junior officers, and he would not have said that any of the women were members of even the lower aristocracy. Yet Alexander Bolugayevski was a prince. He would have expected one or two of Sevastopol's leading citizens to be present. Then he remembered Lord Blaistone's hint that there was something not quite right about this family.

He was required to take Dagmar into dinner, and suddenly it seemed everyone was looking at him. "I feel

33

very conspicuous," he muttered, when they were seated and the family confessor had said grace. "Whoever did the seating? Georgei, I bet."

"Of course he did not," Dagmar said. "I arranged the seating."

His head turned, sharply. "And what made you choose me?"

She rested her white-gloved elbow on the table, and then her chin on her gloved forefinger, while she looked at him for several seconds. "So that you would have to ask me to dance."

He couldn't believe that she could be interested in someone six years her junior. But he wanted *her*, quite desperately. And tonight she was quite superb. She wore a blood-red gown which was held up, it seemed, only by her magnificent breasts, and her hair was swept up in a chignon surmounted by a diamond tiara; the thought of holding her in his arms, if only to waltz, was breath-taking.

Once the toasts had been drunk, one hand tight in his, the other resting lightly on his shoulder, they led the dancing. Now he regretted that extra glass of champagne with his meal. Her face was fuzzy at the edges, while her teeth seemed to gleam at him with an extra sparkle as she smiled. "You waltz very well, Mr MacLain."

"It goes with being an officer, Your Excellency."

The music stopped, briefly, but in that time she was claimed by her next partner. Just as well, he supposed; he had had a growing urge to crush her against him, and kiss her mouth. And then . . . you are very drunk, he told himself. But, so was everybody else. Why not *be* as drunk as everyone else?

He set down his glass, took another, drank that as well, and made his way across the room. Dagmar was, as usual, the centre of a group of people, mainly officers, speaking and smiling as animatedly as ever, but she was watching his approach. "Gentlemen," she said. "Our English guest. Hero of that famous charge."

34

"I am Scots, not English."

"It seems half the English army is Scotch," said one of the officers.

"Scots," Colin corrected him. "Scotch is what you drink, if you can get it."

The man glared at him, but Dagmar had moved to stand beside him. "You are drunk," she remarked in a low voice. "If you go around correcting people all the time you will find yourself fighting a duel."

"But the fellow was wrong."

"Nevertheless."

He gazed at her. "Are you not drunk, Your Excellency?"

"Of course. But I cannot afford to show it until after our guests have gone."

"Then let me dance with you."

"My card is full for the entire evening. I think the occasion is proving too much for you. You have not fully regained your strength, you know. I give you permission to retire."

"*You* give me permission?"

"It is my house, Mr MacLain."

"And I am your prisoner. Very well, Your Excellency, I will retire. Will you come and turn the key on me?"

As usual, her eyes were cool. "Who knows," she remarked. "You will have to wait and see."

The room was swaying as he left it, not even saying goodnight to the Prince or Georgei. He knew he had behaved very badly. The resentment still bubbled inside him, the uncertainty as to the right course to take, the misery when he thought of all those Englishmen and Scotsmen sitting out there shivering in the snow, while he . . . he fell across his bed and was asleep in seconds, and awoke, it seemed only a few seconds later, as his door gently closed.

"Do you always sleep with your boots on?" Dagmar asked.

35

He tried to get up, and slipped down to kneel beside the bed, which was swaying to and fro. The candle had burned down, and he couldn't properly make her out. "And fully dressed," Dagmar pointed out.

She knelt beside him, close enough for him, even in the gloom, to take in her face and realise that she had loosed her hair, which tumbled about her shoulders. She wore an undressing robe, at the moment tightly tied about her waist. "Is the party over?" he asked.

"It ended an hour ago."

"I must apologise . . ."

"For what? Listen, get on to the bed and I will take off your boots."

He struggled to his feet, and fell again, but this time partly across the bed. Dagmar knelt beside him, and half pushed, half dragged him on to the mattress, until only his feet were dangling over the edge. Then she turned her back on him, and straddling his leg, seized the boot in both hands. He gazed at the curve of her back. She was wearing nothing under the robe. She had come here to have sex with him. Dagmar Bolugayevska?

His right boot was off, and now she transferred her attention to his left. When that came off she was breathing heavily, and turned towards him, shrugging away the robe as she did so. He tried to sit up. "Dagmar . . ."

She held her finger to her lips. "Not a word!" She knelt beside him again, unbuttoned his jacket and then his shirt. When he turned his head his nose touched her left nipple. She had forbidden him to speak, but had said nothing about touching. He opened his mouth and sucked the nipple between his lips. "Do not bite," she said severely, pulling the coat and shirt from his shoulders.

Then she pushed him flat, going with him so that he did not have to release her, while his hands slid round her back to find and hold her buttocks. Then she pulled away and he had to let her go. "What a lot of clothes you men do wear," she commented. But then

36

he was as naked as she, and she was lying down on top of him.

Winter sunlight was flooding the room. He looked down at the tawny hair, scattered across her face as she slept. My God! he thought. What happens now? Definitely prison, even if he did not first have to fight a duel with Georgei.

He needed to use the pot, and very gently eased his arm out from beneath her. She rolled on to her back. He slid out of the bed, and the room started going round and round. He knelt, reaching beneath the bed, and found the pot. When he raised his head, she had rolled on her side again, and her eyes were open, gazing at him. "I did not mean to disturb you," he said.

"You should have awakened me. I would have liked to see you pee."

He drove both hands into his hair.

"Does something ail you?" she asked.

"Our situation."

"That we are sharing a bed? We have shared nothing else."

"Eh?"

She smiled, and sat up. "You were not capable."

"My God!" He simply could not remember.

"I do not know whether you are still too weak from your wound, or whether you simply did not find me attractive enough. Or whether, perhaps, you were simply too drunk. I hope it was the last. You are shivering. Why do you not come back to bed?"

He stood up. "I am capable now."

"That I can see. Well, then, I am greatly relieved." She raised the covers, to allow him to look at her body. Now it was light enough to see her properly, to appreciate the voluptuous beauty that she was offering. "Get in."

He obeyed her. He might feel that he had recovered his sexual powers, but his brain was still spinning, and not merely from alcohol. He lay on his back and the sheet and

37

blankets dropped on top of him. "Will you tell me why?" he asked.

She slid down the bed herself, turned on her side, and threw her left leg across his thighs. "Don't move," she said, and propped her head on her hand, inches from his face. "Why what? Why we are here? We are going to fuck, shortly."

"To . . ." He had never heard a woman use that word before, much less a countess. "Why?"

She smiled. "Do you not know? Or want? My God, I have heard this about the English. If you are really not interested, then I shall leave and say no more of it. But . . ." Her other hand slid down his stomach to hold him. "I would say you are very interested indeed."

He disobeyed her, rolling on to his side himself. Their noses touched. "Your Excellency . . ."

"I think Dagmar is now definitely more appropriate."

"Dagmar. Are you not . . .? Well, it is not what ladies do."

"You mean English ladies? I am Russian. Half-Russian, anyway." She kissed his lips, lightly. "But it is not what Russian ladies do either, at least with their guests."

"Why me? I mean . . ."

"You do not think you are sufficiently attractive? I was attracted to you from the moment I first saw you, a battered wreck. But you knew this."

"Well, I . . . I hoped it might be so. But you are six years older than I."

"I think that is a very good relationship," she said, apparently seriously. "As for the rest, I know you better than you know yourself, Mr MacLain. I have cleaned up your bottom more times than I can remember. I have washed your privies, more times than I can remember. I have heard your secret thoughts, when you were delirious. Should I not possess what I have nurtured?"

"Your father . . ."

38

"My father does not interfere with my life. He would not dare."

"Well, then, Georgei . . ."

"Neither would Georgei dare."

"But . . . your prospects . . ."

"You are my prospects," she told him.

Before he could quite determine what she had meant, she had rolled on top of him, and he was inside her, and she was rising above him with great surges. "Hold me," she panted. "Hurt me. Make me come!"

A few seconds later she had collapsed on his chest, her hair scattered across his face, her body still trembling. "I am going to marry you," she whispered in his ear.

Dagmar left him a few minutes later. He tried to think, but before he could do so he was surrounded by servants come to see to his bath and to dress him.

However much he might have dreamed of it, he had never had the slightest intention of going to bed with the woman, much less marrying her.

What *was* he going to do? He was compromised, utterly at her mercy. Except . . . he might know nothing about the opposite sex, but he did know that when they lost their virginity they bled . . . there was no trace of blood on his sheets. He couldn't possibly marry a Russian, an enemy of his country. He'd probably be shot.

He went downstairs, and found the family already started on breakfast. "Ha ha, Mr MacLain. You found our champagne a little strong last night, I fancy," Prince Bolugayevski shouted.

"I'm afraid that is so, sir. I hope I did not disgrace myself."

To his consternation, the Prince looked at his daughter.

"I think you behaved yourself admirably," Dagmar said.

39

Colin looked at Georgei, who was in his field uniform, and clearly about to rejoin his regiment. Georgei winked.

"I will see you in my study, when you have finished your meal," Alexander Bolugayevski said.

They all know, Colin thought desperately. My God, they all know! He raised his head to look at Dagmar, and she blew him a kiss.

"Sit down," Bolugayevski invited, and Colin cautiously sank into the chair in front of the huge ebony desk. "Cigar?"

He took one. "You understand," the Prince said, "that this business has been carried out very informally, and very incorrectly, I may add. But the circumstances are exceptional. There is a war on, you and Dagmar are of different nationalities, and . . . well . . ." He smiled. "Where Dagmar is concerned, business is usually conducted informally – and more often than not incorrectly, as well. But I am delighted that she has accepted your proposal."

"Ah," Colin said. "Well, sir, you see . . ."

Bolugayevski flicked some ash away. "Are you saying that you did not propose to my daughter?"

"Well . . ." Of course I did not, he wanted to shout. It was she proposed to me. But he had bedded her, again at her invitation. "Of course I did, sir," he temporised.

"Because you love her."

"Oh, indeed. Yes. Absolutely." How the devil was he going to get out of this mess? But there was one sure-fire way at least to delay it, and let everyone have second thoughts. "But the fact is, sir, well, as you pointed out at breakfast, I was very drunk."

"*In vino veritas*, Mr MacLain."

"Oh, quite. And I do love your daughter, and wish to marry her." What an accomplished liar he was becoming.

"But the fact is, when I proposed, I was drunk. I had not taken into consideration all the factors involved."

"What factors?"

"Well, sir, I am only twenty."

"And Dagmar is twenty-six. I assure you, that does not concern her in the slightest."

"It's not that, sir. I am a subaltern in the Eleventh Hussars. It is against military law, British military law at any rate, for any officer under the age of thirty to marry without his commanding officer's permission."

"I am sure that can be obtained."

"And then, sir, I could not possibly marry, at my age, without the permission of my parents."

"I would say that too can be arranged."

"I am not sure about that, sir, in the present circumstances. Our two countries are at war. I may be eternally grateful to you and your family for saving my life, and for nursing me back to health, and treating me as guest rather than a prisoner, but that is not how it will be seen in England. Or, indeed, at Balaclava. Why, I could even be accused of treason if I were to marry a Russian lady. In the present circumstances."

"I think, Mr MacLain, that if you ever have to give up soldiering, you should enter the legal profession. I think you would do very well. You do not wish to marry Dagmar, is that it?"

"Oh, good lord, no, sir. I do wish to marry Dagmar. But don't you see it would be much more practical when the war is ended."

"Which may not be for some years."

"Well, sir . . ."

"I do not think we can wait that long. Has it occurred to you that Dagmar may be pregnant? She is certainly compromised."

Colin gulped. The Prince's attitude bore no relation to anything he might have expected from an English father. "In any event, she has made up her mind," Bolugayevski said. "And Dagmar always gets her way. We will go ahead with the wedding. Not here. Dagmar and I are leaving Sevastopol tomorrow morning. You will accompany us."

"Leaving? Just like that? But you are besieged."

"Not really. The way to the east is still open; your people just do not have sufficient men to close it. It will not be a comfortable journey, I'm afraid, but we have done it before."

"But . . . your duties here . . ."

"I have no duties here any longer. The harbour is blocked. My ships can neither get in or get out. So I have decided to hand over my affairs to my chief clerk, at least until this business is resolved. I also have pressing business summoning me home. The messenger arrived yesterday, but I did not let his news interfere with our party. However, that is behind us now, and I must make haste. So: you will be married on Bolugayen and have a honeymoon, and in due course we will write to your commanding officer and to your parents, presenting them with a *fait accompli*, and I have no doubt at all that they will accept the situation."

"But my career . . ."

"I will give you a career. A very good one."

"You don't understand," Colin said urgently. "I am a soldier, because I wish to be a soldier. It is all I wish to do. I am also a soldier who has taken an oath of allegiance to the Queen, God Bless Her. You are trying to make me into a deserter, in time of war. My God, sir, I could be shot."

Bolugayevski waved his hand. "These are a young man's ideals. They are admirable, but they will not last. In a few years you will look back upon them and smile at yourself. As for being shot, well, the British will have to get hold of you, first. I do not think we will see them on Bolugayen. It is many, many miles from the sea."

Colin stood up. "Sir, I have tried to be reasonable. Now I must tell you that, much as I love your daughter, much as you may feel I have wronged her, I refuse to marry her without the permission of Lord Cardigan, and without the permission of my parents, and until this war is ended."

"Sit down," Bolugayevski said.

Colin sat down without intending to. "Now you listen to me, young man," the Prince said. "As you keep reminding me, you are a prisoner of war. You should have died from that wound. My son saved your life, and I saw to it that you recovered. I kept you here, when I could have sent you to a prison camp, where, in your weakened condition, you would have died. Your life is mine, several times over. My daughter wishes to marry you. You think she is a lecherous whore, who is growing desperate as she cannot find a husband." He gave a brief smile. "I will not deny that Dagmar is a creature of the flesh. But that is no fault, as she will devote her flesh entirely to you. But there is a great deal more to it than that. I will not discuss it with you here; we will be in Bolugayen in a few weeks. But then you will learn that your marriage to my daughter is of great importance to my family. I have said, I will make it all right with your family and your superiors. That is important too. And I am offering you a life of great luxury, great power, and the arms of a beautiful woman. You do not strike me as being a fool, Mr MacLain, but I will tell you this: whether you are a fool or not, you *are* coming to Bolugayen to marry Dagmar."

Colin paused in the corridor to regain his temper. He had felt like strangling the Prince. But his good sense had kept him controlled. He could understand the Russians' point of view, however bizarre it might be. They felt that, as they had saved his life, he belonged to them. But just to be kidnapped, as if he were indeed a serf . . . my God, he thought: they are treating me exactly as Georgei treated Jennie Cromb! Save that Jennie had not apparently required kidnapping, at least in the first instance.

He stamped along the corridors and found himself in

43

the great withdrawing room. "Where is the Countess Dagmar?" he demanded of the footman he found there.

"I believe the Countess is in her apartment, sir, preparing for tomorrow's departure."

Colin mounted the stairs, and encountered one of the maids at the top.

"Sir?" the girl inquired.

"I am looking for the Countess Dagmar," Colin said.

"I am here, Mr MacLain." Dagmar stood in the doorway, hands clasped in front of her.

"I would like to speak with you, in private."

"Of course." She waved her hand, and the three maids in the room with her filed out. "Would you like me to close the door?" Dagmar asked.

"I think it would be a very good idea."

She closed it. "Would you like me to lock it?"

"If you dare," he said. "Then you will be unable to summon help."

"Am I going to need help?" She turned the key, then crossed the room and sat down in one of the chairs. "You are very attractive when you are angry. But then, you are very attractive at all times. You have seen Father?"

"Yes, I have seen your father." He drew up the other chair to sit beside her. He was determined to be reasonable, terribly aware of the weakness of his position. "I wish you to know that I have every intention of honouring my obligation towards you."

"I never doubted it for a moment."

"But I wish you to understand that I cannot possibly do so while our two countries are at war, and until I have received permission to marry from my commanding officer and from my parents. Your father does not seem able to appreciate this."

"I am afraid I do not appreciate it either," Dagmar said. "You come here, allow your life to be saved by my family, by *me*, have your way with me, and then tell

44

me that you cannot marry me for perhaps several years? I had supposed you were a gentleman."

"Well," he retorted, beginning to lose his temper, "I never made the mistake of supposing you were a lady."

Pink spots flared in her cheeks. "Nonetheless, you will marry me, Mr MacLain."

He stood up. "And suppose I told you that I shall never consummate the marriage?"

"You have already consummated the marriage, Mr MacLain."

"That I will never speak to you?"

"That is your business, I am sure."

"That I will continue to consider myself a prisoner of war, and will use every endeavour to escape as soon as I can?"

She smiled. "If you can escape from Bolugayen, Mr MacLain, you will be a man amongst men."

"Dagmar," he said. "You must realise that this is absurd. We are living in the middle of the Nineteenth Century. You cannot just decide to marry someone and have it done whether he wishes it or not."

"Ah," she said. "Then you do not, after all, wish to marry me."

His temper bubbled over. "All right, since you will have it, I do not wish to marry you. I was drunk and you took advantage of that. I am aware of what I did, and I am prepared to behave like a gentleman. But I will not be kidnapped like some serf. I will marry you when it becomes possible. Then I suggest that we obtain a divorce, just as rapidly as possible. Will that not satisfy you for the loss of your virginity? Supposing I *did* take your virginity."

She tossed her head. "You are my husband, Mr MacLain, before man and before God. That we solemnise it is a religious requirement. But the deed is done. Now, would you like to fuck me again, as you are sober, and more in command of yourself?"

45

"You unutterable, vulgar bitch! I would like to beat the living daylights out of you."

"That is your privilege, as it is the privilege of every Russian husband. Is that what you propose to do? Oh, do not worry. I shall not resist you."

He stared at her in impotent fury. She was completely in command, both of herself and the situation. In his entire life it had never occurred to him to consider striking a woman, but . . . he swung his hand for her cheek. She gave a little shriek and threw up both hands; these caught the blow but could not resist the force behind it, which knocked her over her chair and on to her hands and knees. "Not my face, you fool," she snapped. "It is not done to mark a woman's face!"

His anger was increasing. He raised his foot, to place it on her buttocks and send her flying flat on the floor. She still seemed concerned only with protecting her face and lay supinely before him, not attempting to move, both hands pressed to her cheeks.

He stood above her, experiencing a series of emotions he had never known before. He was her prisoner, her victim; but she wanted to be his, equally. He realised he could do anything to her at that moment – save, it seemed, mark her face – and she would not object. He wanted to hurt her. He wanted to make her realise that she could not control events, control him, make a mockery of his life. What would she really do, if he beat her? Surely then there would be some response from the male members of this family. How he wished to see both Georgei and his father down the barrel of a duelling pistol; he was not the slightest bit apprehensive of the outcome: he had been the best shot in the regiment.

He scooped at her skirts. There were several of them, and one or two tore as he dragged on them. Her stockinged legs and bare buttocks were exposed, and, still keeping his left foot planted in the middle of her back, he pulled off his belt and gave her a resounding blow on the white flesh. She

46

uttered a little shriek, and he raised the belt again, then looked down at the red weal and felt thoroughly ashamed of himself.

He stepped away from her, threading the belt back round his waist. Dagmar rolled over and sat up, her skirts still above her knees. "Why, Mr MacLain," she said. "One blow? That is no way to treat a lady!"

Chapter 3

THE WIFE

Colin slammed the door behind him and leaned against it. The exertion had his wound throbbing with pain. Well, perhaps he would die. Or perhaps get himself killed. He heard the front door close, and voices.

He ran down the stairs and into the central hall, where Georgei and another officer were being helped out of their greatcoats by the footmen. Georgei grinned at him. "Well, Colin! All arranged?"

Colin went up to him. "I have just beaten your sister on her bare ass," he said.

Georgei nodded. "She enjoys that. As long as you please her, you will get on famously."

"I have just quarrelled with your father!" Colin shouted.

Georgei turned to his companion. "Did I not tell you that he is a most vehement fellow? He will bring some powerful blood into our family. By the way, Colin, you have not been introduced. This is my friend, Constantine Dubaclov. He was not able to be at the ball, poor fellow, because he was on duty."

Colin gave a brief bow, then faced Georgei.

"Sir, I am bound to say that I consider that you and your family have behaved in a most dishonourable manner. Almost you make me regret that I saved your life."

"Ah, but I shall never regret saving yours, Colin. What would you, Constantine? I brought this fellow into the bosom of my family, so what does he do? He seduces my sister and now wishes to be excused from marrying her."

"That is a lie!" Colin snapped.

"But still," Georgei went on as if he had not spoken. "We assume that he is suffering from dementia because of his wound. It will seem different on Bolugayen, eh?"

"Ah, Bolugayen," Dubaclov said. "There is no more beautiful place on earth. You will like it there, Lieutenant MacLain."

Attempting to oppose, or anger, these people, was like attempting to punch his way through a feather mattress. But there surely remained one certain way of solving his dilemma. "You, sir," he told Georgei, "are a liar and a cheat, an abductor of women, a rapist and a villain."

Dubaclov drew a sharp breath, but Georgei continued to smile, although there were pink spots on his cheeks. "Vehement," he remarked. "Always vehement."

Colin swung his hand, and slashed it across Georgei's cheek. The Russian gave a little stagger, then regained his balance. "The choice of place, time and weapons are yours," Colin told him. "Only let there be a choice."

Georgei stroked his chin. "There will be no choice, Colin," he said. "How may a man fight his own brother-in-law? There may come a time when Dagmar no longer desires you as a husband . . ." His eyes gleamed. "Then perhaps I may respond to your challenge." He looked past Colin. "Lieutenant MacLain is not himself," he said. "I wish you to confine him to his room, until further orders. Do not use more force than you have to."

Colin turned, and saw four footmen behind him. He looked back at Georgei. "You are also a coward," he said.

Georgei bowed.

He attempted to get some rest, and was disturbed by the arrival of Yevrentko in the middle of the afternoon. "Your servant, Mr MacLain," the schoolmaster said in English. "I have been hearing all manner of rumours."

"They are probably facts, not rumours," Colin said.

"Then you are betrothed to Her Excellency? You are a very fortunate fellow."

"Do you think so? She sized me up and decided to have me. As if I were a slave on a block."

Yevrentko nodded. "They are like that, these country-bred aristocrats. They know little of the outside world, only their own unlimited power. Your pride is hurt, because she chose you. Now if it had been the other way around, and you had chosen some pretty maid to be your wife, whether she wished it or no, you would find the situation entirely natural."

"You cannot pretend this situation is natural," Colin snapped. "Dagmar Bolugayevska is beautiful, rich, undoubtedly the apple of her father's eye; she could surely have the pick of every unattached young man in Russia. But she picks me, a foreigner who is an enemy of her country, who is six years her junior and who has made it perfectly clear that he does not wish to be her husband."

"It is a private family matter," Yevrentko said.

"Then, am I not entitled to know of it, as I am now virtually a member of the family?"

The schoolmaster hesitated, then shook his head. "It is not for me to say. I but came to wish you goodbye, as I understand you are leaving Sevastopol tomorrow."

"Wait!" Colin seized his arm. "You must tell me the truth of the matter."

"I cannot." Yevrentko looked down at Colin's hand. "Please do not make me invoke the aid of those fellows." For the two footmen had remained in the room.

Colin sighed, and let him go.

That evening a bath was poured for him, and his dinner clothes laid out. "Suppose I do not wish to eat with the family?" he inquired.

The footman bowed. "Then you will be served here, sir. It is entirely as you wish." Colin allowed himself to be dressed and went down to dinner.

Georgei had stayed for the meal, as had his guest, Dubaclov. Prince Bolugayevski was as beamingly good-humoured as ever. And Dagmar was as attractive as ever, wearing an extremely *décolletage* dress, with her hair piled in a chignon. She revealed a huge amount of white flesh. A woman with an unpleasant secret, if Yevrentko's guarded remarks were anything to go by. Or did it involve the entire family? Colin recalled Lord Blaistone's words.

He was welcomed as if no crisis had ever occurred. The talk and laughter was general as they drank champagne before the meal, and then sat at various places scattered around the huge table. Colin said little, but no one seemed to care. He could not believe that they supposed he had accepted the situation. Perhaps they did not care whether he accepted it or not. They held all the trumps. "We must be early to bed, Constantine," the Prince said when they had drunk their brandies. "We are leaving before first light."

Dagmar accompanied Colin into the hall after dinner. "We have a long journey tomorrow. I will wish you a good night."

They gazed at each other. "Thank you," he said.

He was aroused soon after midnight, by his attendants; he had now, he reckoned, to consider them as guards. But clearly, he was never going to have a better chance of escaping than on this journey. It was an idea of which he was soon disabused. There was a caravan of troikas waiting in the courtyard, all mounted on sleds and each to be drawn by two horses, presently surrounded by milling servants loading various boxes. "Normally we attach bells to the ponies, and have a merry journey," Prince Bolugayevski told Colin. "But I think we will dispense with the merriment until we are clear of the isthmus."

The Prince himself got into one of the vehicles with some of his servants. Colin was placed in another, seated beside Dagmar who was, like himself and the Prince, so wrapped up that only her eyes were visible. Two menservants were seated opposite them. The rest of the party took their places, and the cavalcade moved out of the yard of the Bolugayevski Palace, accompanied by a guard of hussars. It was five o'clock, and still very dark; the street was several inches deep in hard-packed white powder. It had been a moonless night, and there were no stars to be seen through the blanket of gray cloud.

Within a few minutes of leaving the palace, they were halted at a checkpoint, and Colin realised they were at the inner defences. If he did manage to escape, any information he could carry to Balaclava would be invaluable. But it was difficult to make out in the darkness more than the parapet and ditch, and the emplaced guns. Then they were allowed through, to be stopped again shortly afterwards at the outer wall; now he could see some towers, looming up in a sinister fashion, and again, ditches and glaces and heavy guns. The Russians were certainly prepared to resist any attempt at a *coup-de-main*.

Then again they were through, and trotting along a wide, embanked road. The darkened houses and forts of the city had disappeared. "This is the dangerous part," Dagmar said. "It will soon be daylight." And added, "It is below freezing out there. A man would not last very long, without a horse to take him to warmth."

He believed her, as he parted the curtains to look out at the white wilderness to either side. But he could not believe that this road, which had to be known to the Allies, was not patrolled. He parted the curtains again as the first light dawned. "You will have us freezing inside as well as out," Dagmar complained.

He ignored her. There was still nothing to be seen, save cold-stunted trees. Then he saw smoke, and roofs; they were coming to a village. Their escort now moved up to either side, and Colin's vista was cut off. But a few moments later there was a shot. The hussars immediately wheeled their horses and rode away to the right, floundering through the snow. Colin craned his neck, and saw, on a rise, a patrol of horsemen; from their uniforms he thought they might be Chasseurs D'Afrique. In any event the Frenchmen knew they were outnumbered, and were retiring. But surely this had to be his chance . . . he heard a click, and looked back into the interior of the troika, to gaze at a pistol, held by one of the servants, and pointed at him.

He looked at Dagmar. "I would not have you do anything foolish, my dearest one," she said.

"And it amuses you to keep me a close prisoner," he said bitterly.

She smiled. "But are you not pleased to have such a pretty gaoler? It could have been a lot worse."

"I gather you have a secret," he said, ignoring the footmen. "Do you not suppose I should share it?"

She made a moue. "Do you not have at least one secret? I have not asked to share any of *them*."

It was roughly three hundred and fifty miles from Sevastopol to Poltava, their destination, and the journey took them a month. For that time they were entirely cut off from the the rest of the world. Even whey they stopped, at villages or towns along the way, *they* were the bearers of what news there was from the south; there was no news from the north.

The most surprising member of the party was Dagmar. If it had been all but impossible to resist her beauty and sexuality in Sevastopol; it was impossible not to admire her fortitude and determination to ignore the hardships of the journey. If she guarded her complexion with the greatest care, never going out of doors without her face covered save for her eyes, she never complained at delays, and

53

when one of the troikas became stuck, she was as willing as anyone to lend her shoulder to push and fall to her hands and knees in the snow to free the vehicle. Indeed, she preferred to do this than let Colin attempt it. "You are still not yet back to your full strength," she would say.

It was a topsy-turvy world, Colin reflected, where he was desperately determined not to let himself fall in love with his wife!

"Poltava!" Dagmar said. "Tomorrow we will be in Poltava."

"Your home is close to Poltava?"

"Oh, yes," she said. "Very close."

In fact, the Bolugayevskis maintained a palace in the city itself, and into the courtyard of this the cavalcade slithered the following day. Here the temperature was consistantly below freezing, as it was now early February. But within the palace all was warmth and glowing candelabra. "Baths," Dagmar declared. "And news."

The steward bowed. "It is not good, Your Excellency. It could happen at any moment."

"I must get out there," the Prince said. "So must you. And your fiancé. Forget the baths."

Dagmar hesitated, then nodded. "You will have to wait until Bolugayen," she told Colin.

"One of your family is ill?"

"My grandmother is dying. Pray we are in time," she said. "I wish for her blessing."

A journey of some three hours brought them into the forecourt of the immense Bolugayevski mansion. "This is the front of our estate," Dagmar told him. "For the next two hundred miles, all is ours." She was not boasting.

The entire drive was lined with people, men, women, and children, standing bare-headed, waiting to honour their master. Before the house there was a crowd of grooms and footmen, huge shaggy dogs and shivering serving maids.

And two utterly beautiful young women. Alexander Bolugayevski embraced them both, briefly, and then hurried inside, one arm round each of their waists. "My sisters," Dagmar said, hurrying behind them, and looking over her shoulder. "You must come too."

Colin followed, stamping snow from his boots as he entered the brilliantly lit vestibule of the house. Footmen came forward to take off his fur coat, as others were doing for Dagmar in front of him.

He gazed at a huge downstairs hall, off which reception rooms led left and right. Each room contained a roaring fire. In every direction there was another army of bowing servants. In front of him there was an immense staircase, dividing as it reached the first-floor gallery. Up this Dagmar was hurrying; in front of her the Prince and his two younger daughters were entering one of the upper reception rooms. "This way, Your Excellency," said the majordomo, and Colin ran up behind his future wife.

He caught her up on the gallery. "Do you think I should intrude?"

"Yes," she said, and checked in the doorway.

Inside the room there were already several people gathered around a daybed on which there lay a woman. All heads turned as Dagmar entered. "Is she . . .?"

The woman on the bed raised her hand, and Dagmar ran forward, dropping to her knees beside her grandmother. "I am glad you came," the Princess Dowager Bolugayevska said, her voice weak but clear. "So glad."

"I have brought someone, dearest Grandmama," Dagmar said. "My fiancé."

"Let him come forward," the dying woman commanded.

Alexander Bolugayevski beckoned Colin. Everyone in the room was looking at him. Colin knelt beside Dagmar feeling exceedingly embarrassed. "What is your name?" the Princess asked.

Colin had to lick his lips. "I am Lieutenant Colin MacLain, of Her Majesty's Eleventh Hussars, Your Highness."

"A hussar!" the Countess said. "Georgei is a hussar. Will you make my Dagmar happy?"

"I . . ." He glanced at Dagmar. "I shall endeavour to do so, Your Highness."

"Then I am happy." She closed her eyes. "I give you my blessing, my children." She sighed.

The doctor moved forward. "She must rest, Your Highnesses."

Alexander nodded, and touched Dagmar on the shoulder. "I will remain."

"And I, Papa," said one of the girls.

Dagmar touched Colin on the arm, and he followed her out, accompanied by the other daughter. Colin gazed at yellow hair and exquisite features and, he estimated, a thin body beneath the heavy gown. "Alexandra is fourteen, Mr MacLain," Dagmar said, perhaps as a warning. "Lieutenant MacLain is going to be your brother-in-law, Alix."

The girl offered him her hand to kiss. He did so. "You have been blessed by Grandmama," she said in a quiet voice. "Perhaps you will bring happiness to Bolugayen."

Colin glanced at Dagmar. "It is my determination that he will," Dagmar said. "And now, Mr MacLain, I think you should have a bath. I certainly mean to."

Nothing had ever felt so good, or, Colin supposed, been so necessary. He could feel the accumulated filth of a month peeling off, even as he felt the accumulated cold of that month being dissipated from finger and toe, ear and nose.

"I am Vassily," said a young man, kneeling behind the tub and somewhat fastidiously washing Colin's hair. "I am to be your personal servant, Your Excellency."

"Does that mean you belong to me?"

"I belong to the Prince, Your Excellency. But to you, also."

"Right. Then you must do as I say."

"Yes, Your Excellency," Vassily said uneasily, as he held a bathrobe for Colin to step into. Colin looked at him for the first time. He was a good-looking fellow, in his early twenties, with yellow hair and . . . unmistakeably Bolugayevski features. But he was a servant, and was clearly concerned about just what his new master might wish of him. "Will Your Excellency take a drink?"

"Not of vodka, right now."

"No, no, Your Excellency. Wine."

"That sounds very civilised."

There was a decanter on the table by the bed, which he hadn't noticed before. In fact, he hadn't noticed much about the room, in his anxiety to get at the bath. Now he realised that apart from being clean, and warm, there was fire roaring in the grate surrounded by thick red and gold carpets matching the wallpaper and several upholstered chairs. The room was dominated by an enormous tester bed.

Vassily poured a goblet of wine. "Take one for yourself," Colin said.

"Your Excellency?"

"It is my wish, Vassily."

Vassily poured for himself. "Now," Colin sat down and stretched his legs. "Tell me about the Bolugayevskis."

"Your Excellency?"

"This family into which I am to be married. Tell me of them. Of yourself, perhaps. Who is your father?"

"The Bolugayevskis are one of the oldest families in Russia, Your Excellency."

"Oh, come now, Vassily. Surely all families are the same age? When did the first Bolugayevski become a prince?"

"I do not know, Your Excellency."

"My great - great - great - great - great - great - great-great-grandfather was ennobled by Peter the Great, Mr Maclain," Alexandra Bolugayevska said.

Both men jumped, Colin to his feet, while Vassily nearly

dropped his glass. Colin clutched the dressing robe around himself. The girl stood inside the door she had opened so silently. "You may leave, Vassily."

Vassily cast a startled glance at his master. But, however embarrassed, Colin understood that if Alexandra Bolugayevska was as inquisitive about him as he was about the entire family, she was a much better bet than the valet as regards information. "You may go, Vassily," he said. "Come back in half an hour, to dress me."

The valet bowed, and hurried from the room, closing the door behind him. "Does your big sister know that you are here?" Colin inquired.

Alexandra went to the table, and to his amazement, poured herself a glass of wine. "She would be annoyed."

"I imagine she would. And do you not suppose that fellow is going to excite the entire servants' hall with the tale of your, shall we say, invasion?"

"Servants' hall?"

He realised again that he was in a situation of which he had no experience. "Servants who attempt to tattle about their masters, or their mistresses," Alexandra said, "are whipped."

"Even if he is your own brother?" It was a shot in the dark, but there could hardly be any other explanation.

"Vassily's mother was a serf," Alexandra explained. "He is not a member of the family."

"Ah! Would you like to sit down?"

She sat in one of the other chairs, some distance away, her glass held elegantly. "But it is not so in England, I have heard," she remarked.

He assumed she was talking about servants in general, and not her unrecognised half-brother in particular. "Not quite so bluntly, perhaps. Servants are sometimes beaten. But if they do not like it, they have the right to leave. And even, if the beating was too severe, to complain to the magistrate."

"In Russia they have no such rights," Alexandra said.

"Besides, the only magistrate on Bolugayen is Papa. He will be holding a *tzemtsvo* court in a few days' time, dealing with all the offences which have been committed in his absence."

"What is a *tzemtsvo* court?"

"The *tzemtsvo* in the village council. The members are senior serfs, and they are responsible for the behaviour of the rest of our people. They have judicial powers, but they cannot sentence. Only Papa can do that."

"And there are people awaiting sentencing?"

"Several people. There will even, I imagine, be one or two executions. You may find it amusing."

"Why?"

"Why are you here, Mr MacLain?"

"I am told it is to marry your sister." She raised her eyebrows. "I don't suppose it will do me any good to tell you this," Colin said. "But I have been kidnapped as a husband for Dagmar."

"Do you expect me to believe that?"

"It is the truth."

Alexandra finished her wine and stood up. "I would really like to know why," Colin said.

"Why don't you ask her?" Alexandra said, and went to the door. "I will send Vassily to you."

"Is it true that there is an Englishwoman on the estate?" he asked Vassily as he was dressed for dinner.

"I believe that may be so, Your Excellency."

"You mean you do not know? You must know."

"There are four thousand people on Bolugayen, Your Excellency. Three thousand eight hundred of them are serfs. I believe the foreign woman is one of those. I do not know them all by name."

Shades of the Deep South in America, Colin thought. Except that he doubted there were that many slaves on any one cotton plantation.

Dagmar waited for him at the foot of the stairs;

she wore black. "Grandmama died two hours ago," she said.

"I am very sorry," he said.

She gazed at him for several seconds, then she nodded. "I believe you. You are a perfect English gentleman, Mr MacLain. Can we not be friends?"

"I will be your friend, Your Excellency, when you have told me the truth of this whole affair, and when you have permitted me to resume my freedom of action, remembering always that I am an English gentleman, and intend to behave as one."

Once more she considered him, her head slightly on one side. Then she said, "Well, I suppose few husbands and wives are actually friends. Will you give me your arm?"

He was tempted to refuse, but reflected that would be ungentlemanly: whatever else, she continued to be his hostess. She tucked her gloved arm through his, and escorted him towards the drawing room. Here the family waited, together with one of the priests, the doctor, and a man and woman. "Father Alexei," Alexander Bolugayevski said. "Dr Simmars. My steward, Nicholas Smyslov, and Madame Smyslova. Lieutenant MacLain."

The steward bowed and his wife gave a brief curtsey. "I am sorry we have to meet in such sadness, Mr MacLain," Smyslov said.

"Permit me to offer you my condolences, Prince," Colin said to Bolugayevski.

"Thank you. I am sorry my son could not be here. But a son-in-law is an acceptable substitute, is he not?"

Colin opened his mouth and closed it again. He would gain nothing by another protest, and it would be bad manners to make a scene in these circumstances.

"The wedding will take place tomorrow morning," Alexander Bolugayevski declared.

Colin's head jerked. "How can that be, Your Excellency? Are you not in mourning?"

Bolugayevski nodded. "It will be a family affair. But it was my mother's dying wish."

Colin stood at his window in his dressing gown and watched the snow clouding down. He wondered where Jennie was, and if she knew of his arrival.

The door opened, and he turned. Dagmar placed the glowing candle on the table beside his bed. She wore an undressing robe over a silk nightgown. "Contemplating your escape?" she asked.

"I would be, were it at all possible."

"I am glad you are sensible." She fluffed out her hair, which was loose. "I gather my baby sister paid you a visit this afternoon."

"She was curious."

"And what did you tell her?"

"The truth. I'm not sure she believed me."

"She is a curious child. However, she will not visit you again, I promise you."

"You haven't harmed her?"

"Of course I haven't harmed her. I merely gave her six strokes of the cane."

"You what?"

"In Russia we are great believers in corporal punishment. When you are legally my husband, I will let you cane her, if you like."

"For my pleasure, you mean?"

"Oh, I am sure you will enjoy it. But in Alexandra's case, there is always a reason. She reads too much. And dreams too much." She smiled. "And perhaps, plots too much. She needs to grow up."

"And you?"

"I grew up long ago." She sat on the bed. "There are some things I wish to explain to you."

"I wish you would."

"Tomorrow, as Papa has said, we will be married. It will have to be a muted ceremony, unfortunately, because we

61

are in mourning. However, I would be very disappointed if you attempted to disrupt it, in any way."

"You mean I would be caned?" he said, sitting in a chair opposite her.

"How may my husband be caned? But there is a custom in this country, and I am sure in England as well, whereby a highborn youth, of either sex, while spared the rod themselves, may yet be punished, by means of a deputy. Is that not true?"

"A whipping-boy. So, if I 'disappoint' you, Vassily will suffer, is that it?"

"Vassily?" She gave a little laugh. "Would the sight of him, exposed naked on a triangle, his back a mass of bleeding lacerations, concern you? I think that would be a waste of time. Fortunately, we possess a more emotive substitute. Or so Georgei assures me."

Colin's head jerked. "Jennie Cromb? You would not dare!"

"Here on Bolugayen I can do whatever I wish. So can you, when you have properly settled in." She stood up. "I have put up with your behaviour, because I understand your notions of masculine superiority, masculine rules. Now we are in my home I need do that no longer. Papa supports me in everything I do, or wish to do. I make the rules here. Tomorrow we will be wed, and you will come to my bed. Then you will be my husband in all ways, at all times. Understand this." He glared at her, but she continued to smile. "As I will be your wife, at all times, and in every possible way. I will wish you good night."

She went to the door, but he was there before her. "Do you realise I could strangle you here and now?"

"No, you could not, Colin. That door is not locked. None of the doors on Bolugayen are locked. And there are four of my people waiting in the corridor. A single cry for help, a single untoward sound, and they would be in here."

"And supposing I was only beating you? I am told you enjoy that."

"Then I would send them away again, Colin. Now let me pass."

He hesitated, his hands curled into fists. To let the anger inside him explode would be utterly self-defeating. But he could not resist saying, "And do you intend to spend the rest of your life with four guards standing at your door?"

"It will not be necessary, when you have come to your senses." She stepped round him and turned the handle. "You will, you know."

"I wish to see the girl. I must know that she has not already been ill-treated."

Dagmar shrugged. "If that is what you wish. You will see her tomorrow morning before the ceremony."

"To speak to."

Another shrug. "All right. But it really would make very little sense for you to tell her any of our intimate secrets. It would only distress her, I am sure, to know that she is a hostage for your good behaviour."

He slept fitfully, anticipating and apprehensive of tomorrow. Vassily was there to bathe and dress him early; the wedding was to take place at eight o'clock. Colin had decided it was a waste of time talking with Vassily; the servant was too conditioned to his situation.

He drank a glass of vodka, and felt better. There was a tap on the door. Nicholas Smyslov stood there. "I am to be your groomsman, Lieutenant," he said. "But first, I believe there is someone you wanted to meet."

He stepped aside, and Colin drew a sharp breath. The woman who entered wore a cloak, and a shawl over her head. But he would have known her eyes anywhere. "Mr Colin?" Her tone was incredulous.

He stepped towards her, then checked. "Do any of these people speak English?"

63

"I have never heard them do so, sir."

"Let me look at you."

She pulled the shawl from her head, letting it lie on her shoulders. Her hair remained as he remembered it, long and straight, an auburn stain on the whiteness of her neck. Her face and complexion were as he remembered them too. He could not see her body beneath the fur coat, but he could remember that as well. Was it possible that she had not changed at all, despite her ordeal? She had spent eighteen months with these people, and borne a child.

"I am told you have a son."

"Yes, sir."

"I should like to see him, some time."

"Yes, sir." Her eyes flickered to Vassily, and back again. Colin realised that she knew the valet, and perhaps very well. "Are you going to be staying here, sir?" she went on.

"It looks as if I may be doing so, for a while," Colin said. "But when I leave, I will take you with me. I promise."

"Why should you wish to do that, sir?" she asked.

By nine o'clock Dagmar was Mrs Colin MacLain. Or was he really Mr Colin Bolugayevski?

There were certificates to sign, and a great deal of embracing. "I am so happy for you," Anna said, as she hugged him.

"Now you can stop pretending," Alexandra suggested, presenting her cheek for a kiss.

"You will excuse us," Dagmar said, and beckoned the servants forward, with fur coats. "My husband and I have a duty to perform."

"Now?" Prince Bolugayevski asked.

"I think now is the best time, Papa. Will you walk with me, Colin?"

Colin was encased in coat and gloves and sat down to have thick boots pulled over his shoes. Dagmar sat opposite him while she was equally equipped to face the morning. The family stood around, awkwardly, as did the Smyslovs and Dr Simmars. "We shan't be long," Dagmar said, wrapping a scarf round and round her face so that only her eyes were visible; her fur hat was pulled down over her forehead.

Footmen opened the doors for them, and they went out of the back of the house. "Did you see Jennie?" Dagmar asked, her voice muffled.

"Yes."

"And thus you are reassured, I hope?" Her boots crunched on the snow as she led him across the lawn.

"Yes. Thank you. Does she belong to you, or your brother?"

"Georgei has given her to me."

"Just like that? As if she were some Negro?"

"Well, really, Colin. Your racial prejudice is showing. Can only Negroes be slaves?"

"Of course, I am mistaken," he said. "So can British army officers."

"I really would like us to be friends." She had reached the end of the lawn, where there was a high hedge, with an arch cut into it. She went through the arch, and emerged on to another lawn, smaller than the first. Here the snow lay as thick as anywhere else, but protruding from it there were several crosses.

"My mother is buried there." Dagmar pointed. "With the son who caused her death. There is my grandfather, and over there are my great grandparents. There and there are my uncles, and there and there my aunts."

"Is this where your grandmother will be buried?"

"Of course." She glanced at him. "You expected a vault?"

"It is more usual, where members of one family are accumulated."

"My great grandfather was, above all other things, a pastoralist. He decreed that we should all lie under the vault of heaven. I will be buried here, in the course of

65

time. As will you, and our children. But I have brought you here today that we may offer a prayer on this grave," Dagmar said.

She had moved to one side of the little park, and Colin stooped beside her, slowly decipering the Cyrillic letters on the cross: ALEXANDER BOLUGAYEVSKI. BORN 4 JUNE 1846; DIED 2 FEBRUARY 1847. MY CROSS TO BEAR. "I named him after Papa," Dagmar said. "This pleased Papa."

He looked up at her. "So there you have it," she said. "He did not even live long enough to make it all worthwhile."

"You mean you were married before?" he asked.

"No, I have not been married before," Dagmar said. "It was the greatest scandal of the year, 1846. I am surprised you did not hear about it in England."

"My God," he said. "So . . ."

"My name was, and still is, banished from polite society. I am not received in either Moscow or St Petersburg. Their majesties refuse to recognise that the Countess Bolugayevska exists. As for marriage . . ."

"But what of the man? The father?"

"The father is irrelevant, now. He was not in a position to marry me."

"And was also ostracised?"

She hesitated for a moment. "No one ever discovered who he was. He withdrew himself from society. Men of talent, of course, can never truly withdraw from public life; they are too valuable. Shall we go in? I am chilled."

He walked at her side. "I am terribly sorry for your tragedy, Dagmar. But . . . could you not have gone away somewhere to have the child, and then farmed it out."

"I . . . we were betrayed, by a servant. All St Petersburg knew that I was pregnant." Dagmar gave a little sigh. "Mama took it badly. I believe it was responsible for her death. This is a great burden for me to bear. Papa . . .

66

Papa stood by me then, and has stood by me ever since. He has also turned his back on society, save where it is necessary for business."

"Again, I am most terribly sorry, Dagmar." They had regained the back porch of the house, and servants were waiting to open the doors for them. "But do you think kidnapping me as a husband can possibly regain your place in society?"

"Of course it cannot. I would not wish it to. I merely wish a husband. And a family. A replacement for little Alexander. Perhaps you have already accomplished that."

"If I have, will you let me go?"

"No," she said. "You are my husband."

Almost he felt sorry for her. But that did not alter his determination to escape, just as soon as he could. Only now he was committed to taking Jennie and her child with him, even if she did not seem all that interested.

The knowledge of what Dagmar had suffered, added to her beauty and sensuality, made it easier for him to act the husband as she wished. Indeed, he reckoned he would have had to be an eunuch to share a bed with a naked Dagmar and not wish to mount her, again and again. She was a glorious sexual companion, eager to give, eager to receive, eager to experiment, always smiling and sometimes even laughing aloud. "I shall fall in love with you," she declared, lying on his chest.

"I would not recommend it."

She laughed. "Because you will fall in love with me. And we shall have an immense family together, which we shall raise in glorious splendour, here on Bolugayen."

"I wouldn't count on that either," he told her.

"Ah, Colin." Prince Bolugayevski sat behind his desk. His study was as large as the average reception room, but with its book-lined walls and the fire roaring in the grate was as warm as any room in this palace.

Nicholas Smyslov stood beside the desk, and bowed as Colin entered. "May I have a word with you, sir?" Colin asked.

"Of course, my dear boy. Of course. Sit down."

"In private, sir?"

The Prince nodded, and glanced at Smyslov, who bowed again, and withdrew. Colin sat down, folding the tails of his coat over his thighs.

"So," Bolugayevski said. "How is married life?"

"Married life is a very happy state, sir."

"That is how it should be. I am very pleased. Then what is troubling you?" He pointed. "You *are* troubled. You are not still fretting over the way it happened, I hope?"

Colin had chosen his words with care. "In certain directions, sir. I have done my best to accommodate myself to your wishes, and those of Dagmar, of course. But I have still acted in an unforgiveable manner, as regards my parents, and my career. You spoke of letters . . ."

"Ah, yes. I shall write them, certainly. And so shall you. But at the moment there is very little point. There will be no movement on the roads until the spring."

"You moved on the roads," Colin pointed out.

"I had a great need to do so, as did the messenger who brought me the news of my mother's illness. Matters like ordinary post will have to wait."

"I do not consider this 'ordinary post', sir," Colin protested. "My career is in jeopardy."

"I doubt that," Bolugayevski said. "The war will hardly be over as yet. Even if the Allies have abandoned the Crimea, they will not have got around to making peace yet."

"The Allies will not abandon the Crimea, sir, until Sevastopol has fallen."

"Then they will be there a long time, and you have even less to worry about, as you will remain a prisoner of war. Now tell me this, do you consider that you have honeymooned for long enough?"

"Why . . ." Colin bit his lip.

Bolugayevski laughed. "Three weeks, is it not? You must have all but worn out your pizzle, boy. Now it is time for you to take your proper place in our affairs. There will be a *tzemstvo* court the day after tomorrow. I have delayed it until my mother was buried, but now there has been a slight thaw she is to be interred tomorrow. Then it will be time to deal with some of the abominable crimes that were committed while I was stuck in Sevastopol. You will sit at my side."

Colin supposed that in time, he would be a JP in England, if he ever got back there. But he felt distinctly odd as he sat beside Prince Bolugayevski at a table in the village hall; Smyslov sat on the other side of the Prince. In contrast to the palace, the room was bare, and distinctly chill, despite the iron stove set against one wall. It was crowded with threadbare humanity, men, women and children; there were even some dogs present. Together they gave off a pungent aroma, mainly of sweat.

But more disturbing than their appearance was their demeanour of abject servitude, even fear. They seemed apprehensive of even being looked at, and would touch their caps or their foreheads at the slightest indication that this might happen. Marshalling them were several men, hardly better dressed and equally fearful of their betters, but filled with authority over those inferior to themselves. Colin was concerned to see that they carried revolvers and whips, and from time to time used the lash, too. "Those are members of my Black Regiment," Smyslov said proudly. "They are our police."

On the left of the room, seated in three rows on benches, were a dozen men. These, Colin gathered, were the members of the *tzemstvo* itself, the village council. They seemed as anxious to please their master

69

as did everyone else. There were a variety of crimes to be answered for, ranging from failure to complete a certain quota of work to petty thieving, and the sentence for each of these offences was a flogging. This was administered immediately, the victim being stripped to the waist and secured with leather straps to the wall. Four women and two children suffered the same painful humiliation as eight of their menfolk, screaming and wailing their agony to their fellows, who watched with stolid faces.

But the principal event was reserved for the end, when two young people were thrust forward. One was a man and one was a woman; neither was more than twenty. Now they stood before the table, heads bowed, shivering. "These are the pair who were found to possess that seditious literature," Smyslov explained.

"You mean those two can read?" Bolugayevski demanded.

"Can you read, Nikolai?" Smyslov inquired.

The young man mumbled a reply.

"He can read, Your Highness," Smyslov said.

"Who gave you this rubbish?" Bolugayevski asked.

The paper was lying on the table; Colin had not noticed it before. Nikolai raised his head. "I found it, Your Highness."

Bolugayevski pointed. "You are lying. You . . . what is your name?"

The young woman jerked to attention. "Natasha, Your Highness." Her mouth trembled as she spoke.

"What is he to you?"

"We are to be married, Your Highness."

Bolugayevski glanced at Smyslov. "You were away, Your Highness. The Princess Dowager gave them permission, last summer."

"Ha!" Bolugayevski commented. "Do you realise that possession of seditious literature is a capital offence?"

"We found it, Your Highness," Natasha protested. "We did not know it was seditious."

70

"But you can read. He can, anyway. Did you not read it?"

Natasha licked her lips. "And having read it, you should have brought it to Monsieur Smyslov. But you kept it, because you intended to circulate it amongst my people. You are sentenced to death. Tell me who gave you this paper, and I will commute that sentence."

The woman looked at her lover. "We found it, Your Highness," Nikolai said again.

Bolugayevski stared at him for some seconds, and Nikolai stared back. The people at the back of the room shuffled their feet. "If we may beg for mercy, Your Highness," said one of the council. "Nikolai is a good lad. And Natasha is also. I am sure if they were suitably punished they would never again accept such a paper."

"That is up to them," Bolugayevski said. "All they have to do is tell me who gave them this paper."

"May I look at it, sir?" Colin asked.

Bolugayevski slid it across the table. Colin picked it up and read: *Obey the Will of the People. The Will of the People cannot be gainsaid. We will bring down the tyrant, and all his lackeys. Wait for the summons. The Will of the People.*

"It is a secret society," Bolugayevski said. "Devoted to sedition. It must be stamped out. Certainly I will have none of it on my estate. Well?" he demanded. "Have you made up your mind?"

"I found the paper," Nikolai insisted. "I found it. Natasha had nothing to do with it. She cannot even read."

"I am sure you told her what was in it," Smyslov said.

"No, your worship, I did not. She knows nothing of it."

"I cannot see any reason for clemency," Bolugayevski announced. "They are guilty of sedition, and of defying

71

me. But I will give the woman a last chance to save herself. Hang the man."

Four of the overseers hurried forward to grasp Nikolai's arms. Two more were already throwing a rope over the rafters. "Your Highness," Colin whispered. "Surely the man must be given the right to appeal?"

"Appeal? What has he got to appeal about?"

"Well . . . the sentence."

"The mandatory sentence for sedition is death. This is sometimes commuted to exile, but I see no reason for that here. The lout has defied me."

"But if he were to appear before a higher body, they might think differently."

"Colin," Bolugayevski said. "I know you are English, and perhaps do not understand these things. There is no higher authority, on Bolugayen, than the Prince."

Colin looked back at the room. The sentence was being carried out, without a murmur of protest from anyone save the girl Natasha, who fell to her knees, screaming her lover's name. Nikolai had been taken beneath the beam, the noose placed around his neck, and four of the overseers were already heaving on the rope. His feet left the ground, kicking desperately, as the rope choked the breath from his lungs. "God, but these peasants take long to die," the Prince grumbled.

"Assist him!" Smyslov commanded, and two of the overseers threw their arms round Nikolai's legs and pulled down with all their strength.

"I believe he is gone, Your Highness," said one of the council, peering at the drooping body.

"And good riddance," Bolugayevski growled. "Well, girl. The name of the man, or woman, who gave you that literature."

The girl had been on her knees, her head sagging. Now she raised it. "Murderer!" she screamed.

Bolugayevski's features stiffened. "I am offering you your life," he told her.

"I will look down on you in hell!" she shouted.

Bolugayevski jerked his head. "Take that carrion down," he commanded. "And hoist the woman in its place."

Chapter 4

THE CATASTROPHE

"I think Lieutenant MacLain needs a glass of vodka," Prince Bolugayevski said as they entered the palace. "But I will have one too. It is devilish cold out there." The footman bowed and hurried off.

Bolugayevski threw his gloves into his hat, being held by another footman. A third was taking off his fur coat. Two more footmen were attending to Colin. "You'll be telling me next that you have never seen a woman hanged," the Prince said.

"I have never seen a woman hanged," Colin said.

The footman returned with a tray and glasses and a decanter. Bolugayevski tossed his first drink off, and the glass was refilled. Colin finished his drink. "You'll excuse me." Not even a whole bottle of vodka was going to remove the memory of that twisting, dying body, that blood-blackening face.

He went into the hall, and the footmen bowed. He went up the great staircase to the first gallery, and faced Alexandra. "Murderer!" she hissed, and walked away from him.

He followed her. "What did you mean by that?"

"Were not Nikolai Raspeen and Natasha Perubovska hanged?" she asked over her shoulder.

"And that concerns you?"

She turned to face him. "Obviously it does not concern *you*!"

"I had nothing to do with it. Save that I was there. And felt sick. It was your loving father who ordered the executions."

"I hate him. Oh, how I hate him. But you . . . you are married to Dagmar. She is just like Papa, in everything."

"So you hate her too?"

Alexandra tossed her head. "Are you going to tell her? Or Papa?"

"You mean they don't know?"

"Well . . ." she flushed.

"I will not tell them. But you must tell me how you knew of that couple, Nikolai and Natasha."

"They are our serfs. Should I not know them?"

"I am told there are nearly four thousand serfs on Bolugayen. Do you know them all by name?" She flushed, and he held her shoulders. "Listen to me, Alexandra. They were condemned for possessing seditious literature. Did you know that?"

"Yes. We were in Poltava, last summer, and this man was handing the sheets out. He gave one to Nikolai. Then the police came, and he ran away, But some of the sheets got scattered, and I picked one up."

"And did what with it?"

"That's my business."

"You mean you still have it? My God! Do you know what your father will do when he finds out?"

"He cannot find out, unless you tell him."

"I am not going to tell him. But you must promise me to destroy that paper. Now."

"Why do you care?"

"You are my sister. Well, virtually."

"Did you really feel sick when you saw Natasha hanged?"

"Yes."

"Would you have spared her life?"

"In England, we do not hang people for possessing pamphlets directed against the Queen."

"England," she said. "I should love to go there. Will you take me there, Colin?"

"Chance would be a fine thing."

"But if you hate Dagmar . . ."

"I never said I hated Dagmar."

"But you do. Now I know you will escape, just as soon as the snows thaw. Will you take me with you?" She pouted. "Don't you like me? I would be as good to you as Dagmar."

"I believe you would," he agreed, wondering if she had the least idea what she was talking about.

"I promise," she said, and to his consternation, threw both arms round his neck and kissed him on the mouth.

"Why, Colin," Dagmar said from the doorway. "Whatever are you doing?"

Colin's arms had gone round the girl's waist to hold her against him. Now he released her, even as Alexandra herself jumped backwards, cannoning into the table. "I was thanking him," Alexandra said, a trifle breathlessly.

"He must have done you a great favour," Dagmar remarked. "Well, I would run along if I were you." After an anxious glance at Colin, Alexandra left. Dagmar walked into the centre of the room and sat in a straight chair, hands clasped on her lap. "Papa tells me you were quite overcome at the court."

"Yes, I was. We do not do things that way in England."

"Those people were would-be revolutionaries."

"Surely the word – 'would-be'?"

"You would prefer to wait until they had actually asassinated someone before bringing them to justice?"

"I would prefer to know that they were at least planning an assassination before hanging them."

"You read that obscene pamphlet. There are things you need to know about Russia."

"Your father has already tried to explain his, and presumably your, point of view."

76

"That we need to keep our serfs in subjection? This is perfectly true. Can you imagine the chaos were they to get the upper hand? Supposing they did, can you imagine the tyranny they would impose upon the country? Upon everyone, including their own class? That always happens when those not bred to rule begin doing so: you have to look no further back than the French Revolution. Quite apart from a total collapse of Russia's place in the world. I know it is customary in the West to regard Tsar Nicholas as a tyrant, but he is at least an educated man, with some sense and sensibility to govern his actions. Put a man of the people in a position of unlimited power, and you would have an unimaginable situation."

"Wasn't Napoleon a man of the people?"

"And didn't he drive France into an unimaginable situation? Napoleon," she said darkly. "He is responsible for all of this because of the influence he, and his ideas, had upon Tsar Alexander. The Tsar dreamed of freeing the serfs, and making Russia into some kind of Utopia. Then he died, suddenly, and mysteriously. But the true misfortune is that he died before he revealed the agreement he had come to with his eldest son, the Grand Duke Constantine. Constantine did not wish to sit on the throne, with all its responsibilities and all of its problems, and Tsar Alexander accepted this. But only his intimates knew of it when he died, and when Tsar Nicholas was pronounced Emperor, even he refused at first to believe it. The result was the revolt in Warsaw in favour of Constantine which we call the Decembrist Plot. It had to be crushed, but it earned Tsar Nicholas a reputation as a hard and ruthless man. Then there was the second revolt in Poland, in 1832. That also had to be crushed. Can he be blamed for becoming ever more harsh and ruthless? Now the situation is compounded because the Grand Duke Alexander, the heir to the throne, is himself surrounded by 'liberal' advisers. And they know that the Tsar is not a well man. So you see, we tremble

77

on the brink of revolution." She smiled. "Another reason why I need a husband who can shoot straight. But not one who turns green at the sight of a hanging."

"And you believe in the principals of the Tsar as opposed to those of the Grand Duke."

"Of course I do. And so must anyone who wishes to preserve the greatness of Russia. In any event, who can possibly feel sympathy with these assassins who call themselves the Will of the People? They are beneath contempt." Dagmar went to the door, paused, and looked over her shoulder. "Do you like my baby sister?"

"Yes, I do. Very much."

"As she obviously likes you. Would you like to fuck her?"

"Would I . . .?" He was never sure when his wife was being deliberately provocative. But then, could he not be deliberately provocative in return? "Yes. I would."

"But you will not do it. Papa would hang you, and lock Alix up in a convent. I should remember that, if I were you."

Even a Russian winter eventually ends. Bolugayen slowly seemed to come to life, like a monster awakening from slumber. People began to smile, and there was a great greasing of cart axles and factory machinery. The cattle were allowed out, and the chickens squawked in their runs, while the crowing of the cocks filled the air. The executions and floggings of February seemed forgotten, at least until the next time the Prince decided to hold court.

It had been the longest confinement Colin had ever experienced. No doubt he should be thankful that he had been honeymooning, and had had Dagmar's arms to retreat to. The rest of the family had eaten and drunk, copiously; they had played games such as chess, and they had played music. But now they too were desperate to get out of doors, and gallop their horses across the suddenly

78

black earth. As was he. His principal occupation over the previous two months, apart from satisfying Dagmar's insatiable sexuality, had been to wade his way slowly through Prince Bolugayevski's huge library.

The other girl, Anna, the most beautiful of the trio, seemed to wish neither to dominate nor be excessively forward. Yet she was clearly highly intelligent, and while he would have liked to get to know her better, he did not wish to give Dagmar something else to hold against him.

Anna also seemed to have a disturbingly close relationship with her father, an intimacy of glance and touch. Colin had to regard the Prince as his enemy, which meant Anna also had to be so considered. Even more did he regard Bolugayevski as an enemy when he discovered that the Prince had appropriated Jennie Cromb as his mistress. He protested to Dagmar, but she merely shrugged and said, "Papa must have his sexual outlets."

And there was nothing he could do about it, even if he could have no doubt that the Prince ill-treated the girl. He saw her from time to time, but she usually looked the other way. To her he was obviously one of the rulers and she one of the serfs. And he could not take a deeper interest in her, conscious as he was that Dagmar was always watching him, and that Dagmar possessed the power of life and death over the unfortunate girl.

With the thaw there came news from the south. Prince Bolugayevski marched through the house, braying his pleasure.

"The British Government has fallen," he told his family. "That is a measure of our success, eh?"

"And Sevastopol?" Dagmar asked.

"Sevastopol is still Russian. It will always be Russian."

"And Georgei?"

"Georgei is having the time of his life. Here, this is his letter. Read it."

The girls perused it, eagerly.

"Now we will be able to write letters of our own, sir," Colin suggested.

"Why, yes, so we shall. I shall attend to it."

But a week later news arrived from St Petersburg: Tsar Nicholas I was dead.

Prince Bolugayevski immediately ordered his estate, and everyone on it, into the deepest mourning. "I shall have to go to Petersburg," he told his family. "I must attend the new Tsar, and pay my respects to the old."

"But . . ." Dagmar bit her lip.

"I am sure the past is the past," the Prince said. "With a new Tsar, a *liberal* Tsar, things will surely change."

Apparently, Colin thought, he was quite happy to support a liberal Tsar, as long as the liberality only applied to him, not his serfs. "Oh, Papa, can I come with you?" Alexandra begged.

"Not this time, my poppet. The roads are still very bad, and I have no idea what sort of reception I will receive. In the summer, if all goes well, we shall all go to St Petersburg. Won't that be fun?"

"Oh, yes, Papa," Alexandra cried.

Anna merely looked thoughtful.

Dagmar was concerned with practicalities. "Who will be in charge here?"

"Why, you, my dear. With Colin, of course. It will be good for him to learn to rule."

"But I will be in charge?" She wanted confirmation.

"Yes." Bolugayevski looked at Smyslov. "You understand?"

"Of course, Your Highness."

"What about the sewing?" Dagmar asked.

"That must proceed as normal. We must live."

"And the ceremony?"

A look of uncertainty crossed Bolugayevski's face. "Perhaps it would be inappropriate."

"We must have the ceremony, Papa," Anna protested.

"The people will be unhappy if we do not, Your Highness," Smyslov agreed.

"But I cannot stay," Bolugayevski said. "I must go to Petersburg. And Georgei is not here."

"Well . . ." Dagmar smiled at Colin. "Colin can act for you."

"Ah! Yes. You will permit this?" He was not asking Colin.

"I will be pleased to permit this, Papa," Dagmar said. "As you say, he must gain the experience of ruling."

"Perhaps you would tell me just what is going on?" Colin asked, after they had waved the Prince and his entourage out of sight. He had been too busy writing letters to his parents, his uncle, and Lord Cardigan, to take much interest in anything else. But now these were on their way, and he felt that a great weight had been removed from his mind, and his conscience; he had explained the situation as best he could without being so ungallant as to say that he had been kidnapped by a Russian countess for her bed. That would have been too humiliating a confession.

"Why, nothing is going on," Dagmar said in response to his question. "But we have to sow the crops."

"And there is a ceremony attached to this?"

"Of course. These people retain many of their superstitions. Even Father Alexei understands this. You know there has always been a ritual ceremony connected with sowing the crops, to ensure a bountiful harvest?"

"My God! You're not going to tell me you practice human sacrifice?"

"Well, no. They used to, down to quite recently. But nowadays, such practises are frowned upon."

"You mean that you would indulge in it, if it were legal?"

She put her head on one side as she gazed at him. "I think it would be fascinating. However, as you say, it is not legal. Yet there has to be a ritual death and rebirth,

81

hopefully productive. So, you see, a maiden is selected by the village elders, and brought up to the house, and made to lie with the master of the estate, who is usually Papa, or in his absence, Georgei, and having been, hopefully, impregnated, she is then buried. Alive, of course."

Colin could not believe his ears. "And that is not a blood sacrifice?"

"She is only buried for an hour or two, and then she is dug up, and everyone is very happy. I believe there was an occasion, before I was born, when the girl was dead when she was recovered, but that was because she had lost her head completely at being buried and suffered a heart attack."

"What a nuisance," Colin said sarcastically.

"It was. We had a very poor crop. On the other hand, there was another occasion, when I was a little girl, when Papa actually did manage to impregnate the girl. Everyone was delighted. And that year we had a very good crop."

"And where is the child?"

"Vassily? He is your valet."

Colin opened his mouth and then closed it again; even if he had recognised that Vassily had to be a Bolugayevski out-child, he had not properly evaluated the relationship. "He is your brother! Your half-brother, anyway."

"Does that mean I am supposed to dine with him? Some men do educate their bastards. It was Papa's decision not to do that for Vassily. However," Dagmar went on, "if you are similarly successful, and wish it, we will educate your son. If it is a son. Second to the son you are going to give me, of course."

"I'm afraid I have no idea what you are talking about."

"Colin," she said, with great patience, "neither Papa nor Georgei can be here for the ceremony. Thus you will have to act for them. You can hardly expect me to."

"That is obscene."

"Oh, you are full of useless words. It is the custom. What can possibly be obscene about a custom? And what are you concerned about? I have given my permission. Besides, are you not feeling the urge to mount someone beside me? This way you can do it with my blessing. As for the girl, I do assure you that she will be the prettiest virgin on the estate."

Colin sat between Dagmar and Anna, on the balcony above the great porch of the Bolugayevski Palace. Alexandra sat next to Anna. Both the younger girls were in a state of high excitement. But then, so was Dagmar, he could tell from the way she constantly licked her lips, and pulled at her gloves. The ladies wore black evening gowns, as they were in mourning, although as the evening air was still chill, they also had fur capes. Behind the princely party were the Smyslovs, Dr Simmars and his wife, and Father Alexei, as well as four of the leading members of the *tzemtsvo* and their wives, specially invited into the palace for this most important occasion of the year.

Up from the village there wound a huge column of torchlight, all the men and women and children on the estate, wearing their very best clothes, come to behold the sacrifice, chanting hymns as they marched. It was still not quite dark, and Colin found himself staring at the little group leading the procession. This consisted of four men, who between them were half dragging, half carrying a woman. Even above the singing he could hear her screams and wails.

Dagmar squeezed his hand. "She is only play-acting. In any event, she will be given enough vodka to make her contented."

"You mean I am required to commit rape."

"Why?" she asked. "Isn't that an exciting thought?"

My God, he thought. It *was* an exciting thought. He had been sucked into this world of unbridled power, unbridled sex, unbridled superstition . . . and the catastrophe was that he was enjoying it. He was as hard as a ramrod at the thought of what he was about to do . . . and then he wondered if Jennie Cromb was in the throng? Of course she was. She would be in the crowd, and she would know what he was about to do. But she, at least, must be feeling some relief at the departure of her master.

The mass of people had reached the drive before the house, and fanned out to either side. Now Colin could see that behind the four men and the woman, there were six more men, carrying a wooden coffin. The ceremony was about to begin.

Father Alexei advanced to the balustrade of the balcony, arms outflung, and blessed the proceedings. "It is time to go down and claim your victim," Dagmar said.

"You mean you don't come with me?"

She blew him a kiss. "Tonight you are the master of all you survey, my lord Prince."

Colin went inside, to the top of the grand staircase. The servants had now assembled in the great hall, and into the hall had come the four men and the woman. The girl! As he went down the stairs he knew she could not be a day over sixteen. She was not truly pretty, but rather, attractively ugly, with a tight little monkey-face and straggling dark hair. But at least the hair looked clean.

Now she was released by her captors, who stepped away from her, leaving her isolated in the centre of the mosaic floor. She stared at Colin, and he stared back at her as he descended the stairs. He had been told exactly what he had to do by Dagmar, and now the excitement was all but overwhelming. "Behold your bride of the night, my lord," said Igor the butler. "Her name is Olga."

The girl attempted a curtsey and Igor presented the tray and the two glasses of vodka. They were bigger glasses than usual. Colin took one, and nodded at the girl, who took the other. She stared at him as she drank, but managed to drain the glass, giving a little shudder as she did so. Colin also drained his glass, then hurled it to the floor, where it shattered. Olga did likewise, and the servants clapped. Colin stepped forward, and saw Olga's lips puckering. But she swallowed her tears as he swept her from the floor, one arm under her knees and the other under her shoulders, and turned . . . and nearly dropped her. For the family and their guests had all gathered on the gallery at the head of the staircase, and they too were clapping, even more enthusiastically.

Colin swallowed, and carried his victim to the right of the staircase: not even for a ritual occasion were the family going to allow one of their serfs into one of their bedrooms, and a small ground-floor parlour had been dedicated to the purpose. Here a roaring fire suggested hell, and all the furniture had been cleared out save for a mattress on the floor, on which had been spread a white sheet; against the wall there was a washstand, with basin and ewer.

Colin carried Olga inside, and the door was closed behind him; he heard the key turning in the lock. He was here until Dagmar chose to let him out. He set Olga on her feet and she kept on going down, to kneel before him. He looked down at her. "We had best be about it."

His initial ardour had dwindled in the publicity of the event, and he was in a hurry. Olga rose to her feet, untied her rope girdle, and lifted her gown over her head. She wore nothing underneath, and had a remarkably full figure, accentuated by the chill to which she had been exposed. But now her lips were trembling again. "I do not please you, my lord."

"You would please any man, Olga," he told her truthfully enough. "I am just a little overcome."

She let the gown drop to the floor, and he realised that she must have been scrubbed time and again for this occasion; if she wore no perfume, she exuded cleanliness and good health. He undressed as rapidly as possible, but he was indeed overcome. Olga gazed at him in consternation. "I do not please you," she said again.

He put his arms round her to hold her against him, and was relieved by at least a twitch.

"We'll see what we can do without that." He kissed her mouth, ran his hands over her body, sought every nook and cranny and was at last rewarded; she gave a shriek as he entered her, for despite his massaging he doubted she was properly prepared. "I am sorry," he said when he was spent.

"I am proud," she panted.

"Will you be able to find a husband?"

"I will have the pick of every husband in the town, for having been deflowered by the Prince."

He grinned, and kissed her. "I am not the Prince. I am a stand-in."

"One day you will be the Prince," she said seriously.

One day! It could happen. But if he ever allowed himself to think like that, he would never escape this place. Olga squirmed on to his stomach, hair flopping on to his face. "Would you like to enter me again?"

"Yes, I would. But I can't, right now. Give me a little while."

"May I touch him?"

"I'd like that."

She stroked him, and he began to harden. She seemed to know all the right things to do, even if she had been a virgin. No doubt the youth of the village had to occupy their time somehow during the long winter months. "You could do it again now," Olga said.

"I believe I could. No, don't get off. Sit on me."

Olga's mouth made an O, but she knelt astride his thighs, and he reached down to guide himself into her . . . and the door opened. Olga gave another little shriek, and rolled over, Colin sat up. There was quite a crowd outside the door, but only Dagmar and another woman entered; the other woman was quite old, and he recognised her as the wife of one of the *tzemtsvo*. "Not too soon, are we?" Dagmar asked.

86

Colin stood up and backed against the wall, holding his hands in front of his penis; Dagmar had not closed the door, and apart from the servants, both Anna and Alexandra were peering at him. Olga was kneeling beside the mattress, also attempting to use her hands as a shield. Dagmar and the woman ignored them both to examine the sheet, and the drops of blood staining the white.

"There we are," Dagmar said. "My congratulations, Colin. Now dress yourself. And you too, girl. The people are waiting."

Olga put on her dress, and was led out into the hall. "She is ready!" the woman shouted.

The servants cheered, and the news was passed back out into the waiting crowd, to more cheers. Dagmar and Colin followed. "You seem to have been enjoying yourself," Dagmar remarked. "Were you about to fuck her a second time?"

"As a matter of fact, yes."

"Did you find her attractive?"

"As a matter of fact, yes."

"You amaze me. Well, as soon as this is done, you can fuck me instead. The thought of you in her has made me quite randy."

Olga was duly placed in her coffin, the lid nailed down, and she was buried, in a grave already hacked out of the still frozen earth. The serfs settled down to a huge meal at which great quantities of vodka were drunk. The family and their guests were also fed, in the house, and afterwards Dagmar and Colin strolled through the trestle tables which had been erected on the drive, greeting their servants. Colin was growing more and more agitated, but at last Dagmar gave the signal, and the spades whipped away the earth. The coffin was lifted out, the lid taken off, and Olga emerged, shivering but smiling and triumphant.

The onlookers cheered and several of the young men seized the girl and lifted her on their shoulders, parading her in front of the house while she was given glass after glass of vodka. Then they carried her down the slope to the village, their elders following, the children rushing around, the dogs barking. "I fancy little Olga may well be deflowered more than once, tonight," Colin said.

"Absolutely," Dagmar agreed. "Tonight she belongs to everyone."

"Yet she will still find a husband?"

"Of course. Who would not be proud to follow where the Prince has led? And if she becomes pregnant, so much the better."

"But the babe will still be considered mine?"

"Well, of course. You are the Prince."

"The acting Prince."

"No matter." She linked her arm through his and they turned back towards the house. "You have done your duty, and it will be the most fruitful year for a long time."

"I suppose it pays to be confident."

She squeezed his arm. "It already is. Simmars tells me that I am probably pregnant."

Colin hadn't realised that she had missed a couple of periods. But a month later there seemed no doubt about it at all. Once again it was an occasion for an enormous celebration; Dagmar wanted her father to share her news, and sent a galloper to Petersburg, as no one expected the Prince back before the summer. "We must take no chances with this one," she said. "You will have to act the Prince in more than just bed."

Colin was actually intrigued to assume the duties of estate manager, always with Smyslov at his shoulder to make sure he did not go wrong. He was first of all astounded at the size of the estate, which covered some two thousand square miles in area. There were several woods in which, according to Smyslov, there were both bears and wolves, not to mention foxes, to provide sport for the Prince and his family.

Then there were enormous areas of pasturage, where the cattle were grazed, guarded always by a considerable body of armed men to protect them from the wild beasts. There were hills and valleys. There were lakes and a river. There were quarries where stone was hewn and lumberjack camps where felled trees were sawn up into logs. There were several villages, inhabited by people to whom the Prince Bolugayevski was only a name but still utterly controlled and dominated their lives. And above all there were the fields, still black and unpromising. But the wheat crop had been sewn and Smyslov assured him that come July they would be a sea of waving stalks, together with acre upon acre of cotton trees, the true fount of the family's wealth.

On Colin's first tour of the property, he and Smyslov rode to the farthest eastern boundary, a journey which took eight days. They sat their horses on a a ridge and looked down on more rolling countryside. "That is foreign land, for us," Smyslov said. "It belongs to Count Rashnikoff."

"Is he one of those who does not recognise the Prince? I mean, socially."

"Yes. It does not bother the Prince. Does it bother you, Mr MacLain?"

"Hardly. I'm quite sure they don't recognise me, either."

Their servants had already pitched camp on the reverse slope of the hill, as it was late afternoon. "We shall rest here for tomorrow, before starting back. Would you like a woman?" Smyslov asked.

"Is that all you people ever think about?"

Smyslov grinned. "Women, and vodka. What else *is* there to think about?"

"I suppose, not much," Colin agreed, certainly if you are a hired hand, existing in the midst of this vast nothingness, he thought. "Except, maybe, God."

"God is for church, on Sundays," Smyslov remarked.

"I'm not sure Father Alexei would agree with you. Anyway, where are you going to find a woman out here?"

"There is a village in the next valley."

"And you can just ride in there and take one of their women?"

Smyslov grinned. "These are Jews."

"On our land?"

"Oh, yes. The Prince allows them to stay there, because they are very industrious people. But he will not have them near the town, or the palace, of course."

"Why not?"

"Because they are Jews."

"Good Lord! Are there many Jews in Russia?"

"Oh, yes," Smyslov said, pouring vodka. "Far too many."

"And they will let you use their women? I have heard they are the most rigid of people in their sexual mores."

"Mr MacLain, they are rigid in everything. That is why they are so disliked. On the other hand, they have to have somewhere to live, so however much they may resent it, they have to accept whatever we inflict upon them." He drank vodka, and grinned. "Call it one of the taxes they have to pay, if you like. I am sending Dimitri over there now, to fetch one for me. I shall tell him to bring one for you, as well."

"Aren't you afraid your wife will find out?"

"My wife hardly expects me to absent myself from her bed for a fortnight without replacing her. I am sure the Countess holds the same opinion of you."

"I see." He wondered if she did. "But I don't think I shall indulge tonight."

Smyslov raised his eyebrows. "Some of these women are really most attractive. And what makes them even more attractive is the fact that they hate us for taking them, and yet they know they must submit, because to resist might mean the destruction of their village." He

90

winked. "There is no more interesting experience than having a woman who hates you, but is helpless."

"I think we are surrounded by all the hate we can stand," Colin said. "I'll bid you goodnight."

He fell asleep to the sound of ribald laughter.

He sought Dagmar when, a week later, he regained the palace. She was in the library, playing chess with Alexandra. "Darling!" She drew him down for a kiss. "I knew you were back; I heard the dogs barking. What do you think of our property?"

"It is very impressive. May I have a word?"

"Of course." She moved a piece.

"In private?"

She raised her eyebrows, but nodded. "What can you possibly say that I shouldn't hear?" Alexandra demanded.

"I wish to speak with my wife," Colin said, patiently.

"Your game is lost anyway," Dagmar said. "Your knight is out of play. You cannot hope to beat me virtually a piece down."

"Ha!" Alexandra commented, and flounced to the door.

"And close it," Dagmar said. "Now, what is troubling you? Come and sit down and tell me all about it."

He sat beside her, and told her about Smyslov and the Jews. "Jews!" she said contemptuously. "They are not worth thinking about."

"They are human beings," he argued. "If you allow them to squat on your land, they must be properly treated. Just to enter their village and seize three of their women, rape them and then send them home again . . . that is barbaric."

"You really should not take up postures until you understand what you are speaking about," she sneered. "You say we treat them as if they were animals? That is because they *are* animals. They are pariahs. It is an act of charity on Papa's part that they are allowed to

91

squat, as you so aptly put it, on our land at all. There are many *boyars* who will not permit them on their property. There are many towns who will not have them inside their limits. Poltava is generous in this, at least under its present governor. It is not possible to be kinder or more humane to such people than we are. To make them move on would be to drive them to destruction. Believe me, they know how well off they are. And if they have to sacrifice the odd maidenhead, that is a small price for them to pay."

"For your extreme generosity in allowing them to live?" Colin got up and went to the door.

"Colin! Don't go off in a rage. It is the way of the world. You cannot change it."

He checked at the door to look back at her. "Not even if I am the Prince?"

She smiled. "But you are not the Prince, Colin, as you keep reminding me. You are only the acting Prince. Papa will soon be home. And Georgei too, whenever this stupid war ends."

He hesitated a moment longer, then threw the door open and stalked into the hall. And checked at the sound of a horn.

Dagmar appeared at the library door. "What's that noise?"

"It's the post!" Instantly he was forgotten as she ran for the stairs. Indeed people were appearing from everywhere as the horn brayed again.

"There'll be a letter from Papa!" Alexandra shouted, running down the next flight of stairs.

"And one from Georgei!" Dagmar cried.

The horseman urged his mount into a gallop as he reached the drive, and saw the crowd of people gathered in the downstairs porch to greet him. He slid from the saddle, unslinging his satchel as he did so, and Igor gave him a glass of vodka. But Colin noted that he was trembling as he extended the bundle of letters. Dagmar snatched them from him, and immediately noticed the official envelope with the black edges. "From . . . Sevastopol! Oh, my God!"

"Georgei!" Alexandra screamed, snatching at the letter.

Dagmar looked about to faint, and Colin hastily put his arm round her waist. Anna took the letter, and slit the envelope with her thumb. Her lips moved as she scanned the words. The servants waited in absolute silence. "Tell me!" Dagmar shouted.

"Georgei is dead," Anna said.

Chapter 5

THE CONSPIRATOR

The man behind the counter looked up as the bell jangled and the door opened. He was a bookseller, and had few customers. Now he regarded the tall, handsome woman with the auburn hair peeping out from beneath her headscarf; both scarf and gown informed him that she was unlikely to buy a book. He frowned, peering at her from behind his spectacles. "Yes?"

"You are Monsieur Woskov?"

"I am Woskov."

"I have the Will to come here," she said.

Woskov uttered a gasp, and although they were alone in the shop gave a glance left and right. "Who sent you?"

"Igor Bondarevski."

The shopkeeper continued to stare at her for several seconds. Then he said, "We had supposed the Will was finished, on Bolugayen."

"Because two were hanged? The Will is stronger than ever."

Woskov was looking more concerned. "You are not Russian," he said.

"Does that matter?"

"Everything matters in this business. Who are you?"

"I am a servant in the Bolugayevski Palace. My name is Jennie Cromb."

"The Englishwoman! I have heard of you. And you

pretend to be of the Will? How do I know you are not a spy?"

"I used the password."

"Ha! You could have been given it by one of the Bolugayevskis. They could have tortured it out of Raspeen or the woman."

"They learned nothing from either of them," Jennie assured him.

"Ha!" he said again. "We have heard nothing from Igor for the past month."

"The estate is in mourning. Have you not heard that Count Bolugayevski is dead?"

"I have heard this. Good riddance!"

"The body arrives in a few days time, for burial," Jennie said. "Prince Bolugayevski is due back as well. Igor is of the opinion that we will never have a better time to strike a decisive blow. The Count is dead. When the Prince is also dead, then we shall see."

"Ha! What shall we see? The estate will be in the hands of the Countess Dagmar. No, she will be the Princess Dagmar. She is a devil, far worse than her father or her brother."

"It is our intention to remove the Countess as well. And her husband. And the Countess Anna. Only the Countess Alexandra of the family will survive. We know she is a liberal. In fact, we are sure she would be one of us, if she dared. She is only afraid of her father and brother . . . and her sister. With them out of the way . . . who can tell?"

"You mean to murder five people, all at once?"

"We mean to *execute* five people, all at once," Jennie pointed out. "As they execute us, in batches."

"I do not like trusting foreigners," Woskov grumbled.

"We are your best hope. Besides, what are you risking? Give me the gun, and then forget about it, and me, and the Will, if you wish."

"You think it is as simple as that? When they take you,

95

they will hand you over to the police. Do you know what they will do to you?"

"They will not take me," Jennie said.

"They will brain your child before your eyes."

"He is not my child. He is Count Bolugayevski's child."

"You are unnatural."

"I have been conditioned to be unnatural."

"And then do you know what they will do? They will force broken glass up your ass."

"I have said, they will not take me." Her voice was even, but there were pink spots in her cheeks.

"And when they do that," Woskov went on, "you will tell them everything they wish to know. You will tell them about me, about this shop, about everything."

"Monsieur Woskov, I have been picked for this, out of all the members of the Will on Bolugayen, because I am the one in whom Igor Bondarevski has the most confidence. Now, will you give me the gun, or not?"

Woskov glared at her, then went to one of the bookcases which lined the walls. From a shelf he took out several books, and from behind them lifted down a cloth bag.

"You considered that well hidden?" Jennie was aghast.

"Nobody buys those books."

She untied the string and looked into the bag.

"Do you know anything about such things?" Woskov asked.

"I will not be the one using it. But show me how it works, anyway," Jennie said, and took the revolver from the bag.

"It is an American weapon, called a Colt," Woskov said. "It has this revolving part, called a chamber, you see? The chamber contains six bullets. You point it, and squeeze the trigger. The head hits the percussion cap on the bullet and fires it, and in the same instant moves the chamber round, so that the next bullet is ready to be fired. All six can be discharged in a matter of a few seconds."

96

"Where are the bullets?"

"Let me see you squeeze the trigger, first."

Jennie levelled the gun at the wall, took a deep breath, and pulled her finger tight. The revolver jerked on to the empty chamber. "You would have missed the side of a house," Woskov said contemptuously.

"I will practice," she promised. "Give me the bullets."

Woskov delved into another bookcase, and produced a box. "There are twelve in there."

"That will do very nicely. Now give me a book."

"Eh?"

"I came in here to make a purchase," she pointed out. "Give me Pushkin."

"Ha! Everyone wants to read Pushkin." He selected a volume and handed it to her. "Can you read?"

"Yes," she said. "I can read." She placed the book beside the revolver and the box of bullets in her satchel. "Thank you. I will not visit you again."

"I should hope not." He watched her walk to the door. She was a beauty. "I will wish you good fortune."

Jennie stepped into the sunlight, and blinked. Then she hurried towards the market, and the rest of the Bolugayevski people. Normally either the Countess Dagmar or one of her sisters came into town on market days, but because they were in mourning the shopping party was commanded by Tatiana Smyslova, who was sitting impatiently in the cart. "Where have you been?" she demanded.

"I purchased a book, madame."

"A book? What book?"

Jennie opened her satchel. Tatiana Smyslova inspected the volume then handed it back. "Stupid girl. Did you not know there is a complete set of Pushkin in the Prince's library?"

"I am not allowed in the Prince's library, madame."

"Anyway, a serf, reading Pushkin? That is an absurdity.

Come along now, hurry up. It is time we were on our way."

Usually when the Bolugayevskis went shopping in Poltava they spent several days at their town palace. But today the palace was shuttered and silent. Almost Jennie felt sorry for them; their entire future had been built around Count Georgei. As had hers. But when she remembered that, her pity dissipated into anger and outrage. Of course she had gone with him of her own free will. He had offered her more money than she had ever dreamed of possessing. Presumably that made her a whore, although she had not been on offer to more than one man. And her dream of a London adventure and a return to Blaistone with her pockets jingling had ended very rapidly. The Count had been courtesy itself on the ride up to town, and when they had stopped for the night at an inn and he had come to her, he had treated her with all the gentleness of a lover. It had been a memorable night; she could have imagined no more romantic or beautiful way to lose her virginity. She had not been able to believe it was happening; he *did* mean to treat her as a lady.

But then they had reached London. He had taken her to his lodgings, and said, "I like to tie my women up. Do you mind?"

She hadn't known what to reply. In view of how he had treated her up to then, she had not believed he could possibly wish to hurt her. She had clung to that belief even when, having stripped and been stretched on her face on the bed and tied by her wrists to the posts, he had gagged her mouth. "Can't have you making a noise and attracting attention," he had said. Then he had stripped himself.

She had presumed she was going to have the experience of her life. And she had had that. He had beaten her mercilessly, and she had been unable to make a sound. Then he had lifted her buttocks and entered her with a series of quite savage thrusts, which had left her bleeding as if cut with a knife.

Then he had released the gag. "If you scream," he said, "I will flog you again. The landlady is well paid."

She had sought only escape, but his servant slept outside the door. And before she could make any plans she had been bundled up and taken out of the house and to the docks, where a Russian ship was waiting to carry the Count back to St Petersburg. She had thought she would go mad, as again she had been tied up, beaten and raped. Her misery had been compounded by seasickness, and an inability to communicate with anyone on board, save for the Count himself and his servant. She had rushed headlong into hell.

He did not beat her every day, or even every week. Sometimes he could be gentle, and make love to her as if she were a lady. But this unpredictability was perhaps the hardest cross to bear, as she never knew when he would become violent. It was impossible to deduce what triggered his moods of anger. But he stopped beating her altogether when he realised she was pregnant. That had been the most fortunate thing that had ever happened to her. By then she had already become caught up in the immensity of time and space that was Russia, something she had never considered on Blaistone. Even the ride up to London, so strange and so exciting, had dwindled into nothing compared with the weeks at sea, the long passage through the Baltic, and the wonder of St Petersburg itself.

She had had no more than a glimpse of the city before they had journeyed on, to Moscow. By the time they had got there her condition was obvious. Count Georgei had taken her to consult a midwife to make sure. Then they had celebrated. She had already become acquainted with vodka, of which the Count and his servants consumed vast quantities and insisted that she do so as well. That night they had drunk champagne, while she had gaped at the onion domes on St Basil's Cathedral and the immense fortifications of the Kremlin. From that moment he had treated her with great kindness; he wanted the babe, although he had made it clear that it was a boy he required. And after Moscow the journey had become pleasant, because they had abandoned their horses and drifted down the Volga on rafts. Although by now the year was well advanced, they seemed to be outstripping winter, and moving steadily south to warmth.

Then a carriage! She had never ridden in a carriage. And *then*, Bolugayen. "This will all be mine, one day," Count Georgei had said, as they topped the last rise and could look down on the palace. "I will share some of it with my son."

"And with his mother?" she had been bold enough to ask.

"Some of it," he had promised.

Certainly she had continued to be well-treated on the estate. She had understood right away that the family did not approve of Georgei's action, or even of his choice of her, a foreigner, as the mother of his first child. But they had accepted it, because Georgei was the future Prince.

The Bolugayevski serfs had regarded her with even more suspicion than the family, at first; she was not only a stranger in a community where every member had known each other all of their lives, but she was the Count's creature. It had taken all of her natural friendliness to win them over at all, and even then she had been aware that there were secrets in the community from which she was barred. She had had no idea just how deadly some of those secrets were. That knowledge had come after the baby had been born.

The tragedy of Georgei Bolugayevski's life, she supposed, was that he had never beheld the son by whom he had set such store. Barred as he was by the excesses of his sister from marrying into polite society, he had intended to educate his bastard to the highest degree, and once he had inherited, to make the boy his heir and cock a snook at the entire Russian establishment. He had even included her in that heady dream of the future, although he had made it plain that he would never marry her.

Her dream lay in the direction of revenge. But as she had no wish to die on the scaffold she had determined that it would be a slow and patient revenge, to be achieved through the medium of her son. But then so much had changed. The war had started, and Georgei had had to go off and join his regiment, only a few weeks before her delivery. At the same time, the Prince had determined to go to his Crimean home and make sure all his shipping interests would not be in danger. Countess Dagmar had decided to accompany him.

That decision had changed Jennie's life. The estate had been left in the care of the Princess Dowager, a stern old lady who disapproved of her grandson's infatuation with a slut, as she considered the relationship to be. The moment the child was born she had informed Jennie that she was as much a serf as anyone else, and would have to work for her keep. The baby boy had been taken away from her, except for his feeds; she had not been allowed to bathe him or even to kiss him goodnight. She had been returned to the kitchens, and caned for good measure.

That had led her immediately into the orbit of Igor Bondarevski the butler, and she had discovered how deeply hated the Bolugayevskis were by their serfs. Igor was a man of many parts; the Will of the People was only one of them. Then, she had found a true Bolugayevski lover in Vassily, and learned that he too was a member of the Will. She had thought it nothing more than a servant's dream world, until the discovery that Nikolai Raspeen and his woman were in possession of seditious literature. Jennie had then understood that she was in the midst of a gigantic conspiracy. She had not sought to enter it herself; the concept had been too terrifying. She had kept away from it, until in February the Prince and Dagmar had returned, bearing with them their captive husband. That he had been Colin MacLain, a man she had always admired, had been a considerable shock, but that he had promised to help her, had seemed the best thing that had ever happened to her, better even that the death of the Dowager Princess.

Then had come the summons to Prince Alexander's bed. She had been plunged into a deeper hell than she had previously experienced. Her hatred had come flooding back, fuelled by the realisation that Colin MacLain had been merely using words to her – he was too much Dagmar's subservient creature ever to attempt to carry out his promise. Thus had come the realisation that she did not wish to wait any longer, on either the growth to manhood of her son, or the chance that Colin might after all turn out better than seemed possible. She had sought an immediate solution to her hatred, some kind of revenge, for the terror and humiliation in which they were forced to live. But there had to be some end in view. To murder the old woman, or the two girls, would have been simple enough. But there would remain Smyslov, and his people, to control events until the Prince and his son could be brought back. Murder, on that scale, was beyond their power. And at the end of it all, the Prince and the Count would still return, breathing vengeance. The Will of the People dreamed, but they did not really wish to die.

But now that Georgei was coming home in a wooden box . . .

The wagons rumbled into the yard at the back of the Bolugayevski Palace, and Jennie hurried inside. She had been allowed to be part of the household since the Princess Dowager's death, as she was both one of the Prince's playthings and the mother of Georgei's son. No decision had yet been taken regarding the babe, now

102

that his father's dreams were ended forever. This was to be Prince Alexander's prerogative – another reason for plotting his death.

"He's been fretful," complained Ludmilla the upstairs maid, who had been looking after the child.

"He is hungry," Jennie said equably, and unfastened her bodice; even after fifteen months she still had some milk. Besides, she loved the feel of him.

"Is there news?" Ludmilla asked anxiously. "Does Sevastopol still stand?"

"There have been some great battles," she said. "But Sevastopol still stands."

The door of the garret bedroom opened, and Vassily stood there. Ludmilla gave a hasty curtsey, and left; it was not merely that Vassily was the Prince's son, even if he was condemned to a lifetime of serfdom – he was also known to have an understanding with Jennie. Now he turned the key behind the maid. "Well?"

"You should not come here like this. Do you not suppose the family will become suspicious?"

"The family!" His tone was contemptuous. "I am the family. Where is it?"

"In the satchel."

He took out the revolver, cradled it almost as tenderly as she was cradling the babe. "It is beautiful. Where are the bullets?"

"In the box."

He opened the box, and took out one of the cartridges. "These are beautiful too."

"Woskov showed me how it works."

"I know how it works." He broke the gun, inserted the bullet into a chamber.

"Not in here," she snapped. He took the bullet back out again. "There are twelve," she told him. "So you can practice."

"I do not need to practice," he said proudly. "I have fired a revolver before. The Prince let me."

"And you did not shoot him, then?" She could be contemptuous too.

"It was not the time." He put the revolver and the cartridges back into the bag and sat beside her on the cot. "I shall not need more than five of them."

"Five?"

He grinned. "One for the Prince, one for Dagmar, one for Anna, one for Smyslov . . . and one for the Englishman."

"What of yourself, after?"

"Who will arrest me? I will be the only surviving Bolugayevski male. Apart from your brat."

She hugged the babe against her. "You'll not harm baby Georgei. What of the Countess Alexandra?"

He raised his eyebrows. "We agreed that Alexandra should live. She must live, to be our princess." He grinned. "I shall rule beside her. Perhaps I shall even marry her."

"Your own half-sister?"

"Well . . . bed her, anyway. I have long wanted to do that."

Prince Alexander Bolugayevski walked his horse slowly down the drive to his palace.

The servants were all in black. The death of the young Count was a far more serious affair than that of the Dowager Princess. Igor Bondarevski himself hurried forward to assist the Prince from the saddle. "Welcome home, Your Highness," he said.

"To what?" Bolugayevski demanded.

The Prince stalked up the steps to the porch, where his daughters, his son-in-law, and his bailiff waited for him. They all wore black. With them was an officer wearing the uniform and insignia of a captain in the Actirski Hussars; he had a black armband on his left sleeve. "Captain Dubaclov, Your Excellency. I visited Bolugayen two years ago, and I dined with you in Sevastopol just before you left. I was Georgei's friend. General

Menschikov gave me compassionate leave to bring his body home."

"Where is he?" Bolugayevski demanded.

Dagmar led her father into the house, and into one of the reception rooms. On a trestle table in the centre of the room the coffin waited. It was open; Georgei had been embalmed for the long journey home. Yet it had been hastily done, and the summer was hot. There was an atmosphere in the room. Equally, the embalming had not been able to do much about the wound; the bullet had taken away half of Georgei's face.

Dagmar remained by the door while her father stood above the corpse. "Who did this?" the Prince asked.

Dagmar sighed. "They say it was an English bullet, Father."

He turned to face her. "And you married one," he snarled.

"A man who once saved Georgei's life, Father."

"For him to become this lump of carrion? Bare your ass." The hand which still held his riding crop twitched, and the thong snapped against his boot.

Dagmar's head came up. "You cannot whip me, Father. I am five months pregnant. With your grandchild!"

He glared at her, then at her stomach, but in the loose gown there was no visible evidence. "Did you not get my letter?" she asked.

"I got your letter." His shoulders suddenly sagged. "My family is destroyed."

"Your family is here, in my belly."

"And the father?"

"Give him the opportunity, and he will prove a worthy son to you."

"An Englishman? Who wishes only to escape you?"

"I do not think he wishes to do that any longer, Father."

Bolugayevski looked down at his son for a last time. "Have him covered up," he said. "No one is to look

105

on him again. He is ugly. And then bring Colin to me."

Dagmar summoned Igor to have the coffin sealed, then took Colin upstairs to the Prince's study.

Bolugayevski sat behind his desk, leaning back in his chair. Dagmar gestured Colin also to a seat, and sat beside him. "I have heard good reports about you," the Prince said. "You impregnated the Queen of the Harvest. That is good. Even I have only ever done that once. Now you can no longer play act. Now you must take my son's place."

"If I can," Colin said. "Did you despatch my letters, sir?"

"Of course I did. And there have been no replies. Have you received any?"

"No, sir. Yet must I write them again, sir, to make sure."

Bolugayevski leaned forward, pointing. "Let me remind you, young man, that you are still a prisoner of war. More, you have a responsibility to your wife, and to your unborn child. And now, even more than that, you have a responsibility to my family. It was an English bullet that struck down Georgei."

"I am sorry, sir. It was a Russian bullet that struck me down, at Balaclava."

The two men glared at each other. "Why must you quarrel, at such a time?" Dagmar asked. "I am sure Colin will continue to fulfil his obligations to me, Father. Perhaps if you were to tell him exactly what you have in mind for him . . ." The Prince raised his eyebrows. "You see," Dagmar went on, "Bolugayen must be ruled, and by a man. It is the law. We have stamped out the Will of the People by your prompt action last March, Papa. But still, we can take no chances on its recurring. By the very nature of things, it is possible that you may die . . ." Bolugayevski cleared his throat. "Before our son grows to manhood," Dagmar continued. "In that case, you, Colin, will have to be the Prince, until our son can inherit."

"Would I *really be* the Prince?" Colin asked.

"There have been many well-born men of English and more especially Scottish descent who were ennobled by the tsars," Dagmar insisted.

"It could be done," Bolugayevski agreed, grudgingly. "We could apply for the necessary letters patent, of adoption and ennoblement, from the Tsar. I had an audience with him, you know."

"Did you, Papa?" Dagmar was suddenly excited.

"That business was not mentioned. However, neither was I invited to a court reception he was holding a few days later."

"Oh." Her shoulders drooped.

"But there are changes in the air," her father went on. "His Majesty is already canvassing opinion both on ending the war and on freeing the serfs. He is summoning a meeting of the *boyars*, as soon as it can be arranged, to discuss this. I am to attend."

"Then you will be re-accepted socially."

"Is that all you can think of? This is a serious situation. It is widely believed that the Tsar intends to free all the Imperial serfs, as soon as it is practical. Well, no one can stop him doing that, although I have no doubt that it will cause trouble. As to his other intentions, I doubt he can actually do either," Bolugayevski went on. "There are too many *boyars* implacably opposed to either course."

"And you of course are one of them, sir," Colin remarked.

"I am. And so must you be, if you wish to be a Bolugayevski."

"I'm afraid I cannot agree to that, sir. I think the Tsar is adopting a most sensible, and correct attitude."

"Why, you . . ."

"Papa!" Dagmar said severely. "And you, Colin. You are behaving like children, with Georgei's body lying

107

downstairs. Colin! Papa is offering you an immense fortune, an immense future. It will also be the fortune and the future of your son." Her gaze softened. "Of your *sons*. Will you reject it?"

Colin looked at her. It was an immense opportunity. But he could never be another Prince Bolugayevski, not in the mould the family required. Then he thought, but if I *am* ever the Prince Bolugayevski, then surely I could do as I please? I could create a new mould, for my son. For my *sons*. Suddenly, it was a most attractive prospect.

"You would have to swear to make your home here in Russia," Dagmar said softly, watching his expression.

He glanced at her, then at the Prince. "I would like to consider the offer, certainly, sir," he said.

Bolugayevski nodded. "We will speak of it after the funeral."

"Tell us the news, Captain Dubaclov," Alexandra begged at dinner.

"Ah, the news," Dubaclov said. "Well, let me see, when last did you hear?"

"We know the enemy were reinforced by some Sardinians in February," Anna said.

"And we heard of the huge bombardment at Easter," Dagmar added.

Dubaclov nodded. "That was a bad business. We suffered six thousand casualties. Their second attack, in June, they came at us, man to man. It was in that fight that Georgei fell. We held them, even if we suffered another five thousand casualties. Do you know what happened after that? I heard of it just as I was leaving. The British commander, Lord Raglan, died. Some say it was of a broken heart because of his failure." He grinned. "More likely it was cholera."

The table was silent for several minutes, then Colin said, "Are these casualties being replaced?"

Dubaclov hesitated before replying. "I am afraid not.

108

The way in and out of Sevastopol is virtually impassable since the Allies have been able to move closer. They allowed me through because I was escorting a dead officer. But replacements . . . no."

"Then Sevastopol is bound to fall."

Dubaclov sighed. "It does seem likely. There is a rumour that the Tsar is contemplating peace."

Alexander Bolugayevski set down his glass. "I have just returned from St Petersburg. I heard no such rumour."

Both Dagmar and Colin looked at him in surprise.

"I am sorry, Your Highness," Dubaclov said. "I am only repeating what I heard in Sevastopol."

"But . . . if the Tsar sues for peace, we will have been defeated," Alexandra said.

"And Georgei will have died for nothing," Anna added, her tone bitter.

Alexander Bolugayevski glared at his daughter, pushed back his chair and left the room. They heard him shouting at Igor. "Send the Englishwoman to me."

Colin made to rise, and Dagmar held his hand. "There is nothing you can do," she said. "Not now. Please be sensible."

Slowly Colin sat down again.

The family waited in the breakfast room. Captain Dubaclov stood as close to Anna as he dared. He had thought Dagmar the most beautiful of women, when he had come here two years ago, and again when he had met her in Sevastopol. But now he had seen Anna. Anna was more beautiful than her sister, her features were softer; she was young, and virginal. She had, so far as he was aware, never left Bolugayen in her life. She was like an unopened rosebud, waiting for a man to come along and teach her all the delights of the world. So she too was a countess. And she was equally a possible princess, in the course of time. Thus her husband would also be a possible prince. To accomplish that, he might even find it possible not to hate the Englishman – or at least to appear not to do so. But Anna hardly seemed aware of his existence. Of course, she, like all her family, was overwhelmed with grief . . . There would be time later.

Dagmar entered on the arm of her husband. Prince Bolugayevski came last. He greeted no one in the room, and no one attempted to greet him. Instead he addressed Father Alexei. "Is all ready?"

"Everything is ready, Your Highness."

The Prince went to the outer door. "What are you waiting for?" he demanded.

They hurried behind him, into the hall. Six footmen lifted the coffin and carried it out of the door and into the garden. The Prince followed, and Dagmar and Colin followed him. How different to the first time he had seen this garden. Now there was no snow, only green grass, no furs, only muslin gowns. Now flowers sprouted to either side. But beyond the leafy archway lay fresh-turned earth. And here, too, the servants had taken up their positions, together with the members of the *tzemtsvo* and their wives; the mass of the serfs waited at the front of the house. If Colin doubted any of them felt genuine grief for the death of the Count, they all had to fear the rage of the Prince, which had already been so terribly displayed.

Colin looked along the row of faces. Igor Bondarevski, stood close to Jennie Cromb, her hair hidden beneath her black bandanna, but her face stark and cold. Everyone in the house had heard her screams last night. Besides Jennie was Vassily, who stared at his father with utter hatred. Filing in behind the family were Smyslov and his wife, and his Black Regiment.

The servants were assembled on the left side of the grave. The family stood on the right. All heads were bowed, staring into the grave, as the ornate wooden box with the brass fittings was slowly lowered, and Father Alexei began his prayers. Colin looked up, and found

110

himself staring at Jennie, who stood almost exactly opposite him, and whose face wore an expression he had never seen before.

A movement caught his eye, and his head half turned to look at Vassily, standing beside Jennie, and whose hand was emerging from the pocket of his tunic. For a moment Colin could not credit what he was seeing, and then Vassily had levelled the revolver, and fired; from a distance of no more than eight feet the bullet slammed into Prince Bolugayevski's stomach.

Chapter 6

THE PRINCESS

There was no immediate response from anyone, save the Prince. He collapsed in an almost straight line and lay on the ground, hands clutched to his belly. Colin realised that the revolver was moving to point at Dagmar. He gave a shout, and struck his wife on the back. Dagmar shrieked, and fell into the grave, to land on the coffin with a thud. Colin had already swung his arm, to send Anna sprawling, while the revolver barked again, and for the second time in his life he felt that numbing thud. The sudden flurry of movement in front of him had distracted Vassily, and he was now firing wild. Alexandra gave a shriek and fell to her knees. Behind her Tatiana Smyslova also cried out as she was hit.

The hammer clicked on an empty chamber, and the shocked onlookers leapt into action. "Take them alive!" Dagmar shouted, holding on to the sides of the grave in an attempt to pull herself up, and gazing at her father as he writhed and groaned; her hat had fallen off and her hair was cascading in every direction. "I want them alive!" But she was already more concerned about Colin, kneeling on the ground with his back to her, hugging himself.

Alexandra was on her hands and knees, moaning, her head drooping; Anna was kneeling beside her.

Sergeant Golkov had drawn his revolver, and had been going to fire at Vassily, but had been checked by Dagmar's command and instead fired into the air. Tatiana Smyslova

112

was lying on her back, screaming again and again. Her husband was kneeling beside her. His Black Regiment were already running forward, to either side of the injured people and the grave, wielding their whips.

Dr Simmars was looking left and right, uncertain who to attend to first. Father Alexei had also dropped to his knees, unhurt; he was praying. Dubaclov had drawn his revolver, but could not make up his mind what to do with it.

Vassily was staring at the mess he had made of the assassination attempt; he could not believe he had not killed anyone. He reached for the six bullets in his pocket. But Igor also reacted. The assassination attempt had been a failure; now it was time to think of oneself. He threw both arms round the young man's waist, and brought him to the ground. "I've got him!" the butler bawled. The rest of the servants surged forward, equally anxious to prove their innocence. Only Jennie remained standing, absolutely still, staring at the mayhem in front of her.

"Help me, you old goat!" Dagmar screamed at Father Alexei, stamping on the lid of her brother's coffin, and tearing at the earth with her hands. Alexei pulled himself together, and grasped her arms to heave her up on to the ground beside her father. "Papa," she said. "Papa!"

Alexander Bolugayevski opened his mouth to reply, and a spurt of blood splashed over her skirt. "Simmars!" she shrieked.

The doctor stumbled forward. He fell to his knees beside the Countess and the Prince, but he knew immediately he was too late. Dagmar crawled to her husband. "Colin . . ."

Colin attempted to grin at her through gritted teeth.

"You!" Dagmar shouted at Smyslov. "Have them carried up to the house." She reached her youngest sister, still crawling.

"I'm hurt!" Alexandra wailed. She was trying to reach behind her. "Oh, I'm hurt. Dagmar . . ."

"You'll be all right," Dagmar told her. "Smyslov . . ."

"My wife is dying, Countess! My wife is dying!" Tears were streaming down the bailiff's face.

"Not while she's making that racket. Stop the blood. Anna! Stop Alix bleeding." She crawled back to Colin, hoicking up her skirt to tear a length from one of her petticoats and stuff it against the back of his shoulder, where the blood was seeping through his coat. "Hold that there."

Panting, she got to her feet, and looked across the grave to where two members of the Black Regiment were assisting Igor in dragging Vassily to his feet. "Help me!" Vassily screamed at Jennie.

But Jennie remained still. "Take her also," Dagmar said.

"To Poltava, Your Excellency?" Golkov asked.

"No. Take them to the cellars, and hold them there. I wish to speak with them before we send for the police. You stay with them."

"Bitch!" Vassily shouted. "Sister bitch!"

"I shall make you speak in another tone, brother dog," Dagmar promised.

Jennie Cromb made no protest as she was marched away behind him, her arms held by two of the Black Regiment. "I will attend to them," Igor said.

Dagmar looked at him. "Sergeant Golkov will attend to them," she said. "Do not harm them, Golkov. I will come as soon as I can. But you will stay with them until I come." Golkov saluted.

"If only I could have understood what he was doing sooner, Your Excellency," Igor said.

"Yes," Dagmar said. "I will speak with you too, later." Her gaze swept those of the terrified servants who were not engaged in assisting the wounded, then she turned back to the family.

"I need help, Countess," Dr Simmars said.

"There is no time to send to Poltava. You will have to do the best you can. I give you *carte blanche* to requisition whoever or whatever you choose."

114

"With respect, Your Excellency, I have some medical knowledge."

Dagmar glanced at the black-bearded man hurrying beside her. "Who are you?" she demanded.

"Mordecai Fine, Your Excellency."

"You are a Jew! Are you one of our Jews?"

"Yes, Your Excellency. Also a doctor."

"I will not have a Jew in the house," Dagmar said. "As for touching my sister or my husband . . ."

"If he knows medicine, we need him, Countess," Simmars said.

Dagmar hesitated a moment, then nodded. "Very well. He can attend Madame Smyslova."

They trooped into the house, Mordecai Fine looking left and right at the furniture and carpets, the paintings, the drapes, the anxious servants – he had never seen anything like this before in his life. Alexander Bolugayevski was carried up the stairs and laid on his bed. Simmars bent over him. The doctor slowly straightened. "The Prince is dead, Countess."

"You mean he died some time ago, doctor," Dagmar told him. "I would have you be straight with me, in all matters." Simmars bowed. "And if my father is dead, as well as my brother," Dagmar said, "then I am now the Princess Bolugayevska. I would have you remember that."

Simmars glanced at his mistress, seeking some evidence of tears, or even distress. "Do you wish . . . ?"

"If my father is dead, there are other people to be attended to. Begin with me."

"Countess?"

"Princess," Dagmar reminded him. "Close the door."

Simmars hesitated, then obeyed. "I wish you to tell me that my baby is all right," Dagmar said.

Simmars licked his lips. "I . . . are you in any pain, Your Excellency?"

"I do not think so. It is difficult to say. I am shaken."

115

"To be sure, I would have to . . . examine you, Your Excellency."

"Then do so." Dagmar went to the settee against the far wall. "Do you wish me to lie, or sit?"

Simmars was trembling. "If you would lie down, Your Excellency."

Dagmar lifted her skirts to her waist and then lay down. Simmars gulped; she did not wear drawers. "Make haste," Dagmar said. "There is a great deal to be done."

"Yes, Your Excellency." Still trembling, Simmars stooped beside those magnificent thighs, ran his hands over that throbbing abdomen.

"Your hands are cold," Dagmar pointed out, as he gently kneaded the flesh. "Should they not be warm?"

"I am sorry, Your Excellency. Would you like me to wash them?"

"There is no time. Well?"

"There is no obvious disorder. To be sure, I would have to . . ." he paused in embarrassment.

"Then do it," Dagmar snapped, and parted her legs.

"If you could . . . draw them up, Your Excellency."

Dagmar put one hand under each of her knees to hold herself in position. Simmars touched her with the utmost caution. "Cold," Dagmar muttered. "But gentle. Well?"

Simmars straightened, reluctantly. "There is no trace of blood, or disorder, Your Excellency. I would say your babe is unharmed."

"Good." Dagmar sat up, pulled her skirts into place. "Now, go about your duties. And Simmars, I am no longer to be addressed as Your Excellency. I am Your Highness."

"Of course, Countess . . . Princess. Your Highness. I will go to Countess Alexandra immediately."

"You will go to Prince Bolugayevski, immediately."

"Prince . . ." Simmars looked at the body.

"My husband, doctor."

116

"Ah. Yes. Immediately, Your Highness."

He hurried from the room, and Dagmar moved closer to the bed to look down on her father. He looked ugly, because he had not been washed, and there was both dirt and blood on his face, and on his clothes. He carried the effluvium of the last violent seconds of his life. She opened the door, and the four servants who had carried their master in, stood to attention. "Send Madame Bondarevska to me," she said.

One of them hurried off, and Dagmar continued to gaze at her father. "You will hear their screams in hell, dearest Papa," she said softly.

The butler's wife stood in the doorway. "Get your women, and wash my father's body," Dagmar said.

Alexandra lay on her bed in a welter of blood, rolling and moaning. Anna and two maidservants stood beside her. "Where exactly was she hit?" Dagmar demanded.

"I don't know," Anna said. "There is so much blood . . ."

Dagmar stood above her sister. "There is no blood now," she said. "No fresh blood."

She grasped Alexandra's shoulder and rolled her over, and Alexandra gave a shriek. Dagmar gazed at the skirt, where the blood was thickest, then stooped and with a twist of her strong hands tore the garment into two. Then she tore the petticoats apart, to expose her sister's body. Now it was easy to see what had happened: the bullet had just nicked the bottom of the curve of the girl's right buttock; the matted clothing had stopped the bleeding for a while, but now the wound was starting to seep again, although it was clearly neither deep nor dangerous, unless it became infected. "Take off these clothes and wash her," Dagmar commanded. "Then bandage her up."

"I am dying," Alexandra moaned. "Oh, God, I am dying."

"You are not dying," Dagmar said. "Although you may not sit down for a while. You should thank Colin for saving

117

your life by pushing you over. Dr Simmars will come to you as soon as he can."

Anna held her arm. "Papa . . . ?"

"Papa is dead," Dagmar told her. She went outside, and listened to a great deal of noise from one of the guest bedrooms. She clucked her tongue in annoyance, and went towards the racket, but as she reached the door it was opened, and Mordecai Fine emerged.

"Ah, Countess. I really need your help."

She gazed at him from beneath arched eyebrows, surprised both by his manner and his request. "My help, doctor?"

"Madame Smyslova has been hit in the lower torso. As far as I can ascertain, as she is certainly not near death at the moment, the bullet must have struck a rib. Possibly it has exited. Possibly it is still in the wound. But in any event, it must be established where it is, and the wound must be cleaned and properly dressed. But Monsieur Smyslov will not allow me to do this."

"Why not?"

"Well, Your Excellency, it involves undressing the lady, and then I must examine her. He says he will not let a Jew touch his wife's body."

"Ah! Well, Dr Simmars will be along in a little while."

"With respect, Countess, the woman is losing blood, and there is a possibility that the bullet has lodged somewhere dangerous. Every second that she is not examined increases the risk to her life."

Dagmar stepped past him and entered the room. Tatiana Smyslova lay on the bed, moaning. Smyslov stood beside his wife, holding her hand, but he gave a hasty bow as Dagmar entered. "The Prince . . .?"

"The Prince is dead, Smyslov."

The bailiff gulped. "Then . . ."

"Under the circumstances, I am now the Princess Bolugayevska. Or certainly, my husband is the Prince. As he is unwell, you will take your orders from me."

Smyslov gulped again. "Yes, Your Highness."

"Very well. Now, Smyslov, do you wish your wife to die?"

"Well, of course not, Your Highness."

"Then you will allow Dr Fine to examine her, and do whatever he considers necessary." Smyslov gulped a third time, and looked at Fine. "I will return later to see how Tatiana is," Dagmar told him, and went to her suite.

Again there was blood, mud, and anxious faces. But Simmars was looking pleased. "His Excellency has a broken shoulder, Your Highness," he said. "But I have removed the bullet and set the bone, and he is resting comfortably."

Dagmar stood above her husband. "I think you meant 'His Highness'. He is unconscious."

"I gave him laudanum, Your Highness. The pain of setting the bone was considerable."

Dagmar looked at the firm, strong, features. She had never given him the opportunity to prove his strength. But he did have strength, which would have to be channelled – and controlled. "Well, you had better take your laudanum along to Madame Smyslova, and then my sister," she said. "I will see you later. You," she said to one of the footmen. "Stay here and watch the Prince. I wish to be informed the moment he awakens."

"The Prince, Your Highness?" The man was confused.

"Yes," Dagmar said, and followed Simmars outside.

She went down the great staircase. Madame Simmarsa, Father Alexei and Captain Dubaclov were standing in an anxious huddle.

"The Prince . . .?" Father Alexei said.

"My father is dead," Dagmar told them.

"Without the unction," Alexei muttered. "This is a catastrophe."

"You are welcome to go up and pray for him," Dagmar

said. "Madame Simmarsa, I think your husband could do with some help, with bandages."

"Of course, Your Highness." Madame Simmarsa hurried up the stairs behind the priest.

"If there is anything I can do," Dubaclov said.

"Yes, there is. Come with me." Dagmar went into the servants' lobby, from where the stairs led down to the cellars. Here she encountered Bondarevski.

"The Prince . . . ?"

"Prince Alexander is dead, Igor. Prince Colin is resting, but he will survive."

Bondarevski swallowed. "The grave . . ." Dubaclov ventured.

"Yes. Igor, have my brother's coffin brought back into the house. We shall have to have another funeral."

Bondarevski licked his lips. "The Prince . . ."

"The late Prince will have to be embalmed. Yes, you can send in to Poltava now."

"And Colonel Vorontsov, Your Highness?"

Dagmar nodded. "Him as well. As well as General Lebedeff. Haste now."

Bondarevski bowed and hurried off. "You are going to hand the assassin over to the police?" Dubaclov asked. "I had got the impression you intended to deal with him yourself."

"Them." Dagmar led him down the steps. "There are more than one. No, I wish them interrogated by the police, and tried, and executed, with the greatest publicity: they will be publicly hanged in Poltava. But I wish to . . . speak with them first. Do you understand me?"

Dubaclov had once wanted to marry this woman. And now he wanted to marry her sister. "I hope not," he said in a low voice.

Dagmar was at the door to the main cellar. She checked, and looked over her shoulder. "Are you not a soldier? A soldier needs to be hard. A Russian soldier, at any rate." She went into the room, where torches flared in

120

the sconces on the walls. This cellar was used for meat storage, and indeed there were three freshly slaughtered pig carcasses hanging from iron hooks in the centre of the room. Hanging beside them, from their wrists, were Vassily and Jennie; their feet could just reach the floor. Standing around them were Golkov and two more of his people.

Dagmar went up to them, nose twitching slightly at the high smell of the meat. Vassily's head had been drooping, but he brought it up as his half-sister stood in front of him. There was a bruise on his cheek. "I said he was not to be beaten, Golkov," Dagmar said.

"I am sorry, Your Highness. But he fought us."

"And the woman?" Jennie Cromb's face was also marked.

Golkov grinned. "She did not fight us."

"But you manhandled her anyway. All right, Sergeant. You and your people wait outside."

"But Your Highness . . ."

"I have given you an order, Golkov."

The sergeant then saluted, and gestured his men to the door. "And close it," Dagmar said.

The door clanged shut. "Well, Vassily," Dagmar said. "You have killed your father. Did you know that?"

"My only regret is that I did not kill you as well."

"Oh, yes," Dagmar agreed. "You will regret that. How much you regret it depends entirely upon me. I have sent for Colonel Vorontsov, but I do not suppose he will reach here until tonight. Then he will take you back to Poltava, and treat you very badly. Do you wish that to happen?"

"Does it matter what I wish, bitch-sister?"

"I'm sure it does, at least to you."

"Are you offering me clemency?"

"No. You killed Papa. However, I am offering you the choice between several weeks, or perhaps even months, of agony, followed by a rope, or a single bullet in the head now, without any previous pain at all."

121

Vassily glanced at Dubaclov, who still wore his revolver. "You have no right to execute me without a trial."

"My dear brother, as I am now Princess Bolugayevska, I have the right to do anything I choose, here on Bolugayen. You need to remember this. But for publicity purposes, you would be shot attempting to escape."

Vassily's breath rasped as he inhaled. "What is it you wish to know?"

"The names of your accomplices. Where you got the revolver; it is not one of ours. Where the Will of the People meet in Poltava. I will think of the questions. All you have to do is answer them. First tell me this: when you were being arrested, you shouted out, Help me. To whom were you speaking?"

"Everybody."

"You hoped my servants would assist you? I see. But you were looking at Jennie."

"She was closest."

"I do not believe you," Dagmar said. "I believe there are certain of my servants who are still members of the Will of the People, and are your accomplices. I wish to know who they are." Her tone suddenly lost its banter. "Now!"

Vassily inhaled again. "I do not know what you are talking about. I hate my father. I have always hated him. Thus I determined to kill him, once I knew that Georgei was dead."

"And thus you would have only me to deal with," Dagmar said. "I think you have made a mistake, brother. But you meant to kill me as well. Had my husband not pushed me into the grave you would have done so. So you see, your wish to kill only our father will not stand up. You intended to kill the entire family, Vassily. Tell me who commanded you to do this?"

"I hate you all," Vassily said.

"The police will get it out of him," Dubaclov suggested.

122

"Of course they will. But why should I not get it out of him first? I can be just as searching as any policeman."

"He is your brother," Dubaclov protested.

"No," Dagmar riposted. "It may please him to think of himself as my brother. But he is merely the product of my father's semen, carelessly distributed." She turned to Jennie. "But you are not even my father's child," she remarked. "And you have ample cause to hate my father. You are a member of the Will of the People, are you not?"

Jennie gazed at her.

"She knows nothing of this business," Vassily said.

"How gallant you are, brother. Are you one of her lovers?"

"She knows nothing of it," Vassily said again.

"We shall see. I am going to ask you the same questions, Jennie. And I expect you to answer. First, was it you Vassily was appealing to, at the graveside?"

"I do not know," Jennie replied, her voice low.

"All right. Are you a member of the Will of the People?"

"Yes," Jennie said.

"Well, now, there is cooperation, eh, Captain?"

Dubaclov gave a sigh of relief.

"And Vassily?" Dagmar said.

"I do not know."

"Of course he is, as he fired the gun. However, obviously the pair of you are not alone in this conspiracy. I wish to know the other members of this obscene organisation. Is Igor a member?"

"I do not know," Jennie said.

"Then tell me who is."

"I do not know."

"Do you seriously suppose you can defy me, simply because you bore my brother's son? He is nothing, now. Do you understand that?" She patted her stomach. "I carry the next heir to Bolugayen, here in my womb. And

123

even if I did not, there is no way I would ever allow Georgei's brat to inherit. Now give me names."

Jennie licked her lips. "I do not know any names, Your Highness."

Dagmar seized the neck of Jennie's blouse, tore it down to her waist, then seized each side of the material and ripped it apart. Beneath was a single shift. Dagmar ripped this in turn, exposing Jennie's breasts, heaving as she closed her eyes. "Is that not a pretty sight?" Dagmar asked Dubaclov.

Dubaclov stared at the exposed flesh.

Dagmar released Jennie's waistband, and gave a jerk on the skirt; it settled on the floor around her ankles, to leave Jennie naked. "Oh, yes," Dagmar said. "A pretty sight. Dubaclov, would you not like to mount her?"

"I . . ." Dubaclov shifted his feet, uncertain whether she was laying a trap for him.

"Of course you would," Dagmar said. "But now is not the time. There may never be a time, for her. Fetch me one of yonder meathooks."

"Your Highness," Dubaclov protested. "Please!"

"Fetch it!" Dagmar snapped.

Dubaclov went across the room and took down one of the meathooks from the wall. This was about four feet long, its end curved into a hook, its sharp-pointed tip capable of being driven firmly into any carcase. "Thank you," Dagmar said, taking it from him. She turned it over, so that the hook was downwards, then inserted it between Jennie's legs, thrusting it through, and at the same time raising it so that it stroked Jennie's genitals. Jennie's eyes flopped open at the touch of the steel.

Dagmar turned the meathook over, hook now uppermost, and drew it forward, so that the tip just touched the flesh at the base of Jennie's spine. "Do you realise," Dagmar asked, "that if I pull on this hook, hard enough, I can tear you in two?"

124

Jennie gasped, and her body seemed to sag. "I shall enjoy doing that," Dagmar said, softly. "Tell me who else is in the conspiracy with you."

Jennie's mouth clamped shut.

"You are a courageous little bitch," Dagmar said. "I will do it, you know."

"For God's sake, Your Highness . . ." Dubaclov protested.

Dagmar glanced at him. "And you call yourself a man? Are you afraid of the sight of blood? Of the sound of a woman's screams?" Dubaclov bit his lip. "And you would marry my sister?" This time Dubaclov's mouth fell open in consternation. "Oh, yes," Dagmar said. "I have seen the way you have looked at her. Or did you just hope to fuck her and then make your escape?"

"I . . . I . . ." Dubaclov glanced desperately at the door.

Dagmar smiled. "I think you would make a good brother-in-law, Captain Dubaclov. Constantine. I will accept you into the family. If you are truly a man."

"Your Highness overwhelms me."

"If you are truly a man, Captain," Dagmar repeated, and looked at Jennie. "Now, bitch, are you ready to tell me what I wish to know?"

"I know nothing," Jennie said, and tensed her muscles for the agonising pain she anticipated.

"She knows nothing!" Vassily shrieked. "I am the one you should ask."

"You are the one I am asking," Dagmar said. "But she is the one who will suffer if you do not tell me what I wish to know. Now!" She pulled the meathook towards her, just enough to mark Jennie's flesh. Jennie's entire body tensed, her breasts and stomach and thighs arching forward.

"Igor," Vassily gabbled. "Igor is the leader of the Will here on Bolugayen. Igor, and . . ." He reeled off a string of names, only stopping when he ran out of breath.

"Where did you get the revolver?"

"From the bookseller, Woskov, in Poltava."

"When?"

"The last shopping expedition."

Dagmar turned the meathook over and slowly withdrew it from between Jennie's legs. Jennie gasped, and her body slumped. "But you did not go on the last shopping expedition," Dagmar said softly. "Jennie went."

"So did Madame Smyslova," Vassily panted.

"That is true. And very disturbing. Ah, well, no doubt Monsieur Woskov will tell us the truth. But you are condemned out of your own mouth, brother. Quite apart from having been caught red-handed."

"Do what you wish with me," Vassily begged. "But let Jennie go. She is innocent."

"We shall see. Thank you, Vassily." She handed the meathook to Dubaclov. "Replace that, Captain." Dubaclov obeyed, and turned to watch in consternation as Dagmar released Vassily's breeches and pulled them down. "Bring me that stake," she said.

Dubaclov picked up the wooden stick, one of several that stood against the wall, and handed it to her. Dagmar grasped the stake in both hands and stood to one side of Vassily. Vassily's eyes opened wide in fear. "Just in case you manage to escape both justice and the police," Dagmar told him. "I am going to make sure that *you* do not father any more Bolugayevskis."

She swung the stick, and Vassily's body jerked as the wood smashed into his thighs. Dagmar took a step back to adjust the range and swung the stick again. This time it thudded into Vassily's genitals, and he uttered an animal-like scream. Dagmar swung again and again, while Vassily jerked and screamed.

Dagmar hit her half-brother twelve times. Between his legs was a bloody mess and blood had gathered on the floor beneath him. He was still conscious, but could do nothing more than whimper. Dagmar threw the stick on the floor and went to the door. She stepped through, and Golkov and his men stood to attention. They were in a state of some agitation, having heard the screams. "The police will be here later on," Dagmar said. "You will remain on guard here until then. I do not wish any of the servants to speak with those two. Especially Igor. Do you understand me?"

"Yes, Your Highness."

"You may amuse yourselves with the woman, if you wish."

Golkov grinned. "And the man, Your Highness?"

Dagmar raised her eyebrows. "Why, you are a man of unsuspected depths, sergeant. By all means, the man as well, if you wish. If you can find anything of his to amuse yourself with."

Dubaclov followed her to the steps. "You promised to let the woman go," he muttered. "You promised your brother a single bullet in the brain."

"No, no, Captain," Dagmar corrected. "Vassily offered to tell me what I wanted, if I would let her go. I never actually accepted his proposal. As for the bullet, he refused that offer, when it was made."

"You are a devil."

Dagmar, halfway up the steps, paused to look down at him. "I am a Bolugayevska. It remains to be seen, Captain, whether you are capable of belonging to my family. Come now, to my room, and we will find that out." She smiled at him as he hesitated, unsure of what she had just said. "You wanted to fuck that woman, didn't you, Constantine? Well, I found her equally attractive. But I am much more attractive. And if you wish to marry my sister, you must also belong to me."

"But . . . are you not pregnant, Your Highness?"

Dagmar tapped him on the shoulder with her fan. "My dear Constantine, I did not say I was going to let you fuck me."

*　　*　　*

Colin blinked at the light, and felt a resurgence of the pain. "I seem to be making a habit of this," he muttered.

Dagmar kissed him on the forehead. "I intend to make sure it does not happen again. Your shoulder is broken, but Simmars tells me it will mend."

"My God, was the fellow mad?"

"You mean Vassily? No, he was not mad. He is nothing more than a hired assassin."

"But to shoot his own father . . . How is the Prince?"

"Papa is dead."

Colin gave a little gasp, amd his face twisted with pain.

"That means," Dagmar said carefully, "that the Prince Bolugayevski lies before me."

His eyebrows raised. "You cannot be serious."

"Certainly I am serious."

"I am so very sorry about your father."

"He lived a full life."

"I must be honest and tell you I never liked him."

"And I will be honest in return and tell you that he never liked you. But he is history, now. You are the future."

"Prince Bolugayevski," Colin muttered. "My God! Whatever will they say in England?"

"I am sure they will congratulate you most heartily," Dagmar said. "Now you must hurry up and get well. There is a great deal to be done."

Michael Vorontsov had been appointed to Poltava simply because there had been no sign of sedition there. Now he could not be sure whether this outbreak of violence was going to earn him promotion or censure. But although this was his second visit to Bolugayen in connection with this business, he was very nervous as he stood to attention when the Princess Bolugayevska entered the room. Then he clicked his heels as she presented her hand for him to kiss. "Your Highness. I

128

can only repeat my condolences. This is a most tragic business."

"Thank you, Colonel. It is good of you to call. Yes, it is a sad business. When one thinks of people with whom one has grown up . . . Please be seated."

Vorontsov seated himself, as did Dagmar, ringing a little silver bell as she did so. "We will have tea, Igor."

The butler bowed. Vorontsov opened his mouth in surprise, and Dagmar touched her lips with her forefinger. Igor withdrew, closing the doors behind him. "You are concerned, Colonel."

"Your Highness, you know that man is accused of being a member of the Will of the People?"

"I do."

"I have a warrant for his arrest."

Dagmar smiled. "And he is about to serve you tea. I assure you that it will not be poisoned; he assumes himself to be safe. Tell me, Colonel, have you also a warrant for the arrest of Madame Smyslova?"

Vorontsov swallowed.

"And several other of my people, I fancy. I assume you learned this from my bastard brother, Vassily. Or was it from the Englishwoman?"

"I am afraid your brother seems to have been rather badly beaten, Your Highness . . ."

"I know," Dagmar said. "I did the beating."

Vorontsov gulped.

"But you did question the Englishwoman?"

"Yes, we did, Your Highness. She was reluctant to talk to us, but we managed to persuade her."

"I am sure you found that very enjoyable," Dagmar said. "And you have the bookseller, Woskov?"

"I'm afraid not, Your Highness."

Dagmar raised her eyebrows. "You didn't let him escape?"

"No, no. But when my people knocked on his door, he shot himself."

129

"What a pity. But you have enough."

"Oh, indeed. And when I take the butler, and Madame Smyslova, into town . . ."

"That would be even more amusing, would it not, Colonel? To be able to interrogate a member of the middle class? However, I must ask you to forego that pleasure, at least for the time being."

"Your Highness?"

"What I would like you to do, Colonel," Dagmar said, "is arrest those people who have been accused by my step-brother, or by the Englishwoman. But not Igor, and not Madame Smyslova."

"I do not understand, Your Highness."

"It is very simple . . . ah, Igor. Thank you."

Igor placed the tray on the table, and poured. Vorontsov gazed at him, and Igor attempted not to notice. The door closed again. "As I was saying, Colonel. There was a cell of this secret society on Bolugayen. My father and I thought we had weeded out the main part last February."

"Bondarevski is the ringleader," Vorontsov said.

"I understand this. I will be responsible for him. The same goes for Tatiana Smyslova."

Vorontsov stroked his moustache. "This is a dangerous business, Your Highness."

"I do not think so." Dagmar sipped tea. "You will give me those two warrants, and serve the rest."

"If that is what you wish, Your Highness. But I can take no responsibility for anything that may happen here, because of your misplaced clemency."

Dagmar smiled at him. "Who said anything about clemency, Colonel?"

Dagmar stood with Anna, Captain Dubaclov and Smyslov on the front porch of the palace to watch the arrested servants being driven away in the police wagons. Dagmar glanced at Igor, who was also standing by the door. "You

130

will have to replace those people, Igor. I will receive your list after luncheon."

Igor bowed.

"Your Highness," Dubaclov said. "May I ask when the funeral of your father and your brother will take place?"

"As soon as the Prince is able to attend it, Captain. Why are you in such a hurry?"

"Because I must rejoin my regiment, Your Highness. There is a war on."

"If you wish to remain, Captain, for the funerals, I will write your commanding officer and obtain an extended furlough for you." She went up the stairs.

Dubaclov looked after her. "How I admire her. She is so strong."

"Her strength is frightening," Anna remarked, and went into the card room.

Dubaclov followed. "What makes you say that?"

"You were with her when she questioned Jennie and Vassily. Vassily could not walk when the police took him away. He had to be dragged." She turned to face him. "What did she do to him?"

"She terrified them both, that is all." And afterwards, he thought, she terrified me. He had felt he was being savaged by a gorgon, had never known when she might bite him hard enough to destroy his manhood. Yet, to experience that again, with this lovely, innocent creature . . . And Dagmar had given him her blessing.

"I would like to be that strong," Anna said. He turned and grasped her hands. "I am so glad you are not that strong, Anna."

"Why, Captain . . ." she smiled. "You're blushing."

"Anna . . ." Still holding her hands he led her across the room to the settee by the window, and sat down. "I will have to rejoin my regiment, very soon."

"If Dagmar says she will arrange it for you to stay, then you will stay." She made no effort to free her hands.

"Would you like me to stay, Anna? Dear Anna."

131

"Why, Captain . . ."

"Would you? If you would, I would ask you to marry me."

"Marry? Oh, my."

"Wouldn't you like to do that."

"I've never thought of it." Now at last she tugged her hands free, and half turned away from him; her cheeks were as pink as his.

"I know I am not the son of a prince, or even a count, Anna. But I have every prospect of becoming one, if I make General. All things are possible when we are at war. I do love you, Anna. I adore you."

"Good heavens," she said. "Whatever will Dagmar say?"

"This seems a very good selection, Igor." Dagmar reclined on her chaise longue. "I approve. You may start training these people in their duties immediately."

"Thank you, Your Highness."

"And Igor, I wish you to be sure that you train them only in their duties as servants."

"Your Highness?" The blood was draining from Igor's cheeks.

"I have something here you should read," Dagmar said, and picked up the warrant which had been lying beside her on the couch. She held it out, and with a shaking hand Igor took it and unfolded it. His trembling increased as he read it, and he fell to his knees. "I have persuaded Colonel Vorontsov not to serve that warrant, Igor, for the time being," Dagmar said.

"Your Highness, it is a lie."

"It is not a lie that you created a cell of the Will of the People here on Bolugayen," Dagmar said. "A cell that was responsible for the death of my father." She swung her legs to the floor and sat up. Igor fell forward to grovel, his head on the carpet. "When I first realised that, I felt like having you flayed alive," Dagmar said. "I may still do that, one day. But then, I reflected, you are a good butler, Igor. I need good and faithful people about me in the difficult times ahead. I am sure that now we understand each other, you will be, good and faithful."

"I will serve you unto death, Your Highness," Igor mumbled.

"Of course you will. And just so that you do not forget that promise, I wish you to know that I have arranged with Colonel Vorontsov that should anything, anything at all, Igor, ever happen to me, I will have your wife, your two daughters, and your three sons, all flayed alive, before your eyes. This is regardless of whether you have anything to do with what happens or not. Do you understand this?"

"Your Highness . . ." Tears streamed down Igor's face.

"Good," Dagmar said. "Our understanding will, of course, remain entirely private, between you and me. Should anyone learn of it, I will regard it as an attempt upon my life, with the consequences I have outlined to you. Now go and wash your face, have a glass of vodka, and send Monsieur Smyslov to me."

Igor scrambled to his feet and backed to the door. When he opened it, Anna and Dubaclov were standing there.

"How are you feeling?" Dagmar asked her husband.

"Much stronger today."

"I can hardly wait for you to be really well again. There is so much to be done. I am not sure I am up to it."

"You, Dagmar?"

She smiled. "I will still be happier with you at my side. But there are some things which cannot wait. There is Papa's funeral. And Georgei's."

"But I thought . . ."

"We could not continue with the ceremony, with the Prince lying wounded. You must be there, my love."

"Oh. Yes. Right. Then let's get it done. Do you mean

those two coffins have been lying in the house for the past month?"

"I have had them put in the cellar. Still, I agree it is something that should be done."

"You are an amazing woman, Dagmar. You have got to be about the most pragmatic person I have ever met. Don't you feel any grief at all, for your father and brother?"

"Of course I feel grief. But do you expect me to weep all day, and wear black all the time? I am not some peasant woman. I am the Princess Bolugayevska. Now there is something else that needs attending to: Constantine Dubaclov wishes to marry Anna."

"Good heavens."

"I have given my permission in principle. But of course the actual decision must be made by you."

"She's your sister, Dagmar."

"She is your responsibility, as Prince Bolugayevski."

"Oh, come now. I'm not really the Prince. I may hold the title, as your husband, but . . ."

"I have written St Petersburg with the news, and my letter has been endorsed by the Governor of Poltava. Bolugayen must have a prince, and he must be, in our circumstances, the husband of the eldest surviving daughter. You will have the power, Colin. And I will be at your side to see that it is properly used."

"I don't doubt it for a moment."

Dagmar ignored his comment. "So, will you receive Anna and Dubaclov, and give them your blessing?"

He considered. "I do not really care for Dubaclov."

"I think he will make Anna an excellent husband. And she needs a husband."

"You mean you wish to be rid of her?"

"On the contrary. I wish to be sure she remains here. I would like us to offer Dubaclov a position, here on Bolugayen. I think we are going to need all the loyal people we can get, over the next few years."

"And you reckon Dubaclov will be loyal to us?"

"Of course," Dagmar said.

"Now tell me what has happened to Jennie Cromb."

Dagmar frowned. "You know she was involved?"

"I cannot believe that. She made no move to help Vassily at the graveside. You have not let the police take her, I hope? I would be extremely concerned about *that*."

Dagmar considered him for several seconds, then smiled. "There is nothing for you to concern yourself with, my love. I have put Jennie in a safe place, where the police will not look for her."

"Where?"

Dagmar hesitated only briefly. "I have sent her over to the Jewish village, in the care of Dr Fine. She will be safe there until this business blows over."

Chapter 7

THE PRINCE

The late Prince Alexander Bolugayevski and his only son were buried a week later. Several notables from Poltava came out for the funeral including both the Governor, Baron Lebedeff, and his wife, as well as Colonel Vorontsov – with a large escort of policemen. Afterwards the guests gathered in the mansion for luncheon.

"Well, Prince," Lebedeff said, raising his glass of champagne. "Here is to a prosperous life. I assume you are remaining here?"

"I don't have anywhere else to go, Baron," Colin confessed. "I'm still technically a prisoner of war."

"Yes," Lebedeff commented. "But I wonder for how much longer. You have heard the news?"

Colin frowned at him. "What news? I have heard little these past six weeks."

"You do not know that Sevastopol has fallen?"

"By God! No, I had not heard that. How did it happen?"

"Very simply, it was stormed by the Allies. The French were the main factor. The British assault was beaten off. But the French carried out a considerable feat of arms. They attacked entirely without warning, and in several different columns, but yet every column acted at exactly the same moment. It has been suggested than every battalion commander had checked his watch against every other's, and thus they all were in complete unison as regards time. I personally cannot credit this."

"It could be done," Colin said. "Synchronisation of time. Now there is a development."

"It has never been done before," Lebedeff grumbled. "However, they captured the Malakoff Tower, which was the dominant aspect of the fortifications, and then forced their way into the city. Casualties were enormous. I believe the Allies lost ten thousand men."

"And the Russians?"

Lebedeff made a face. "The figure is being put as high as thirteen thousand. There can be no doubt that we have received a most resounding defeat. Already there is talk that the Tsar has sent out peace feelers. Do you know, Russia has never been defeated in any war? Certainly not one fought on Russian soil. Not even Napoleon I could do that. Now this upstart Napoleon III is doing what the great man could not."

"With a *little* help from the British, surely?" Colin suggested. His brain was tumbling. From his sick bed he had written again, to his parents and Cardigan as well as to the War Office, bringing them up to date on his situation, but had still not received a reply. Or at least, not been shown one. He had reflected that his situation was prevented from reaching a critical stage because he was still a prisoner of war. But if there was to be peace . . . what *was* he going to do? If there were times when he actively disliked his wife, and he knew he could never love her, she seemed to be prepared to give him all the riches of the earth . . . in exchange for a subaltern's pay. And a change of nationalities, to be sure.

Lebedeff seemed able to read his thoughts. "You would be a fool to give all this up, Your Highness."

Colin glanced at him. "Do you know what it entails, Baron?"

"I know what it *means*, Your Highness. Enormous

137

wealth, enormous prestige . . . oh, I know your wife has gone through a difficult period, but . . ."

"What do you know of that period, Baron?"

"Absolutely nothing," Lebedeff said, hastily.

"Not even the name of the man?"

"Good heavens, no. It happened before I came to Poltava. In any event, I gather it was the most closely guarded secret one could imagine. Not even the servants knew of it."

"How can you be sure of that, Baron? If you were not here at the time?"

"Simply because, Your Highness, servants gossip. It is what they are best at. And the Bolugayevski servants go into Poltava often enough. But not a word of it has ever been spoken. Of course, you can always find out by asking your wife."

Colin gave a short laugh. "Do you suppose she would tell me?"

"I am sure you could persuade her."

"By beating her, you mean? But if I did it sufficiently to force her to answer my questions she would probably have me locked up."

"How may that be, Your Highness? You are the Prince Bolugayevski. Or you will be, once your letters patent arrive. They will certainly be here in a month. And as they were requested by the Princess herself, in the most glowing terms, well . . . she must wish you to rule here."

"And that will put me even beyond the anger of my wife?"

Lebedeff laughed. "You say the quaintest things, Your Highness."

"I think that went off very well," Dagmar said, when the last of the guests had departed, "and you were just magnificent, my darling. But you are looking tired. I think you should go to bed."

Colin had no objection to that. "You must be getting

138

pretty fed-up with nursing an invalid," he remarked, as she helped him undress; since the shooting and the arrest of Vassily she had not replaced his valet, and had tended him entirely herself.

"I enjoy it," she said. "But of course I wish you to get well. I wish to have sex with you, and in a month or so that will be impossible for a further six months." She kissed him. "And there is the trial. Both Vorontsov and Lebedeff are anxious to have that completed before, well . . . Vassily is not very well. I'm afraid Smyslov's men beat him rather badly when they arrested him. Well, he deserved it, killing his own father, but it would be a shame were he to die before he can be hanged."

"Why do I have to be present?"

"You do not *have* to be present, you are the Prince Bolugayevski. But I thought it would be splendid for the Prince Bolugayevski to give evidence. It will show everyone that we have the welfare of the entire community at heart, that we uphold the dignity and the majesty of the law . . . and it will introduce you to the public, who at present are hardly aware of your existence."

"What about Jennie?"

"I think it would be best for Jennie to keep a very low profile for a while longer; she can come to no harm over in the Jewish village, and Dr Fine assures me that she is well looked after."

He watched her come towards him, breasts and hair trembling, lips smiling. She wished to arouse, and no man could watch Dagmar Bolugayevska without being aroused, even if, at five months, she was just beginning to swell. Yet every time she did this to him he hated himself, and her. He had not meant to raise the subject, despite Lebedeff's suggestion, but it came out before he could stop himself. "May I ask you a question?"

"Of course."

"To which I would like an absolutely truthful answer."

"You shall have it, my darling." She crawled into the bed.

"Will you admit that you chose me as a husband because you were determined to have a husband, and there was no Russian of any social standing who would marry you?"

She made a moue. "It is unkind of you to put it so bluntly, but since I have promised to answer you truthfully, yes, that is correct. Not that I have regretted my choice for a moment."

"But would I not be right in assuming that the man you would most have liked to marry is the father of your child? Your first child."

A watchful look came into Dagmar's eyes. "I have told you that was not possible."

"Because he was married, or because your parents would not have permitted it?"

Dagmar gave a somewhat savage smile. "Both."

"That is what I supposed. But now, both your mother and father are dead, and you are the Princess Bolugayevska. You have very kindly bestowed the executive power of this family on me. But have you made no effort at all to contact your first lover, to find out if he is free? *You* were certainly free, to divorce me and marry whomever you chose. Perhaps he would have done the same. Then your first lover could be Prince Bolugayevski, instead of me."

"It was not possible," Dagmar said. Her lips twisted as she spoke. "My first lover is dead."

Prince Bolugayevski! It was impossible to get the concept out of his mind, even if it was equally impossible to accept the reality of it. The most powerful man in Poltava, and for a thousand miles around! Colin MacLain, Subaltern in the 11th Hussars, twenty-one and a half years old! Then his decision was made! To remain here, and be a Russian, and perhaps rise in the service of the Tsar. But an enemy of his country! No, not this Tsar. This Tsar by all accounts was a man who wanted only the best, for his people as well as his country.

He sat up. Beside him, Dagmar breathed deeply. She was a woman who considered that all life was there to be manipulated. But in doing that, she had given him the power to do some manipulating himself. He got out of bed. He could not dress himself, without a great deal of effort which would undoubtedly wake Dagmar, so he inserted himself into a dressing robe, quietly opened the door, and stepped outside.

Once out of the room, he was surrounded by stealthy sounds as the servants went about their business of readying the house for the appearance of their master and mistresses. But did not only their master matter? His sense of power grew with every minute. He had the wildest desire to display it and enjoy it. He was drunk with the thought of it.

He went down the grand staircase. At the sight of him, all the footmen and maidservants, busily sweeping and dusting, paused to bow. He nodded to them, and went past them out on to the front porch. Girls were weeding and gardeners pruning, watched by Igor. "Good morning, Igor," he said.

The butler had not heard him approach, and nearly fell over as he bowed. "Good morning, Your Highness."

"What time does Monsieur Smyslov come up?"

"Usually about ten, Your Highness."

"Very good. Have a horse saddled for me."

"Now, Your Highness?"

"Now, Igor."

He returned up the stairs and to his bedroom. Dagmar was sitting up. "Wherever have you been."

"I have been speaking with Igor. I wish to go for a ride."

"It is too soon. You will hurt your shoulder."

"I am a cavalryman. Every day I do not ride is a lost day."

She made a *moue*. "You realise I cannot come with you . . .?"

141

"I would not expect you to. But tell me this: do you have a meeting with Smyslov every day?"

"Yes. It is necessary, if I am to keep my finger on the pulse of the estate."

"Of course. But it will no longer be necessary for *you* to attend it. I will see to it from now on. As of this moment, your sole concern is being a mother."

Dagmar opened her mouth as if she would have protested, then changed her mind. "As you wish, Your Highness," she smiled.

He kissed her forhead. "You did say you wished me to rule, my love."

Igor and a groom waited with Colin's horse, and assisted him into the saddle. He walked his mount out of the yard and down the slope to the town; he knew he could hardly do more than walk, for fear of hurting his shoulder, but it was so good to be again in the saddle, and out in the open air, and . . . lord of all he surveyed. It was harvest time, and the serfs, men and women, were streaming out of the town to the fields. All paused to bow and salute their master. All his. Every last one.

Then he thought of Jennie. Banished to the Jewish village.

He wheeled his horse to return to the palace; he was not strong enough to ride to the village, nor could he spare the several days it would require. In any event, the Prince Bolugayevski did not do things like that. He would send a messenger, requiring that the woman be sent to him. Then he saw a horseman approaching, and drew rein. There was something familiar about the heavy, black-bearded man, who now doffed his hat as he came closer. "Good morning, Your Highness. I trust you will forgive this intrusion?"

"Dr Fine!"

"Thank you for remembering me, sir."

"You are the very man I wish to see," Colin said.

"Indeed, sir? I hope no one is ill at the mansion."

"Not to my knowledge. May I ask your business?"

Fine looked astonished; he was not used to being addressed in such civil terms by a Bolugayevski. "Why, Your Highness, I came to see you."

"Did you, now. Concerning what?"

Fine licked his lips. "I had hoped, sir, that being an English gentleman, you might be sympathetic towards the situation of my people."

"Ah. Well, I am prepared to listen. You'll come in and breakfast with me, doctor."

Fine looked more astonished yet. "You are most kind, Your Highness."

"Now tell me," Colin said, as they walked their horses into the mansion yard. "How is the woman Jennie Cromb?"

"I do not know, sir. I am afraid she is probably not very well. Those fellows are devils. And a pretty woman . . . my heart bleeds for her."

Colin drew rein. "What are you talking about? Which fellows?"

"Why, sir, the police," Fine also halted his horse.

Colin stared at him. "Is Mademoiselle Cromb not in your village?"

"Why, no, sir. There is no reason for her to be."

"But she *was* in your village?"

"No, sir. She was handed over to the police on the afternoon of the late Prince's death, so far as I know."

"Who did this?" Colin spat out the words.

"Why . . . the Princess Bolugayevska, I imagine, Your Highness. But . . ."

Colin slid from the saddle and threw his reins to the groom who came hurrying up. Igor came out of the house to bow to his master, and Colin stamped past him, heedless of the gathering pain in his shoulder. He went up the stairs to the gallery, turned towards his apartment, and

143

encountered Dagmar, fully dressed, just emerging from the doorway.

"Why, Colin," she said, "I did not expect you back so soon." Then she frowned. "What has happened? You have had a fall!"

Colin stood in front of her. "You sent Jennie Cromb to the police? I wish the truth."

Dagmar's features tightened. "And I think you have overtired yourself by your foolish exertion," she said. "Come and lie down."

"I wish the truth. Now!" Colin said.

"You are making an exhibition of yourself, in front of the servants," Dagmar said. "Now come inside."

"The truth!" Colin shouted. "I am tired of lies. You have lied to me, one way or another, from the moment of our first meeting. Now I wish to know, where is Jennie Cromb?"

"You dare to shout at me?" Dagmar exploded, and moved her right hand. Colin had no idea whether she had been going to strike him or not, but his own reaction was instantaneous, driven by long pent up anger and frustration. His good right hand still held his riding crop, and before he understood what he was doing he had whipped it across her shoulders, from whence it rode up to slash into her face. Dagmar gave a shriek, and fell to her hands and knees.

"I will deal with you, properly, when I return from Poltava," Colin said, and went to the stairs.

"You bastard!" Dagmar shrieked; blood was dribbling from her split cheek. "You . . . come back here!" Colin ignored her. Dagmar scrambled to her feet and ran to the balustrade. "Stop him!" she screamed.

Colin gazed at the servants as he went down the stairs. Igor looked as if he would have obeyed his mistress, then saw the expression in Colin's eyes and stepped back into the throng. "Stop him!" Dagmar shrieked again, but still no one moved. She had told them all he was their master.

144

Colin went outside, where Fine waited. He had dismounted, but the groom still held both their horses. "You'll come with me," Colin told the doctor.

Fine mounted. "You did not know of this, Your Highness?"

"I did not know of it," Colin said. "I was told the woman was with you."

They rode in silence until the walls of the city were in sight. Then Fine observed, "The police are a law unto themselves, Your Highness."

"Their law does not affect the Prince Bolugayevski," Colin said. He was endeavouring to keep calm, not to give way to the fury in his heart. If Jennie lived, he would save her. If she was dead, he would avenge her. He did not care what might happen afterwards.

They rode to the governor's palace, and attracted no attention. Even the majordomo at the palace door had no idea who sought the governor, although he could recognise the quality of Colin's clothes. "You have a card, Your Excellency?"

"No, I do not have a card," Colin told him. "I am the Prince Bolugayevski."

"The Prince . . ." The man goggled. "His Excellency is in a meeting, Your Highness. I will see . . ." He scurried off.

"He does not seem to believe me," Colin said.

Fine was looking nervous, while various footmen stood around uncertainly. A moment later Lebedeff hurried into the hall. "Your Highness, what a pleasant surprise. I did not know you were up and about. And you have not even been offered a chair and a glass of wine?" He looked at Fine in bewilderment.

"Dr Fine is my personal physician," Colin explained. It was Fine's turn to look bewildered.

"Ah, doctor," Lebedeff said. "You'll come in, Your Highness, And you, doctor. Yes, indeed. Lewitski, wine for our guests. I assume you have breakfasted?"

"As a matter of fact, no, Baron," Colin said. "But no matter. I have not the time for that."

Lebedeff ushered them into a book-lined study. "Do you know, Your Highness, I was about to come out to see you? Your letters patent have arrived."

Colin sat down. "So soon? You told me they were unlikely to be here for another month."

"Yes. Well, I suspect that with all the unrest in the country following the death of the Tsar and now the fall of Sevastopol, his majesty is anxious to have people he can rely on in positions of authority."

Colin raised his eyebrows. "And he imagines he can rely on me? Someone must have been stretching the truth a little. Does he not know I am English? Or rather, Scottish?"

"You will have to ask the Princess about that, Your Highness. She was the one who, perhaps, stretched the truth a little. Anyway, your papers are here. I trust you are pleased about that?"

"Very pleased, Baron. I will assume it makes my immediate task the more simple. Your police are holding one of my people in their cells. I wish her released."

"May I ask the name of this person?"

"Jennie Cromb."

"The Englishwoman! Ah. Yes. I understand. However, Your Highness, I must inform you that this woman has made a complete confession of her part in the assassination of your father-in-law."

"I have no doubt that she was, shall I say, persuaded to make that confession."

"Oh, well, you know what the police are like. But the fact is, she has admitted that it was she who procured the weapon. That makes her an accessory before the fact of the murder, and therefore as guilty as Vassily Bolugayevski himself. They are to be tried together."

"Nevertheless," Colin said. "I wish you to sign an order for her release. I, the Prince Bolugayevski, wish you to do this for me, Baron Lebedeff."

146

Lebedeff stroked his moustache, glanced at Fine, and then cleared his throat. "It would be very irregular. The woman is a confessed murderess. Of a prince," he added, as if suggesting that if Jennie had murdered some lesser person, the matter would be more easily resolved. Lewitski appeared with a tray, decanter and glasses, and poured.

Colin sipped. The alcohol gave him a glow of strength. "Has the Prince Bolugayevski not got the power of life or death over his serfs?"

"Well . . . within reason."

"You mean that if I carelessly murder one or two of them I may have to account for my actions to my peers, who will, of course, exonerate me of any blame in the matter. I should remind you, Your Excellency, that I have the right to hold court on my property, for any crime committed *on* my property. It was my wife's decision that this business should be handed over to the police here in Poltava."

"Well, the assassination of a prince is hardly a parochial matter, Your Highness."

"Yet the right to try the case remains mine."

"Well, legally, yes, Your Highness."

"Then I am rescinding my wife's original order. I wish the woman released into my custody immediately."

"And the other people who were arrested?"

Colin had only intended to get Jennie out of the hands of the police, whether she was guilty or not. Now he realised that with Dagmar and Vorontsov handling the business, there might well be a good number of innocent people involved. "Yes," he said. "I will take them all back."

"And what of Vassily Bolugayevski?"

Colin hesitated. Vassily was most certainly guilty of murder; he was an eye witness to that. "You may keep Vassily, and try him, Your Excellency."

"You are most generous, Your Highness," Lebedeff said sarcastically.

*   *   *

147

Colonel Vorontsov stood to attention as the Prince Bolugayevski and Dr Fine entered his office. "Your Highness! May I be of service?"

"Yes," Colin said, and gave him the governor's order.

Vorontsov frowned as he read it. "This is most irregular, Your Highness."

"So I believe," Colin agreed. "Nevertheless, I wish that order implemented. Now."

"May I ask if the Princess Bolugayevska authorised this, Your Highness?"

"Colonel Vorontsov, what my wife may, or may not, choose to authorise is neither here nor there. You have in your hand an order from Baron Lebedeff to release all prisoners held in regard to the murder of the late Prince Bolugayevski into my custody, with the exception of Vassily Bolugayevski. Now, I do not have any people with me, save for Dr Fine. Therefore you will deliver the prisoners to Bolugayen before dusk this evening. Is that understood? However, I will take the woman Jennie Cromb with me now. I wish to see her now, in her cell."

Vorontsov gulped. "You know she is here?"

"Of course I know she is here, man."

A puzzled look crossed Vorontsov's face. Then he seemed to pull himself together. "You understand that she has confessed to providing the weapon for Vassily Bolugayevski to kill his father?"

"I understand that she has made a confession. But you are in the business of securing confessions, are you not, Colonel?"

"What I am trying to say, Your Highness, is that the woman is a self-confessed accessory before the fact of a murder, and has been treated as such."

"I wish to see her, Colonel. Now."

Vorontsov hesitated, then rang the bell on his desk. An orderly entered. "The Prince Bolugayevski wishes to see the prisoner Cromb," he said.

148

"No, no, Colonel," Colin said. "I wish *you* to take me to the prisoner, in her cell."

Vorontsov licked his lips, then went to the door. "If you will accompany me, Your Highness."

Colin had the impression, when first entering the building, that the very walls seemed impregnated with fear. But as he and Fine followed Vorontsov and the orderly down the steps into the cells, he became aware of a sense of despair. It was compounded of the stench, of the various noises that escaped the cells to either side, of the lumbering figures of the gaolers, one of whom, at an order from Vorontsov, led them into the cell block, carrying a flaring torch. Colin glanced at Fine, and saw that the doctor was as shocked as himself. "Are there any of your people in here?" he asked.

"I would say so. Even if not from my village," the doctor replied.

"This is something I shall have to look into," Colin promised.

They descended another level, and were now in the midst of scurrying rats. There was no daylight down here, and the walls dripped dampness. The orderly was carrying a torch, however, and Vorontsov checked the numbers. "One hundred and twelve," he said. "This one."

The warder turned the key, with difficulty, and the door swung open, the hinges creaking. Clearly it was not opened very often; there was a small trap next to the floor through which food could be pushed, but exercising the prisoners or allowing them toilet facilities was not something in which the police indulged. Colin stepped inside, checking at the stench. "Bring that light," he told the orderly.

The torch flared above his head. The woman on the floor was already gathering herself into a trembling ball, shrouded only in her hair; she possessed neither clothes nor any kind of blanket – not even straw. "No," she muttered. "Please, no."

149

"You understand, Your Highness," Vorontsov said, "that she is here at the express command of your wife. I have disobeyed the Princess: she gave me instructions that the prisoner should die before the trial."

Colin bent over the bag of trembling bones. "The trial is still two weeks off, is it not? I imagine you are on schedule." He thrust one arm under Jennie's knees and another under her shoulders, and straightened, looking at Vorontsov. "That I do not kill you, now, Colonel, is that I am conscious you were but obeying my wife's command. Now get out of my way."

Colin wrapped Jennie in his coat, and carried her to the Bolugayevski Palace in Poltava for Fine to examine. Clearly any kind of travel was out of the question. The servants were astounded to see their prince arriving unannounced on the doorstep, but they began airing rooms and beds, in one of which Colin laid Jennie. She had done nothing but tremble on the way from the police headquarters, keeping her eyes shut. Now she opened them, gazed at her surroundings, and closed them again. Colin and Fine stood together, looking at the ribs protruding through the flesh, the mere sacks of breasts, the thin legs. "Once she had the finest figure in the world," Colin said.

"She will regain her figure, with care," Fine said. "But the rest . . ." – he pointed to the bruises, the whip weals on her back and buttocks – "much depends on how capable she was of closing her mind."

"It looks pretty closed now," Colin said.

"Yes," Fine said. "Thus even more depends upon how successful you are in opening it again. To sunlight rather than shadow."

"It will be your success," Colin told him.

Fine raised his head. "She is your sole responsibility as of this moment," Colin said. "You will stay here, and

150

you will nurse her back to health. But the moment it is possible, I wish her brought out to Bolugayen."

"But, Your Highness . . ."

"Are you married? I will have your wife come here and keep you company."

"My wife is dead, Your Highness. I have a son . . ."

"Very well. He will be brought here. Do not fail me in this, doctor. Bring Mademoiselle Cromb back to her full health and you may ask of me what you will. Anatole!" He called the butler. "Do you know who I am?"

"You are Princess Dagmar's husband, sir."

"Yes, but I am also the Prince Bolugayevski. Remember this. I am returning to Bolugayen, but I will be back shortly. From this moment Dr Fine is in charge here. You will do whatever he commands, supply him with whatever he requires. He has the fullest authority to act in my name in all matters within this building and its grounds. Do you understand me?"

Anatole looked from Colin to Fine and back again. "Yes, Your Highness."

"Very good. I will be back as soon as I can, doctor, but you understand there are certain things that I must attend to, on the estate."

Fine nodded, his expression indicating that he wished his new employer luck.

Colin was returning to a crisis. But it was a crisis he had no doubt he could resolve. He enjoyed a tremendous sensation of power, together with an equal surge of energy. He had been a prisoner for too long. There was so much he could do, with the power and wealth he had been given. So much that needed to be done. So much that *would* be done. He drew rein at the top of the last hill above the mansion, and looked down at his estate. He had never seen anything so indicative of prosperity. Then he saw the horsemen, waiting, half-way down the hill.

He walked his mount towards them, and identified

Smyslov, and Golkov, accompanied by ten of the Black Regiment. "You will pardon me, Your Highness," Smyslov said as Colin drew near. "But I have orders to place you under arrest."

"Whose orders?"

"The Princess Bolugayevska, Your Highness."

"I see. And having arrested me, what were you to do with me?" Colin inquired.

"Take you to the Princess, Your Highness."

"Well, I am going to the mansion in any event. So you will be saved the trouble."

"I am afraid I must ask you for your weapons, Your Highness."

"I am sorry to disappoint you, Smyslov, but I do not have any weapons." Colin opened his coat to let them see for themselves. "Unless my crop is so considered."

Smyslov hesitated, acutely embarrassed. "I think not, Smyslov," Colin said, and urged his horse forward. The others fell into place behind him, but Smyslov rode beside him.

"I do beg of you to be careful, Your Highness," he said. "I have never seen Her Highness in such a mood."

Colin grinned. "I assure you that the mood is going to worsen, Smyslov."

They rode up the drive, and dismounted. Smyslov gestured his people to remain outside while he accompanied Colin into the front hall. Dagmar, who had clearly been watching from the windows, awaited him. With her were Igor and several footmen, as well as Dubaclov. Anna and Alexandra stood at the top of the stairs, faces tight with apprehension. "So," Dagmar remarked; her head was bound up in a vast bandage, but she could speak quite easily. "You have had the temerity to return."

"This is my home, is it not?" Colin inquired. "You made it my home, my dear. How is your cheek?"

"My cheek will get better," she said. "Before you."

152

"Or before Jennie Cromb, no doubt. But you will be sorry to learn that your friend Vorontsov had not yet completed the task you set him. Jennie Cromb is alive, and she will be well. What is more, she will return here, with the other people you so carelessly condemned."

Dagmar's face seemed to freeze. "Are you mad?" she demanded. "Seize him," she told Igor. "Bind him, and confine him. Don't worry about his shoulder. If it breaks again that is his bad luck. And what he deserves."

Igor gestured his people forward, and Colin heard a movement behind him, where Smyslov was drawing his revolver. "If any one of you lays a finger on me," he said quietly, "I will have you hanged."

Igor checked, looking at his mistress. "He gives himself airs," Dagmar sneered. "He thinks he is the Prince Bolugayevski. I made you that, husband, and I can unmake you. Your letters patent have not yet arrived. Now they never will. I will send to the Tsar . . ."

"I hate to disappoint you, but my letters patent arrived last night," Colin said, and took them from his breast pocket. "They were given to me by Baron Lebedeff this morning."

Dagmar marched towards him, and snatched the letters from his hand. "There are, of course, copies both in Poltava and St Petersburg," Colin reminded her. "So call off your dogs, and come upstairs with me. I have some things to say to you."

She glared at him, then turned to Igor. "I said, seize him."

"But Your Highness, the Prince . . ."

"He is the Prince. But he has clearly lost his senses." She turned back to Colin. "Oh, there is a list as long as my arm of action which could only be the result of madness. Lebedeff and Vorontsov will both supply evidence against you. I shall confine you for the protection of us all. Seize him!"

Still the servants hesitated, aware that they were signing

their own death warrants if they arrested a prince without due authority, as Dagmar recognised. "I give you the authority to do this," she said. "I will inform the Governor of what I have done."

"And I say that my wife has no authority in this house or on this estate," Colin said.

The servants looked from one to the other. Colin knew this was the moment of crisis; he had not supposed Dagmar would go this far. He had no physical power to fight these people. He could only use their age-old fear of authority to his advantage, but he was the newcomer here – they had known and feared Dagmar for twenty-seven years. "Smyslov," Dagmar said. "If you fail me, you know what I shall do."

Colin heard the click of a revolver being cocked behind him. "You will surrender, please, Your Highness," Smyslov said.

Dubaclov also drew his revolver. Colin took a deep breath, realising that he might be about to die, and Anna spoke from the gallery. "You cannot touch him," she said. "He is the Prince Bolugayevski."

Dubaclov paused in consternation at the interruption, delivered in such an authoritative tone. "It appears that my sister has also lost her senses," Dagmar said contemptuously. "I will deal with you later, miss. Now, bind him."

"I know your secret, Dagmar," Anna said quietly.

Dagmar turned to look at her sister, the blood draining from her face. "Would you like me to tell them all?" Anna asked. "Tell the servants? Tell Dubaclov?"

Dubaclov stared at his fiancée with his mouth open.

"You are a lying little bitch," Dagmar said, every word a drop of venom from her lips.

"Am I?" Anna asked. "I *share* your secret, sister dear. Do you think he would be satisfied with just *you*?"

Dagmar seemed to shudder, from head to toe. Then she threw back her head and uttered a primeval shriek,

154

and ran at the stairs. Colin ran behind her, and caught her arm. She turned and swung her hand at him, but he evaded the blow easily enough. "Igor," he snapped. "Your mistress has lost her sensses. Help me."

Igor hesitated a last time, then signalled two of the maidservants forward. "Take Her Highness to her apartment," Colin said. "And stay with her until I come." He looked at Smyslov. "You had best put away that weapon, Smyslov."

Smyslov bit his lip. "You do not understand, Your Highness. The Princess . . ."

"It is the Princess who is demented," Anna said. "You will take your orders from the Prince."

Smyslov looked from one to the other. "I am capable of understanding anything, Smyslov," Colin said. "Certainly where my wife is concerned. I will tell you this: serve me faithfully, and you will have nothing to fear from my wife." He looked at Igor. "That also goes for you, Igor."

Igor looked at Smyslov, and the bailiff holstered his revolver. Dubaclov merely looked thunderstruck. The maids were half helping, half forcing Dagmar up the stairs. "You had better go with them, Alexandra," Colin said.

"No!" Alexandra said. "I hate her." She turned and ran along the gallery to her room.

"I will go with them," Anna said.

It was Colin's turn to say, "No!" She looked down at him. "I wish to speak with you."

She considered, then inclined her head in half a nod.

"And you, Dubaclov?" Colin asked.

"I . . ." Dubaclov holstered his revolver. "I also wish to speak with you, Countess."

Anna looked at Colin. "I think she will speak with me first," Colin said, and went up the stairs. From the head he looked down at the petrified servants. "Get these people back to work, Igor," he said. "And you, Smyslov. I will speak with you both later. Anna?"

155

She wore a defiant expression on she went into one of the upstairs reception rooms. Colin followed.

He closed the doors and gazed at her. She sat on a settee in front of the window. "I would say I owe you a great deal," he remarked, going towards her.

"I would say you owe me everything."

"I accept that. But don't you owe me anything in return? Such as an explanation?" She gave a little shiver. He sat beside her. "Whatever secret you share with Dagmar, and is sufficiently important to cause her to lose her senses, she will undoubtedly recover, and wish to do something about it. I'm sure you understand that Dagmar is capable of doing anything, to protect such a secret. Therefore your only defence is to share it with me, and I will protect both you and myself."

"How do I know I can trust you?"

"I could give you the word of an English gentleman. I could say that you have to trust me, because you can trust no one else. And I can also say that I know what the secret is, what it has to be."

She shot him a glance. "And you still married her?"

"Well, I did not really have very much choice, Anna. Besides, I knew nothing of any secret until after we were married. I only knew she had one. So . . . Georgei was the father of her child. Am I right?" Anna stared at him. "And he also had a go at you, is that it? I'm not as shocked as you thought I would be."

Anna continued to stare at him for some seconds, then she gave a short laugh. "What are you going to do, with your 'knowledge'?"

Colin frowned; she had sounded contemptuous. "Use it to our advantage. Does Dubaclov know of this?"

"Of course he does not. No one knows of it."

"Nor can they. Do you still intend to marry him?"

"Are you going to tell Dagmar what you know?"

"I will have to, won't I."

"She'll laugh at you."

156

"You haven't answered me about Dubaclov."

"Marrying me to him was Dagmar's idea."

"And you don't love him."

"Love *him*?"

"That is very encouraging. I don't like the fellow either. I'll see him off, if you wish."

"Thank you."

"He hasn't, er . . ."

"He does not know that I am not a virgin," she said. "I would not let him come to me."

"Anna, you will have to marry some day, you know. And your husband will have to know you are not a virgin."

"I would prefer the secret remained mine. And yours."

"And Dagmar's?"

"Yes. And Dagmar's. She does not love you," Anna said. "As of now, she will hate you."

"And you would love me?"

"Yes. Will you not love me?"

"I imagine I probably could, very easily. But it is quite impossible, Anna. I am married to your sister. Who is also going to be the mother of my child."

"I also will be the mother of your child, Colin, if you wish. I am not asking you to divorce Dagmar. But why should this secret not be as securely kept as the other? Who is to know, or would dare say, what we do with our midnight hours?"

"My dear girl, that has got to be the most immoral suggestion I have ever heard."

"You are the Prince Bolugayevski. Here on Bolugayen the Prince Bolugayevski may do whatever he chooses. As my father has always done."

He stared at her, and she stared back. "Good God!" he muttered.

"So there you have the truth. *That* is the knowledge that will make Dagmar your slave."

"Good God," he said again. "Your mother knew!"

"And killed herself. And her unborn babe."

"You knew that?"

"No. I was only eight years old when it happened."

"And . . . when did . . ."

"I was fourteen when Papa came to me. Just before he went to Sevastopol. But he has been to me since returning."

"The man must have been an utter monster."

"You have lived with us long enough to understand that."

"And Alexandra?"

Anna shook her head. "They killed him before he could go to her as well."

"And you say no one knows of it, save us three?"

"Unless Papa told Jennie. But I doubt he would have done that."

"But the scandal, your ostracism . . ."

"It was sufficient that the Countess Dagmar Bolugayevska became pregnant out of wedlock." Anna smiled. "But I think her real crime, to the gossip hungry matrons of St Petersburg, was that she would never tell them the name of the father."

She paused, and Colin sat down on the far side of the room. "Well, then," she said. "Have I filled you with horror, at such devious goings-on? They are not so uncommon in the heart of this vast country. You are the Prince Bolugayevski. Here you are lord of everything you can see."

"Were I to take advantage of what you are offering, I would be lowering myself to the level of your father."

"You have already done that, Colin, simply by accepting his position and his power. Dear Colin." She got up and came to him, standing beside him. "For you *not* to accept what I am offering would mean you are a fool. Would you not agree?"

Part Two

THE MASTER

"'Gold is for the mistress – silver for the maid –
Copper for the craftsman cunning at his trade.'
'Good!' said the Baron, sitting in his hall,
'But Iron – Cold Iron – is master of them all.'"

Rudyard Kipling
Cold Iron.

SIX YEARS LATER

Chapter 8

THE AMERICAN

The stagecoach drew to a halt in the main square of Poltava, and was immediately surrounded by a seething crowd of men, women, and children, seeking news, seeking mail, seeking employment. Charles Cromb got down, brushed himself off, and waited for his bag to be unloaded. The American was tall and powerfully built, and wore a ribbon-tweed cape over his black frock-coat and matching trousers. Travelling in this country reminded him of travelling west of the Mississippi, save that there were no Indians. But a whole hell of a lot more restrictions.

And a whole lot more weather. It had taken him two months to get here from England. It was now late April and there were still patches of snow outside the city.

Several little boys were gabbling at him. He had picked up Russian over the past few weeks, but he couldn't understand them. He did gather they wanted to carry his bag, however, so he nodded to one of them, who promptly asked him a question. "Police?" he said. "*Policia?*"

"Ah, *spassebo*," the boy said, and hurried off. Charles followed, the disappointed urchins trailing behind.

The police station was not far, and Charles found himself facing a large man wearing a green uniform and sitting behind a desk beneath a huge portrait of the young Tsar. Charles gave him the passport with which he had been issued in Sevastopol. The sergeant opened it suspiciously, carefully turning the pages; obviously he had no idea what it was. "Passport," Charles explained. "I was told to bring it here the moment I arrived in Poltava."

The sergeant blinked at him, and remarked, "Eeengleesh."

"Only by descent, bud. I am American."

"Eeengleesh," the sergeant repeated, and gave orders to an underling. Charles was to follow this fellow, and did so, having regained his passport. They went up a flight of stairs, along a corridor, and up another flight of stairs. Charles was out of breath when they arrived at a closed door. The constable knocked, and the door was opened, to reveal four male secretaries. The constable explained the situation, and one of the secretaries took the passport from Charles, opened an inner door, and spoke to the person beyond. Then he beckoned Charles.

Charles went forward, and gazed at a man, also wearing uniform, quite young, judging by his unlined face with thick black hair. "I am Colonel Vorontsov," the man said in English, and glanced at the passport. "You are a long way from home, Mr Cromb."

"You could say that, Colonel."

Vorontsov waved him to a chair, and then sat behind his desk. The secretary bowed and withdrew, closing the door. Charles sat down. "You have business in Poltava?" Vorontsov asked.

"May I ask you a question, Colonel?" Vorontsov raised his eyebrows. "What's with this country? You know, it's possible to travel from New York to San Francisco without a single solitary soul asking your business. Here, wherever I stop, I have to report to the police, and answer a whole lot of questions. What are you guys frightened of?"

Vorontsov regarded him for some seconds. "We are not frightened of anyone, Mr Cromb. It is my business to keep the peace. There is unrest in the country, inspired by a few anarchists. Perhaps you do not have anarchists in America."

"We have Indians."

162

Vorontsov gave a faint smile. "And we have Mongols. But not in Poltava. You have not answered my question."

Charles sighed. "I am on my way to pay a visit to a place called Bolugayen."

Suddenly Vorontsov was interested. "Do you know the Bolugayevskis?"

"No, I don't. But I am looking for a cousin of mine who is believed to be in Russia, and on that estate."

"You are related to the Prince?"

"Afraid not, Colonel. This is a woman, who may be living with them."

Vorontsov rested his chin on his hand. "Of course! Jennie Cromb!"

Charles frowned at him. "You know my cousin?"

"Yes," Vorontsov said. "We have an acquaintance. Tell me, Mr Cromb, have you come to Russia to take your cousin back to America?"

"Well, that will obviously have to depend upon whether Jennie wishes to come with me. When you say, back to America, I should point out that she has never been there. Now you tell me: is she a serf?"

"There are no longer any serfs in Russia," Vorontsov said, regretfully. "By edict of the Tsar, they were all freed, last month."

"But that's great. If the serfs are free, then Jennie is free too. If she ever was a serf."

"She came here as a serf, certainly," Vorontsov said. "But then . . . I must tell you, Mr Cromb, that your cousin became involved in subversive activities."

"What subversive activities?"

"The assassination of Prince Bolugayevski. She belonged to an organisation called the Will of the People. This organisation still exists, and is bent on a course of assassination of public figures."

"Good God! And you say my cousin was a member of it?"

163

"She was undoubtedly a member of the conspiracy which plotted the death of the Prince, and carried out the assassination. She should have been hanged. Had I my way, she *would* have been hanged. However, the new Prince Bolugayevski thought otherwise."

"Thank God for that. This new prince being the Britisher, right?"

"That is correct, Mr Cromb."

"You'll understand, Colonel, that I find it difficult to accept that a cousin of mine could possibly be involved in a murder."

"No doubt. However, I strongly recommend that you do take her out of Russia, and back to America, if that is at all possible."

"Would that be some kind of a threat, Colonel?"

"It is advice, Mr Cromb. You should understand that your cousin has never been exonerated, acquitted or amnestied for her crime. She was removed from my custody by the simple decision of Prince Bolugayevski. Her file is still in that cabinet over there, and it is still open."

"Because you hope to nail her again, one day?"

Vorontsov smiled. "I am a patient man, Mr Cromb." He held out the passport. "I will wish you a pleasant stay at Bolugayen."

When he attempted to hire a horse and a guide out to the Bolugayevski estate, Charles was advised that the Prince had a house in the city, and that there would be the best place to find what he wanted. So he took himself along to the Bolugayevski Palace in Poltava, and stood on the pavement to stare at it. It *was* a palace. As for his brownstone in Boston, so carefully selected by his father to represent his rise in the world . . . He went up the steps and rang the bell. The door was opened by a footman, wearing blue and gold livery. "I don't suppose you speak English?" Charles inquired.

164

The footman held up his hand, and stepped back into the house, half closing the door. Clearly, with a Britisher as Prince, the language would not be unknown in this house. The door was opened again, by another man, clearly also a servant although far more resplendently dressed than his underling, in the same colours. "You Engleesh?" he asked.

"Ah . . ." But to go into the rigmarole would delay things enormously, he knew. "Yes."

"You have business?"

"I wish to go to Bolugayen."

"Why? You know the Prince?"

"I wish to meet him. Can you supply me with a horse and a guide?"

The butler looked bewildered. and then another voice spoke, from inside the house. The door swung in. "You come," the butler said.

Charles stepped inside, and again paused, as he took in the parquet floor, the paintings and ikons on the walls, the carved panelling, and the great staircase leading up to a first floor gallery. And then realised that nothing in this house mattered beside the woman who was standing halfway down the staircase. Of a good height, and slender, her figure obscured by the flowing white gown, nipped in at her waist by a pale blue sash, she possessed an exquisitely handsome face; the features were too strong for pure beauty, but were compellingly attractive, and were framed in a mane of soft golden hair, which floated on her shoulders. He put her age down as early twenties, and realised that if it were possible to fall in love at first sight, then he had just done so.

"You must forgive Anatole," she said, her voice, low and yet clear. Her English was flawless. "He finds English a most difficult language."

Charles had to clear his throat before he could speak. "And you don't?"

"I have more time for learning. Do you know the Prince?"

"No, ma'am, I've never met him. But I look forward to doing so."

She came down the stairs and turned away from him, going into one of the reception rooms, a vast chamber decorated in blue and gold. Charles glanced at Anatole, who nodded. He followed the woman who went to a settee and sat down with a rustle of taffeta. "Anatole will bring tea," she said. "Or would you prefer vodka?"

"Ah . . . tea would be fine, ma'am."

"Do you have a card?"

"No, ma'am. My name is Charles Cromb."

The mention of his name clearly increased her interest. But she did not immediately follow it up. "I am Anna Bolugayevska," she said.

Charles swallowed. "And you're a princess?"

"No, Mr Cromb. I am a countess. My sister is the Princess Bolugayevska. Tell me, I have never heard an accent like yours before. What part of England are you from?"

"I'm an American," Charles explained.

"I see. But you are related to Jennie?"

"I'm her cousin. Can you tell me where she is?"

"She is on Bolugayen."

"And she is well?"

"She is very well, Mr Cromb."

"Say, that's tremendous. D'you think I'd be welcome if I paid her a visit?"

"I'm sure you'd be welcome, Mr Cromb."

"Well, great. I was kind of hoping I could raise a guide, here. I don't know the country."

"I will take you out to Bolugayen myself, Mr Cromb. I am going there tomorrow."

"Well, I couldn't ask for anything more than that, Countess. Tomorrow, eh? Could you recommend me to an hotel for the night?"

166

"My dear Mr Cromb, you are my guest. You'll stay here."

"Here?" Charles looked left and right.

"Anatole will tell your man where to put your things."

"My man?"

"Don't you have a man? A servant?"

"To tell you the truth, Countess, I don't."

"You have travelled all the way from . . . America, without a servant?"

"I guess we do things differently over there."

"Yes," she agreed. "Then Anatole will show you to your apartment. I will receive you at seven." She rang a little glass bell on the table beside her.

Charles accumulated not one, but three servants, all male, and all supercilious, which increased as they unpacked his bag. There was a whispered consultation, and one of them departed hurriedly. Charles was having a bath, but he could see what was going on. Anatole, who had been summoned, stood beside the tub, looking anxious. "No suit," he explained.

"There are two suits in there," Charles replied. "Those guys hung them in the cupboard."

"No dinner suit," Anatole said.

"Dinner suit? Oh, you mean, white tie? No, I don't travel with that kind of gear."

"No possible dine with Countess with no suit," Anatole declared.

"Well, now . . ." Charles stepped out of the tub and was promptly enveloped in a huge warm towel by one of the valets. "You'll have to inform the Countess that I'm not respectable, I guess. I'll eat alone."

He wasn't too bothered. He was in a state of euphoria at his surroundings and his hostess, and at being so readily accepted where he had expected a difficult passage. Anatole returned with a dinner suit, as well as several more helpers. With their assistance, Charles was dressed.

167

"Whose suit is this, anyway?" he asked as he took a turn in front of the full length mirror set into the wardrobe door.

"It is the Prince's suit, Your Excellency."

It took Charles a few moments to realise it was he being addressed; no one had ever called him "Your Excellency" before.

"Now, you come. Reception in small drawing room."

"Small party, eh?" Charles asked, as he followed the butler to the stairs.

"Countess alone this evening, Your Excellency," Anatole told him.

Holy shit! Charles thought. He was alone in this huge house with that gorgeous girl . . . apart from a few dozen servants. She couldn't be married, because she had introduced herself as Anna Bolugayevska. Holy *shit*! On the other hand, he reminded himself he had come here to rescue Jennie from the clutches of these people, one of whom, probably this girl's brother, had carried her off.

Further thought was precluded, as he arrived at the doorway to the "small" drawing room. It would have held sixty people without any two having to brush shoulders. Anna Bolugayevska was waiting. She wore a blue evening gown, with white elbow length gloves; her hair was upswept in a chignon, secured by a band which sparkled with diamonds, and there were hardly less valuable stones glittering from the rings on her fingers, the bracelets on her arms. But for all the jewellery, the room was dominated by the whiteness of her skin and the depths of the décolletage of her dress. Charles had some difficulty in breathing.

"You look very smart, Mr Cromb," Anna remarked. "Were you not obviously in a hurry to reach Bolugayen I would have my brother-in-law's tailor come in tomorrow; you obviously need some clothes. Would you like me to do that? It would only mean a delay of twenty-four hours."

Charles licked his lips. "But . . . don't you want to get home?"

168

"I am home, Mr Cromb. In one of our homes, to be sure."

Anatole served champagne. "May I say that you are absolutely beautiful, Countess?" Charles ventured, raising his fluted glass.

Anna smiled. "Why, thank you, Mr Cromb. Welcome to Bolugayevski Palace. Your health!" She drank, finishing the glass in a single swallow, and then, to his consternation, hurled it into the blazing fireplace. He could do nothing less than follow her example. "Sit here, beside me," she commanded. "Now tell me about yourself." He did so. "You own a shipping company." She seemed impressed, but he suspected she was merely being polite. "And now you are seeking Jennie? Because you knew of her situation?"

"I didn't know of her situation. I just wanted to look up my family. But I heard something about it, in England."

"You mean, how she was carried off by my brother?"

Charles gulped; he had anticipated having to feel his way with great caution.

"Georgei was like that," Anna said. "I suppose we all are. But then, we are Bolugayevskis."

Anatole now summoned them to dinner.

The dining room was more in the nature of a hall, and the oak table was forty feet long. He was seated at one end, and looked past the rows of chairs and the glowing candelabra to Anna, who was at the other end. At that distance he could not make out her face. There were six footmen waiting to serve him, so completely that he was not even allowed to wipe his own lips with his damask napkin. A similar number attended to Anna. He tried to see what she was going to do with her wine glass, but to his relief, having drunk, she replaced it on the table.

Obviously there could be no conversation, and the meal took a long time. But at last she rose, swept into another

169

drawing room, and seated herself. Anatole hurried forward with goblets of brandy. Charles was feeling a little fuzzy from the wine on top of the champagne; his normal drink was whisky. Now he watched Anna drain a glass of brandy as it if had been water, to have it immediately refilled by Anatole.

He also knew a growing sense of excitement. He was alone with this gorgeous creature, who was rapidly getting drunk. And she had invited him to remain here, with her, for another two days. The question was, was he going to take advantage of it? Dare he? But he couldn't help but feel it would be no crime, after what this girl's brother had done to Jennie.

"I'm afraid Georgei treated her rather badly," Anna remarked, as if able to read his thoughts. "But that too was his way. Then she was passed on to Papa, and he treated her worse."

"You can just sit there, and say those things?" he asked.

Anna shrugged. "It is the truth. And you cannot avenge her, as both my brother and my father are dead."

"According to your chief of police, here, Jennie was accused of complicity in that crime, and arrested."

Anna raised her eyebrows, while Anatole refilled her glass. "You have met Vorontsov?"

"It was necessary to present my passport."

"And he told you about Jennie? What did he tell you?"

"That she had been arrested. But then released, by order of the Prince."

Anna nodded. "That is true. Do you have any idea of what the word 'arrested' means in Russia? Did Vorontsov tell you?"

Charles frowned at her. "What are you getting at?"

"I am telling you about this cousin you have come so far to find. She was raped, a great many times, by the police. Including Vorontsov. At the time of her arrest, I

170

mean. She had been raped by my brother and my father, and, I imagine, more than one of the servants, before then." Charles gulped. "Then she was beaten with canes, on her bare buttocks, Mr Cromb," Anna went on. "Then she was subjected to even more unpleasant mistreatment, such as having her nipples pierced with needles or broken glass pushed into her anus."

"My God!" Charles exclaimed. "You . . ."

"Then, as she would not implicate anyone, she was systematically starved to death. She was all but dead when Prince Colin rescued her. That was five years ago. She is now fully recovered, physically, and is very well. But an experience like that leaves a profound effect."

"Are you trying to tell me that she is mad?"

"No. No, Jennie is not mad. She is a very strong woman, mentally and physically. You should be proud of her. What I am trying to say is that you will find that she has changed, from your memory of her."

"I have no memory of her, Countess. I never met her."

"Well, then, it will be an experience for you."

He leaned forward. "Why was this man Vorontsov not punished for such a crime?"

"Vorontsov? He is a policeman, Mr Cromb. Policemen cannot commit crimes. At least, not in Russia."

"Oh, yeah? Well . . ."

"You mean to rush out and challenge him to a duel?" Anna smiled. "He would simply have you arrested. And if you were to kill him, you would be hanged. That would be rather a waste."

Charles ignored the compliment, aware only of a seething sense of outrage. "You mean nothing can be done about him?"

"Not unless you intend to start a revolution, and that also leads to a hanging. The Prince overruled him, because he is the Prince, but not even Colin could actually bring him to book. Besides, Vorontsov was only acting on the orders of the Princess."

171

"The Princess?"

"My sister Dagmar. She is the Princess Bolugayevska."

"Then who is this guy Colin? Are we talking about the Britisher, MacLain?"

"That is correct. My sister's husband."

Charles scratched his head; he no longer felt the slightest inhibition in her company. "Let me get this straight. Your sister has Jennie arrested for murdering her Dad, who is also your Dad, and this MacLain character comes along and uses his clout as the new Prince to have Jennie released. Now that couldn't happen in the States."

"But then," she pointed out, "you don't have princes in the States. Or," she added thoughtfully, "Bolugayevskis."

"So, Jennie was, or is, this MacLain's mistress, and your sister was jealous."

Anna Bolugayevska's eyes were cool. "No, Mr Cromb. You have got that wrong. Jennie is not, and never was, Colin's mistress."

"Then I don't get it at all. But this arresting and releasing must've caused a bit of a ruckus at home."

"Why, yes, Mr Cromb, it did cause, as you put it, a bit of a ruckus at home."

"But Jennie is still living there, with this MacLain, and your sister . . . is that what they call a *ménage a trois*?"

Anna regarded him for several seconds, then got up. "Why, yes, Mr Cromb. You could describe our situation as a *ménage a trois*. Now I shall go to bed. I recommend you do the same. We have had enough to drink."

Charles struggled to his feet, keeping his balance with difficulty. "But say, Countess, if Jennie didn't kill your old man, who did?"

Anna Bolugayevska had reached the door, which was being held open for her by Anatole. "Why, my brother killed my father, Mr Cromb. My other brother, Vassily. Didn't Colonel Vorontsov tell you that?"

Sleep was a disjointed affair, composed of many broken

images. Charles was quite annoyed when the drapes were drawn and he was forced to awake. A footman presented him with a card, on which was written, in English, "I shall breakfast on the back terrace, at nine."

"What time is it?" he snapped. "Time! Clock!" He drew a circle in the air and then gestured the two hands. The footman produced his own fob watch and showed it to him; it was twenty past eight. Charles shaved, washed and dressed with haste, afraid that if he was late she might take herself off. He reached the terrace, which looked out over the grounds, at three minutes to nine.

Anna Bolugayevska, in white muslin fluttering in the slight breeze, was drinking white wine, and Anatole was waiting with a glass for him. "Why, Mr Cromb," she said. "How nice to see you. I was afraid you might not be feeling well."

"I've felt better," he admitted.

"You will have to become used to our habits, if you are going to be our guest."

He sat down. "About last night," he ventured. "I figure that you were just trying to scare me off."

"I have no idea what you are talking about, Mr Cromb."

"Well, all that stuff . . . it couldn't possibly be true."

She raised her head. "We Bolugayevskis are guilty of a great number of crimes, Mr Cromb. But it would never occur to any one of us to lie, about anything. Except perhaps Dagmar."

"Okay. You've told me about your family. And I've told you all about me. Now will you tell me all about you?"

"What is it you wish to know?"

"Everything."

"Why, Mr Cromb, are you flirting with me?"

"I guess I am, Countess. Does that offend you?"

"Good heavens, no. A woman is hardly a woman if she does not enjoy a flirtation. Now, let me see. I am the second daughter and third child of Prince Alexander Bolugayevski and Princess Dagmar Bolugayevska. Both

173

my parents are dead. My father was murdered, as you know, and I am afraid my mother committed suicide. Some time ago."

"Oh, say, Countess, I'm real sorry about that."

"I was very small. But I know she was deeply unhappy, about . . . things. However, now I am twenty-one."

"And unmarried? Your Russian guys are slow."

"I was engaged once, when I was sixteen. but it was very brief." She gave a secret little smile. "The Prince did not approve."

"Your father?"

"No, the present Prince."

"This guy MacLain."

"Yes, this guy MacLain." She had clearly never uttered a phrase like that in her life before.

"But still, that *was* five years ago. In the States, you'd have men clustering round you like bees round the honey pot."

"I am afraid the Prince would not permit that either."

"Sounds a real tyrant, your English prince. But say, if he's that stand-offish, why d'you reckon he'll welcome me?"

"Because you are Jennie's cousin, Mr Cromb. Now . . ." She became brusquely efficient. "The tailors come in at nine. I have told them that the suits must be ready by this evening."

"Now that surely can't be possible."

"Why not? I have instructed them."

"And you are the Countess Bolugayevska."

"Why, yes, Mr Cromb. When you have been measured, would you care to take a drive around the city?"

Charles' new clothes were waiting for him that afternoon, when they returned to the Bolugayevski Palace after picnicking on the bank of the Vorskla River, which ran by the city. By then he was in a state of euphoric shock. The picnic had been quite idyllic. Charles had never had the

174

time or the inclination to take a woman on a picnic before, if he had done so it would have been just the two of them and they would have sat on the grass, and drunk beer while they ate their sandwiches. Anna Bolugayevska's idea of a picnic was to drink champagne out of crystal flutes while she ate spoonfulls of caviar, seated in comfortable folding chairs and being served by Anatole, while the footmen stood at a respectful distance. He had felt obliged to ask, "Do you ever do anything all by yourself, Countess?"

And she had smiled. "There is no reason for my people to inhibit you, Mr Cromb; none of these can understand English, save for Anatole. So flirt away."

"Flirting is not only a matter of words, Countess."

"You mean you wish to touch me? To fuck me, here on the banks of the river?" Once again she had reduced him to speechlessness. Anna had continued to smile. "Obviously that is not possible, in front of the footmen. Or even Anatole." Then to his consternation, she clapped her hands. "Anatole, give me your bugle."

Anatole hurried forward to hand her the trumpet. "Now take yourself and your people away," Anna said. "Far away. I will blow the bugle when you may return."

Anatole bowed and he and the other three men disappeared.

"I am going to bathe," Anna said. "The water will be very cold, but the more invigorating for that. Will you bathe with me, Mr Cromb?"

"Well, heck, Countess . . ."

"However, I dislike undressing in front of men," Anna said. "So I would be much obliged if you would turn your back on me until I say you may turn again." She smiled. "You may use the time to undress, yourself."

He felt a tremendous combination of relief and disappointment. "You mean you have a costume you're going to change into. Right. But the fact is, I don't have a costume, unless your guys have brought one along for me."

175

"Mr Cromb, I do not wear a costume to bathe. Now, will you kindly turn your back."

He didn't know what to say. But he got up and turned his back, feeling a variety of emotions, sexual arousal the most prominent. She couldn't possibly mean . . . "Thank you, Mr Cromb, you may turn round now."

He turned, and here was absolute perfection, from the whiteness of her shoulders, and breasts, entrancingly heavy and pink-nippled, to the surprisingly slender thighs and the spread of pale silk at her groin, down the straight-ness of her well-muscled legs. "Why, Mr Cromb," she said. "Are you *not* going to bathe?" She turned away from him. Her hair was still up and there was no protection for her equally white back and buttocks, as she sat on the bank and slid into the water, which came above her waist.

Charles tore at his clothes. He had no idea what she intended, but he had to get in there with her. He ran at the bank, and she turned to look at him in turn. "Why, Mr Cromb," she remarked. "You *are* a big fellow."

He slid down the bank, shuddered because the water was indeed very cold, and reached for her. She stepped back, frowning. "Please, Mr Cromb."

"But . . . for Christ's sake, Countess . . ."

"I have no intention of being raped, Mr Cromb. Nor had I expected it of you. Do not worry, the cold water will soon have a soothing effect."

Definitely he was in a world he had never imagined could exist. He had bathed naked with a Russian countess, who had engaged him in pleasant conversation while allowing him to look at her as much as he liked . . . but then she had been looking at him. But she had not permitted him to go any further than look.

"That was the wildest experience I ever had," Charles said. "I'm sorry I was rude."

Anna smiled. "You are strange to our customs. I forgive you."

"Well, I've never done anything like that before. But you said, well . . ."

"You would like to fuck me, is that it?"

Tentatively he picked up her hand; she made no effort to free herself. "Do you know what I would like to do, more than anything else in the world?" he asked.

"To fuck me."

"You mistake me, Countess. Of course I wish to make love with you. But more than anything else I would like to take you back to America with me. As my wife, of course."

"Do you know, Mr Cromb, I believe you have the instincts of a gentleman," she remarked. "I think it would be simply delightful to come to America with you. But I am afraid it is not possible."

"You mean you would fuck me but not marry me."

She smiled. "I never said that I would fuck you either, Mr Cromb. I merely observed that *you* wished to fuck *me*. Which was correct, was it not?"

"Because I am *not* a gentleman, is that it?"

"No, Mr Cromb," she said quietly. "Because I am already suited. The Bolugayevska you should marry is my sister Alix. She is just as attractive as I. And she is a virgin."

Chapter 9

THE BETROTHAL

"You are now on Bolugayen, Mr Cromb," Anna Bolugayevska said, pointing down into the valley. Charles had been surprised at her decision to ride out of Poltava. Her landau rumbled along some distance behind them, followed by the wagonloads of purchases she had made during her stay in the city. Then he had realised that she actually did enjoy riding. She made a picture in her dark blue double-breasted tunic over a matching skirt, her flowing red scarf, her black silk hat, and her hair caught in a snood.

She had not invited him to breakfast with her; this morning her note had merely informed him of the hour they were leaving, early enough to give him time to breakfast in his room. She had been politeness itself, but the intimate camaraderie of the previous day had been entirely absent.

He contented himself with saying, "Very impressive", as he looked at the mansion, the outbuildings and the stables, and in the distance the roofs of the houses and the church steeple all nestling so pastorally in the midst of a sea of white cotton-buds.

But as ever, Anna had the last word. "And it's all ours. No matter what the Tsar may say." She kicked her horse and cantered down the slope, followed by her various attendants.

Charles followed, hooves clattering on the gravel of the

forecourt, above which the house rose. Grooms hurried forward to grasp their bridles, footmen appeared to assist in the unloading of the wagons as they came into the yard. Anna was assisted from the saddle by a somewhat elderly man, redolent of authority.

"This is Igor," she told Charles. "Igor is our butler." She spoke rapidly in Russian. "I have told him to prepare an apartment for you in the guest wing," she explained. "You will be staying with us for a while." Her eyebrows assumed an entrancing arch. "You *will* be staying for a while, Mr Cromb?"

"I reckon that depends on the Prince, Countess."

"Well, then, let us ask him." Her gloved fingers twined in his and she led him up the steps, to where a man waited. Prince Bolugayevski could not be thirty years old. He was a handsome man, his fair hair brushed straight back from his forehead. His clothes were of the very best quality. "Darling," Anna said, in English. "I have brought you a guest."

Charles gulped as she released him, ran forward, put her arms round her brother-in-law's neck, and kissed him on the mouth. It was a warm, intimate kiss, to which the Prince responded. I am already suited, she had said. But . . . the Prince?

Neither looked the least embarrassed as they released each other and Anna beckoned Charles forward; if the Prince was frowning, it was because he recognised something in the new arrival. "Have we met, sir?"

"His name is Charles Cromb, Colin. And he is Jennie's cousin."

"Good heavens!" Colin held out his hand. "Welcome! But . . . I don't remember you from Blaistone."

"I'm Charlie Cromb's son. My father left Blaistone before either of us was born, I fancy, Prince."

"Well, come in. Come in. Jennie's out at the moment, riding. With Alix. But I'm pleased you've met Anna."

"I've invited Mr Cromb to stay for a while," Anna said.

179

"Of course."

The Prince walked into his house, past bowing servants. Anna tucked her arm through Charles's, and followed. "You see," she said, "I told you he'd be pleased to see you. Now, I'm sure you need a wash and brush up after your ride. Igor will show you to your apartment."

The Prince, who had reached the door to one of the downstairs reception rooms, turned back towards them. "When you are ready, we will have a talk."

"Come in, Mr Cromb," the Prince invited, when Igor opened the doors of the study for him. "I'd have you meet my sons. Well, Georgei is adopted to be sure. But he is Jennie's son."

The six-year-old boy came forward and offered his hand with great dignity. "Father tells me you are my uncle, sir," he said, in English.

The boy had auburn hair, and his resemblance to Jennie was marked. "I guess I am."

"And you come from America. I should like to go to America, one day."

"Well, perhaps you shall." Charles glanced at the Prince.

"I am sure you shall, Georgei," Colin said. "Peter."

The second boy was perhaps a year younger, and smaller. But he too moved with conscious dignity. "Welcome to Bolugayen, sir," he said in a high, clear voice.

"Peter will be six this year," Colin explained. "He is my son. Thank you, boys, now off you go. Mr Yevrentko is waiting for you."

The two boys bowed to their father, and left the room. Charles looked around him. The room was really too large to be described as a study; the acres of book-lined walls more suggested a library. The Prince gestured him to a leather-upholstered armchair, and came round the huge walnut desk to seat himself in another.

"The Countess Anna has explained to me the reasons

behind your visit," the Prince said. "Tell me, how did you know where your cousin was living?"

"I went to Blaistone Manor. All of the family has disappeared. You might say Jennie had disappeared too, as far as Blaistone was concerned. But they did know the name of the fellow who carried her off."

"Did you see Lord Blaistone?"

"It was he gave me the information. He showed some interest in you."

"Did he, by God? But you know my situation?"

"I am sure it could be resolved. After all, the war is six years in the past."

"Perhaps I do not wish it resolved, Mr Cromb. I carry a great deal of guilt on my shoulders, for several causes. I think it should probably stay there."

"I'm afraid I don't understand."

"One needs to live in Russia to understand. Anna also tells me you saw Vorontsov."

"I did."

"And is it your ambition to carry your cousin back to the States?"

"That has to be up to her. And you, I guess. I just knew I had to find her."

"Which is an admirable determination. Are you financially sound?"

"I own a shipping line."

"Not necessarily the same thing." Colin smiled. "I also own a shipping line."

"In addition to all this?"

"My predecessor believed in diversity, and who is to say he was not correct to do so. We live in changing times."

"Like losing all your serfs?"

"I haven't lost them, Mr Cromb. I merely no longer own them."

"Still, quite a change, eh?"

"What the Tsar decrees, happens. He freed all the Imperial serfs some years ago."

"Does that mean Jennie is now free?"

"Jennie has been free for several years, Mr Cromb. I gave her her freedom the moment I became Prince."

"And she has remained here, of her own free will?"

"Jennie has suffered a great deal since coming to Russia, but now there is nowhere else that she could be as well off and as contented. At least until your arrival."

"And she is now your mistress?" Despite Anna's dismissal of that possibility, he had to be sure. The Prince raised his eyebrows. "Forgive me, Prince," Charles said. "But it seems to me that everyone around here calls a spade a spade."

"You mean, Anna," the Prince said. "But that goes for all the sisters. No, Mr Cromb, Jennie has never been my mistress. Anna says she told you what was done to her, by the police."

"Yes."

"Well, then, you will understand, she no longer enjoys matters of the flesh. She is regarded as a sister here, by both my wife and sisters-in-law, and by myself."

"But Anna said there is nothing the matter with her mind."

"Why, no, Mr Cromb. She has her son, she has a great many friends amongst my people, and I believe she is happy. I wish her to remain so."

"Colonel Vorontsov still has a file on her. Her case is still open. It seems to me that only you stand between her and a hangman's rope. Can any woman be happy knowing she exists on such a thin knife edge?"

Colin smiled. "I imagine she knows that I have no intention of dying, in the immediate future."

"Then let me ask you one more question, if you won't think me presumptious. Your serfs are freed. How does that affect your wealth, and your power? Power which stands between Jennie and the rope."

"Very little. His Majesty has sought to reform our system of life, but he has no intention of overturning

182

either the social or economic fabric of the nation. The freeing of the serfs is to be a gradual process. This year was only the commencement. People who have for generations been bound need a long period of adjustment before they can be turned loose."

"I never thought to hear an Englishman express such a point of view, with respect, Prince."

"Shall I say that I have become Russianised, Mr Cromb?" He gave one of his boyish grins. "Or would you prefer, corrupted? Now come, the girls have returned."

Charles followed the Prince into the hall, where two women, were just handing their silk riding hats and crops to waiting footmen, while Igor hovered with a tray of glasses of brandy. "I've a surprise for you," the Prince said. "Jennie!"

She was taller and far more lovely than Charles had expected.

"I'm Charles Cromb, Jennie," Charles said. "Your father and mine were brothers."

Jennie hesitated, glanced at the Prince, then held out her hand. Charles decided to shake it rather than kiss it. "I do not understand," she said.

"Mr Cromb has come looking for you," the Prince said.

Jennie gazed at Charles. "Well, in a manner of speaking," Charles explained. "I went to England to look up my Dad's family, as we don't really have any family in the States."

"My mother sent you here?"

Charles frowned. "Your mother is dead, Jennie. Didn't you know that?"

"No, I didn't know that. Did you see my sisters?" she asked.

"'Fraid not. I couldn't find them. Seems that when your Ma died, they up and left Blaistone."

"You mean they are probably dead too?"

"Well, I doubt that," Charles protested. "I guess they're married, but as they didn't keep in touch with Blaistone, I couldn't trace their married names. So, that left you. Lord Blaistone told me where to come."

"I must go and change," Jennie said. At the foot of the stairs she paused and looked over her shoulder. "Will you stay?"

Charles looked at the Prince, who nodded. "Your cousin is welcome to stay for as long as he chooses."

"Thank you."

"She's going to have a cry." Charles turned in some confusion. "I'm Alix," the girl said. She was only a girl, definitely younger than the sister she so strongly resembled. Both features and hair were similar to Anna's, but there was a quality of softness, in both the eyes and the mouth, that Anna had totally lacked.

"My pleasure, Countess."

"I must go and change for lunch. But this afternoon, you must tell me all about America. I so want to go there." She followed Jennie up the stairs.

"May I say, Prince, that you have gotten yourself surrounded by truly beautiful women."

"You could say I am the most fortunate of men. Now you must come and meet my wife."

Charles followed the Prince up the stairs and along the gallery to an apartment on the far side of the house. Double doors admitted the two men into an even larger and brighter room, high-ceilinged and decorated mostly in white. Two women sat in the bay window, industriously stitching. Both looked up at the entry of the Prince, and one hastily stood up as well. But she, dark-haired and gamine-featured, was never a Bolugayevska. The other, who did not rise, had to be the Princess, for she had the family features, only colder; her hair was also darker than her sisters and she was clearly some years older. A heavy layer of powder could not hide the scar on her cheek.

"Papa!" A little girl, who had been playing quietly in the corner, came running across the carpet.

"This is my daughter, Catherine," the Prince told Charles. "And this is Catherine's mother, Olga." Olga gave a hasty curtsey.

"Do we have a guest?" Dagmar inquired, quietly, speaking English – her voice as cold as her eyes.

"Mr Charles Cromb, my dear," the Prince said.

Dagmar frowned. "Cromb?"

"I am Jennie's cousin, Princess," Charles said.

Dagmar gazed at him, as if not sure that he should have addressed her at all. "Mr Cromb will be staying with us for a while," the Prince said.

"And is he going to take that creature away with him when he leaves?"

Charles looked at the Prince in consternation. "Somehow, my dear, I doubt that," the Prince said. "I thought you might like to meet him. Shall we go down, Mr Cromb? I do not think the Princess will be joining us for lunch."

Charles gave a bow, and moved to the door. The Prince put his daughter down after giving her another squeeze, and followed. "Quickly, Mr Cromb," he recommended.

Charles hesitated, looked over his shoulder, and saw the vase hurtling in his direction.

There were eleven for lunch, including Charles. Apart from the three women, Anna, Alexandra and Jennie, and the Prince, there were Mr and Mrs Smyslov, who were the estate bailiff and his wife, the family priest, Father Alexei, and Dr Fine, the family physician, and his son David; these two intrigued him, because they were definitely Jewish, yet were treated with total intimacy by the rest of the family. Fine himself was a young middle-aged man with a full black beard and strong features; Charles gathered he was a widower. David, was eighteen, good-looking with intense dark eyes. Both clearly worshipped the Prince. The Smyslovs, he felt, were afraid of their master. As, perhaps, was the priest. The eleventh diner was the young prince's tutor, Yuri Yevrentko.

As the table was big enough to seat forty without discomfort, the place settings were some distance apart, but he discovered that he was much closer to Anna than anyone else. "I gather you have met the Dagger, Mr Cromb," Anna remarked.

"The Dagger?"

"My sister, the Princess."

"Ah. I have met the Princess, yes, Countess. And a lady called Olga."

"Oh, yes, Catherine's mother."

"It seems to me that the Prince has a regular harem."

Anna smiled. "Not so you'd notice. Olga happened to be the Queen of the Harvest one year, and the Prince got her pregnant. The Prince attempts to do this every year, of course, but this was only the second time it has happened within living memory. So, the babe was brought into the house, and when Olga's marriage turned out badly, the Prince brought her too. But he has not again taken her to his bed." Her tone indicated that *she* had made certain of that. "Now tell me, what do you think of my baby sister?"

Charles glanced down the table to where Alexandra was in animated conversation with the Smyslovs. "I think she is very beautiful."

"Is she as beautiful as I?"

"She may become so, with time," Charles said, again picking his words with great care.

Another gentle laugh. "Would you like to fuck her?"

"Countess, you say the damnedest things."

"Would you still rather fuck me?"

She was getting to him at last. "Yes, Countess. I'd rather fuck you. But that's your brother-in-law's privilege, isn't it?"

She showed not the slightest reaction. "Why, yes, Mr Cromb. Mind you, I could ask him if he'd allow *you* the privilege, just the once, perhaps. Would you like me to do that?"

"Don't you ever tire of tormenting people, Countess?"

He watched her eyebrows move. "I am perfectly serious, Mr Cromb. I find you a most attractive man."

"Just as you were serious when you suggested that a Yankee whose father came up from the bottom end of society should contemplate marriage to your sister?"

"We live in changing times, Mr Cromb," Anna said, perhaps unconsciously quoting her lover. And now she was indeed speaking seriously. "I suspect, were she encouraged to think about it, Alix might find you most attractive as well. I know that the Prince would very much like to see my baby sister married. And . . . well, there are problems. I think he might look upon your suit very favourably."

"Don't you think I should know what these problems are, before I make a proposal?"

Anna ate for some seconds before replying. "Alix has no problems which can possibly affect you, in America, Mr Cromb," she said. "She is twenty years old, and in every way healthy. And a virgin, as I told you. I will wish you success in your enterprise. And indeed, I will help you in every way I can."

"You say the Prince is eager to marry the Countess Alexandra off," Charles ventured. "But should he not be even more eager to marry *you* off, Countess?"

Anna gave her secret smile. "No. He is not the least anxious to marry me off, Mr Cromb. Nor do I have any desire to be married."

"You'd love America," Charles said. "I live by the sea, the bay, that's Quincy Bay, really, and the Atlantic Ocean. It's tremendous. But west of the Alleghenies we have prairies every bit as enormous as this one."

It was dusk, and the sun was sinking. It was the end of April and still fairly early in the evening, and the family

187

had not yet assembled for dinner. At last he had been allowed this time alone with Jennie. He was, actually, very nervous. He could not look at her without his imagination taking control of his mind as he remembered what she had suffered. And she remained so very attractive. More than either of the far more lovely Bolugayevska sisters he longed to take her in his arms, hold her against him, stroke her hair and allow some of his strength to flow into her body. But quite apart from the fact that she was his cousin, he had the Prince's warning that she would undoubtedly reject him.

"You make it sound a paradise," she murmured. She watched the sunset, rather than him.

"It is. Or can be. Jennie . . ." He picked up her hand and she made no resistance. "You and I are possibly the only family either of us have in the world. It is certainly my duty to care for you, protect you and nurture you. But I wish you to know that I have feelings for you far beyond any call of duty. Will you let me take care of you, for the rest of your days?"

She squeezed his fingers. "I would love you to be able to do that. But . . . Bolugayen is all the home I have ever truly known. It was terrible in the beginning, but since Mr MacLain became Prince, why, it has been a heaven on earth. Do you know that Bolugayen is about the only estate in Russia where the freeing of the serfs has not been accompanied by some disturbance?"

"You are in love with him. You know you can never be more to him than a mistress."

"But I know I admire him, more than anyone else in the world. Love, the sort of love of which you speak, has nothing to do with it. He is well satisfied, and . . . so am I."

She had given him a cue to try another tack. "He sure has a peculiar set-up here. Doesn't that bother you?"

"You don't understand their circumstances."

"I would very much like to. Everyone hints at some

188

deep, dark secret which puts them beyond the social pale
. . ." He hesitated. "But you know of it."

"Certainly I do. But it is not my place to tell you.
Anyway, I believe it will soon be ended. The family's
ostracism, I mean. Mr MacLain intends to take us all
to St Petersburg this summer, and I believe we are to
be invited to a reception by the Tsar and Tsarina. Mr
MacLain went to St Petersburg himself, four years ago,
at the Tsar's invitation, to discuss the freeing of the serfs.
The Tsar liked Mr MacLain, and told him that, in a few
years time, he would be able to receive us socially. That
time has now come."

"And that is important to you."

"It is important to the family, Charles."

"I can see that the idea of coming to America with
me can hardly compare with the prospect of attending
the Tsar's reception," he observed, not sure whether he
intended the remark to be sarcastic or not.

In any event, Jennie did not take offence. "Why do you
not come with us? Surely, having come this far, you can
stay another few months."

"And do you think I would be invited to this reception
as well?"

"Of course. The invitation will be extended to the entire
family, and you will be one of the family. You are my
cousin."

It was an enormously attractive prospect. Not merely
to attend a tsar's reception, but the idea of spending the
entire summer here in this idyllic spot. Jennie squeezed
his hand again. "At least consider it," she suggested.

Charles had been resident on Bolugayen for just over a
week when the Prince invited him to ride with him. "May
I come too?" Alexandra asked.

"No, you may not," the Prince told her. She pouted,
but did not argue. The two men, followed at a respectful
distance by two grooms, walked their horses out of the

mansion yard and along the road to the town, before turning off on to one of the bridle paths which led through the cotton fields to the stretches of open pasture beyond.

The Prince gestured at the somewhat bare-looking fields. "Isn't it one of the wonders of nature that under all of that earth there is a whole generative process under way."

"What are your feelings when you look out at this, and consider that it is all yours?"

"Why, satisfaction, you might say, Cromb."

"And never a backwards glance?"

"One should only ever look forward." He touched his horse with his spurs, and broke into a canter. Charles followed, and they galloped for a couple of minutes, before the Prince drew rein in a cloud of steam. "Jennie tells me she has invited you to remain here until July, and then come to Moscow with us."

"She did. I hope she was not being presumptuous?"

"Jennie? She can never be presumptuous on Bolugayen. I would be delighted. So would the girls."

"And the Princess?"

"The Princess will raise no objections."

They walked their horses over the springy turf, the mansion and the town now in the valley behind them. "You mean you would take your wife to St Petersburg, to meet the Tsar? When you know she hates you? That is what Alix told me, anyway."

"Oh, Dagmar hates me, certainly. But it has long been her dream to be presented at court. Better late than never, eh?" He looked at the American. "Do you like Alix?"

"I think she is very charming."

"This is an odd family, Cromb. I imagine you have discovered something of it."

"Something."

"I suppose you could best describe the girls as predatory, when it comes to men. I suppose it is because of their peculiar background."

190

"Which I gather you hope to expiate this summer."

"Why, yes. But they are inclined to fix their gaze upon a man, and say to themselves, and each other, I want him . . . and have him."

"We have women like that even in Boston, Prince. But they are somewhat more subtle about their methods. However, Alix has shown no signs of grabbing me."

"Unlike Anna, you mean." Indicating that the Prince was more observant than he appeared; or did Anna have the habit of teasing him as well? It was, in any event, the first suggestion that the Prince *did* know what had happened in Poltava.

"I'm sorry. I have done nothing to encourage her. At least, since . . . I understood her situation."

"Nor should I, if I were you. I would not be happy about that." He paused to let the import of his words sink in. "However, if you were to ask me for Alexandra's hand, I would be very happy about that."

Charles drew rein. "Well, now, Prince, it seems to me that you have adopted a great many of the characteristics of this family. I'm not blaming you for that, as you're now the head of it. But as I'm a stranger, you are going to have to explain a few things to me."

The Prince had also halted. "Explain what?"

"Well, sir, I came to your estate looking for my cousin Jennie. I may say that I am both delighted and relieved to find her so well and so contented. That being so, I have abandoned my original idea of taking her back to the States with me, even if I still feel it would be the best thing for her. However, the point I am making is that neither you nor any of your sisters-in-law had any idea I was coming. In fact, as Jennie didn't know I existed until I appeared, there was no possibility of you knowing that either, right?"

"Right," agreed the Prince, with a faint grin.

"So I turn up at your town house, and am made to feel as welcome as a long lost brother by your . . . sister-in-law.

191

Okay, you tell me this is their way. She flirted with me, and maybe I took her too seriously at the time. But, having checked me before I went overboard – I guess she's told you all of this – she then suggests that I make a play for her sister. This on a two-day acquaintance, her sister not yet having met me. Now, sir, I have been here just on a week, and you are making the same suggestion. I know you have just told me that these young women size a man up and say, I'll have that one, and go out and get him, but the fact is that Alix has never shown the slightest interest in me, save as a stranger who can tell her about strange places. So . . . what gives?"

The Prince resumed walking his horse, and Charles again fell into place at his side.

"What gives, Cromb, is that I am the head of this family, and that therefore it is my business to secure the most advantageous marriage for my sister-in-law as much as for my children, when they reach an appropriate age. Alix is now past the stage when she should have been married. Circumstances have made it impossible for me thus far to find her a husband."

"But, according to Jennie, circumstances are about to change, Prince. Aren't you taking the whole shebang to St Petersburg this summer? To be presented at court, as you put it? You have to be able to find Alix a husband then."

"No doubt I could. But I would prefer not to."

"You mean because of the ancient scandal, whatever it was?"

"No. It has nothing to do with the scandal. I wish my sister-in-law to marry outside of Russia."

"I don't get it. You seriously want to send her off with someone she has only known a week . . ."

"My dear Cromb, at least she has known you a week and has revealed no distaste for you. Do you suppose she would even have *met* a suitable husband here in Russia? He would not use his belt on her ass every night?"

192

"I take your point. But still, you would at least know something of these gentlemen, of their background and financial situation. You would be certain that you would not be condemning your sister to a lifetime of poverty."

"You own a shipping line."

"I have told you this, Prince. You do not know that it is true."

"As you are Jennie's cousin, I suspect it is true. Besides, I would make a settlement on you that would relieve you, and Alix, of any financial worries for the rest of your life."

"So there just remains the question of why you are so desperate to have Alix out of Russia."

The Prince rode in silence for some minutes, then he said, "What I have to say to you, Cromb, is in the most utter confidence. It must not even be repeated to Alix. And on no account can it ever be revealed to Jennie." Colin frowned. "My father-in-law was, as you know, killed by an organisation known as the Will of the People. This group have apparently managed to infiltrate almost every aspect of Russian life. They certainly infiltrated Bolugayen."

"But I don't see how this affects the Countess Alexandra. You can't mean that she is a member of this Will of the People conspiracy?"

"I believe she is. Or certainly was. Call it a flirtation, if you like. A young girl, sensitive enough to be aware of the enormous injustices she could see about her, injustices inflicted by or in the name of her father, free to wander about Poltava as she chose, to listen to what she chose . . ."

"You ever asked her about it?"

"Not in so many words. But she has virtually confessed it to me. As has Jennie. The plot was not only to kill Bolugayevski, you know. It was to kill Dagmar, Anna and myself, at the same time, and leave Alexandra as Princess Bolugayevska."

193

"Holy shit! You say Jennie planned to kill you as well?"

"I think she now realises that would have been a sad mistake," the Prince said, quite seriously. "The point is, that we have Vorontsov in Poltava, and probably quite a few police chiefs in other provincial capitals, just waiting for Alix to make a mistake. At the present time they have no evidence that I could not refute. But times change, and people; and circumstances."

"Yes, but surely, now the serfs have been emancipated, these Will of the People no longer have any reason to assassinate anybody?"

"Unfortunately, they think they do. They regard the emancipation as a gigantic hoax."

"You want Alix out, with me playing the knight in shining armour? Trouble is, Prince, in America we have a quaint little custom. It's called being in love with your wife."

"Would you find it so difficult to be in love with Alix?"

"I think I might find it rather easy, in the course of time. But there are a few little hurdles to jump. The first is that I am not at the moment in love with her."

"I know. You are in love with Anna."

"There's no law against being in love with another man's mistress, Prince, so long as you don't try to do anything about it."

"Oh, quite. Alix is very like her sister."

"She can't be *very*, Prince, seeing that she's a member of this Will of the People organisation and Anna is not."

"I would have said that difference should make her more attractive to you. It proves that she is a liberal rather than an ultra-conservative. Anna is certainly an ultra-conservative."

"It also proves that she has a streak of anarchy in her. I'm not sure that would go down very well with the ladies of Boston who are likely to ask my wife to tea. But there's

194

a more important point than that. I am a wealthy man, but that's by American standards, not Russian. I don't live in a palace, and while I have help around the house, I don't have servants standing at my elbow every moment of the day and night . . ." – he glanced at the patient grooms, who had remained out of earshot throughout the ride – "just in case I stub my toe. And I have no intention of accepting charity from you or any other man."

"I am sure Alix would be able to adapt, Charles." The Prince reached across and clasped his gloved hand. "I should be really pleased were you to agree to consider my proposition."

Charles looked down the sweep of the dinner table, past the acres of jewel-bedecked neckline which competed in splendour with the acres of silver cutlery and crystal glassware. He looked across the table at Alix as she chatted with the Smyslovs.

"Have you made up your mind?" Anna asked.

His head jerked. "Do you and the Prince have no secrets from each other?"

"None at all. Oh, I know you would rather carry *me* off, Mr Cromb. But as that is impossible, you could do a lot worse than Alix."

"You'll understand that I find the whole thing rather sudden."

"You are the answer to a prayer. These things are always sudden. Colin was the answer to a prayer."

"Not everyone's prayer, surely, Countess."

She smiled. "In your case, there will be no dissenters. Save for Dagmar, to be sure. But she dissents from everything, and her opinion no longer matters."

"Do you, then, hate her?"

"I have no cause to hate anyone, Mr Cromb. May I call you brother?"

"If there is no possibility of your ever calling me anything better, I guess you may."

"That is splendid." She gave a quick nod of her head, and the message was clearly immediately relayed to the Prince, who stood up.

"Ladies and gentlemen," he said. "It is my great pleasure, this evening, to announce the betrothal of my sister-in-law Alexandra, to Mr Charles Cromb, of Boston, Massachusetts."

There was a roar of applause and hand-clapping. Charles looked across the table at Alexandra. Presumably she had been briefed, because although pink spots had gathered in her cheeks, she did not look otherwise disconcerted by the announcement.

"Speech!" Anna cried. "Speech!"

Slowly Charles rose to his feet. He thought it probable that he was more surprised than anyone at the table. But as he began to speak there was a tinkling crash; David Fine had dropped his glass.

Charles lay on his back and tried to remember the events of the evening, the vast quantities of vodka and wine and brandy he had consumed.

But now . . . there were things to be done. Letters to be written, certainly, to Bowen his chief clerk to inform him that his return would be delayed until the early autumn – Alexandra had no intention of missing the rehabilitation of her family or a meeting with the Tsar and Tsarina – and that when he did he would be bringing with him a Russian countess as his bride. That would set the tongues wagging.

But first, some fresh air. His valets were as usual waiting for him to make a move, and had him bathed and shaved and dressed in half an hour, which left him feeling distinctly better. He went downstairs, where the huge house was just beginning to stir. Then in the distance he heard the braying of the post horn.

The arrival of the post was always an exciting occasion on Bolugayen. Anna and Alix appeared in their dressing

196

gowns, hair loose, cheeks still flushed with sleep. The Prince, fully dressed, came running down the stairs. Igor Bondarevski had greeted the mailman and taken the satchel. He was now carefully arranging the various letters and parcels on one of the hall tables.

"That'll be the lace I ordered from Kiev," Anna said. "Oh, I do hope they've got it right this time."

The Prince was thumbing through the letters. "My word," he remarked. "There's one here for you, Charles."

Charles took the envelope, and recognised Bowen's handwriting. He slit the paper with his thumb, took out the several sheets of paper, unfolded them, and read with a slowly gathering frown.

"Not bad news, I hope," the Prince said.

Charles raised his head; his mind was spinning. "We are at war," he said, scarcely believing the word himself.

"You mean the United States? At war with whom?"

"At war with ourselves, Prince."

Chapter 10

THE MARRIAGE

The Prince looked bewildered. "A civil war, in America? But what can there be a civil war about, in such a country?"

"Slavery, Prince. Slavery. There were rumblings before I left, when Lincoln received the nomination. But now . . . the southern states have seceded, declared themselves independent, and fired upon a Union fort. The President has declared war, and called for seventy-five thousand volunteers. My clerk writes that he also seeks the support of all shipowners, certainly in the north."

"Does that mean you will have to return?"

"At once, sir."

"Now there is a catastrophe, to be sure."

Charles looked up the stairs to where the three women, for the sisters had been joined by Jennie, were gazing at him. "I do wish you to believe, Countess Alexandra," Charles said, "that this unfortunate turn of events will make no difference whatsoever to our plans, unless you so will it."

"But . . ." Alexandra's tongue came out and circled her lips. "I cannot go with you. Not now." The St Petersburg visit loomed far larger in her mind than her marriage.

"I quite understand this," Charles said. "I will have to ask you to wait for me. This war cannot last very long."

"Of course I will wait for you, Mr Cromb," Alexandra said.

Charles looked at Anna, but she was watching her lover.

"No," the Prince said. "There can be no delay."

"With respect, Prince, but I really do not feel I can take the Countess back with me at this minute," protested Charles. "The country appears to be in a turmoil, and I imagine I will be obliged to leave Boston almost the moment I get there. Sadly, I have no family in America. It would place the Countess in an intolerable position to be dumped in the middle of a strange country, which is at war, and with not a soul to turn to."

"I entirely agree," the Prince said. "Under no circumstances could I permit Alexandra to go with you at such a time. But equally, under no circumstances can I condemn her to some kind of open-ended engagement, which may last for years. You say this war will soon be over. Wars have a habit of lasting longer than anyone expects them to. I merely wish the marriage to be celebrated before Charles departs, that is all."

"Oh!" Alexandra looked decidedly taken aback.

"With respect, Prince," said Charles. "I must leave immediately. Today, if possible."

"I think tomorrow, Charles," the Prince said. "One day is not going to make all that much difference when you are in any event contemplating a journey of several weeks."

"But, the banns . . ."

"In my authority as Lord of Bolugayen, I command that the banns be dispensed with," the Prince declared. "The marriage will take place this morning." He turned to an equally thunderstruck Igor. "You will send a messenger into town to inform Father Alexei that his services are required, immediately, and you will invite the members of the *tzemstvo* and their wives to the wedding of the Countess Alexandra to Mr Charles Cromb. Tell them that they are also invited to the wedding luncheon, which you will instruct Boris to prepare. You will extend the same invitation to the Smyslovs. Off with you, now."

Igor hurried away.

"But Colin," Alexandra protested, "I have no gown."

"Of course you have a gown," Anna told her. "You will wear Mama's wedding gown, as did Dagmar."

"I am not as big as Dagmar," Alexandra wailed.

"Then we will cut it down for you. Come along, Jennie. Oh, and Yevrentko," – for the tutor had also appeared on the ground floor – "tell Madame Rospowa that we need her immediately."

She grasped Alexandra's arm and bustled her off, Jennie following, while Yevrentko hurried to the servants quarters to find the seamstress.

The Prince took Charles's arm. "You had better come with me and have a brandy; you look as though you could do with it."

"Yes," Charles agreed.

"Charles, I realise this is a very sudden turn of events, but we must know how to react to such things. Am I not right in supposing that the moment my sister-in-law becomes the wife of an American citizen she herself becomes an American citizen?"

"Yes, I believe she does. By God, Prince . . ."

The Prince smiled. "As such, she would immediately be placed above the usual punishments for breaking Russian laws, certainly in such matters as sedition, while obviously, as an American, she could never be charged with treason. The worst that could be done to her would be deportation to the country of which she is a national." He held up his hand. "Believe me, Charles, I intend to do everything in my power to keep her out of mischief until you are in a position to carry her off. But it is better to be safe than sorry."

"You like to play with a lot of wild cards."

"I enjoy gambling. But I like to keep an ace in the hole, as they say. Now I suggest you go and prepare yourself for your wedding. While I go and inform my wife."

Charles had hoped to have at least a moment alone with

Alexandra before the ceremony, just to communicate with her on this suddenly changed level, to attempt to discover what she thought about it all. He knew only three things about his wife, and two of those things were not necessarily to her advantage: she was both a Bolugayevska and was, or had been, an anarchist capable of plotting the death of her own father – or perhaps those were merely two sides of the same coin. In her favour was the single fact that she had expressed a wish to visit the United States.

But there had been no prospect of a *tête-a-tête*; perhaps Anna and the Prince, who were the instigators of this entire business, were afraid of what might arise from such a meeting. It was of course disturbing to be undergoing what was in effect a shotgun marriage, when he had never even kissed the girl.

But there she was, standing beside him, her hand in his, her face just visible beneath the gauze veil which hung from her white satin headdress – a family heirloom older than her dress – looking up at him with her enormous blue eyes, while Father Alexei intoned the service. What he was actually saying Charles had no idea, for it was all in Russian, and he had to rely on Jennie's nods to reply when appropriate; his cousin was acting as matron of honour, and stood beside his bride. But now he was being gestured at to place the ring – another family heirloom – on Alexandra's finger, and he gathered that they were man and wife.

The drinking began immediately. Charles had made a resolution to remain sober, but it was difficult, as glass after glass of champagne was handed to him. It seemed that everyone in the room had to kiss the bride, and then hurl his or her glass into the fireplace. But then, all the women had to kiss the groom, while the men shook his hand, each congratulation accompanied by another drink and a shattering of glass.

*   *   *

201

The wedding feast dissolved into wine and drunken laughter. Charles realised that his glass was again full, and that the room was slowly rotating about his head. He blinked, and belched, and tried to stand up – and had to down again; thank God he was apparently not required to make a speech. But he certainly needed to empty his bladder.

He pushed himself up again, grinned owlishly at the many faces around him, staggered towards the door, and continued on his way to the Prince's study and the downstairs privy that lay beyond. He pushed the doors open and stumbled in, releasing his breeches as he did so. He reflected that there was no feeling comparable, for a man, at least, of relieving himself when the necessity had been present for too long. He gave a great sigh of satisfaction, pulled the chain, and heard a movement behind him. He turned, saw that the study doors had been closed, and that Anna was turning the key in the lock.

Hastily he completed the fastening of his breeches, while she smiled at him. "You *are* a modest fellow."

He had drunk sufficient to leave him entirely at ease, even with her barbs. "And are you not forbidden fruit?"

Her smile widened as she came towards him. "Is that not the sweetest tasting of all?"

"Countess, this is my wedding night approaching me."

"Which is why I am here. I am exercising my *droit de seigneur*."

"You?"

"Well . . ." She had now come right up to him. "I do not think Dagmar would care to. Or in fact, that you might care to with her; she might well slip a knife into your ribs between thrusts." She put her arms round his neck and stood on tiptoe to kiss him on the mouth.

"Countess," he said, when she took her mouth away, "I am too drunk to play games. You are taking a grave risk."

"Who said anything about playing games?" she asked. "You are not too drunk to perform, I hope?" She moved

202

away from him, and sat on the desk, raising her legs to rest her slippers on the arms of the Prince's chair; her skirts slid back over her knees to her thighs, and Charles realised she was not wearing drawers. There could be no turning back now: this was what he had wanted from the first moment he had laid eyes on this woman. But he could still not believe that she wanted it too. Besides . . . "And when the Prince comes in?"

"The Prince will not come in," she said. She allowed her knees to drop apart. "I should hate to suppose I had misjudged you, brother."

He moved forward, kicked the chair to one side, and was in her arms. Now she wrapped her legs round his thighs to bring him against her. His hands slid round her shoulders and he fumbled at the small buttons at the back of her bodice, feeling more than one rip away in his anxiety, but then, as her hands slid inside his drawers, his own could come back to the front and hold those magnificent breasts. "God," he muttered as he caressed her. "I fell in love with you the moment I saw you."

"You mean you fell in love with these. And this." She hugged him close again, and now it was flesh to flesh.

"And what part of me did you fall in love with?" he whispered into her ear as he drove himself into her.

She did not reply until he was spent, but that was only a matter of seconds. Then she still clung to him. "Women do not love as men," she said, her head tilting back, her eyes a gleam of pleasure. "Which is not to say that I did not long to have you inside me. Or would not wish it again."

"That will not be practical for a little while."

"You mean never." She gave a delicious gurgle of laughter. "I must leave some of you for my baby sister. And then, you are departing tomorrow, are you not?"

He was reluctant to leave her embrace, found her breasts again, and bent his head to suck her nipples. "Must it be never?" he mumbled against her flesh.

203

"Only if you would have it so."

He raised his head, kissed her mouth. "You mean the decision is mine? Well, then . . ."

"I mean, you will have to come back to me, when you have fought and won your war."

"And you will be here, waiting for me?"

"How possessive you are," she said. "I will certainly be here. As to whether I shall be waiting for you, that will depend upon the circumstances."

He stepped away from her. "Will you tell the Prince of this?"

"I do not know."

He raised his head in surprise, having expected a negative answer. She smiled. "Are you afraid of him?"

"In an equal land, no. Here on Bolugayen, he would have the advantage."

"Then I shall not tell him until after you have left." She eased herself off the desk, went into the privy where there was a basin and ewer, and returned with a wet cloth to wash him. "I would not have my baby sister become suspicious of you. Or me."

She dried him, and Charles dressed himself, his mind in a spin at having shared so much intimacy with such a beautiful woman. And with fear for her, too. "Are *you* not afraid of the Prince? Of what he might do to you?"

"No," she said. "I would enjoy whatever he might do to me."

He caught her arm. "Do you love him?"

Her eyes became opaque. "He is my man."

"But insufficient."

She kissed him. "You are too arrogant. But then, so is Colin."

"I love you," he said. "I adore you. Say the word, and I would carry you off, regardless of the danger."

"I will not say the word, Charles. I do not wish you to be hurt."

204

"At least say that you have some feeling for me." He was behaving like a schoolboy, he knew.

She kissed him. "I have invited you to return, and not only to collect Alix. Now we must rejoin the party; it will soon be time for you meet the people. And then it will be time for you to perform again, with Alix. You leave first. I will come when the coast is clear."

Time to perform again – with his wife. Charles did not know if he would be able to. Not only physically, but his New England personality was now riddled with guilt: married not two hours, and he had committed adultery! But it was not yet time, for as Anna had warned him, he and his bride had first to meet the people. They had completed their meal, and now flooded up the hill, hundreds of them, with their children and their dogs. The Prince beckoned Charles and Alexandra, and he and Dagmar walked the couple out on to the downstairs porch, where they were greeted by an enormous upsurge of congratulatory cheers. Then there was singing and dancing, in which the bride and groom were required to join. Charles had no knowledge of either the words or the steps, but he found himself cavorting about the front drive, his arms wrapped round two buxom matrons, performing various movements with his feet and singing as lustily as any of them, while Alexandra faced him, supported by two of the men, face flushed and legs kicking, veil vanished and carefully dressed golden hair coming down in streaks on to her shoulders.

At least, he reflected, he was being very rapidly sobered up, and so presumably was Alexandra, unlike the rest of the wedding party, which had now gone from champagne to vodka. And the marriage needed to be consummated. The Prince signalled Igor, and the butler blew a blast on his bugle. The music and dancing stopped, and the steaming tenants bowed to their betters. Still laughing and panting, Alexandra took Charles's hand and led him up the steps.

*   *   *

Charles was relieved, and indeed, delighted, to discover that his session with Anna had not inhibited him in any way, especially when presented with a carbon copy of her, physically, and a young woman who replaced inexperience with total enthusiasm. When he was spent she lay on him, legs still twined round his, hair collapsed in a mess on his face, while she kissed him again and again. "I think I have waited all of my life for this," she said. "Oh, Charles, you're not going to be away for very long, are you?"

"I hope not. But it will be at least a few months."

"And I will have to wait that time," she said sadly. "Will you fuck lots of women when we are separated?"

"Right now that is an impossible concept," he said. "Will you fuck lots of men?"

She pouted. "I do not think Anna and Colin would let me."

He raised his eyebrows. "You mean you would like to?"

"Well . . . it is such a delightful sensation. Dagmar always told me it would hurt like blazes. But it didn't hurt at all. Not really."

"Don't you have any morals at all?"

She kissed him. "Of course I have morals."

"But they don't apply to sex."

"Well, of course not. Sex is too enjoyable to have morals about. It would be like attempting to apply morals to drinking."

"Some people do, you know. Especially in Boston."

"Then I shan't like it. When are you going to fuck me again?"

"Soon. Listen to me. I wish you to behave yourself when I am away. I am not talking about sex. But there *are* things that are more important. Life and death, to mention only two."

She frowned at him, then rolled off him and lay on her back. "Colin has been telling tales about me."

206

He rose on his elbow to look at her. "He has told me nothing that I should not know, as your husband. Now, I would like you to swear to me, as my wife, that you will never have anything more to do with the Will of the People."

He had expected a pout in reply, but instead her face took on a quite unexpected expression: for a moment she looked almost like Anna. "You do not understand," she said.

"I think I understand more than you suppose. I can understand both that there was a reason for their existence, up till this March, and that you were attracted to their ideals. But you must understand, Alix," he went on, "that all that is now history. There is no longer any reason for the Will of the People to exist. All that they were fighting for has been achieved."

"Because the serfs have been freed? Do you call being up to your ears in debt for the rest of your life being freed? The serfs are worse off now than when they *were* serfs."

He squeezed her fingers. "I must still ask you to have nothing to do with these people, Alix. You may be right, and very little has changed, for the serfs. But at least it is a step in the right direction. There is light at the end of the tunnel. To attempt to hasten things by revolution or murder is not only criminal, it will be counter-productive. You must see that. That is what is happening in my country now, and has been happening for some years. But now we are going to end it. A great many lives and a good deal of property are going to be destroyed. All because people are not prepared to work patiently for what they are trying to achieve."

Alexandra lay down again.

"So will you promise me that you will never again have anything to do with these people?"

She smiled, and rolled on to his chest again. "We are supposed to fuck on our wedding night. Not talk politics."

207

Chapter 11

THE TSAR

"You must write and keep us informed of what is happening," the Prince said. "What you are doing, and how your war is going."

"I shall do that." Charles squeezed his new brother-in-law's hands. "I owe you a great deal. I shall not forget it."

"The feeling is mutual. I look forward to your return."

Charles faced Dagmar, who had herself come down to bid him farewell. "It has been a great pleasure, Your Highness. I look forward to our next meeting."

"If there is to be one," she said coldly.

Jennie held him close. "I wish I could have come with you," she said.

"I am sure you still can."

She shook her head. "This is my home. But just to know you are there, and caring . . . your visit has made me very happy. Do take care." Her eyes were filled with tears.

He could think of nothing to say to Anna, merely bent to kiss her knuckles, but as he held her hand to do so, was rewarded with a quick squeeze. "Do obey the Prince," she said, "and write as often as you can."

Then Alexandra was in his arms, hugging him with all her strength. But she was not weeping. Charles had an idea weeping was not part of this family's regular behaviour. "Do hurry back," she begged.

"I shall count every minute." He hugged her one

last time, then ran down the steps to where Igor was holding his horse. Smyslov was going to accompany him to Poltava, and see him safely on to the coach to Sevastopol. The two men and the four servants walked their horses out of the grounds, pausing at the top to look back down at the valley and the mansion and the people who remained on the porch, waving kerchiefs. Then they were gone.

"And good riddance," Dagmar remarked.

"Oh, Dagmar!" Alexandra said.

"Do you think he will come back?" Anna asked.

"Of course he will not come back," Dagmar said. "He came here, was treated like royalty, took Alexandra to bed . . . what has he got to come back for?" She looked at Jennie as she spoke, and Jennie flushed, then turned and went into the house.

"That was quite uncalled for," Colin said. "He will come back, and he will make Alix a good husband. It only remains to be seen if Alix will make him a good wife."

Alexandra stuck out her tongue at him. "And," she said, "you can't cane me. Only my husband has the right to do that, now."

"I can see it's going to be a long war," Colin remarked. "Well, I must go down to the mill; I gather there is something the matter with the machinery."

"I will come with you," Anna said.

Dagmar snorted and returned to her apartment.

"Well?" Anna asked, as they walked their horses down the drive. "Are you pleased?"

"I am certainly relieved."

"And you do believe Cromb will come back for Alix?"

"I do believe that, if he is not killed."

Anna gave a little shiver.

"That would distress you?"

"Yes," she said. "It would distress me very much."

Colin looked straight ahead, giving a nod to the people they passed on the road, all of whom bowed before their

209

master. they mounted their horses. "How many times did you have him?"

"Just the once. How did you know?"

"I know the look in your eye, my darling. I wonder I do not cane *you*."

She gave one of her delicious gurgles of laughter. "Because you know I would enjoy it too much. Anyway, have I no rights? Did I not give you all of this?"

"Yes, you did. And I will never forget it."

Another laugh. "I will never let you forget it, my darling. Does the thought of Cromb inside me make you want me more, or less?"

He glanced at her. "More."

"Well, then, have me. Now." He looked left and right, and she laughed a third time. "We can go into the wood." She turned her horse off the road and cantered towards the trees.

Colin followed. "We have something like a hundred beds at the mansion, and you wish to lie on the grass?"

"Why not? It's romantic. Exciting. Different." She ducked her head beneath swaying branches, and looked over her shoulder to make sure they were alone. Not that there was anyone on Bolugayen who would dare interrupt the Prince and his lady, particularly as no one could doubt what they were doing.

"Oh, isn't it exciting?" Alexandra craned her neck as she dashed from window to window of the railway carriage. She had been desperately excited for weeks, since their journey had begun. But it had grown to a crescendo when they reached Moscow, and boarded the train.

None of the sisters, much less the two children – Olga and Catherine had been left at home – had ever been to Moscow before, much less the capital, St Petersburg. "Oh!" Alexandra cried. "Isn't it beautiful?"

Colin had sent ahead, and their carriage was waiting for them, to take them to their residence in the city.

The Bolugayevski Palace had been opened and the servants were lined up to greet them. But these were complete strangers, as the house itself was strange, and, because of nearly twenty years of neglect, oddly old-fashioned. "All of these drapes will have to go, for a start," Dagmar declared. "And those carpets. You!" she pointed at the butler. "What is your name?"

"Oleg, Your Highness."

"You heard me. Have these dreadful things out, and new ones in, by this evening."

Oleg gulped, and looked at Colin. "Do as the Princess commands," Colin said.

Dagmar was already climbing the grand staircase to the first floor gallery, looking into the reception rooms. "Everything," she said. "Who are you?"

The middle-aged woman curtseyed. "I am Madame Anastasia, Your Highness. The housekeeper."

"I wish these rooms stripped. Where are the bedrooms?"

"Up here, Your Highness." The woman was trembling as she led Dagmar up another flight of stairs. The others merely watched her go, then looked at Colin.

"I think we'll let Dagmar sort out the housekeeping," he said. "Would you like to go for a walk?"

"Oh, yes," they agreed without hesitation.

The ball was the following week. The three sisters had spent every day shopping and the house was filled with the rustle of taffeta and the cries of comment. Colin had by now sorted out the sleeping arrangements in the completely refurbished house. He occupied the master bedroom, with Dagmar's room on his right, and Anna's on his left. Alexandra and Jennie had their rooms further along the hall, and the two boys and their nannies shared another, next door to Yevrentko. If Madame Anastasia found it odd that the Prince and Princess did not choose to share a room, she knew better

211

than to make any comment; Colin had no doubt that the arrival of the Prince accompanied by four quite beautiful women, even if two of them were his sisters-in-law, was in any event a fruitful source of gossip below stairs and from thence out into the markets and shops of the city.

Now he waited in the front hall, as they came down the stairs. Dagmar, as befitted her rank and title, led, wearing pale blue, and with a diamond tiara crowning her yellow-brown chignon. Anna was next, wearing pale green, with her hair loose, as befitted an unmarried young woman, although it was kept under control by another tiara, somewhat less resplendent than her sister's. Alexandra was third, in pale pink; her hair was upswept, and she too wore a tiara. All the sisters' gowns displayed plunging *décolletages*, and they wore matching white elbow length gloves. Jennie came last. She had had to be persuaded by Anna and Colin to come at all; it had not ever been her hope to one day meet royalty. She wore dark blue, with her auburn hair loose, held by a plain band rather than any jewellery, and her neckline was modestly high. But she was still the most attractive of the quartet.

"You look lovely, Mama," Peter said.

"And so do you, Mama," Georgei said loyally.

"You all look lovely," Colin told them. "Now boys, off to bed."

The two boys solemnly shook hands with him, kissed the hands of their mothers and aunts, and trooped up the stairs to where Yevrentko and the nannies were waiting. Colin escorted the ladies to the carriages. He had chosen to use two to avoid any crushing of the gowns; he and Dagmar rode in the first one, and the three younger women in the second. "Are you not nervous?" Dagmar asked, as they moved away.

"Not really."

"I suppose you met royalty often when you lived in England."

"As a matter of fact, I never met Her Majesty. But we do not have quite the reverence for our royal family that you have for yours. Don't worry: I shall treat the Tsar with due deference; you must remember that we have met before. But *you* are nervous."

"I have waited all of my life for this moment. Thirty-three years. And now it is too late."

"Nothing is ever too late."

"Indeed? When my life has been ruined, and I am virtually a prisoner in my own home?"

"That is surely your choice, my dear."

"My marriage is a sham. Is that my choice as well? Five years, and you have not been to my bed!"

"I had supposed you might scratch out my eyes, were I to do so."

"What you mean is, you are afraid Anna might scratch out your eyes. To be ruled by such a whore!"

"That is hardly the way to speak of your sister. And I would argue that she is scarcely more of a whore than yourself, Dagmar. But I would hate us to quarrel, tonight."

"We shall not quarrel, tonight. I shall be the most perfect wife to you, tonight."

"Prince Bolugayevski," the Tsar said. "It is so long since last we met. And in the interim I have heard a great deal about you." He was a big man, almost as big as Colin himself; forty-two years old, he wore the fashionable side-whiskers with a clean-shaven chin, to give his already bold features an accession of strength. He was dressed in a white tunic over red breeches, with a crimson ribbon across his chest. "Not least," the Tsar added, in English, "that you are a well-situated man." He switched back to Russian. "The Tsarina."

Colin bowed over the Empress's hand. She had begun

life as Princess Marie of Hesse-Darmstadt, and was thus a German by origin. Once she had been reputed to be a beauty, but he now beheld a somewhat overweight woman with florid features. She apparently liked *his* looks, however, for she gave him a bright smile. "I have heard of you too, Prince Bolugayevski," she said archly. "And that you are a naughty fellow."

Colin wondered just what she *had* heard of him. "May I present my wife, the Princess Bolugayevska?" he said.

Dagmar was standing in front of her sisters and Jennie. Her cheeks were pink, and she was breathing deeply. This was, as she had said in the coach, an occasion that should have happened some seventeen years ago. Now she gave a deep curtsey before the Tsar, who held her hands to raise her up. "My dear Princess," he said. "It has been too long."

Dagmar seemed unable to speak as she was presented in turn to the Tsarina. By then Alexander was lost in the superior beauty of Anna. "The Countess Anna Bolugayevska, Your Majesty," Colin explained.

"You mean you are not married, mademoiselle?" the Tsar asked.

"I am not so blessed, Your Majesty," Anna replied.

"Well," the Tsar remarked. "Well, well, well."

"Mrs Charles Cromb, Your Majesty," Colin said. Alexander gazed at Alexandra, as if unable to believe his eyes that there was yet a third of these magnificent women. "Mrs Cromb is also my sister-in-law, Your Majesty," Colin explained. "But she is married to an American shipowner."

"Ah," the Tsar said. "Does he come from the South, or the North of that country?"

"He comes from Boston, Your Majesty. And is there now, I believe, using his ships for the advantage of the northern states."

"Capital," Alexander said. "Capital. You are to be

congratulated, my dear." Alexandra gave another curtsey, and passed on to greet the Empress.

"And Miss Jennie Cromb, Your Majesty."

This time the Tsar's eyes positively gleamed as he stared at Jennie. "Another sister-in-law, no doubt, Prince?"

"Actually, a cousin by marriage, Your Majesty."

"By God, sir, but I should like to join you for breakfast one day, indeed I would. Well, Prince, your ladies will certainly brighten St Petersburg for a season. I bid you welcome."

Colin bowed.

It was now possible to take in their surroundings. Their arrival, in the midst of innumerable other carriages, a *melée* of snorting horses, shouting drivers, bellowing majordomos, high-pitched exclamations, had been chaotic. Their entry, up huge double staircases lined with glittering cuirassiers, had been awe-inspiring, but they had been proceeding as part of a long procession of people. If the Bolugayevska women, with their looks and their jewels, and their very strangeness as no one present had ever seen them before, had attracted a good deal of attention, *they* had been interested only in the coming presentation, for which they again had had to wait in line for some time, while their fingers had grown increasingly clammy inside their gloves, and Colin had watched beads of perspiration glistening on those swan-like necks.

But now the ordeal was over, and they could look around them at the hundreds of other guests, who were looking at *them* as they were escorted to an alcove by one of the flunkeys. Here there was a settee and two straight chairs. Colin sat in the centre of the settee, with Dagmar on his right and Anna on his left. Jennie sat in one of the chairs and Alexandra in the other.

The orchestra, which had been playing muted music in

215

the background, now increased its volume, and a ripple of sound went through the chamber. "Do you remember when last we waltzed, Colin?" Dagmar asked. "My God, how long ago it seems. How long ago it *was*."

"I will waltz with you now, Dagmar," he promised. "As soon as it is permitted." For they had to wait on the Tsar. But now Alexander rose, and offered his arm to the Tsarina. She gathered her train in her other hand, and descended the steps at his side. They moved together into the first steps, and then whirled their way the entire length of the chamber. As they reached the end, all the other dancers took the floor, a kaleidoscope of brilliant uniforms and bare shoulders, of jewellery and medal ribbons, of gleaming smiles and flashing eyes.

Colin escorted Dagmar on to the floor, and they danced together, while he kept his eyes on the other three. But they were the three most beautiful women in the room, and within a few minutes they too were dancing. He thought the evening could be pronounced a success.

Colin danced the second number with Anna. "Do you realise this is the first time you and I have ever danced together?" he asked.

"I did not even know you danced at all."

"It is part of the training of every British army officer," he said. "Now, tell me, who was that handsome young guards officer who had you in his arms just now?"

"I really cannot remember. But he asked if he could call, so we shall find out then."

"You mean you gave him permission?"

She smiled at him. "Of course. I am young, unattached, lonely. I need to be admired and courted."

"But you said . . ."

"It is my ogre of a brother-in-law who must see these fellows off. *N'est-ce pas?*"

216

"When you are this devilish, I long to kiss you."

"Patience," she laughed. "Oh, patience." He wondered what all these young bloods, and old bloods too, who were watching them so enviously, would say, or do, if they knew that when the ball was over this gorgeous creature would come to his bed?

The music ceased, and he escorted her back to their alcove, surprised to find that they had been joined by another woman, who was sitting next to Dagmar and talking most animatedly. The conversation ceased as Colin and Anna approached, but the woman looked up and gave them both a gracious smile. She was handsome rather than pretty, with a voluptuous figure and a wealth of dark hair. "Colin, my dear," Dagmar said. "This is the Countess Dolgoruka, one of Her Majesty's ladies."

"Countess." Colin bent over her hand. "Dolgoruka? Is that not a Polish name?"

"I am Polish, Your Highness," the Countess said. "But I have discovered that I have the same name as one of your charming sisters-in-law."

Colin looked at Anna. "No, no," Alexandra said. "The Countess has the same name as me."

"Isn't that quaint?" Alexandra Dolgoruka remarked. "Your bevy of beauties is causing quite a stir, Your Highness. I was saying to the Princess that I should very much like to entertain her to tea, if that is permissible?"

"Well, certainly it is," Colin agreed.

"How nice. I shall send a formal invitation. I am sure we shall have lots to talk about." She stood up. "It has been a great pleasure meeting you, Your Highness. Ladies." She swept away.

Colin sat beside Dagmar. "She looks a formidable young woman."

"She is. I believe she was the Tsar's mistress, once."

"And is still employed by the Empress? You see, my dear, we are not the only family with an irregular domestic life."

217

The music had struck up again, but no one took the floor. Colin looked up to discover the problem, and saw that the Tsar had left his dais, and was walking across the room towards them. Every head turned to follow his progress, fans stopped fluttering, whispers ceased. Colin hastily stood up as he realised that Alexander was indeed coming to him. The sisters and Jennie stood also. "Prince Bolugayevski," Alexander said. "May I impose upon you by asking one of your so lovely ladies to dance with me."

"We are honoured, Your Majesty."

Dagmar swelled with importance. Alexander made her a short bow, then turned to Jennie. "Mademoiselle Cromb, would you do me the honour?"

"I have never been so insulted in my life," Dagmar declared, as they drove home in the small hours. "For His Majesty to dance with that . . . that . . ."

"Cousin?" Colin suggested. He had had a lot to drink, was very tired, and was absolutely delighted at Jennie's triumph.

"I was going to say, serving girl," Dagmar remarked.

"But you didn't really use those words, did you?" Colin asked. "I just nodded off for a moment."

"Ha! As I was saying, for His Majesty to dance with her once was bad enough. But three times . . . it was an insult to Russian womanhood."

"He was certainly smitten. Probably because she is so different to Russian women. I mean, Anna and Alexandra are as fair as can be, and yet their skin does not have the translucent quality of Jennie's."

"I wonder what Vorontsov and his people saw when they were forcing broken glass up her asshole," Dagmar said.

"Dagmar," Colin said, "if you ever say anything like that again, I am going to beat you so black and blue you will not be able to show yourself in public for a month."

"Ha!" she commented. "You mean, when I take tea with the Countess Dolgoruka, you do not wish me to tell her of Jennie's background? Surely the Tsar has a right to know that the woman with whom he has made a public spectacle of himself with was once arrested by his own police?"

"If he is to know, I will tell him," Colin said. "I would remember that, if I were you."

Dagmar subsided into silence, but she was clearly simmering. He was relieved when they regained the Bolugayevski Palace and he was able to escape her and join the younger women, who were in a state of high excitement. At least, Anna and Alexandra were. Jennie merely looked petrified. "Something to tell your grandchildren," Colin smiled.

"If she ever has any," Alexandra commented.

"Oh, she will," Anna declared. "By the Tsar."

"Are you crazy?" Jennie demanded.

"He wishes to make you his mistress. Well, everyone could see that."

"That is absurd," Jennie declared, cheeks pink.

"It is well known," Anna said firmly, "that when the Tsar dances three times with any woman, he wishes to make her his mistress. And if she happens to have his child, why, her fortune is made. The Tsar already has an out child, by Olga Kalinovskaya. She is Polish too, you know, just like the Dolgoruka. He has a weakness for non-Russian women."

Jennie looked at Colin. "What am I to do?"

He gave her a hug. "Don't panic, for a start. It hasn't happened yet."

"You cannot possibly refuse the Tsar," Anna said. "No one can."

"I am going to be no man's mistress," Jennie insisted. And flushed. "Certainly not his."

The invitation arrived the following morning. It came in

the form of a uniformed messenger who carried a key, and a note. Jennie showed it to Colin; her hands were trembling. *Should you oblige me by using this key, my messenger will show you the lock. At four o'clock this afternoon. Please oblige me, and I shall be ever thine.* The note was not signed. "Well, that last promise is a lie for a start," Jennie said, "if he has a regular harem."

"Maybe he is faithful to them all, in his fashion," Colin commented.

"You mean you wish me to go."

"I do not wish you to do anything you do not wish to. However, this may be a great opportunity for you."

She gazed at him for several seconds, an expression he had never seen before on her face. "At least," he said, "you have until four o'clock this afternoon to make up your mind."

"Do you think she will go?" Anna lay in Colin's arms, as they liked to do after lunch.

"I really have no idea. I have told her that the decision must be entirely hers."

She rose on her elbow. "What will happen if she goes?"

"She will become the Tsar's mistress, and, by projection, we will become the Tsar's favourite people, at least for a while."

"How the wheel does turn," Anna commented. "And what will happen if she does not go?"

"Then I think we will all pack our bags and return to Bolugayen."

"And you left that decision to *her*?"

"After all she has gone through, do you seriously expect me to command her to have sex with anyone, much less someone she has only met once, and is the representative of the government at whose hands she suffered so much?"

"Who is also the Tsar," Anna said reverently, lying down again. "Shall I go and speak with her?"

"Under no circumstances," Colin said.

Alexandra lay across the foot of Jennie's bed, watching her perfume herself following her bath. "So you are going," Alexandra remarked.

"I haven't made up my mind," Jennie said, hunting through her wardrobe.

"But . . . all these preparations . . ."

"There is nothing wrong in preparing," Jennie said.

Alexandra sat up and hugged her knees. "I wish he'd asked me. I'd have gone like a shot."

"You'd have been committing adultery." Jennie put on her shift and then fitted herself into her corset. "Give me a hand with these straps."

"Oh, pooh." Alexandra stood behind her to pull the corset as tight as possible. "Everyone commits adultery. Colin and Anna commit adultery every day of their lives. Anyway, you can't really commit adultery, with a tsar. I'd tell Charles, of course. Do you think he'd mind?"

"I really don't know." Jennie surveyed her wardrobe. They seemed to have done nothing but shop and employ seamstresses since arriving in St Petersburg, in a determined effort to catch up with current fashion; they had even bought themselves crinolines, garments they had never worn on Bolugayen. Now she dropped hers over her shoulders, and adjusted the straps.

"He's your cousin," Alexandra pointed out

"And I know him no better than you do. In fact, I do not know him as well as you, because I am not married to him. But I would say he would object."

"Oh, pooh." Alexandra commented again. "He couldn't object, if it was the Tsar."

"Americans don't have tsars," Jennie reminded her.

"You *are* going," Alexandra deduced.

Jennie surveyed her racks of new clothes. Yes, she

221

thought, I am going. Because the Tsar has commanded it, and not to go would be to fail Colin. Oh, Colin, she thought. She did not blame him for anything; she owed him her life. That he had never touched more than her hand, never intruded upon her privacy, never treated her as anything less than a dearly-loved sister, had been bewildering at first. She had lain awake in her bed, awaiting the turning of the door handle. Then she had reckoned that he was still so in love with Anna that he had no time for anyone else. But gradually it had dawned on her that Colin, being the ultimate gentleman, would never approach her, not because of what she had experienced, but because to him she was still a scullery maid.

The odd thing was that she felt, had there been no one else, he might have married her. But while his peculiar code of honour permitted him to have a countess as a mistress, it would never do to treat a scullery maid in the same way. And, she had reflected sadly, even had he married her, it would have been out of pity.

Thus she had accepted a loveless life, save for little Georgei – and he had too much of his father in him. But that did not mean she could not love. With every year, every month, every day she had lived in the shadow of the Prince, she had fallen more deeply in love with him. Without his being the least aware of it. But then, she had hardly been aware of it herself until the so strange appearance of her cousin, with his wish to carry her back to America with him. She did not doubt for an instant that Charles could give her as much protection and indeed, luxury, in America as Colin could in Russia, and she knew she would have abandoned Georgei without a backwards glance, sure that he was going to grow up to be a Russian aristocrat. But she could not make herself abandon Colin. It was then that she had realised that she loved him, without reservation, and that were he ever to crook his little finger she would crawl into his bed without hesitation, regardless of what memories might thus by aroused. But he had never done that. Instead he was sending her to the bed of another. And she would go, although this might perhaps arouse even more ghastly memories, because it was what he wanted.

From her wardrobe she selected a green silk dress and a grey paletot trimmed with claret-coloured velvet bands and buttons with an attached shoulder cape; the ensemble had a grey velvet bonnet, trimmed with claret and grey-coloured plumes. Her ribbons were grey and her gloves, her undersleeves white. Her gloves were grey. Alexandra clapped her hands in delight. "You look superb! You *are* going, then."

"Yes," Jennie said. "I am going."

A closed landau drew up at the Bolugayevski Palace on the stroke of four.

She got into the carriage and the door was closed on her.

The key was in her reticule, clutched in her hand. But she could not help but wonder if she was being kidnapped, if some fresh awful fate awaited her. Then she thought of the Tsar's handsome features; he had not looked like a satyr.

They entered a wood. She had to trust her driver, and even more, her driver's master. But soon enough they came to a small lodge, set quite alone and surrounded by trees. The coach stopped, and the driver jumped down to open the door and assist her out.

"The key is for the front door, mademoiselle," he said, and got back on to his seat.

Jennie watched the landau rumble out of sight, and looked left and right. She was alone. If anyone had lured her here to do her a mischief he, or she, would never have a better opportunity. She had a sudden urgent desire to be inside the house, whatever she might find there. She ran up the few steps, extracted the key from her reticule and thrust it into the hole. It turned easily, and she was inside, closing the

223

door behind her. Then she put the key back in her purse and looked around her.

The room was small, but exquisitely furnished, and although there was no sign of anyone else in the house, it was obvious that there had been someone here recently; there was not a speck of dust to be seen, and in the grate, although it was a warm summer afternoon, there was a roaring fire. In the far corner there was an easel, on which was pinned a large sheet of paper. In the tray there were a collection of crayons of every colour.

A single staircase led up to the first floor. Jennie went up, and looked into the one bedroom. Here too everything was spotlessly clean, and the drapes had been drawn and the covers turned back on the large tester bed. She stood at the window and looked out at the park, and saw a single horseman approaching. Her breathing quickened in time to the pounding of her heart. But she could not be found waiting in the bedroom.

She hurried down the stairs, and sat on the settee. A moment later she heard boots on the floor of the porch. Then a key turned and the door opened. The Tsar wore civilian clothes and looked extremely ordinary, although he remained a handsome man. Now he took off his silk hat and his cape, and placed them on a chair by the door, while gazing at her. Jennie hastily stood up. "You have done me a great honour, mademoiselle," Alexander said. "Will you not take off your coat?"

"Perhaps I should keep it on, Your Majesty," Jennie said.

He raised his eyebrows. "Are you cold, mademoiselle?"

"No, Your Majesty. It is simply that I do not know for how long I shall be staying."

"Do you not know why I invited you here?"

"Yes, Your Majesty. But I fear that you may have been acting under a misapprehension."

"In what way?"

"May I ask what you saw in me, Your Majesty?"

224

Alexander sat down, intrigued. "I saw an entrancingly lovely woman, who also struck me as being an unusually intelligent one. I like the combination. Are you going to claim that you are not lovely? In which case I recommend that you look in the mirror. Or that you are not intelligent? I think that is a decision you should leave to me."

"Does my past not interest you, sire?"

His frown returned. "Are you then a criminal?"

Jennie drew a deep breath. "I have been arrested by the police, sire."

"On what charge?"

"Sedition, and conspiracy to murder."

"Indeed? Those are very serious crimes. Capital crimes. Yet you stand before me."

"I was released, by order of Prince Bolugayevski."

"Who thus must have assumed you innocent. I am perfectly happy to trust his judgement."

"Thank you, sire. What I am trying to say is, that I was a prisoner of the police in Poltava for six weeks. I was interrogated by them."

Alexander gazed at her for several seconds. "I understand," he said at last. "It is a bloody business. Are you then in some way mutilated?"

"No, sire. But . . ."

"Have you then come here to tell me that the very thought of a man repels you?"

"I do not know, sire."

"Oh, come now. Are you not Bolugayevski's mistress?"

"I am no man's mistress, sire."

Now the stare was one of surprise.

"He is well-suited, already, sire," Jennie said, carefully.

"By God, but I would say you could be right," Alexander agreed. He got up, stood in front of her, held her chin in his hand, and kissed her mouth. "I am sorry for what happened. The police have been given so many powers by my predecessors that it will take me a long time to change them, if it is ever possible to do so.

There *is* much sedition in Russia, still. I had hoped that once the serfs were freed . . . but then, it is early days yet." He smiled, and kissed her again. "I did not bring you here to talk politics, mademoiselle."

Jennie could not believe her ears. "You mean you wish me to stay, sire?"

He kissed her a third time. "I would like to sketch you." He walked to the easel and from beside it picked up a thick rug. This he unrolled on the floor in the middle of the room. "You do not find it cold in here?"

Jennie shook her head. "It is very warm, sire."

"Good. I find it so. Well, then, would you lie on the rug? Use a cushion for your head, but lie half on your side, facing me." Slowly Jennie took off her hat, and placed it in a chair. "Oh, let your hair down," the Tsar commanded. "Your hair is your crowning glory." Jennie pulled out the pins and the auburn locks tumbled past her shoulders. "Capital."

She picked up a cushion from the settee and laid it on the rug, then knelt beside it. It was a very long time since she had lain on the floor, and she had no idea what to do with her crinoline. "Shall I help you?" he asked, and held her hands to raise her to her feet, before going round behind her to start untying bows and unfastening buttons.

"But . . . you said you wish to paint me," she protested.

"Well, not paint. I am no good at painting. I will draw you," Her gown was loose and he eased it forward from her shoulders.

"You mean you wish to draw me in the nude?" Jennie asked, stupidly.

"Of course. How else may one draw, or paint, a beautiful woman, but in the nude. Attractive clothes may make a plain woman look more attractive, but they can only detract from true beauty." Jennie's gown collapsed in a heap round her ankles. Already he was

226

scooping her petticoats from her thighs to lift over her head. In her wildest dreams she had never envisaged herself being undressed by a tsar. "Do you know," he said chattily, as he untied the crinoline in turn. "I think this the ugliest of garments. But I suppose one must follow fashion."

He unbuckled her corset, still standing behind her, then made her sit in a chair, while he knelt before her to unlace her boots. This is absurd, she thought. He is the autocrat of all the Russias, and he is kneeling before me like a servant. The boots removed, the Tsar slid his hands up her stockings, past her knees, to her thighs, to find her garters, sliding beneath the hem of her drawers. Jennie gave a little sigh and closed her eyes. "You do not find me repulsive?" Alexander asked.

Jennie opened her eyes again. "No, sire. You have a most pleasant touch."

He smiled at her. "I am glad of that." His hands slid higher yet, to find the silk of her pubes. "Do you know, I think the sketch will have to come later."

Chapter 12

THE ARRANGEMENT

Alexandra was breathless as she burst into Colin's study. "Jennie's home!" Colin looked at his fob watch. It was a quarter to ten. The family had already dined, desperate to converse between themselves about what Jennie might be doing, but prevented from speculating by Colin's expression. Thus after the meal he had retired to this seclusion, to wait, and let the sisters get on with their clatter.

What did he feel? He really had no idea. Envy, certainly. His memory kept casting back nine years to that unforgettable day on the bank of the bog. He supposed he had fallen in love with her then, and been shocked at himself for doing so. Lord Blaistone's nephew did not fall in love with a scullery maid. But his love had grown, with every passing year, except that with every passing year it had become more and more confused with responsibility. To be able to rescue Jennie from Vorontsov and his thugs had made him feel at once heroic and ashamed. To watch her slowly returning to health and strength and beauty had been the greatest experience of his life. But how could one express love, to a woman who had suffered so much, who owed him so much, who could only submit to him out of gratitude. And now, the Tsar. Presumably, to be desired by the most omnipotent man in Europe, had to be the greatest of compliments. One which she would have rejected out of hand. Then she had understood that it was what her master wanted, and she had accepted her fate.

Had he again pushed her into servitude? Or had he found the ultimate answer to her dreams? "Good," he said. "You could ask her to stop in and wish me goodnight."

"Oh . . ." Alexandra flounced to the door. "Don't you have any feelings at all?"

"I can't afford any," Colin retorted.

Jennie came in a few minutes later, after a brief knock. Colin stood up. "Can you forgive me?"

"What is there to forgive." She took off her hat and gloves. "I am sorry I am late."

He peered at her. There was a certain dishevelment about her clothes, and even more about her hair, and there were pink spots in her cheeks. But she did not look distressed in any way. "Have you eaten?"

"Yes." She sat down.

"Would you like a glass of brandy?"

"Yes, thank you. I would."

He poured two, gave her one, and sat down himself, in front of his desk, and beside her. Jennie drank, deeply. "I am to have a house of my own, servants, a carriage, and an allowance." She raised her head to look at him. "If I choose."

"Then you pleased him."

"Apparently. So he wishes me to become his whore."

"I do not think the mistress of an emperor can ever merely be called a whore," Colin ventured, still uncertain of her mood.

"I told him of Vorontsov, and the police," Jennie said. "And he did not seem to care. Rather it increased his interest in me."

"I can imagine it would."

"He sketched me, naked, lying on the floor."

"He is an artist?"

"He can draw."

They gazed at each other. "Are you going to accept?" Colin asked.

229

"Would you like me to?"

"The decision has to be entirely yours. What of Georgei?"

"I have not mentioned him. I . . . if I am to be the Tsar's mistress, I would not wish him to live with me. He is your adopted son. I am content with that." She gave him another long look. "You are to go away."

"Eh?"

Almost she smiled. "I think the Tsar thinks that I am your mistress."

"I see. So I am to be banished."

"It is hardly a banishment. You are to go to Warsaw, as vice to the Governor-General of Poland."

"What?" He was utterly astonished. "Me? He does realise that I am English, and that I am only twenty-eight years old?"

"He admires both the English and youth. He certainly admires you, even if he is also jealous of you. He feels you are the man for the job. There is a great deal of unrest in Poland, apparently. He means to send for you himself, tomorrow, and explain it to you."

"I see." Colin stroked his chin. No man could refuse a command, or even a request, of the Tsar.

And no woman? "If you wish, I would come with you," Jennie said.

"No," he said. "I do not think I could take you, my dear, without causing scandal. But . . . unless he definitely repels you, I would accept the Tsar's offer. I do not like the thought of you being on Bolugayen, with me absent."

"Is not Anna my friend?" Jennie asked.

"Anna is a law unto herself, Jennie. And Dagmar . . ."

"Dagmar hates me. Well, I hate her."

"Thus it is best for me to be there. Go to the Tsar. Make him happy, and become wealthy and powerful in your own right. That is what you deserve, and that is what you need."

230

"A scullery maid," she murmured, "mistress to an emperor."

"There have been successful scullery maids before," he reminded her.

"And when I am cast aside? I do not believe the Tsar has ever kept a mistress for more than a year, apart from Olga Kalinovskaya. And she retains his interest only because she is the mother of his son."

"By the time he casts you aside you will be rich, because he also never lets a mistress go without making sure of her future. While if you also were to become a mother . . ."

"And . . . a future living alone in a house in this city?"

"A future doing whatever you choose. There will always be a home for you on Bolugayen. Once I return."

"You are too generous to me," she said, and went to the door. "There are arrangements to be made. I will keep you informed. Oh, by the way, Mr MacLain, I have not yet told the sisters."

"I shall tell no one, until you give me permission to do so," Colin agreed.

"Thank you." She closed the door behind herself, leaving him stroking his chin.

The Tsar was in the company of several of his leading advisers, most of whom were soldiers. "The fact of the matter is, Prince Bolugayevski," Alexander explained, "that it seems that I have been too easy on the Poles since my father died. It seems they are forming secret societies, and openly inviting France and Austria to aid them in gaining their independence. Can you believe it?"

"I am assured by Count Hetzendorf that Austria will have nothing to do with aiding any revolution, Your Majesty," said Count Abramov. "They remember 1848 too well. A successful revolution in Poland could well overspill into Habsburg lands."

"Hetzendorf can make whatever promises he wishes," Grabowski snorted. "The fact is that these 'patriots', as

231

they call themselves, cross the border into Austrian Poland as and when they choose. They use the Carpathians as bases, return when they are ready, and seem able to obtain all the arms and ammunition they wish."

"I am sure the Emperor Franz Josef will do all he can to help," Alexander said. "I have written, outlining the situation, and anticipate a reply very shortly. I am less sanguine about that madman in Paris. He has been on a wave of euphoria since he beat the Austrians."

"He's no fighter," Grabowksi said. "The Austrians virtually beat themselves by their incompetence. Is it not true that Napoleon was sick to his stomach when he saw the dead and wounded after Solferino?"

"Napoleon will hardly ever be required to see the dead and dying after a battle in Poland, supposing there ever is one," Tarnowski remarked. "So that will not stop him backing the insurgents with money and arms. And rhetoric."

"With respect, Your Majesty," Colin interjected. "Have we reached the stage of insurgency?"

"Not as yet," the Tsar said. "But there are all the signs. Secret societies, like this dreadful Will of the People here in Russia. But the Poles are more deceitful than the Russians. They hide their intentions behind committees, like the Committee for the Improvement of Agriculture, which the Okhrana inform me is nothing more than a cover for meetings planning armed revolt. This simply must be prevented."

"Take every tenth man and hang him," Grabowski said. "That would soon bring them to heel."

"I am sure it would," the Tsar said. "But it would do our international reputation no good at all, apart from being a crushing weight on my conscience."

Grabowski's expression indicated that he cared little for Russia's international reputation and even less for the Tsar's conscience.

"What I propose to do," the Tsar went on, "is to take

232

firm steps to forestall this tide of revolution, without descending to the methods of a tyrant."

Colin watched the various ministers exchange glances. They obviously did not accept that such an approach was practical, or likely to be successful. "In the first place," the Tsar announced, "I am sending my brother, the Grand Duke Constantine, to Warsaw as Governor-General. He is on his way here now from his country estate. He will have the fullest authority to act in my name, and to take whatever measures may be necessary for the restoration of order. However, I have already determined as to the measures to be taken. Thus I am sending, as the Grand Duke's deputy, the Prince Bolugayevski."

Heads turned, and Colin flushed. "This is for a variety of reasons, gentlemen," the Tsar said. "It is not enough for us to stamp on the Poles. We wish them, we need them, as participants in our empire, not as a running sore. Thus it is necessary to face facts. All of my military commanders learned their business and rose to their commands under my late father. They are all . . ." he glanced at Grabowski, "talented soldiers and able men. But they are Russian, and they are regarded by the Poles as men of the *ancien régime*, men to be feared, not loved, and men, sadly, not to be trusted. That is, of course, the Polish point of view. My aim is to send them men who will clearly be of my own liberal disposition. The Grand Duke is certainly that. Prince Bolugayevski has the merit not only of being well known to be perhaps the most liberal and popular landowner in Russia, but he is also English, that is to say he is by definition of a liberal tradition." He paused, to look around the sceptical faces surrounding him. "Your task will not be an easy one, Prince," Alexander said. "I am advised by Count Wielopolski, who is our man on the spot – he is a Pole but utterly loyal to our government – that it may be necessary to syphon off some of the more radical elements by reintroducing at least a limited form of conscription. I leave this in your hands. But it must be

233

done in a humane, fair, and acceptable manner. Do you understand me?"

"I do, Your Majesty."

"Then will you accept this post?"

"I am honoured, Your Majesty. May I ask for how long is the appointment."

"Until the business is completed, Prince."

Colin swallowed. "I understand, Your Majesty."

"Good. Well, gentlemen, I thank you. Prince Bolugayevski, I wish you to remain." Colin bowed, and the ministers filed from the room. None of them was the least happy with his appointment, Colin knew. "The Tsarina would like a word with you, Prince," Alexander said. "I think you should know that it was on Her Majesty's recommendation that I gave you this posting. Thus I hope you are pleased."

"Very pleased, Your Majesty," Colin lied, while his brain did handsprings. The Tsarina? A woman he had only met once in his life and with whom he had not exchanged half a dozen words? But a woman who also knew that he was Jennie Cromb's master, if not her lover. He needed to think, to consider the implications of this fact, but there was no time, for Alexander was already escorting him from the council chamber into a small reception room, where the Empress was waiting. With her was a very large young man, the Tsarevich Alexander, at seventeen already taller and broader than his father. "Your Majesty!" Colin kissed the Tsarina's hand. "Your Highness!" He bowed to the Tsarevich.

"You will be pleased to know that Prince Bolugayevski has accepted the position, my dear," Alexander said.

"Oh, I am delighted," Marie said. "I know you will make a success of it, Prince. It is so brave of you."

"Brave, Your Majesty?"

"Well, all those assassinations . . . ." She flushed as she looked at her husband.

234

The Tsar cleared his throat. "There have been some attempted assassinations of our people," he agreed. "One or two have succeeded. But I am sure Prince Bolugayevski is not concerned with attempted assassinations. He is a soldier."

"Then I will congratulate you upon your success, Prince," Marie said.

"Should you not wait *on* the success of his mission, Mama?" the Tsarevich demanded.

"It is certain to succeed," his mother asserted.

"The Poles will never be brought to heel by soft words," the boy said. "No rebels ever are."

"Presumably you agree with Grabowski," his father snapped. "That every tenth man should be hanged."

"By no means, Papa. But I certainly believe that every man, or woman found with arms in his or her possession, or with seditious literature, should be hanged."

The Tsar understood that the family difference might be embarrassing to an outsider. "I am sure you have a great deal to do, Prince," he said. "I would like you to depart for Warsaw as soon as possible."

Colin kissed the Tsarina's hand again, bowed to the Tsarevich again, and was escorted from the room by the Tsar. "He is a hothead," Alexander remarked. "I suppose most boys are. Were you a hothead at his age, Bolugayevski?"

"Why, I suppose I was, Your Majesty."

"And shed it with experience. Alex will undoubtedly do the same." The door had been closed behind them by one of the waiting flunkeys. Now the Tsar held Colin's arm and led him into one of the window alcoves. "There is another matter I wish to discuss."

"Yes, Your Majesty. Mademoiselle Cromb asked me to tell you that she awaits your pleasure."

Alexander's face lit up. "Oh, capital. Capital. I will tell you, Prince, that I have never been so enchanted." His face grew serious. "May I ask what is your exact relationship with the young lady? I know you extracted her from the hands of the police, somewhat illegally, I have been informed. Do not mistake me, I am glad that you did bend a few rules in her favour. But since then . . ."

"Mademoiselle Cromb is my ward, Your Majesty. We have never shared a bed."

Alexander gazed at him for several seconds, then smiled. "Your candour is refreshing, Prince." He held out his hand. "I will wish you every fortune in Poland, and after. And I wish you to know that your, ah, ward, will be taken care of in every possible way. In any event, she will be much safer here in Petersburg than she could ever be in Warsaw. Indeed, Prince, I would strongly recommend that you do not take your wife or any of her sisters wth you. It is, after all, hopefully only for a few months."

Colin squeezed the proffered fingers. "Thank you, Your Majesty. I will take your advice. May I ask *you* a question?"

"Of course."

"Does Her Majesty know of this projected liaison?"

"Of course she does not. Oh, certainly she will find out soon enough; it is impossible to keep a secret in St Petersburg. But if you are worried about Jennie's safety, I do assure you that Her Majesty has never interfered in my, shall we say, private life. I give you my word that Jennie will come to no harm."

Colin bowed.

He walked slowly towards the staircase, and was arrested by a hand on his arm. He turned in surprise, neither having heard the woman approach nor been alerted as to her presence by any changes of expression in the guardsmen who stood sentry along the hall. "Countess!" he bowed.

"You are going to Warsaw?" Alexandra Dolgoruka said. "How I envy you. It is my home."

"Are you not allowed to return there?"

236

"I am required to remain at Her Majesty's side," Alexandra said. "However . . . I should be much obliged if you would call on my family. Here is my card, with the address."

"I shall be honoured to do so, Countess."

Alexandra gave a roguish smile. "I have a sister, Catherine, who I am sure would interest you. She is much prettier than I, and she is only sixteen."

"Do you think I need to be interested, Countess?"

"All men need to be interested, Your Highness, from time to time. Although, I suppose, someone in your happy position needs such an interest less than most. May I ask, will you be taking all your, ah, family, to Warsaw?"

"I have not yet considered the position, Countess." Was she fishing, or was she truly unaware that Jennie at least would certainly be remaining. "I have been advised by the Tsar that it would be unwise to do so. Now, may I ask you a question in return?"

She smiled. "One to which I hope I will be able to give a more positive reply. Ask away, Prince Bolugayevski."

"His Majesty has told me that I was recommended for this posting by the Tsarina. Have you any idea why she should have selected me?"

"Why, Prince . . ." Alexandra Dolgoruka squeezed his arm. "Did you not know? Your wife especially requested the favour of Her Majesty."

Colin dismounted in the courtyard of the Bolugayevski Palace and went into the hall. Oleg bowed as he took his hat and coat. "Are the ladies in?" Colin asked.

"Indeed, Your Highness."

"Will you inform them all that I would like to speak with them. I wish them to attend me in the study. Now. I also wish Monsieur Yevrentko to be present."

Oleg bowed again, and Colin went up the stairs. He knew he had to keep very calm, and very cool. He also needed to make some very important decisions. He sat behind his desk, and a few minutes later Yevrentko knocked and came in. "You sent for me, Your Highness?"

"Yes. Will you sit down, over there?" Colin pointed to the smaller, secretary's desk in the corner, and Yevrentko took his seat. "Now," Colin said, "I wish you to copy down everything that is said. Do you understand?"

"Yes, Your Highness." The schoolmaster prepared himself a pen and an inkwell, and a block of paper.

A moment later Dagmar came in, followed by her sisters and Jennie. "Really, Colin," Dagmar said. "We are not servants, you know, to be peremptorily summoned from whatever we are doing."

"This is important," Colin said. "Sit down. All of you."

They seated themselves in front of him, casting curious glances at Yevrentko. "I have to inform you that I have just been appointed vice-Governor-General of Poland," Colin said. There was a moment of stunned silence. Jennie's expression did not change. Alexandra seemed to be absorbing the news, and then clapped her hands. Anna looked both thunderstruck and delighted. Dagmar also looked delighted, and clapped her hands, but she had acted a shade quickly. "But of course you already knew this, Dagmar," Colin said.

"Well . . ." she flushed. "I did mention you to Her Majesty."

"I've always wanted to visit Warsaw," Anna said.

"Unfortunately," Colin said, "because Poland is virtually in a state of insurrection, I can take none of you with me."

"What?" Anna and Alexandra cried together.

"Except of course, my wife."

"Me?" Dagmar cried. "I have no intention of going to Warsaw. And you cannot make me."

"Of course I cannot," Colin agreed. "Because you have already discussed that matter also with the Tsarina, and

238

I am sure you made it clear to her that you did not wish to go."

"Well," Dagmar said sulkily, "according to Alexandra Dolgoruka, Warsaw is a very dangerous place. There have been several assassinations there recently. I do not wish to be assassinated."

"And you recommended that Colin be sent there?" Anna bristled.

"Well . . . somebody has to go and sort out the Poles."

"I do not think that Dagmar actually hopes that I will be assassinated," Colin said. "Although I may be wrong. What she desires is that I shall be absent from Bolugayen for an appreciable period. A period in which she hopes to resume her rule over the estate."

"Why . . .!" Dagmar began.

"And everyone on it," Colin added. Dagmar snorted, and glanced at Jennie, who flushed. "I am therefore making the following arrangements," Colin said. "Firstly, Jennie will be remaining here in St Petersburg, under the protection of a most august person." He glanced from face to face to make sure they all understood his meaning.

"Oooh, Jennie!" Alexandra squealed. "I am so happy for you." Dagmar's face had frozen.

"Secondly," Colin went on, "I have every intention of completing the Warsaw business within six months. That is to say, I shall be back in Bolugayen next March. And thirdly, I have decided that in my absence, the management and conduct of Bolugayen Estate will be entirely and solely in the hands of the Countess Anna Bolugayevska. This includes the management and upbringing of my three children, Count Peter, Georgei, and Catherine. In the event of my death, the Countess Anna will continue to exercise these prerogatives until Prince Peter is of age."

Silence fell again, disturbed only by the scratching of Yevrentko's pen. Colin gazed at Anna, who gave a little smile. Then Dagmar leapt to her feet.

"You cannot do this!" she shouted. "I am your wife. I am the Princess Bolugayevska!"

"And I am the Prince Bolugayevski, with the sole right to determine who shall manage my estate."

"You bastard!" Dagmar shouted. "You pig! You . . ."

"Are you ready, Yevrentko?" Colin asked. Yevrentko's hands were trembling as he laid the paper on the desk. "Now," Colin said. "We shall all sign this paper, testifying that we do so of our own free will, and that you all freely agree to my dispositions."

"I will see you damned," Dagmar declared.

"Anna?" Colin invited. Anna bent over the desk and signed.

"Alexandra?" Alexandra glanced at her eldest sister, then signed.

"Jennie." Jennie's face remained impassive as she signed.

"Yevrentko. Leave a space above your signature." Yevrentko obeyed; his hand was still trembling.

"And you, Dagmar. Above Yevrentko."

"Sign that? Never."

"Very well. Yevrentko, will you sit down and take some more dictation. This is the testimony of Prince Colin Bolugayevski concerning the true facts of the conception and birth of the first son of the Princess Dagmar Bolugayevska."

"You cannot do that!" Dagmar screamed.

"I am about to do so," Colin pointed out. "Anna will lend her testimony to mine."

"You . . . bastards! All of you." Dagmar panted. "Very well. Give me that paper."

"If you attempt to destroy it, Dagmar, I am going to hit you, very hard, in the face," Colin said.

Dagmar snorted, bent over the desk on which Yevrentko had laid the paper, and scrawled her name. "Thank you," Colin said. "Now, Yevrentko, I would like you to make two exact copies of that paper. When you have done that, we shall all again sign each copy. I will take one of the papers with me, the Countess Anna will take one with her, and the third will be registered and lodged with the Imperial archivist, here in St Petersburg. I trust that will satisfy everyone." Dagmar snorted again.

"You are an absolute devil," Anna said, as she shared his bed that night. "Do you know, when I first saw you, I thought you had very little backbone. That opinion altered of course when you took possession of Bolugayen, and of me. But even so I do not believe I truly understood the strength of your character until today."

He kissed her nose. "I assume you are paying me a compliment."

"Of course. Colin, I have changed my mind: I *would* like to have your son."

"Just like that?"

"If I cease taking precautions, it will certainly happen."

"There is the small problem that I am leaving for Warsaw the day after tomorrow."

"I know. I would come with you, whatever the risks, had you not given me the task of holding Bolugayen."

"Can you not do it?"

"Oh, I can do it. I shall do it. It is just that I would rather be with you. However, we have those two days . . . I should very much like you to return to Bolugayen next spring and find me heavy with child."

He took her in his arms, and then frowned. "You do realise that our son can never replace Peter as heir?"

"Of course I understand that, my darling." She nestled against him. "My son will be Peter's sure right arm. I only wish my final fulfillment as a woman."

He was seen off by the entire household, as he rode out of the yard towards the railway station. "Do you know, this is the first time we have been separated, in seven years?" Alexandra asked.

"You speak as if you were his wife," Dagmar said disparagingly, and went back into the house. "Well, Anna, what are your commands?"

"That we return to Bolugayen immediately," Anna said. "I have already given the servants instructions to pack this place up."

"But . . . the season is not yet over," Alexandra protested. "Colin said nothing about going back to Bolugayen so soon."

"I am making the arrangements now," Anna said. "And I would remind you that you are a married woman. Jennie, I don't know what your plans are . . ."

"I understand that my new house is awaiting me," Jennie said. "I shall leave this afternoon."

"I am going for a walk," Alexandra declared, and called for her bonnet and parasol.

"Well, then," Anna said. "You and I had better pack, Dagmar."

"I am staying here," Dagmar announced. Anna turned to frown at her. "At least for a while," Dagmar said.

"And if I forbid it?"

"You cannot forbid it. That infamous piece of paper you possess gives you absolute powers on Bolugayen. It gives you no powers over me, personally. And certainly not while we are in St Petersburg. In any event," Dagmar said, "I have been requested to remain, by Her Majesty. Not even Colin could make me leave in those circumstances. The Tsarina wishes to see more of me. She has taken a great liking to me."

"Very well," Anna said. With Dagmar in St Petersburg, life on Bolugayen would be that much more simple. As she had warned Colin, she did not doubt that her sister hated as much as ever, but there was nothing she could do against that formidable piece of paper. "You do understand, Dagmar, that if you should even attempt to harm Jennie, Colin would very likely break your neck?"

"I am not interested in the affairs of a harlot," Dagmar informed her.

"You also understand that I intend to take both Peter and Georgei back with me. They at least are covered by Colin's instructions both on and off of Bolugayen."

"I am sure you will carry out my husband's instructions to the letter," Dagmar said, and went upstairs.

Alexandra walked along the Nevski Prospect, looking at the water and the islands. Never had she felt so out of sorts, so trapped. In a few weeks time she would be twenty-one years old, and she was a married woman . . . and she was more trapped than ever. All her life she had waited, to be able to leave Bolugayen. Her dream had been St Petersburg. And at last that dream had come true, just as her dream of sexual fulfillment and sexual liberation had come true. She had been the happiest of women. She had no great desire to go to America, which was from everything she had heard a most backward country. She recognised that it would eventually be necessary to do so, supposing Charles ever came back to her. But Charles was a fading memory, already. And in the meantime, there was St Petersburg, acres of handsome young men in magnificent uniforms, like those who had danced with her at the Imperial ball . . . and she was being whisked back to Bolugayen, after not even a month in this heaven.

She knew there was no use in begging Anna to let her stay. Anna was glorying in her power, power that ultimately resided in the amount of support she could command. At the moment, both Colin and Anna considered that she was firmly in their camp. Well, she was. She didn't really like either of her sisters, but she adored Colin, as everyone knew, even if they were all wrong in their reasoning. She loved him for what he stood for, for what he had achieved for Bolugayen and its people. She felt that men like Colin MacLain were the true hope for Russia. But that was something she could not even confide in Colin.

So Anna would never leave her in St Petersburg under the care of Dagmar, just in case she was suborned. It was home for her, and a period of utterly boring waiting, until either Charles or Colin came home . . . "Your Excellency, what a happy surprise."

Alexandra turned, frowning, at the tall, lank young man in the black suit, who was raising his hat and bowing. "Good heavens!" she remarked. "David Fine."

"May I say that you are looking more beautiful than ever, Countess?"

"Why, that is very kind of you, David."

"I could not believe my eyes, when I saw you."

"But you knew we were coming to St Petersburg?"

"I did. And I wanted to call at the palace, but . . ." he flushed.

"You were scared," she chided.

"Well, I didn't want to intrude. But to see you on the street, all by yourself . . ."

"Makes a change, doesn't it? Well, it's been very nice meeting you, David, but I must get on."

"Oh! I . . ." He bit his lip. "I was going to ask you to dine with me."

Alexandra raised her eyebrows. "You, were going to ask me, to have a meal with you?"

"I suppose you think I'm being presumptuous, Your Excellency."

Alexandra opened her mouth to say, yes, and then remembered, firstly, that she couldn't do that any more, and secondly, that this boy was madly in love with her. And thirdly, that she was going back to Bolugayen tomorrow. "I don't think that is at all presumptuous, David," she said. "I think that is very sweet of you. When would you like to take me out?"

"It is all right?" he asked anxiously. "You being married, and . . . everything?"

244

"My husband will not object," Alexandra said.

"Then . . ."

"It will have to be tonight," Alexandra told him. "I am leaving St Petersburg tomorrow."

"Oh!" His face fell.

"I feel the same," she agreed. "Where shall I meet you?"

"Ah . . . should I not call for you?"

"No," she said. "I will meet you here. At seven o'clock."

"Post!" Anna announced. "One for you, Alix. From Charles."

"Well?" Anna was far more excited than she was.

"Oh, it's not going well. The war I mean. There has been a battle at some placed called . . . Bull Run?" She looked at the date at the top of the page. "Good lord! This was written back at the end of July."

"And it got here in two months? That's very good," Anna said. "What about the battle?"

"Well, Charles says they are expecting the rebels to attack Washington at any moment. That's the capital. Oh, dear."

"That's terrible," Anna said.

"He thinks the war may well last a long time," Alexandra muttered, turning over the sheet. "It could be a year or more."

"Shit!" Anna remarked. "Ah, well. At least we know he's all right."

"Ha!" Alexandra commented. "A husband with whom I have spent one night and who is now going to be gone for more than a year? What kind of marriage is that?"

"It is the marriage Colin wanted," Anna said severely.

"Ha!" Alexandra commented again. "Well, I am going out."

"In the evening? By yourself? You have an assignation?"

"As a matter of fact, I have," Alexandra said.

"Who with?"

"I don't have to tell you that."

"You do," Anna pointed out. "Or I shan't let you go."

"Oh . . ." Alexandra stamped her foot, and then smiled. "It is with David Fine. We met, today, on the Prospect, and he invited me to dine with him."

"David Fine? That mouse?"

"He has changed," Alexandra said. "I think a few months in St Petersburg has done him good. I think it may be rather amusing."

"You had better take some money. I shouldn't think he has any."

"As I said, I think it may be rather amusing."

Anna regarded her sister for several seconds. "Very well," she said. "I don't suppose it will do any good to tell you to behave yourself. So I shall tell you, at least, to remember who you are, and who he is."

Alexandra stuck out her tongue at her.

She was pleasantly excited. David Fine had indeed filled out in the few months he had been in the city; there was an alertness, a confidence about him he had entirely lacked on Bolugayen. But he remained very aware of his position as regards her. And, as Anna had suggested, he must still be very poor. She wondered where he would take her? He was waiting for her on the Prospect, looking out at the water. "Countess!" He seized her hands. "I did not think you would come."

"Then why are you here? And for tonight, David, I think it would be best for you to address me as Mrs Cromb. That is my name, you know."

"Mrs Cromb," he said. "Yes. I had forgotten."

She raised her eyebrows. "Equally, I should not go to any very popular restaurant, where I might be recognised."

246

"I thought you might like to come to a little place my friends and I patronise."

"That would be ideal," she agreed. They delved into the side streets of St Petersburg. Alexandra enjoyed a rising sense of excitement.

"It is down here," he explained.

They went down a smaller alleyway. Now they were in the midst of crowds of people, some of whom jostled her, others who greeted David, and then gave her curious looks. But then she was being shown into a low-ceilinged, smoke-filled room where there were people and tables, with cheap cloth covers, and candles, and bottles.

"The food is very good," David assured her. "The wine, well, it is not up to Bolugayen standard. But the vodka is the same." Alexandra found herself sitting at a table and surrounded by eager young men and women sitting beside her, staring at her, and prattling away in a variety of accents. She was introduced as Mrs Cromb, as she had instructed, but that led to even more questions and explanations, as it was not a Russian name, while the evident quality of her clothes, the spotless health of her hands and complexion, indicated that she certainly did not belong in the society of impoverished students.

But she found it all exciting, a side of life she had never experienced before. The evening passed very quickly, and when she first looked at her lapel watch it was nearly ten. By then she was full of vodka and cheap wine as well as food, but she supposed she should be getting home. "We leave tomorrow," she murmured to David, sitting beside her. "Will you take me home, now?"

He stood up, and she followed him, to be immediately seized and hugged and kissed by the people around her. Never had she been treated with such easy familiarity – and never had she enjoyed it so much. But then she and David had reached the steps leading up to the street. They were at the door when it was suddenly thrown open, and they found themselves facing a man in uniform.

247

Chapter 13

THE PLOT

Alexandra gave a little gasp of alarm. David reacted more quickly, spinning round and shouting, "Police!"

There was pandemonium behind them as the lanterns were hastily doused. In front of them there came the blast of several whistles, and Alexandra realised there was a great number of police, all trying to get in the door. She looked for David, but he had jumped over the bannisters into the well of the restaurant. Before she could make up her mind to do the same, her arms were grasped. "Got one of the bitches," a policeman growled.

"Let me go, you bastard," Alexandra shouted. His response was to hit her in the stomach. Nothing like that had ever happened to her before, and she found herself kneeling on the step, gasping for breath and vomiting at the same time. Then her arms were seized and dragged behind her back, and she felt the touch of steel followed by a click. "You can't handcuff me!" she shouted. "I am the Countess Alexandra Bolugayevska!"

"They all say that," the policeman laughed, grasping her shoulders to drag her up, and push her out into the evening air, to a horse-drawn closed wagon. The back doors of it were opened and she was seized round the thighs and thrown into the interior. Desperately she rolled over. She gazed at two of the policemen, who were grinning at her in the gloom. "She's a looker," one said.

"Yeah," agreed his companion. "She could be carrying

a concealed weapon." He glanced over his shoulder, at the racket coming up the stairs from the restaurant. "The captain won't be back for a while."

They climbed into the wagon, and Alexandra tried to use her heels to push herself away from them, but they merely caught her ankles and pulled her back, causing her skirts to ride up. "You can have the bottom half," the first policeman said, and knelt beside her shoulder to tear open the bodice of the gown.

"You bastards!" she screamed. "I'll have you hanged."

"Listen," he said. "Shut up, or I'll hit you again."

Alexandra, opening her mouth to scream, closed it again as he tore open her petticoats and found her breasts. Then she whimpered as the other man threw up her skirts and delved through her drawers, driving his fingers into her vagina and anus. "Oh, God," she whispered. "Oh, God!"

She wondered why she did not faint, with outrage and fury, that she, Alexandra Bolugayevska, could be so mistreated. But now they let her go, for voices, screams and shouts were coming closer. Then more people were thrown into the wagon; Alexandra pushed herself as far up the floor as she could to avoid them, but even so bodies thumped into hers, bruising her and winding her. Then the doors were slammed shut, and the wagon began to move, jolting over the cobbles.

A few minutes later the wagon clattered into a court-yard, and the doors were opened to allow the prisoners to be dragged out. Alexandra was last. "Please," she said, as her feet hit the cobbles. "Please take me to your captain. I must speak with him."

"He'll be speaking with you, soon enough, darling," the policeman grinned.

Alexandra was pushed into the doorway, together with the other seven prisoners. Now there were lights and they could look at each other; she recognised them as people

249

who had been drinking with David and herself earlier that evening.

They were pushed along the corridor and into a room. From one wall a huge portrait of the Tsar looked down on them. "Sit down," commanded a police sergeant, and they obeyed, except for Alexandra.

"I am the Countess Alexandra Bolugayevska," she declared, summoning all her courage. "I demand to see your commanding officer."

"I said sit down," the sergeant said, and suddenly moved his right hand. The whip uncoiled and slashed across her shoulders. She uttered a shriek and fell to the floor, this time banging the back of her head. "Get up!" shouted the sergeant, flicking the whip again. Alexandra pushed herself to her feet.

Colonel Dimitri Taimanov had been to the opera, where he had been delighted to meet his old friend Colonel Constantine Dubaclov – they had served together in the Crimea – even if he frowned at the uniform. "You have been transferred," he remarked.

"I transferred myself," Dubaclov said. "The Hussars are all very well in time of war, but in time of peace they do nothing but parade. The Cossacks are constantly in action."

"Carrying out pogroms against the Jews, eh?" Taimanov laughed.

"When we are called upon to do so, certainly," Dubaclov said modestly. "But right now I have some hopes of Poland, if matters there develop."

"Ah, yes, Poland." Taimanov slapped him on the shoulder. "Tell me, Constantine, have you never married?"

"Never," Dubaclov said, a trifle grimly.

"But . . . were you not engaged once?"

"To a Bolugayevska. Very briefly. The engagement was terminated by that Englishman, when he became Prince."

"And has now gone to Poland, as vice to the Grand Duke?"

"Yes," Dubaclov said, grimly.

"And you would serve under him?"

"I would do anything to bring him down," Dubaclov said. "Serving under him might give me the opportunity."

Taimanov studied him for a few moments, then he slapped him on the shoulder again. "I wish you joy. Now, are you in the mood for some amusement?"

"I am always in the mood for amusement, Dimitri."

"My people were carrying out a raid this evening, on an establishment haunted by students, many of whom are Jews. It is a perfect hotbed of sedition, plots against the government. They will have completed their task by now. Shall we go and talk with some of these people?"

"Talk?" Dubaclov queried. Taimanov winked.

The cab dropped them in the courtyard, and they went inside the station building, past saluting policemen, to be greeted by Captain Karpov.

"The raid was a success, Your Excellency. We took eight prisoners."

"Have you interrogated them yet?"

"I waited, Your Excellency. I felt you would wish to question them yourself."

"Good man. They are in the chamber?"

"Yes, Your Excellency."

Taimanov beckoned Dubaclov and led him into a small office. "Here we see with the eyes of the Tsar," the policeman said with a grin. He stood against the wall and peered into the eyepiece. "Do you like pretty girls, or pretty boys, Constantine? We have a couple of each in there."

"I'm afraid I prefer girls, Dimitri." Dubaclov was apologetic, as he knew his friend's tastes.

"Well, take your pick."

Taimanov stepped aside, and Dubaclov looked through the eyepiece. He saw eight very delapidated, very frightened young people. Then he frowned, and stepped back. "The third woman from the right in the back row."

Taimanov looked. "Yes, she is attractive. Although she seems to have been knocked about a bit."

"Who is she?"

"My dear fellow, I have no idea. She will no doubt tell us when we begun to tickle her a little."

"She has not already told you?"

Taimanov looked at Karpov, who had accompanied the two colonels into the room.

"She keeps screaming that she is the countess something-or-other," Karpov said, "but when she was beaten she shut up."

"My God!" Dubaclov muttered.

"You are not going to tell me she *is* a countess?" Taimanov demanded.

"She is the Countess Alexandra Bolugayevska," Dubaclov told him.

"With respect, Your Excellency," protested the captain. "She was picked up in a beer hall which is well-known to be a meeting place for dissidents."

"That does not alter the fact that you have the youngest of the Bolugayevska sisters in there."

"Do you wish me to let her go?" Taimanov asked.

"Just like that? There will be the most devil of a fuss."

"She was associating with known dissidents," Karpov insisted.

"The affair needs to be handled with delicacy," Dubaclov said. His brain was racing. His greatest wish was somehow to bring that family down, save perhaps for Dagmar. He had never had any idea how it was to be done. But now . . .

"Well?" Taimanov damanded.

"There could be serious consequences," Dubaclov said.

"As you reminded me earlier, Dimitri, this girl's brother-in-law is now vice-Governor-General of Poland. Clearly he has the ear of the Tsar. Will you handle it as I recommend?"

"Certainly," Taimanov agreed.

"It will also be amusing, and I promise you, with no repercussions."

"Tell me what you wish me to do."

"I wish you to interrogate the Countess before any of the others. You have a special room for this?"

"Of course."

"Can it be overlooked?"

"There is an arrangement."

"Very well. Treat her exactly as you would treat any other prisoner, as of course, in view of the circumstances of her arrest, you cannot be expected to believe her claim that she is a Bolugayevska. At an appropriate moment I will enter, and rescue her."

"You understand that it is normal procedure for the woman to be raped, before questioning begins?" Taimanov asked. "This puts them in a very submissive frame of mind," he added, as if understanding that some kind of an explanation might be necessary.

"I do not think that would be a good idea," Dubaclov said. "I wish nothing quite so irrevocable done to her. That would make my task too difficult. Just tickle her up a little; that should be sufficiently amusing."

Taimanov stroked his chin. "And afterwards?"

"I swear it, on our eternal friendship, and as I am an old friend of the family, that you will hear no more of it."

"Suppose she confesses before you get there, Your Excellency?" Karpov inquired.

"I doubt she will do that, Captain."

Dublacov was taken to a small chamber situated above the interrogation room. Here there was a window through which he could look down on the room, but as the glass

253

was tinted no one in the room could see him. He could not hear what might be said below him, but he was not interested in what might be said. The interrogation room itself contained a desk, behind which there was a comfortable chair. In front of the desk there was a straight chair, and to one side of the desk there was a plain bench; the bench was bolted to the floor. Against the wall, beyond the bench, there was a high cupboard.

Dubaclov watched Taimanov and Karpov enter the room. Taimanov sat behind the desk, while Karpov stood to one side. A few moments later the door opened again, and four policemen entered, pushing Alexandra before them. He had always considered her the least beautiful of the sisters, but she remained, even in her present condition, a most attractive woman.

There was an exchange of words between Taimanov and Alexandra, with the Countess speaking with some vehemence. Then Alexandra started to shout, her face crimson, her yellow hair flailing to and fro as she moved her head. Taimanov gave an order and one of the policemen slapped Alexandra's face. She stopped shouting and gasped for breath. The four policemen now stripped her, passing her back and fourth like a toy to be unwrapped as they ripped the layers of expensive cloth. Alexandra was panting and now beginning to weep, but she was obviously too shocked by what was happening to her to attempt to fight them.

When she was naked, she was pushed and pulled to the bench and made to sit astride it. Her body was then thrust forward, and her wrists secured by cords to the two legs. Her ankles were similarly secured, to the centre legs, leaving her pinned face down to the bench from her thighs up, with her legs apart. Taimanov had left the desk to stand above Alexandra, while Karpov opened the cupboard and took out a thin cane, which he whipped to and fro so that it was obiously making a swishing sound, because Alexandra's head came up and she twisted it right and left, clearly again protesting. Then both men bent forward to peer at the scar on her right buttock, prodding her and laughing.

Dubaclov left the observation room and went down the steps. As he reached the corridor a howl of mingled pain, outrage and humiliation drifted through the building as Karpov delivered the first blow. Dubaclov waited for the second blow and the second scream, this time of real anguish, before he knocked. The door was opened by one of the constables, who were not in the private arrangement between the two colonels. "Colonel Taimanov asked me to call. Colonel Dubaclov."

"Constantine, my dear fellow," Taimanov hurried forward to greet him as the door was held wide.

"I am told you arrested some of the scum," Dubaclov said.

"Oh, indeed. We have had a successful evening. Have you ever seen such a delicious ass? Although I must say, someone appears to have chopped a piece out of it."

Alexandra, who had undoubtedly heard his name, raised her head at the same moment. "Dubaclov!" she shrieked. "Help me! Constantine!"

"My word," Dubaclov remarked.

"Do you know this woman?" Taimanov sounded suitably astonished.

"That is the Countess Alexandra Bolugayevska," Dubaclov said. "My dear fellow, there must be some mistake."

"Well, to be sure, she did claim to be a countess," Taimanov said, and looked at Karpov.

He continued with his allotted role. "She was arrested in the company of known dissidents, Your Excellency."

"Surely not," Dubaclov said, moving closer to the naked girl.

"Constantine!" Alexandra shouted. "Help me, for the love of God! They are killing me."

"Of course I shall help you, Alix," Dubaclov said.

255

"Release her this instant," he commanded the police-men.

They looked at Taimanov, who nodded. Dubaclov took off his greatcoat and wrapped Alexandra in it, and she clung to his arm, still crying. "That woman is under arrest, Your Excellency," Karpov protested. "Even if she is a countess."

"I will make myself responsible for her, Dimitri," Dubaclov said. "If she is proved guilty of anything, you will let me know."

"Well," Taimanov said. "It is very irregular."

"I will have you hanged," Alexandra snapped at him; her tears were drying.

"I think you should impress upon the Countess the seriousness of her situation, Constantine," Taimanov said severely.

"Oh, I shall," Dubaclov promised. "But now I shall take her home."

One of the policemen summoned a cab, and Dubaclov held Alexandra in his arms as they drove to the Bolugayevski Palace.

"Do you know what they *did* to me?" Alexandra asked.

"No, I don't, as a matter of fact," he lied. "Why do you not tell me?"

"I will tell the *Tsar*," she said angrily.

"I think you need to think about that," he suggested.

"Alexandra!" Anna peered at her sister. "My God! Have you been in a fight?"

"Anna!" Alexandra hurled herself into Anna's arms.

Anna looked past her at Dubaclov. She made a most attractive sight, for she had been in bed, and had pulled on nothing more than an undressing robe. "Dubaclov?" she asked. "Did you do this?"

"Of course I did not, Your Excellency. But it is a serious business," he said, and glanced at the servants, hovering curiously.

256

"Go away," Anna told them. "Go back to bed. You, Oleg! Fetch a brandy decanter and some glasses."

Reluctantly they retired, Oleg scurrying off to do his mistress's bidding. "What on earth is happening?" Dagmar descended the stairs, also wearing a dressing gown.

"Princess." Dubaclov bowed. "I'm afraid the Countess Alexandra has been arrested."

"Arrested?" Alexandra shouted, releasing Anna. "I have been beaten, raped, whipped . . ."

"Alex, please," Dagmar said. "You are being quite indecent." She was referring less to what her sister claimed had happened to her than to the way Dubaclov's coat, several sizes too large, was swinging open.

"We will go in there," Anna decided, and grasped Alexandra's arm to push her into one of the downstairs parlours.

Dubaclov and Dagmar gazed at each other. He would have spoken, but she gave a quick shake of her head; Oleg the butler was just emerging from the pantry with a tray containing the brandy decanter and four glasses. Dagmar and Dubaclov followed him into the parlour, where Anna had seated Alexandra on a settee and was rearranging the coat. "Thank you, Oleg," she said, and the butler bowed and left.

"Close the doors, please, Colonel," Anna said. "Now. Tell me what happened?"

"I have told you what happened," Alexandra shouted. "I was seized by these policemen, virtually raped, punched, beaten, stripped, caned . . . God, it hurts." She shifted her position. "If Constantine had not come along God knows what they would have done to me."

"But that is outrageous," Anna declared. "Those men must be punished. Do you know who they are, Colonel?"

"Yes, I do, Your Excellency. However, the business is not quite as straightforward as it seems."

"Straightforward?" Alexandra shouted. "I am going to the Tsar."

"I think we should hear what Constantine has to say," Dagmar suggested.

"Go on, Colonel," Anna invited, her tone remaining cold.

"Well, Your Excellencies, the Countess was in the company of a group of well-known dissidents when she was arrested."

"Who were you with, Alix?" Anna asked.

"I was having supper with David Fine," Alexandra said sulkily. "I told you that. He is my friend. There was nothing illicit about it. He took me to dinner in a little bistro close to his lodgings, and suddenly the police burst in."

"This bistro, as the Countess calls it, is apparently well known to the police as a haunt of dissidents," Dubaclov pointed out. "And indeed, it is at present the headquarters of a gang who are plotting the assassination of the Tsar."

"Good heavens," Dagmar said again.

"In fact, it is pretty certain that the people arrested with the Countess will be hanged, or at the very least exiled to Siberia for the rest of their lives."

Alexandra stared at him in horror.

"I see," Anna said. "But surely you do not suspect my sister of being a member of such a gang?"

"Of course I do not, Your Excellency. But it is a matter of evidence. The police were only doing their job. And if any of the other arrested people were to implicate the Countess . . ."

"The man Fine?" Dagmar said.

"He was not arrested," Alexandra said. "He got away."

"He does not sound like a very reliable escort to me," Anna said. "But the police had no right to arrest my sister, much less ill-treat her. Quite apart from being of noble rank, she is an American citizen by virtue of her marriage to Mr Charles Cromb."

"Your Excellency, if the Countess is implicated in a plot

258

against the life of the Tsar I do not think the fact that she is married to an American will have much effect on her sentence."

Anna bit her lip. "Oh, I wish Colin were here."

"If I may be permitted to offer some advice . . ." Dubaclov ventured.

Anna looked at him. "Yes?"

"Well, Your Excellency, I would suggest that you take the Countess back to Bolugayen, and keep her there, until this affair blows over."

"Will that stop her being, as you put it, implicated?"

"Well, Your Excellency, I happen to be a friend of Colonel Taimanov, which is why I was able to help the Countess in the first place. I think I can persuade him not to press charges against her, and indeed not to mention her in his report at all, if I can also assure him that she is returning to your estate and will not be back in St Petersburg for the foreseeable future."

"That is terrible!" Alexandra declared. "I am not guilty of anything."

"Nevertheless, what Colonel Dubaclov says makes sense," Anna said. "Certainly until Colin comes home. Thank you, Colonel. We are most grateful for your help. And now, Alix, I think it is time you went to bed. You'll excuse us, Colonel."

Dagmar and Dubaclov looked at each other as the younger sisters disappeared.

"Perhaps you would be good enough to close the door again, Constantine," Dagmar suggested. Dubaclov obeyed. "Now, come and drink your brandy, and tell me the truth of the matter."

"You have heard the truth, Your Highness."

"I think you should call me Dagmar. After all, we are old friends, are we not?" Dubaclov flushed, and Dagmar rested her hand on his. "So, after having been expelled from Bolugayen most ignominiously, you decided to save my sister, nonetheless. You are a perfect paragon, Constantine. Unfortunately, I know that you are *not* a perfect paragon. So I would like the truth."

Dubaclov had been doing some very rapid thinking. He had to make his way back into the heart of the family. Alexandra had been nothing more than an idea. But here was an invitation. "Then, if you will forgive me, Your Highness," he said. "I am sure you know how much I treasure the memory of those precious moments you and I spent together, how deeply resentful I was, and am, at the way you were treated by your husband and your sister." He paused, but Dagmar's expression never changed. He reckoned she was doing some calculating of her own. "But I had deemed us separated forever," he went on. "Until tonight. My finding Alexandra in a police cell was entirely an accident, but I recognised at once that it was a way to see you again. Perhaps to touch you again . . ." He put down his glass and picked up her hand.

She made no effort to free herself, but said, "You are an even bigger scoundrel than I had supposed, Constantine." She smiled. "But I think I could do with the help of a scoundrel. What would you desire more than anything else in the world?"

Dubaclov drew a deep breath. "To hold you naked in my arms."

"Me? Not Anna?"

"You," he lied, firmly.

"I find that a very attractive suggestion."

"Well, then, Your Highness . . ." He took her in his arms.

"Not quite so fast, Constantine," Dagmar said. "A good thing loses nothing by being anticipated for a little while. You have not asked me *my* dearest dream."

He licked his lips. "Tell me."

"To regain control of Bolugayen."

He pulled his head back.

"By any means possible," Dagmar said.

"But . . . you are the Prince's wife . . . The Prince is away, is he not?"

"Yes, and he will be coming back, unless we are very fortunate." Dubaclov stroked his chin. "There is also my sister Anna," Dagmar remarked. "She is the Prince's mistress. Did you know that?"

Dubaclov swallowed. "No, Your Highness, I did not know that."

"Do you resent that, Constantine?"

"Very much."

"As do I. I think you and I have a great deal in common. The point is that the Prince has given Anna full control over all things on Bolugayen even should he die. Of course, *should* he die, it might be possible to do something about his arrangements. I, for example, would need a husband. Bolugayen would need a prince. And incidentally, as I am sure you are not as disinterested as you pretend, Anna would need a new lover. I would be quite happy about this."

Dubaclov realised that his mouth was open, and hastily closed it again. This woman was offering him everything he had ever dreamed of. "However, there are one or two other small problems," Dagmar said.

"They shall be resolved."

"I am sure of it. But for one, at least, I will again need your help. My husband has gone out of his way to make himself popular with our people on Bolugayen. And he has succeeded, and is highly considered by the Tsar. He is also very popular with the Governor of Poltava, Baron Lebedeff. These are factors that will have to be considered when the Prince dies, in case Anna attempts to oppose me. She will be able to call on considerable support, from His Majesty down. What we need is a crisis which will be perceived as one only you and I can resolve. It is well known that a few years ago there was a cell of the Will of the People on Bolugayen, and the Englishwoman was deeply involved. Now, it is supposed that the cell no

261

longer exists, and as a matter of fact it does not. But can it not be recreated?"

Dubaclov frowned. "I am not sure that I understand you, Princess."

"Use your imagination, Constantine. My sister was arrested tonight, in the company of known conspirators."

"Yes, but I am quite sure she did not belong to their group."

"That is not relevant. What is relevant is the name of the man she has confessed to meeting: David Fine."

"I still do not understand," Dubaclov admitted.

"Fine, Constantine, Fine. This lout's father is the Prince's personal physician. Do you not remember?"

"By God!" Dubaclov muttered.

"So, you see, Fine took Alexandra to this den of iniquity. Why, do you suppose? Now he has got away. What you need to do is find him, and make him confess that he is a member of the Will of the People and that he is part of an assassination plot. Once that is done, you will have no difficulty in obtaining a warrant not only for his arrest, but for the destruction of the entire Jewish community on Bolugayen. Given the Tsar's known fear of assassination, he will probably sign the warrant himself. Then you will bring your people down to Poltava, link up with Colonel Vorontsov, and carry out your pogrom. This will serve a dual purpose. In the first place, Anna will undoubtedly oppose you, as will Alexandra, but if you hold the Tsar's warrant, they will be placed beyond the law and will need my protection. And in the second place, such an exhibition of legal ferocity as you will loose will terrify the rest of my people into supporting me, especially if I intercede to prevent you from carrying out a pogrom against *them*."

"With respect, Princess, but you have a very devious mind," Dubaclov said.

Dagmar recalled that this man had been somewhat

faint-hearted at the time of her father's death. "Am I not offering you the greatest of prizes?"

"Indeed. And you may be sure I will support you to the hilt. But I confess that I am concerned about the Englishwoman. It is well known that the Tsar always listens to the advice of his mistresses. And she will be implacably opposed to us."

"I have said, you may leave the Englishwoman to me, Constantine. By the time all our plans are ready, she will no longer be in a position to oppose us."

"Then there is but one other matter you have not considered: Alexandra. If I have Taimanov track Fine down and break him, and he involves Alexandra in his confession, we may not be able to save her."

Dagmar gazed at him. "Then she will have to be sacrificed, Constantine. This is the future we are considering. Our future. But is it not possible for *your* people to find Fine, and extract a confession from him? I have heard the Cossacks are expert at that sort of thing."

Dubaclov gulped. "Tell me what I must do first."

"First, you will find David Fine. Secondly, you will handle the Polish affair. You understand that this must be carried out in the utmost secrecy, by someone you can trust."

"I understand, Princess. But you must understand this may take some time to arrange."

"I understand," Dagmar said. "But not too much time, I hope. All our plans rest on this."

"And in the meantime?"

"I will commence dealing with Jennie Cromb. But first of all, Constantine, as you are here, and it has been so very long, I think we should consummate our partnership, properly."

"You and Dubaclov seemed to have a lot to say to each other, last night," Anna remarked at breakfast.

"We did have a lot to say to each other," Dagmar

said, equably. "Like me, Dubaclov is profoundly disturbed by this whole affair. How is Alix this morning, by the way?"

"In a terrible state. Both her face and her ass are swollen. However, we are definitely leaving today. I really think it would be best if you were to come with us."

"And I think it would be best for me to remain here, just to make sure that Dubaclov can keep his word and suppress any suggestion that Alix might be involved in this absurd plot." Anna regarded her for several seconds, but Dagmar met her gaze without any discomfiture. "Are you going to tell Colin what happened?"

"Yes, I will write to him," Anna said. "I think I will do that now, and post it from here. That has got to be quicker than from Bolugayen." She stood up.

"Then I shall wish you *bon voyage* now," Dagmar said. "I shall not be here where you depart, as I am taking tea with the Countess Dolgoruka."

Again Anna studied her for several seconds, then she nodded. "We shall expect you on Bolugayen whenever you can spare the time to join us." She went into the writing room, closed the doors, and sat at the desk. For several seconds she tapped her lip with her pen before writing. When she did, she commenced her letter, "Dearest Charles . . ."

"My dear Dagmar," Alexandra Dolgoruka said, sympathetically squeezing Dagmar's hand. "What a terrible thing."

"Alix is utterly innocent, of course," Dagmar said. "She just has this terrible weakness for involving herself in bad company."

"Of course," Alexandra said.

"I am more concerned about other aspects of the matter."

Alexandra Dolgoruka poured tea. "What other aspects?"

"Well . . . the Tsar's new mistress, for example."

264

Alexandra frowned. "Is she not a member of your household?"

"She is, or was, a member of my husband's household. I am not allowed to interfere in such matters."

"Ah," Alexandra said.

"What is more important is that she belongs to a secret society. Perhaps you have heard of it," Dagmar said ingenuously. "It is called the Will of the People."

Alexandra's jaw dropped, and then came up again with a snap. "The Tsar's mistress belongs to an organisation which is sworn to murder him?"

"Have they really?" Dagmar asked, more ingenuously yet.

"You are sure of this?"

"My dear Alexandra, she was part of the conspiracy which resulted in the death of my father."

"And was not executed?"

"She was reprieved by my husband. He said it was because the facts against her were not proved, that her confession was extracted under torture and therefore invalid, but of course it was because they are both English."

"And presumably she was also his mistress?"

"Oh, undoubtedly. He is an absolute *roué*. How I regret the day Papa forced me to marry him. But none of us then understood the nature of the beast. Or ever supposed he would be Prince Bolugayevski."

"The Tsar's doing," Alexandra said, darkly. "But this is a most serious matter. Why did you not mention it before?"

"Simply because I have only just found out that the woman has become the Tsar's mistress. The question is, what are we to do about it?"

"It is no simple matter," Alexandra said. "In the first place, I would imagine that the Tsar already knows at least something of this woman's background. The police will certainly have informed him of it. When he becomes infatuated with a woman, he is *totally* infatuated. I speak from experience."

"Then is there nothing to be done?"

"There is a great deal that can be done. The Tsar's infatuations can pass very quickly, if he is given reason to relocate his affections. If, for example, your friend Dubaclov were to find some link between the English-woman and those people arrested, that would at least cause His Majesty to have some doubts about her. And if, at that same time, he were to meet someone even more attractive than the Englishwoman . . ."

"Who do you have in mind?" Dagmar asked. "He obviously does not find *me* very attractive." She touched her scarred cheek.

"Oh, no," Alexandra said. "With respect, Your Highness, he likes them young. Even the Englishwoman is somewhat old for the position. No, no, what we require is someone *very* young, very fresh, very virginal . . . the complete contrast, indeed, to the Englishwoman."

"And where are we going to find such a woman?" Dagmar asked. "I'm afraid my own sisters do not qualify, at least when it comes to being fresh and virginal."

Alexandra Dolgoruka tapped her teeth with her fan. "I think I may know the very woman we want. All that is required is that she be brought to St Petersburg."

"Prince Bolugayevski! My word, sir, but it is good to see you." Count Dolgoruki hurried into the hall of his Warsaw home, waving the card Colin had sent in by the butler. "Welcome to my home, Your Highness. Welcome. We knew of your arrival, of course." The Count was of middle height, with rather large features and heavy shoulders. Colin was surprised that he was supposed to have a daughter as beautiful as Alexandra had described, but the surprise vanished as he met the two other members of the family.

"Your Highness!" The Countess curtsied. "My daughter

266

Catherine." The girl was quite startlingly attractive, with curling yellow hair and pert features. "I believe you have met our cousin Alexandra."

"I have had that pleasure, Countess."

"She writes such exciting things about St Petersburg," Catherine said eagerly. "I am to go there."

Colin raised his eyebrows. "Alexandra thinks Catherine will do very well in St Petersburg," Dolgoruki explained.

"I am sure she will," Colin agreed.

"Now tell us what you think of Warsaw, and its people, Your Highness," the Countess said, brightly. "Is the Grand Duke well settled in?"

"Oh, indeed, and he is enchanted with your city, as am I. I must apologise for not calling before, but we have been very busy."

"Of course, Your Highness, of course," Dolgoruki said. "But still, now that it is a new year, we must hope for better things."

"Yes," Colin agreed. "I think you are very lucky to be leaving Warsaw, mademoiselle," he told Catherine Dolgoruka.

"What is that noise?" inquired the Countess.

They went to the windows, and the butler came in. "A great crowd in the city centre, Your Excellencies."

"Doing what?"

"Protesting, Your Excellency. They are always protesting."

"Fetch me my hat and coat and have my horse brought round," Colin said. "And I must beg you to excuse me, Countess. Mademoiselle, I wish you a happy visit to St Petersburg."

He mounted his horse, his breath clouding in the cold February night air. His servants fell in behind him, and they trotted down the street to the edge of the great square. Here there was a detachment of Cossacks, overseeing the mob, which was ranged in front of the

Governor-General's palace, separated from it by the high wrought-iron railings, and making a great deal of noise. Not that they were getting too close to the railings, which, Colin knew, would be guarded by a regiment of infantry. "What are your orders?" he asked the captain in command of the cavalry.

"To charge if any assault is made on the palace, Your Highness."

"Well, we must avoid bloodshed if possible. We do not wish a recurrence of last year's massacre." He urged his horse forward.

"You Highness!" the captain protested. "I cannot answer for your safety if you ride into that mob."

"I will answer for my own safety, Captain," Colin said. Heads turned as he forced his way into the midst of the crowd, and there were some hostile gestures. But he was recognised by several of the people, and in the five months that he had been in Warsaw he had become a popular figure.

He advanced until he was in the very midst of the mob, and then drew rein. The noise around him was tremendous, and he could see now that there were quite a few people gathered on the balcony of the Governor-General's palace, watching him. He drew his revolver, pointed it into the air, and fired three times. There was an immediate upsurge of noise, then it died away into a complete hush as it was realised that the shots had been fired by the lone horseman in their midst. "You know me," Colin shouted. "I am Prince Bolugayevski. I, and the Grand Duke, have been sent here to deal fairly with you. This we have done, and shall do."

"No conscription!" someone shouted. The cry was taken up.

Colin raised his hands, and the noise died. "Conscription is a necessary and universal part of Russian life," he shouted. "But there will be no hardship. Any man who can prove he is needed at home will be exempted."

The crowd jostled and growled, but much of the hostility was ebbing. "Now you must go home," Colin shouted. "Gatherings such as this are illegal. Disperse peacefully now, and no action will be taken against you."

More jostling and muttering, but a good many people were beginning to sidle off towards the streets leading into the square. Colin turned his horse and walked it back towards the Cossack regiment, intending to give it orders to return to barracks. He had not gone more than a few feet, however, when a shot rang out.

Chapter 14

THE REVENGE

As usual, Jennie waited in the downstairs hall of her house to receive the Tsar. He was attended by several bodyguards, but these were dismissed at the door; he knew he was safe once inside his mistress's house, because her butler and all her male servants were members of the Okhrana, the secret police. Jennie sometimes found it difficult to determine whether they were there for their monarch's protection, or to make sure his latest toy did not stray.

But there was no overcoming her sense of impermanency. Even this house, which she had been assured was hers in perpetuity, whatever her future relationship with the Tsar, remained nothing more than a transient camp site to her, for all the wealth of rich drapes and exquisite furniture, the expensive wines, the crockery and cutlery which was far superior even to that on Bolugayen. She was here simply because Colin wanted her to be.

As for the Tsar himself . . . she arranged her features into a smile as the butler removed Alexander's civilian hat and coat; she went forward with her arms outstretched, as he liked best. Usually. Today his embrace was perfunctory, and then he was leading her up the stairs to the bedroom without his usual stop at his easel. She followed him through the door, closing it behind her. Everything was as he liked it to be, the roaring fire in the grate, the decanter of wine and the two glasses, the chaise longue on which he liked her to lounge, naked . . . but today he sat on it himself. She poured two glasses of wine, gave him one. "Is something the matter, sire?"

He sighed. "What exactly is Prince Bolugayevski to you?"

Jennie could not stop herself frowning as she tried to guess what was coming next. "I was employed by his uncle in England, and then I became his serf here in Russia."

"But he saved your life when you were charged with murder?"

"Yes, sire."

"So, is the link merely gratitude? Or something stronger."

"I have never been his mistress, sire. I have told you this. The link has always been gratitude. It is stronger now, because my cousin is married to his sister-in-law. May I ask what has happened?"

The Tsar waved his hand. "There has been trouble in Poland. Warsaw. Trouble! There is virtually open warfare! Civil war . . . A rebellion. It is very upsetting."

"And you blame the Prince?"

"I suppose in a way he is to blame. It was his being shot that sparked the whole thing off."

"Shot?" Jennie knelt beside him. "Prince Bolugayevski has been shot?" Alexander nodded. "Is he . . . ?" She bit her lip.

"He is very badly hurt. As to whether he will survive, my brother's report says it is uncertain."

"Oh, my God! Sire . . ." She drew a deep breath. "Would you give me permission to go to him?"

"Certainly not."

"But . . ."

"You can carry gratitude, if that is all you feel for him, too far. I need you here."

Jennie bit her lip again, and bowed her head, while his fingers sought her buttons. She sometimes thought he enjoyed undressing her more than making love to her. But

271

it was difficult for her to be enthusiastic. "We both have too much on our minds," the Tsar said.

"I am sorry, sire."

"Things will look brighter in a day or two," Alexander said. "I will return then. Do not bother to come down."

It was the first ripple ever to have affected their relationship. Jennie went to the window to watch him leave. As he walked his horse to the gate, a phaeton with its roof down, remarkable in view of the cold, clattered by on the street. The driver drew rein to raise his hat to the Tsar, and the two women in the car also inclined their heads, and leaned forward to speak with the Emperor. Jennie frowned as she studied them through the steam that was their breaths. They were both well wrapped up in fur coats against the February chill, and also wore fur hats, but she recognised the Countess Alexandra Dolgoruka immediately. Beside her was an extremely beautiful girl, far more attractive than her . . . cousin? Their features so closely resembled each other that it had to be. The Tsar was certainly attracted. He remained speaking with them for several minutes, and then rode beside the phaeton until it was lost to sight.

The next morning a letter arrived, bearing the Imperial crest. Jennie opened it with a slowing of her heart. *My dearest Jennie,* The Tsar had written, *upon reflection I have come to the conclusion that my attitude yesterday was quite wrong. I appreciate how much you feel you owe Prince Bolugayevski, and thus I can understand your concern at his misfortune. I therefore give you my permission to travel to Warsaw to be with the Prince, and play your part, hopefully, in restoring him to health. You may remain in Warsaw for as long as you wish, and should you so desire, you may return with him to Bolugayen, as soon as he is able to travel. Assuring you always of my esteem. Alexander.*

"The Prince is very weak, you understand," said Dr Winawer. "I am not sure I should let you see him

272

at all, mademoiselle. But if you are sent by His Majesty . . ."

"Which I am," Jennie pointed out. "Tell me, will he recover?"

"Oh, certainly, providing there is no infection. What he is suffering from now is principally loss of blood." The doctor opened the door, and the two nuns seated inside the bedroom hastily rose as the tall, auburn-haired woman entered. Colin's eyes were shut, but he breathed evenly. "The Prince was fortunate," Dr Winawer said. "The shot was fired from a distance, and struck the lower chest. He has broken three ribs, but they will mend. As I have said, his principal problem is loss of blood. But that too he will recover, given time. It is very gratifying that the Tsar should send a representative."

"Yes," Jennie said, and sat beside the bed. "Have they found out who did it?"

"Indeed, it was one of the Cossack regiment which was supporting him. Some people say it was an accidental discharge of his carbine. But it is difficult to be certain."

"Has the man not been arrested and interrogated?"

"Sadly, no. He was immediately shot and killed by the man beside him."

"Then it was not an accident."

The doctor shrugged. "We shall never know. The man who killed him claimed to have acted instinctively."

Jennie watched Colin's eyelids flutter. "Leave us."

"But mademoiselle . . ."

"Leave us," Jennie repeated. The doctor went to the door. "And take the nuns with you," Jennie commanded.

For a few seconds Colin stared at her, uncomprehendingly. Then he muttered, "Jennie?"

"The original bad penny," she smiled.

"But . . . the Tsar?"

"I think the Tsar has found a new toy. Thus I must seek a new employer."

273

His hands moved, feebly, and she caught his fingers. "I did you a great wrong," he said.

"You gave me a great experience, Colin. You have nothing to reproach yourself with. Now your only business is to get well."

"To have you here . . ." His head turned. "But . . ."

"Anna could not come right now," Jennie said gently. "She returned to Bolugayen last September. Do you not remember?"

"Yes," he said, vaguely. "She wrote to me that she was returning, and I have had a letter since. But will she not come?"

"I doubt the news has reached Bolugayen as yet," Jennie said. "You know what the mails are like, in winter. Now you must rest."

"Will you stay?"

"I will stay, Colin, for as long as you wish me to."

Because of the pain, Dr Winawer kept Colin sedated with laudanum most of the time. Thus Jennie would sit by his bed and watch his face, holding his hands, waiting. At least she had the certainty that he *was* going to get well, Dr Winawer's certainty. She herself was terrified at every return of the fever, every onset of delirium. As now. He moved restlessly, twisting his head to and fro, muttering, but she could not make out what he was saying.

She got up, dampened a cloth in the basin on the table, and laid it on his forehead. His movements quietened, and she sat down again, but when she went to move the towel his hand suddenly closed on her wrist. His grip was surprisingly strong, and she made no effort to free herself, waiting for his fingers to relax. Instead they moved up her sleeve. "Colin," she whispered. "It is Jennie."

He did not seem able to hear her, and his hand moved higher yet to her shoulder. She found herself trembling as the fingers then slipped down, to stroke her breast. "Colin," she said. "Anna is not here."

He sighed, still holding her breast. "Jennie," he muttered. "Oh, Jennie." His eyes remained closed, and he was clearly delirious. But in his torment he had spoken her name! Jennie unbuttoned her blouse to let his fingers drift inside.

The next day she sat beside his bed to read him the *Gazette*. This morning he was perfectly awake and lucid. "Dr Winawer says it will be several weeks before you are well enough to sit on a horse," she said. "But you really are looking so much better than I had expected. The report we received in St Petersburg was that your life was in danger."

"I imagine that was the Grand Duke exaggerating," Colin said. "Like all weak men, he tends to overreact to bad news. But several weeks . . . did that news reach Bolugayen?"

"It would have been sent on, although I have no idea how long it will take to get there; the roads are very bad. I only reached Warsaw so quickly because of the train."

"I imagine, once she receives the news the Grand Duke Constantine has been spreading about, Anna will come here, come hell or high water."

"You must not fret about it. In any event, I doubt she will risk leaving Bolugayen."

Colin frowned. "Smyslov could manage the place. Or even Alix . . ."

"When last did you hear from Anna?" Jennie was also frowning.

"It was just after Christmas." Suddenly he was agitated. "Why, is there something wrong? Tell me!"

"Did she not write you about Alix?"

"Alix? Has something happened to Alix?"

"I am exciting you. It is not good. I will tell you when you are stronger."

"You will tell me now, Jennie. Or I will not grow stronger."

"Alix was arrested by the police. Just after you left St Petersburg."

"My God! What for? And why was I not told?"

"Do not fret, my dearest Colin," Jennie said. "It has all been sorted out, well, for the time being, at least."

"Tell me what happened."

Colin's frown was back. "Did you say, Dubaclov?"

"You must remember Dubaclov," Jennie said.

"I remember Dubaclov very well," Colin said. "And you say he rescued Alix from the police? He hates Alix. He hates all of us, except possibly Dagmar."

"Perhaps he has changed."

"Not Dubaclov. If he got her away from the police it was with an ulterior motive."

"You *are* agitated," Jennie said, and gave him a glass of water.

Colin drank greedily. But he would not leave the subject. "Did Anna not comment on it? It must have bothered her as well, because she never mentioned it in her letters. Obviously she did not wish to worry me."

"Which was very thoughtful of her," Jennie agreed, now with just a hint of sarcasm. "However, there is a reason for Dubaclov's action, as Anna understands. It appears that after bringing Alix home, and Anna had thanked him and taken Alix up to bed, he remained with Dagmar for virtually the rest of the night. And since then she has been seeing him quite regularly. It is causing a certain amount of gossip."

Colin tried to sit up, and she had to ease him back on to the pillow. "My God!" he said.

"Well," Jennie said. "If they wish to get together, why not let them? It may ease some of Dagmar's feelings towards the rest of us. You're surely no longer jealous of her?"

"You do not understand," Colin said. "Dagmar would never have sex with a man like Dubaclov just for the

276

pleasure of it. There has to be an ulterior motive. And Dubaclov transferred to the Cossacks some time ago. I read it in the *Gazette*. My God! The Cossacks! There was a fresh detachment arrived in Warsaw just before Christmas. They were part of the covering force the night I was shot."

Jennie frowned. "You can't be serious."

"I am very serious."

"You think Dubaclov planned your murder?"

"I think Dagmar planned my murder, Jennie. Where is Dagmar now?"

"Why, she was in St Petersburg when I left, as I say, seeing Dubaclov quite regularly."

"And waiting for news of my death."

"Then we must certainly send a correction, and quickly."

Colin glanced at her. "I wonder," he said.

Jennie sat beside him. "I don't understand."

"If I am right, and Dagmar did plan my murder, and discovers that the assassin failed, she will merely plan another assassination attempt. She has no doubt been planning this one for the past seven years."

"You will need proof, Colin. And if this assassin is dead . . ."

"The only proof can be supplied by Dagmar and Dubaclov themselves. I think we must let them do that for us, Jennie, or they will be a menace to us for the rest of our lives. What of Anna and Alix?" he continued.

"You do not suppose Dagmar is going to harm her own sisters, do you?"

"Well . . . I am quite sure she hates them, Anna, at any rate, as much as she hates you and me."

"That may be. But she is in St Petersburg, and Anna and Alix are in Bolugayen, and Anna is protected by my deposition. Dagmar cannot affect things there. But it will be very interesting to see just what she does do, assuming I am very seriously hurt, maybe dying."

"Will Winawer support you? And the nuns?"

"Winawer, like most men, will do anything if he is paid enough. I think the same thing can be said for the nuns. I am not asking them to lie. It is simply a matter of not sending any further reports to St Petersburg, if the first one was that gloomy."

"And me? I came here to be at your side. To nurse you back to health."

"You will remain here, attempting to do just that, too overcome by grief at the thought I might die to write any letters." His hand moved on hers. "Would you not be overcome by grief at my death?"

She kissed his fingers. "I would join you in death, dearest Colin. I would have nothing more to live for." She raised her head, flushing, to meet his gaze.

"Have I really been that much of a fool?" he said thoughtfully, and raised his head as there was a knock on the door.

The nuns were trembling with fear, and indignation. "Your Highness, there are men . . ."

They were pushed aside by the uniformed captain, who had four men at his back.

"Prince Bolugayevski?"

Despite Jennie's attempt to restrain him, Colin struggled to his feet. "What do you mean by bursting in here like this?"

The captain produced a sheet of paper. "I have a warrant here for your arrest, Your Highness." He glanced at Jennie. "And for the lady."

"The Princess is here, Your Excellency." Igor Bondarevski hovered in the doorway of Anna's sewing room.

Anna frowned at him. "Dagmar? Now?"

"It is definitely the Princess's crest, Your Excellency."

Anna handed her tapestry to Olga, got up, and went on to the gallery. In early March the snow was still thick on the ground, and Bolugayen had, as usual, been cut off

278

from the outside world for some weeks. Further north the weather must be far more severe. Yet here was Dagmar, getting down from her troika in a flurry of fur and stamping into the hall, flicking snow from her boots. "I did not expect you back until Easter, at the least," Anna said. "Wasn't the journey awful?"

"The journey was awful," Dagmar agreed. "But I felt I should come home."

"You mean Her Majesty no longer asks you to tea?" Anna inquired.

"I had tea with Her Majesty the day before I left St Petersburg," Dagmar said. "However, I have never lacked a sense of duty. Have you enjoyed your five months as *chatelaine* of Bolugayen?"

"I have endeavoured to do my duty," Anna said. "I would have enjoyed it more had Colin been here with me."

"Yes," Dagmar said with some satisfaction. "However, I doubt he will be returned before the summer. What is left of him."

Anna frowned at her, while an icy hand seemed to clutch at her heart. "What is left of him? What do you mean?"

Dagmar addressed Igor. "What are you standing there for, fool? I wish tea." She stalked to the foot of the great staircase, and looked up it, at Olga and little Catherine, and at Yevrentko and the two boys, who had all emerged on to the gallery to see what the excitement was about. "My husband has been very badly wounded, in Warsaw."

"Oh, my God!" Anna cried.

"Papa!" Peter shouted, running down the stairs; Dagmar scooped him into her arms. Olga clapped both hands to her throat. Catherine began to cry. Georgei remained stony-faced, while Yevrentko looked terrified.

"I must go to him," Anna said, herself hurrying for the stairs.

"I would think that a considerable waste of time, as you

would not be allowed to see him," Dagmar told her. "He is also under arrest, on a charge of treason. Together with his other concubine, Jennie Cromb."

Anna, already halfway up the stairs, stopped and turned to glare at her sister. "Arrested? Colin? With Jennie? Jennie was never his mistress." It was more important to her to establish that than find out the truth of what was going on.

"I do not suppose you are aware that there has been an attempt on the life of the Tsar. Colin and Jennie are implicated."

"You are a lying bitch!" Anna shouted.

Dagmar's face was cold. "I must warn you, little sister, that I have had enough of your airs and your insults."

Anna went back down the steps towards her. "And you suppose you can come here, with your lies . . ."

"Ah, Igor," Dagmar said. "Put the tea in the small parlour. Now go and fetch four of your men, and at the same time summon Monsieur Smyslov."

"You will do no such thing," Anna said. Igor hesitated, trembling, looking from one sister to the other.

"I suppose the Countess Anna has been filling your mind with all manner of rubbish," Dagmar said. "What has she told you?"

Igor licked his lips. "That the Prince has placed her in charge of Bolugayen, Your Highness. During his absence."

"Why, that is absolutely true, Igor," Dagmar said. "No doubt the Countess showed you the Prince's letter of instruction?"

"Yes, Your Highness."

"Well, I have to tell you that such a letter no longer has any legal meaning whatsoever. It has been cancelled by order of the Tsar."

"That is a lie," Anna snapped.

"What did you say?" Alexandra had appeared on the gallery as well. Now she ran down the stairs, face ashen.

"Ah, Alix. I have something to say to you as well, later. Colin is arrested. For links with the Will of the People, who have attempted to kill the Tsar." Dagmar opened her reticule, took out the newspaper cutting, and threw it on the floor. Anna didn't move. "I have also received an official notification from the Tsar," Dagmar went on. "You may read it, if you wish." Anna's knees gave way and she sat down, on the bottom step. Alexandra hurried to put her arm round her shoulder, then stooped to pick up the cutting and read it, her lips trembling. "What a pretty pair you make," Dagmar sneered. "Were you both in love with him? And no doubt Jennie as well. You will be pleased to know, Anna, that Jennie hurried off to Warsaw to be with him and escape the police. Oh, she is in it up to the hilt. Sheer jealousy, of course, because she was no longer wanted in St Petersburg. The Tsar has found a new plaything. Well, I imagine she knows what to look forward to, at the hands of the police. It will be a new experience for Colin."

"You are a fiend," Anna muttered.

"Why, yes, I can be a fiend, to those who oppose me. Who *have* opposed me for so very long."

Anna raised her head. "If you lay a finger on me . . ."

"I would not dream of laying a finger on you, Anna. But I intend that others should do so. Ah, Smyslov. Read that." She took the cutting from Alexandra's hand and gave it to the bailiff. Smyslov read it in total consternation. "You will, no doubt, recall the conversation we had after my father's death?" Dagmar asked.

Smyslov nodded, glancing at Igor as he did so. Igor was shivering. "I believe Prince Colin held a similar conversation with you, after he behaved so badly to me," Dagmar said.

"He had the warrants," Smyslov muttered.

"Well, I now have the warrants. Do you understand me?"

281

"Yes, Your Highness. Will you be taking over the estate?"

"For the time being," Dagmar said. "Until the arrival of the next Prince Bolugayevski."

"The next . . ." Anna looked up with her mouth open.

"I have decided to marry again," Dagmar said. "The moment Colin either dies or is executed. To Colonel Dubaclov. He is looking forward to it."

Anna leapt to her feet. "You are mad. You have to be mad. That guttersnipe?"

"Now that really is the limit," Dagmar said. "Igor, take the Countess Anna to her room. You have my permission to cane her. Cane her till she bleeds." Igor looked at his mistress in horror, then at Anna. "And then," Dagmar went on, "you have my permission to fuck her till she faints. Your people can help you. In fact, they can fuck her as well."

"You would not *dare*!" Anna snapped. "Do you think I am some servant? Do you not think I shall reveal your secret?"

"Why, yes," Dagmar said. "Let us reveal our secret, darling sister." She looked at the men. "What the Countess would like to tell you is that we both committed incest with our father. We were forced to it. I suffered most, as I had a child by Papa. There, now you have it." The men stared at her. "But if I were you, Igor, and you, Smyslov, I should keep it to yourselves, or I shall be very angry. And if anyone has any ideas about gaining an advantage over me by tattling to Colonel Dubaclov, I have already told him everything, so it will not work. And as for St Petersburg, I have turned my back on it. Bolugayen is my home, and Bolugayen is where I intend to be, for the rest of my days. Now, Anna, you asked me if I considered you a servant. Yes. As of now I intend to treat you as a servant. But I do understand that you will have to be taught the meaning of discipline. I think Constantine will see to that when he arrives. For the time being, I am merely punishing you for your rudeness. But I also consider you a whore. It is my intention that you shall be treated as a whore, for the rest of your natural life. Igor!"

Anna looked from her to Igor. Her brain seemed paralysed by the sudden overturn of her authority, her very existence. "If you will come with me, Your Excellency," the butler said.

"If you touch me . . ."

"Of course you must touch her, Igor," Dagmar said. "You have my *carte blanche* to do anything you like to her. But do not hurt her so that it will show. Except on her ass."

Igor's face was working with a variety of emotions. Anna took a step backwards, and felt herself against the bannister. Alexandra was also on her feet now. "You cannot be serious, Dagmar!"

Dagmar pointed at her. "And you, miss, had better mind what you say. You are in deeper trouble than anyone, if I choose. Or if Constantine chooses. Remember this." Alexandra's shoulders drooped, and she began to weep. "Now go to your room," Dagmar commanded. "And stay there until I send for you."

Alexandra looked at Anna, opened her mouth as if she would have protested again, then closed it again and went up the stairs. "Well, Igor?" Dagmar demanded.

Igor stepped forward. "Help me!" Anna shouted at Smyslov.

Smyslov licked his lips, looked at Dagmar, and remained still. Igor reached for Anna, and she struck at him, but he caught her wrist, pulled her forward, and drove his shoulder into her midriff. She gasped as the air was forced from her lungs, and before she could recover he had lifted her from the floor, his arm wrapped round her thighs, while her head and hair trailed down his back. This was the man who for the past six years and more had obeyed her every command. "Put me down," she shouted. "Igor, put me down immediately."

"Remember, Igor," Dagmar said. "I want to hear her scream. I want everyone in the house to hear her scream."

Smyslov took out his handkerchief and wiped his neck. "Your Highness . . ."

"She deserves everything that is going to happen to her," Dagmar said. "She is a treacherous little bitch. Now tell me, where is Fine?"

"Countess Anna gave him permission to go over to the Jewish village, Your Highness. There is some religious holiday to be observed."

"Ah," Dagmar said. "That is the best place for him. I can tell you, Smyslov, that when Colonel Dubaclov gets here, we are going to do something about those Jews."

Smyslov shifted his feet uneasily. For five years Bolugayen had been a happy place, a peaceful and contented place. Now . . . "Shall I announce the Prince's arrest in the town?" he asked.

"Will there be a reaction?"

"The Prince was very popular."

"And I am not, is that what you are telling me?" Smyslov shifted his feet some more. "I wish the truth, Nicholas," Dagmar said, softly.

"I think it is that the people associate you with your father, and serfdom, Your Highness," he said. "I know it is not possible, but they will suppose that you will somehow manage to reimpose serfdom."

"Who said it is not possible?"

"But . . . the law . . ."

"I do not intend to break the law. But is it not true that the Prince was very lenient regarding non-payment of mortgage fees, and even the *corvée*?"

"Well . . . the Prince wished everyone to be happy."

"And that, as you well know, Nicholas, is an impossibility. Not *everyone* can be happy. The happiness we need to concentrate on is our own. So for the time being we will not announce the arrest of the Prince."

"The servants will speak of it."

"But they do not know, either, for certain. So it will be rumour. And in a few hours' time Colonel Dubaclov will be here."

"One man, Your Highness? If there should be trouble . . ."

Dagmar smiled. "The Colonel will be accompanied by a squadron of Cossacks, Smyslov. And he will also have with him Colonel Vorontsov and a detachment of police from Poltava. I assure you that there is nothing for you to be afraid of. As long as you do as I tell you."

The people of Bolugayen turned out in the snow to watch the squadron of Cossacks riding down the road from Poltava. Behind them was a detachment of mounted policemen. The people looked at each other, unsure whether to fear the Cossacks or the police more. Then they saw that in the midst of the policemen there was a cart, and in the cart there was a man, his hands bound behind him. He wore no coat, and shivered in the cold; his flesh was almost blue. "David Fine!"

The whisper spread through the onlookers as the prisoner was recognised. "David Fine!"

No one had known what to believe for the past twenty-four hours. Was it rumour, or fact, that the Prince was under arrest for treason? Was it rumour, or fact, that the Princess Dagmar had returned like an avenging fury? Was it rumour, or fact, that she had had her own sister caned and raped? Was it rumour, or fact, that she intended to have all the arrears of mortgage payments and *corvée* called in? But here was fact, staring them in the face.

The cavalcade drew up in front of the mansion, and David Fine was thrown down from his cart. With his hands bound he could not protect his face, which was cut on the ice protruding amidst the hard-packed snow. Two Cossacks

285

seized his shoulders and dragged him up, pulling him up the steps and then throwing him down again, at Dagmar's feet. Standing at Dagmar's shoulder, Alexandra gave a gasp of horror, and clasped her throat. Constantine Dubaclov signalled his men to dismount, and did so himself. Colonel Vorontsov followed him up the steps.

"Your Highness," Dubaclov said. "We have the most serious news."

"Is it about the Prince?" Dagmar might be acting a role, but she did it to perfection.

"It is even more serious than that," Dubaclov said. "Colonel Vorontsov?"

Vorontsov cleared his throat. "This creature" – he nudged David Fine with his toe, and David shivered – "has confessed to his part in the attempted assassination of the Tsar. What is more, he has confessed that the plot originated in his own village, here in Bolugayen."

"Our Jews?" Dagmar made a magnificent job of appearing horrified.

"I am afraid so, Your Highness. I have here an order from His Majesty commanding that a pogrom be launched against them. There are to be no survivors."

"Our Jews?" Dagmar asked. "What a catastrophe. Still . . ." She gave a brave smile. "I know you must carry out your orders, Colonel." She in turn nudged David Fine with her toe. "What about this one?"

"No!" Alexandra shrieked, running down the stairs and throwing her arms around David's neck.

"Ahem!" Dubaclov said, loudly.

"Yes, I understand," Dagmar said. "Allow me to deal with this matter, Colonel. But for the time being, can you not leave this boy alive? At least until you return from the Jewish village." She smiled again. "I do assure you that he is not going to escape."

"I think it is all going very well." Dagmar sat with the two

286

colonels in one of the ground floor drawing-rooms, while Igor served them champagne.

"We will leave tomorrow," Vorontsov said. "We should be back in under a fortnight. I would feel much happier if you allowed me to leave some of my men here."

Dagmar turned to Dubaclov. "I think it would be wisest, Princess," Dubaclov said. "Begin as we mean to go on, eh? The slightest show of revolt must be crushed with the utmost severity, Now is the time, Dagmar. The Tsar is in the mood for it."

"Well, then, leave me four of your men, Vorontsov," Dagmar said. "Now tell me, is there news from St Petersburg?"

"I left immediately after you," Dubaclov said.

Dagmar looked at Vorontsov. "There has been no news as yet, Your Highness. Presumably, when the weather improves . . ."

"The weather!" Dagmar snorted. "Well, I hope that the Prince and his doxy are trussed up side by side by now, both screaming their heads off. Then tell me about Lebedeff."

"The Baron was very unhappy, Your Highness. He refused to accept that the entire Jewish community in Bolugayen could be implicated in the plot against the Tsar. He wished me to delay action until after we had obtained confirmation from St Petersburg . . ."

"That could take weeks. Even months."

"I explained that to the Baron, Your Highness. Thus he accepted the situation."

"Baron Lebedeff is a silly old woman," Dagmar said. "Well, I am going upstairs. Good night, Vorontsov." Vorontsov hastily stood up and bowed. "Dubaclov!" Dagmar called to the colonel. He too stood up, flushing. "Good night, Colonel." Vorontsov bowed again. Dubaclov followed Dagmar out of the room and to the stairs. "Dare we be so obvious?" he asked. "Your husband still lives."

"Perhaps," Dagmar said. "But here on Bolugayen we do whatever we wish." She climbed the stairs in front of him, knowing that he would be watching her hips moving beneath the gown. "Tell me," she said over her shoulder. "You have not inquired after Anna."

"Did she oppose you?"

"She attempted to do so, certainly. I had to punish her, quite severely. But I wondered if you would not also like to punish her? She treated you very badly."

She had reached the gallery. Two maids stood there, curtsying. Dagmar waved her hand and they hurried away.

"You mean you would let me do so?" Dubaclov asked.

"Would you like to? I think it could be quite amusing, I think it would be amusing to watch. Shall we go and visit her?"

Dubaclov swallowed. He wanted this woman, both because of her animal sexuality and because of what she was offering him, that princedom of which he had always dreamed. And he wanted her despite knowing that she was indeed an animal, the product of nearly two centuries of unbridled omnipotence, untouchable wealth, unimaginable arrogance, come together in a single human being who considered that the world had wronged her. She was probably the most vicious woman in Russia. But she was his pathway to that omnipotence, that wealth, that arrogance . . . and if she was going to throw in the sister he really wanted to possess . . . "I think you would enjoy that too," Dagmar smiled, and took his hand.

Anna sat up as the key turned and the door opened. The room was in darkness, as she had not bothered to light the candle. She did not wish to look in her mirror and see herself. She did not suppose she would ever wish to do that again. At least, not until she had killed Dagmar. But if they were coming back to torment her again . . . She pushed herself up. She had been lying on her face across her bed, because it was too painful to lie on her back. Her buttocks ached from the caning, and besides lying on her back made her remember too much. She had not screamed when she had been caned. But she had screamed when the fourth man had mounted her.

She closed her eyes. She could not bear to look at any of their hateful faces. The door closed again, softly. That certainly was not Dagmar. And there was only one intruder. Anna tensed her muscles. "Your Highness?" Yevrentko whispered.

Anna gave a little gasp and leapt off the bed, carrying a pillow with her to hold against herself as she turned to face him. "Have you been sent torment me?" she asked. "Once I had supposed you loved me."

"Your Highness, I do love you. I adore you. I would die for you now. Would you not like to escape this place?"

Anna sat on the bed. "Is it possible?"

"I would help you. I would escape with you."

"You would be hanged."

"I have said I will die for you. Would you not escape with me?"

"Where could we go?"

"We could go south, to Sevastopol, Your Highness. We could get there before any pursuers. No one in Sevastopol knows what has happened here. To them, you are still mistress of Bolugayen. You could command a place on one of your ships, and we would be away."

America, she thought. We could sail to America. And Charles! But . . . "What of Alix?"

"Your Highness . . ."

"We cannot leave Alix here. Besides, we are fleeing to her husband."

Yevrentko gulped. "It will add to the risk."

"We will have to accept that. When?"

"The Princess is still entertaining Dubaclov and Vorontsov, but they will be retiring soon. Then the servants. I estimate by midnight it will be possible to make a move. I will have to go and see the Countess Alexandra now, and then I will return for you just after midnight. You must be very warmly dressed, and you must bring all the jewellery you have."

Anna nodded. "Make sure Alix does the same. Now tell me what reward you require for this."

"Your Highness, my reward is serving you."

Anna held out her hand, and he kissed her knuckles . . . and the door opened. "Well, well," Dagmar said, raising the candle above her head. Yevrentko scrambled to his feet. Anna took a step backwards, still clutching the pillow against herself. Dagmar glanced from his face to Anna's. "Hatching some plot? You slimy little toad. Well, you are dismissed. Ring that bell."

Trembling, Yevrentko obeyed. "You cannot dismiss Yevrentko," Anna said. "What will the boys do for a tutor?"

"I will find another tutor," Dagmar said. "Ah, Igor. Get four of your men, and have Monsieur Yevrentko flogged until he bleeds. Tomorrow he will be expelled from Bolugayen. And Yevrentko, if I ever see you again I will have you shot. Take him out, Igor."

Igor gulped and looked at Yevrentko, and then at Anna. Anna's knees gave way and she sat on the bed, her shoulders hunched.

Yevrentko stumbled through the door. Igor followed.

"Now, Anna," Dagmar said, "perhaps you should tell Constantine and I what you and that lout were talking about. I think you should close the door, Constantine. I think she is going to need to be persuaded."

Chapter 15

THE ESCAPE

The Tsar strode into the small reception room and the two men waiting for him came to attention. Jennie merely held her hat before herself, protectively. Alexander looked across the faces, pausing for a moment at Jennie's before returning to Colin's. "You are not harmed? I gave orders that you were not to be harmed. Or Mademoiselle Cromb."

"We have not been harmed, Your Majesty," Colin said. "Not physically."

"Harrumph," the Tsar commented, and sat behind the one desk in the room. "You have met Colonel Taimanov?"

"I met the Colonel this morning, Your Majesty."

It was Taimanov's turn to clear his throat.

"Yes. Well, you will understand," Alexander said. "That I was forced to act on the advice given to me. I am always forced to act on the advice given to me," he added, somewhat plaintively. "I am only glad that it has turned out well."

"What has turned out well, Your Majesty?"

"Well . . . Taimanov?"

The Police Colonel cleared his throat again. "You will understand that the deposition against you, and Mademoselle Cromb, was made by the man Fine."

Colin listened to Jennie's sharp intake of breath. "No, I did not know that, Colonel," he said. "Fine? You mean, David Fine, from Bolugayen?"

291

"That is correct, Your Highness."

"David Fine accused me, and Mademoiselle Cromb, of being in a plot to assassinate the Tsar?"

"Yes. This was a most serious accusation, as I am sure you appreciate, Your Highness, and it was absolutely necessary to act on the instant. His Majesty agreed to this."

"But I stipulated that there was to be no ill-treatment," Alexander said again. "At least until the charge was confirmed."

"Thank you, Your Majesty," Colin said. "May I ask if the man Fine volunteered this information?"

"Well, no, Your Highness. These people never do volunteer any information."

"I see. He was tortured into making a confession implicating Mademoiselle Cromb and myself?"

"He made a confession under interrogation," Taimanov said carefully.

"Which he has now withdrawn."

"No, no. He has not withdrawn his confession. He has, in fact, disappeared, and may well be dead. But in the course of our investigations, we arrested several more of these people, and confronted them with Fine's statement. I must confess . . ." – Taimanov flushed – "that they laughed. They denied that David Fine had ever been a member of the Will of the People. They said that he had attempted to join, but had been refused admittance, both because he was so young and because he was a hothead. As for his implication of you and Mademoiselle Cromb, they laughed at that too. We do not employ foreigners and princes to do our work, they said."

"And on the strength of that denial you decided to drop the charges against us?"

Taimanov's flush deepened. "Well, no, Your Highness. There were other factors."

"Tell me of these factors."

292

Taimanov looked at the Tsar. "Tell him," Alexander said.

Taimanov drew a deep breath. "As I say, these people, all of whom confessed to their membership of the Will of the People, and to their part in the plot to assassinate His Majesty, denied the implication of the man Fine. This struck me as unusual, and perhaps sinister. Because, Your Highness, Fine had not been arrested by my people. He had been arrested by a Cossack patrol, and had been taken first of all to their commander . . ." – another deep breath – "Colonel Dubaclov."

"Dubaclov!" Colin spat out the word. "Constantine Dubaclov?"

"That is correct, Your Highness. It was Dubaclov who interrogated him."

"Did you not interrogate him yourself?"

"I never saw him. As I say, soon after his interrogation and his confession, which he signed, he disappeared. You know what the Cossacks are like."

"By God," Colin muttered.

"Well, of course this was highly irregular. But I did have a signed confession implicating you and Mademoiselle Cromb. I had to act. Regretfully, Your Highness. But in view of the later depositions, I decided to take the matter up with Colonel Dubaclov. But the Colonel had already left St Petersburg." Again he looked at the Tsar.

"You know what women are, Prince," Alexander said, looking distinctly embarrassed. "They get carried away. It seems that your wife has, ah, been seeing this man Dubaclov." He paused. "Were you aware of that?"

"No, Your Majesty," Colin lied. "And I find it hard to credit. Dubaclov was once, briefly, engaged to be married to my wife's sister, Anna. I did not consider him a suitable husband for a Bolugayevska, and so, when I became Prince, I terminated the betrothal."

"Which is certainly a reason for him to hate you. And it would appear that he has suborned your wife.

293

Apparently he went to her with the story of what he claimed to have discovered, and she in turn went to the Countess Dolgoruka and my wife. They believed her. Well, why should they not have done so? The upshot of it was that they came to me, your wife in tears, Prince, telling me of her long years of mistreatment, of how you kept her virtually under lock and key and had given the management of Bolugayen to the Countess Anna, and begging for redress. She also convinced them, and they convinced me, that under the rule of yourself and the Countess Anna, Bolugayen has become a nest of sedition and rebellion, particularly in the Jewish village."

"So what did you do, Your Highness?" Colin asked, icy fingers closing on his heart.

"Well, Prince, you must remember that you were under arrest, guilty, as I was informed, of being party to the plot to assassinate me. Perhaps I acted hastily. I revoked your powers as Prince and gave them to your wife. I also issued an order for a pogrom to be carried out upon the Jews on Bolugayen." He sighed. "I am sorry."

"So the Princess left Moscow, with Dubaclov and his Cossacks," Colin said quietly. "Do you know, Your Majesty, that Bolugayen was the most peaceful, most happy and contented, estate in all Russia, when I left it?" If it was possible for the autocrat of all the Russias to hang his head, Alexander did so.

"It is worse than that, Your Highness," Taimanov said. Colin looked at him. "As I was saying, knowing that Dubaclov had been the one to take the confession from the man Fine, a confession now proved to be false, or even, perhaps, fabricated, I sought him out. And as he was not at his lodgings, it seemed obvious to seek him at the Bolugayevski Palace. In view of the gossip, you understand."

"But you say he had already left. With my wife."

"I am afraid so, Your Highness. However, I interrogated the housekeeper, Madame Anastasia, and the

294

butler, Oleg Penkarski, and both of them told the same story, of overhearing conversations between the Princess and Colonel Dubaclov in which the name Fine was mentioned, as well as yours and the 'Warsaw business'. The whole thing smacks of conspiracy. Especially with regard to the attempt on your life."

"Yes, it does," Colin agreed, and turned back to the Tsar. "Will you allow me to set matters right, Your Majesty? In so far as I can."

The Tsar gestured to the sheets of paper on the desk. "I have already had letters patent drawn up, entirely restoring your powers and prerogatives as Prince Bolugayevski, and discharging those issued to your wife. I have also had warrants drawn up for the arrest of Colonel Dubaclov, and your wife, if you feel it necessary, on charges of conspiracy to commit murder."

"Thank you, Your Majesty. May I ask when the Princess left St Petersburg?"

"Immediately she received her warrants. That is, ten days ago."

"Ten days. My God! You'll excuse me, Your Majesty. I must make haste."

Alexander frowned. "Are you strong enough to ride eight hundred miles? In the snow?"

"I will see to the Prince's health, Your Majesty," Jennie said.

Alexander looked at her for the first time. "I am sure of it," he said.

"But I will need support," Colin said.

"Colonel Taimanov?"

"I shall see to it, Your Majesty. I would request permission to accompany the Prince." Alexander raised his eyebrows. "This is a personal matter to me too, Your Majesty," Taimanov said. "I regarded Dubaclov as a friend. Now I feel that he has betrayed that friendship, for his own ends."

Alexander nodded. "Then fetch him back here. Now

295

leave us." Taimanov saluted, and left the room. "I wish you to know that I am very sorry at the way things have turned out," Alexander said. "I acted hastily. I wish your forgiveness for that."

"Your Majesty?" Colin was astounded. He had never expected to hear the autocrat of all the Russias apologise, to anyone. "There is nothing to forgive."

"To know that there are people, out there, waiting to kill you . . ." Alexander shuddered. "They will get me in the end, you know, Prince. I feel it in my bones."

"Your Majesty . . ." Again Colin did not know what to say. He dared not look at Jennie.

Alexander squared his shoulders. "But not today, eh? And you have much to do. I will wish you God speed, Prince. Is there anything more I can do for you?"

"Yes, Your Majesty. Pray that I reach Bolugayen in time."

The servants gathered outside the house to watch the Cossacks and the police ride out. The men had camped in the grounds of the Bolugayevski Mansion overnight, and the smoke from their fires still hung on the still air. Today was a fine one, with blue skies, but it was still very cold, and most of the ground was covered in snow; the troopers slapped their gloved hands together as they waited for their commanders. Dagmar came on to the porch with Vorontsov and Dubaclov. "I hope you are up to it, after such a busy night," she chided her lover.

"I have never felt more up to it in my life, Your Highness," he assured her.

"Which did you enjoy more? Fucking her? Caning her? Or just tormenting her?"

"They were all most enjoyable, Your Highness."

"Well, she will still be here when you come back. Now, don't forget. I wish Fine alive. I am going to hang him beside his son."

296

"Alive," Dubaclov promised, and mounted. "It should take about ten days for us to do the job and return."

"I shall be waiting for you."

Vorontsov kissed Dagmar's hand. "My people are at your absolute command, Your Highness. I have told Sergeant Bogatyrchuk this."

"Thank you, Colonel. I do not expect to need them."

She went up to the balcony above the porch to wave them out of sight. They looked splendid; forty Cossacks and twelve policemen. Both units wore grey-green coats and fur hats; carbines hung from their saddles, as did their whips and their swords; the Cossacks were also armed with lances, in boots behind their right stirrups. They were equipped for any eventuality. Not that Dagmar considered there would be much of a retaliation from a bunch of unarmed Jews. There were people on the road leading to the town, and these also stopped to stare at the military. Like all true Russians, they feared the Cossacks. And the police. They also hated them, Dagmar knew. But there was no one down there with the courage to take a stance against them. Nor would there ever be. She was determined.

There was a fresh disturbance from below her, and Yuri Yevrentko was marched out by Igor and several footmen. The tutor looked thoroughly dishevelled, his clothes hastily pulled back on to his body following his flogging. "Wait there," Dagmar commanded, and went down the stairs. Yevrentko trembled as she approached. She looked him up and down, then pointed to the two satchels standing on the floor beside him. "What are those?"

Yevrentko licked his lips. "My books and my clothes, Your Highness."

"Books? Open it." Igor hastily opened the bag. "Empty it," Dagmar commanded.

Igor upended the bag and several books, old but leather-bound and carefully preserved, fell to the floor.

"Your Highness," Yevrentko protested. "That is my livelihood."

"I take away your livelihood," Dagmar said, and kicked the books, which scattered across the floor.

"Your Highness!" Yevrentko screamed, and pulled himself free to drop to his hands and knees and scrabble after his library.

"Bind that fellow," Dagmar said. "And burn that rubbish. We'll have him suborning no more princely houses with his so-called learning." Yevrentko burst into tears as his arms were pulled behind his back and secured, and one of the footmen began gathering up the books. Dagmar stepped up to him, took his spectacles from his nose, dropped them on the floor, and stepped on them, listening to the crunching, splintering sound with a smile. "Now you will see only what you should see. Get him off my property."

Yevrentko was bundled down the steps to the waiting horses.

"I did not say he could ride," Dagmar said.

"But, Your Highness, he cannot walk to Poltava, in the snow," Igor protested. "He would freeze to death."

"Is that any concern of mine?" Dagmar inquired. "Very well. I am a soft-hearted ninny, I suppose. He may ride to the beginning of Bolugayen. But he will walk the rest of the way."

Igor opened his mouth as if he would have protested further, then thought better of it, and saw that Yevrentko was placed in the saddle. He mounted himself, signalled two of the grooms to accompany him, and the little party walked down the drive. As they departed, they passed Nicholas Smyslov riding up from the town. "Tell Monsieur Smyslov to attend me," Dagmar said, and went inside.

"Hunting in the winter has a special excitement," Mordecai Fine remarked, pulling his coat tighter round himself to resist the freezing air.

298

"But requires less skill," Shem Cohen suggested. "The tracks are too simple to follow in the snow."

"But the animals are more dangerous, because those that are not hibernating are hungry," argued Akiba Stein. The three men walked their horses across a wide field of shallow snow; they were close to home now. Each led a pack animal, and across the saddle of each of these there was the carcass of a wolf.

"What we need to remember," Fine said, "is that only seven years ago we were not even allowed to carry arms, much less hunt with them."

Cohen nodded. "It was a fortunate day when you visited the mansion and encountered the Prince."

"I think he would have been our friend anyway," Fine said.

Stein drew rein. They were at the foot of the last shallow hill before their village. Now he sniffed the clear, still winter air. "What is that smell?"

Fine sniffed also. "Woodsmoke. They have been burning rubbish."

"There must have been a lot of rubbish," Cohen said, and urged his horse forward, up the slope. At the top he drew rein, and waited for his companions to catch up with him. He made no sound, just stared down into the valley. Fine and Stein also stared, unable to believe what they were looking at, unable to accept the scattered, blackened timbers which were all that remained of what had once been their homes, the wisps of smoke which continued to rise from the still glowing wood. Fine kicked his horse and sent it floundering down the slope. The animal halted of its own accord as it neared the burned-out village. It was too cold for there to be any stench of death. But there was death in front of them: twelve male bodies, stripped naked and laid out in a row on the snow.

Fine slid from the saddle to look at them. They had all been castrated, but he guessed that nearly all the mutilations had been committed after death, for they all

299

also had gunshot wounds or sabre cuts to their heads and torsos. He stepped past them, and looked at the second row. These were females and children, also stripped. These too had been mutilated, and very few of these also carried wounds inflicted before their horrible deaths.

Cohen stood beside him, then uttered a howl and dropped to his knees: he had identified his wife. "Who can have done this?" Stein muttered. "Were they men, or beasts?"

Fine looked at the hoofprints in the snow. "They were Cossacks."

"But . . . the Prince would never have allowed this."

"The Prince is not here," Cohen said, getting to his feet. Fine had never heard such a tone before.

"You mean the Countess sent the Cossacks here?"

Fine walked down what had once been the village street. Here lay, scattered about, the dogs and cats which had been massacred along with their masters and mistresses. But there had been more than two dozen people in the village. He stopped before what had been the tabernacle. This too had been burned to the ground, and its timbers also still smouldered. But he stepped amidst the charred wood, and found what he was looking for – some twenty incinerated remains, including that of the rabbi. Clearly they had barricaded themselves inside, and the Cossacks had fired the place with them in it. Had they been the lucky ones? "All dead," Stein said. "All dead. Save us."

They looked back to where Cohen was remounting his horse.

"Where are you going?" Fine asked.

"I am going to kill whoever is responsible for this," Cohen said.

"With a sporting rifle? Or even three sporting rifles?"

"I will go with him," Stein said, returning to his own horse. "Will you come, Mordecai?"

Fine looked at the ruin around him. He was a man of peace. Under the benevolent rule of Prince Colin he had watched Bolugayen flourish as never before, watched his own people grow in stature and self-confidence. But now . . . This could only be the result of David's madness. With the Prince away, Anna must have succumbed to the pressures brought to bear by outside forces, and allowed the Cossacks to come in. In which case, she *was* guilty. But she had been his friend. Do I have any friends? he asked himself. David gone, if not dead, a fugitive for the rest of his life. My people destroyed. What do I have left save to kill in vengeance, and again and again, until I myself am killed. Even the Countess Anna. He walked back to his horse and mounted. "I am with you," he said.

"Anatole," Charles Cromb said. "Do you not remember me?" He spoke Russian; he had spent every spare moment over the past year learning the language.

"Your Excellency!" Anatole certainly remembered Charles. But he was uneasy, and glanced even more uneasily at the big sailor standing at Charles's shoulder.

"This is Silas," Charles explained. "The last time I arrived without a servant, remember? You guys seemed to be upset about that, so this time I thought there'd be no mistake. Aren't you going to let us in, Anatole?" Anatole opened the door, and the two Americans stamped into the hall, shedding snow as they did so. "I'll tell you, Anatole," Charles said. "We have had one hell of a journey up from Sevastopol. Now tell me what's been happening?"

Footmen helped them out of their coats, and Silas looked around him in wonder. The skipper had told him about this palace, but he hadn't really believed him. "Happening, Your Excellency?" Anatole asked.

"I got a letter from the Countess Anna, just before Christmas," Charles told him. "It had been written back in September, but things have been a bit confused Stateside. In the letter the Countess said there was some kind of trouble, involving my wife, and that I should be here. So I came as soon as I could, war or no war. Didn't seem much point in writing, as I can travel as fast as any letter. Trouble is, as I said, the Countess's letter was dated September, and here we are virtually in March. I want to know what's been happening."

"I do not know, Your Excellency." Anatole snapped his fingers and gave instructions in Russian, and a footman hurried off to fetch a tray of vodka and glasses. Anatole showed Charles into one of the downstairs reception rooms, and looked more uncertain than ever as Silas followed his captain; but at least the two men had taken off their caps.

"Anatole," Charles said. "It is my intention to go out to Bolugayen first thing tomorrow morning. But I wish to have some idea of what I'm going to. The Countess Anna wrote that she was taking Madame Cromb back home to Bolugayen. Now you tell me, are they there?"

The footmen arrived. Silas looked at the clear liquid with a puzzled expression, then lifted the glass and sniffed. "That is the damndest smelling rum I ever did see, skipper," he commented, in English. "Fact is, it don't smell at all."

"That's because it isn't rum, Silas. But it's still drinkable." Charles set his mate an example. "I asked you a question, Anatole."

"The Countess and Madame Cromb returned to Bolugayen last September, Your Excellency."

"So they are there now. Right. And there's been no trouble?"

"No trouble, Your Excellency. Well . . ."

"Give, Anatole."

Anatole licked his lips. "There has been no trouble, Your Excellency. But twelve days ago the Princess Dagmar came home. She spent the night here before going out to Bolugayen."

"And that's bad news, is it?"

"I do not know, Your Excellency. But the day after the Princess was here, a squadron of Cossacks came to

302

Poltava. They were also going to Bolugayen. They only stopped by the city to pick up some policemen. Colonel Vorontsov went himself."

"All to Bolugayen? That does sound like trouble. But I guess the Countess Anna must have sent for them. She's in charge there while the Prince is in Poland, right? That's what she put in her letter."

"I believe that is so, Your Excellency."

"I still think we should get out there as rapidly as possible. Have some horses arranged for us at first light tomorrow morning, Anatole." However much he was looking forward to seeing Alexandra again, and making sure she was all right, it was the thought that Anna was in Bolugayen while Colin was in Warsaw that was quickening his heartbeat.

Anatole looked as if he might have said something further, but changed his mind. Instead he looked towards the two footmen who were hovering in the doorway. The two men spoke to each other in such rapid Russian that Charles could not follow them, but he caught the name Yevrentko. "What's that?" he demanded. "Yevrentko is here?"

"He wishes to speak with you, Your Excellency. Apparently he saw you on the street."

"Then bring him in."

"Yes, Your Excellency. But . . ."

Charles went to the door, and the footman stepped aside to admit the man who was waiting at the front door. His clothes were torn and mudstained, his face was bruised, and twisted with pain and misery, and he looked half-starved. "Yevrentko?" Charles went to him. "Is it really you?"

Yevrentko fell to his knees. "Monsieur Cromb? Oh, Monsieur Cromb! Thank God I have found you."

"Anatole! Vodka!" Anatole signalled a footman forward, and Yevrentko drank greedily. "And I think you'd better lay on some food. Come to think of it, we could eat too." Charles himself gave Yevrentko a second glass of vodka, then assisted him into the sitting room. Anatole ordered the meal to be prepared. "Now tell me what happened to you?" Charles asked. "Where are your glasses?"

"The Princess smashed them, Your Excellency. She burned my books. My books!" His voice rose an octave.

"The Princess? Are we talking about the Princess Dagmar?"

"Yes, Your Excellency. She is a devil. A devil!"

"Calm down. What was the Countess Anna doing while all this was going on?"

"The Countess Anna! Oh, the Countess Anna!" Yevrentko buried his face in his hands and began to weep.

Colin refilled his glass. "Yes, the Countess Anna. You are not going to tell me that she stood by and watched her sister beat you up?"

"The Countess Anna is no more," Yevrentko wailed.

"What did you say?" Charles grabbed the schoolmaster by the lapels and jerked him to his feet. The vodka glass fell to the floor and smashed. Anatole signalled a footman. "You're telling me the Countess is dead?"

"No, Your Excellency, no." Yevrentko trembled. "She is locked up. Imprisoned. She has been caned, raped, debauched, by order of the Princess."

"By God!" Charles released him, and Yevrentko slowly sank back into his chair. Charles could feel every part of his body tingling with fury. "What about my wife?"

"I do not think she has been ill-treated, Your Excellency. But she is also locked up."

Charles nodded. "You say there are Cossacks and policemen on the estate? Doing Dagmar's bidding, I'll bet."

"Yes, Your Excellency. But . . ."

Charles had turned to face Anatole. "Where do you stand in this, Anatole?" Anatole looked more embarrassed than ever. "You'd better pick the right side,

304

Anatole," Charles said, "because, when the Prince comes home . . ." Anatole cleared his throat. "Give," Charles commanded.

"The Prince has been arrested, Your Excellency. By order of the Tsar."

"I cannot believe that."

"It has been in the newspapers, Your Excellency. And the Princess confirmed it when she was here. The Prince was involved in a plot to kill the Tsar, and he has been arrested, along with Mademoiselle Cromb. They are saying he will be hanged."

It was Charles' turn to sit down.

"Looks like a tricky business, skipper," Silas commented. "Long odds if we can't get no help."

Yevrentko raised his head. "The Cossacks have gone on," he said, now also speaking English. "They left eleven days ago. The day I was thrown out to starve. I have starved, monsieur. For ten days on the streets of Poltava, begging . . . and then I saw you . . ." He began to weep all over again.

"There's food on its way," Charles assured him. "But you say the Cossacks have gone? Gone where?"

"They were to carry out a pogrom against the Jews. Most of the police went with them, and Colonel Vorontsov. There are only four policemen at the house. But they will be back, any day now."

"Then whatever we're gonna do, we'd better do it now. What about the people in the town?"

"They hate the Princess. Given the lead . . ." Yevrentko gulped.

"This legal?" Silas asked.

Charles gave a savage grin. "No. We'd be starting a revolution. You game?"

"I'd like to know what you're aiming to do."

"Well, I'll tell you, Silas." Charles stood up again. "It doesn't look as if I can do anything about my cousin, except make diplomatic representations and pray they're in time. But I reckon I can do something about my wife and sister-in-law." He kept his voice even with an effort. "So you and me'll pay Bolugayen a visit. I mean to go there, collect my wife and the Countess Anna, and then get the hell down to Sevastopol and rejoin the ship."

"Can we make that, skip?"

"I believe we can."

"What about these guys?"

"Only these two know what we're planning. The rest don't speak English. But you do, don't you, Anatole?"

"I will say nothing, Your Excellency."

"I believe you, Anatole. And I'll tell you why: you're coming with us."

"Me, Your Excellency? In the snow? I am too old, Your Excellency."

"You look in great shape to me, Anatole."

"The Princess will crucify me if I help you."

"Maybe. Trouble is, I'm gonna crucify you if you *don't* help me, and I'm the one in the chair, right? Don't worry about your future; I'll give you a job in the States. The two countesses will appreciate having a Russian butler about the house."

Anatole commenced to shiver almost as vigorously as Yevrentko. But Yevrentko now stopped shivering. "I would like to come with you, sir."

"You?"

"The Princess treated me like a dog, sir."

"There's a point. But can you see without your specs?"

"I won't let you down, sir."

"Okay. Seems like we have ourselves an army, Silas. Let's go."

"We'll need weapons, skipper."

"Silas, this house is full of weapons. Just choose your poison."

Dogmar went to Alexandra's room, and Alexandra scrambled off the bed where; she had been lying, fully dressed.

306

"What was that screaming?"

"Anna having hysterics."

"You have been torturing her again."

"My dear Alix, I have not yet begun to torture her. I am indulging her in what she likes best, whoring. I may well get around to torturing her when Constantine gets back. I look forward to that."

Alexandra drew a deep breath. "I would like to visit David Fine."

"Your lover?"

"He is not my lover. But, yes, I wish to visit him."

"To see if he still has his balls? Or to have some fun with him? Come along, then." Dagmar went down the stairs, listening to the rustle of her sister's skirts behind her. "You may say he is not your lover, but do you know that the rascal had the temerity to declare his love for you?"

"He does love me," Alexandra said.

"Well, well." Dagmar opened the door leading down to the cellars. One of the footmen hurried forward, but she waved him away. "We do not want to be interrupted." She went down the steps. "Has he fucked you?"

"Of course he has not."

"You are so chaste," Dagmar said contemptuously. "Or is it just that he did not have the opportunity. Would you like to fuck him?"

"You are nauseating," Alexandra said.

"Be careful, little sister," Dagmar recommended. "Or you may find that I can be very nauseating indeed." She opened the door to the meat cellar, and Alexandra gave a little gasp. David Fine hung from one of the meathooks. He was naked, his body a mass of bruises and lacerations. His head hung, and he scarcely seemed to breathe. He had a fortnight's growth of beard.

"What have you *done* to him?" Alexandra screamed.

"Very little, as yet. Just tickled him up a little."

"But . . . he's dead!"

"No, no. Look." Dagmar went to the barrel of water

307

which stood against the wall, dipped the ladle, and threw some water into David's face. His head jerked, and he gave a little shiver. His eyes opened, and he blinked at his tormentress. "There, you see," Dagmar said. "And he is fed two square meals a day. I want him to be fully aware of what is going on. Especially when he is hanged. Now, what shall we do today, David?"

David Fine inhaled, and his head half-turned as he realised there was someone else in the room. Then he saw Alexandra, and he gave a little moan, and closed his eyes again. "He thinks you have abandoned him," Dagmar said. "Well, you have, haven't you, my dear? What would you like to do with him? Would you like to castrate him? It can be such fun. I castrated Vassily, you know, with a piece of wood. It could have been one of those very pieces of wood there. Bring one to me."

Alexandra looked at the staves, leaning against the wall.

"You are going to scream, as you have never screamed before," Dagmar told David. "And do you know, your screams are going to grow higher and higher."

Alexandra wrapped her fingers round the length of wood, drew a long breath, and brought it down on Dagmar's head with all of her strength.

Dagmar did not utter a sound; her knees gave way and she struck the floor with a thump. "You have killed her!" David gasped.

Alexandra knelt beside her sister. She felt not the slightest remorse. Hitting Dagmar was something she had dreamed of doing ever since she could remember, since Dagmar had first caned her. But when she put her head next to Dagmar's breasts she could hear the irregular thumping of the heart.

"No," she said. "But I will." She reached for the stake again.

"No," David said. "You cannot kill your own sister."

308

Alexandra looked up at him. "You can ask for her life, after what she has done to you?" She stood up and against him on tiptoe, to release his wrists. When she did so, he fell to his knees beside Dagmar.

"Why did you do this?" he asked.

"To save you."

"But . . . you will be in terrible trouble."

"I will not be here. Neither will you."

"But . . ."

"Listen, do as I say. Help me."

Between them they raised Dagmar to her feet, and David held her against him while Alexandra carried her wrists above her head and secured them to the meathook. "She'll scream the place down," David said.

"No, she won't." Alexandra lifted Dagmar's skirt and tore strips from her petticoat. These she rolled into a ball and stuffed them into Dagmar's mouth. Dagmar was beginning to regain consciousness now. Alexandra tore another strip from her petticoat to bind the gag into place. When she was finished she was panting, but Dagmar was helpless, although she could move her legs; her toes just reached the floor. David Fine watched in amazement. "Now listen," Alexandra said. "I am going to go upstairs and fetch some clothing for you to wear. I will tell the servants not to come down here. I believe they will obey me, but if any of them does come down, you must hit them on the head. Right?"

David gulped. He had never hit anyone on the head in his life. Alexandra held his arms and shook him. "It is them or us, David. You must understand that."

He nodded. "I do not understand why you should risk your own life to save me."

"Silly boy," she said. "I will be back in ten minutes." She looked at her sister, who was now fully conscious. Dagmar's eyes were rolling and she was trying to stamp her legs and making shrilling sounds through the gag. "If you want to beat her, you do it," Alexandra said. "Or you

309

can fuck her if you like. After what she has done to you, you can do anything you like to her."

"You people frighten me," David said. "I don't want to do anything to her. I don't even want to look at her."

"Ten minutes," Alexandra promised. She went up the stairs, closed the cellar door behind her. The footman waited patiently in the hall. "Listen, Paul," Alexandra said. "The Princess bid me tell you that under no circumstances is she to be disturbed. Do you understand me?"

"Yes, Your Excellency."

She went first of all to Dagmar's apartment. She knew where everything was, had no difficulty in finding Dagmar's jewels and money. There was enough comfortably to finance a journey to Sevastopol and then a voyage to America.

She crammed everything she regarded to be of any value into a large satchel, and was turning to leave when she saw the pearl-handled revolver. She had no idea Dagmar owned a revolver. She picked it up and broke it – it was fully loaded with six bullets. She put that in her satchel as well. Then she hunted through Colin's wardrobes.

David and Colin were about the same height, and although Colin was by far the heavier man, the clothes would be an adequate fit, especially concealed under a greatcoat. She hurried along to her own apartment. As she past the door to Anna's apartment she hesitated. Should she take Anna with her? But Anna would wish to take command, run things. Anna was just too strong! She would have to find her own salvation. Anyway, there were people in there; Alexandra could hear the maids chattering as they cleaned the rooms. And she couldn't possibly wait for them to finish.

She returned to her own apartment, and dressed in the warmest clothes she had, adding a heavy coat and gloves, drawing thick boots over her stockings. Then she filled another satchel with some changes of underclothes; she'd be able to buy anything she'd forgotten in Sevastopol before they put to sea. And then? She was going to her husband. With David? Charles was a kindly man. He would understand about David.

That they had travelled together, as man and wife, for several weeks? They would have to travel as man and wife. She didn't know if she loved David. But she wanted to *be* loved by David. All of her life she had wanted to be loved, adored, by someone, and there had never been anyone other than David. And besides, as she had probably saved his life, he would love her even more desperately. Charles would understand.

Alexandra put the revolver in her coat pocket, slung the two satchels over her shoulder, and went downstairs, where the footman remained on duty. "I told you that the Princess does not wish to be disturbed, Paul," she said.

"But this is my post, Your Excellency," he protested.

"I am telling you to go away," Alexandra said in her most imperious tones. The footman hesitated, then bowed and left the corridor. Alexandra ran down the stairs, where David was waiting anxiously. Dagmar glared at them both, her eyes seeming almost about to pop out of her head. "Get dressed," Alexandra told David. She stood in front of her sister. "You will give yourself a seizure, if you keep that up," she said. "You should count your blessings. I told him he could do whatever he liked with you, and he refused even to touch you." Dagmar hissed through her nostrils. "Well," Alexandra said, "I suppose someone will be down here eventually. But not for a while. Goodbye."

Dagmar tried to kick at her, but was hampered by her skirt. David was now dressed, looking decidedly baggy, but he would be warm; that was the main thing. "Drink this." Alexandra held out the vodka bottle. "It will give you strength." David gulped at the drink, and Alexandra led him to the stairs. "Pull your hat well down over your eyes," she said. "And leave the talking to me."

311

She led him up the stairs and and marched towards the porch, beckoning David to follow her. Two of Vorontsov's policemen sat in the porch. Both stood to attention as they saw the Countess. "Good afternoon," Alexandra said. The men looked at her, and then at David. "Well," Alexandra said. "Open the door."

One of the policemen immediately opened the door. The other remained at attention, but he spoke. "The Princess Bolugayevska gave us instructions that no one was to leave the house, Your Excellency."

"Well, she has given me permission to leave," Alexandra said. "You may ask her, when next you see her." She went down the steps, David at her shoulder.

"Your Excellency," he muttered. "This will not work."

"It *is* working," she told him. "Just stay at my shoulder." He followed her round the building to the stables, where there was only one groom on duty. No one was expected to be going out on a winter's afternoon; it would be dark in half an hour. "Saddle my horse," Alexandra commanded. "And Countess Anna's." They were the two best, she knew. The man goggled at her. "Hurry up," Alexandra snapped. "Or I shall have you whipped."

"I was told . . ."

"I am telling you," Alexandra said, twitching her crop.

He hurried off, and Alexandra stamped up and down.

"Where are we going?" David asked.

"In the first instance, Poltava. Then we will ride south, for Sevastopol. From there we will take ship for America."

"America?"

"My husband is there. I am going to my husband." She stood against him and touched his cheek. "And you will come with me."

"Your Excellency . . ."

"You may call me Alix, if you wish."

"Alix." He spoke the word as if it was the key to great happiness.

312

"You may kiss me, if you wish." He hesitated, looking down on her face, then slowly lowered his face to hers. They did no more than brush their lips together, before the groom cleared his throat. "Thank you, Olaf."

He gave her a leg up, and she settled into the saddle. David mounted beside her. She touched her horse with her heel, and he walked out of the stable into the gloom of the late afternoon . . . and faced Sergeant Bogatyrchuk, marching across the snow towards them, accompanied by the third of his constables. "Good evening, Sergeant," Alexandra said courteously.

"Your Excellency! May I ask where you are going?" Like everyone else, he frowned at David, trying to decide whether this well-dressed man was indeed the prisoner brought from St Petersburg.

"For a ride." She touched her horse again, but as the animal moved forward, Bogatyrchuk caught the bridle. "Whatever are you doing?" she snapped.

"With respect, Your Excellency, but the Princess Bolugayevska gave me instructions that no one was to leave the grounds."

"Well, she has given *me* permission," Alexandra declared. "Stand aside."

"With respect, Your Excellency . . ."

"Stand aside, or I shall ride you down," Alexandra shouted, again kicking her animal. But the sergeant, a big man, retained his hold on the bridle so that the horse slewed round and Alexandra was all but unseated. "David!" she screamed.

David urged his horse forward, and its shoulder struck Bogatyrchuk on the back. The sergeant fell to his hands and knees. "David, is it?" Bogatyrchuk gasped.

"Ride," Alexandra shouted, and David urged his horse out of the yard.

"David, by God!" Bogatyrchuk said, getting to his feet, and drawing his revolver to level it at David.

"Never!" Alexandra cried, drawing her own revolver,

and firing it. She had never used a hand gun before, and was amazed at how easy it was. At a range of only a few feet she could not miss. Bogatyrchuk uttered a shriek as the green of his greatcoat became stained with red, and fell forward on to his face. The policeman drew his own weapon, and Alexandra sent two shots in his direction. She did not know whether she had hit him or not, but he tumbled over, and then she too was out of the yard and spurring for the gate.

David wheeled his horse as she rode towards him. He saw Sergeant Bogatyrchuk sprawled on the ground, and realised that Alexandra had probably killed him. He saw the policeman slowing rising to his knees. Then he saw a flash of light. The man was firing at him. "Ride!" Alexandra screamed. "For God's sake, ride."

Her own mount was charging out of the yard, hardly under control. He kicked his horse and galloped behind her. They clattered on to the drive and a few moments later were through the gates. "Free!" Alexandra shouted. "Free!"

She turned her horse on to the road towards Poltava. To either side the snow was thick on the fields, but the road itself was reasonably clear. David urged his horse forward to reach her side. "Your Excellency," he gasped. "Alix! We cannot gallop, all the way to Poltava."

She drew rein. "They will follow," she panted.

"Not for awhile. We have a good start."

She glanced at him, then walked her horse up the road. He stayed at her shoulder. "Listen," she said. "In my satchel there is money and jewels. Enough to take you to America."

"You mean, to take us."

"No," she said, "not me. You." She tumbled from the saddle.

Chapter 16

THE WILL OF
THE PEOPLE

It was already dark by the time Charles, accompanied by Silas, Anatole and Yevrentko, left Poltava. Charles was in no hurry. His blood still boiled at the thought of what had happened to Anna, and might be happening to her at that very moment. He meant to rescue her, but to do that he needed to catch the rest of Bolugayen unawares, and that was best done after they had all gone to bed. Thus it was past ten when they reached the estate boundary. Here they drew rein, to take a swig of vodka each – it was bitterly cold – and to listen, and prepare. "Check your weapons," Charles said.

Once everything was found to be in good order, they moved forward again. There was not a sound to break the stillness of the night, until two horses appeared out of the darkness, their hooves unheard because of the snow. But only one had a rider, who had now seen them, and promptly levelled his right arm. "Stand aside, or I shoot!"

Charles frowned as he recognised the voice. "David Fine?" he asked. "I am Charles Cromb."

"Monsieur Cromb!" David urged the horses forward. "Oh, Monsieur Cromb!"

"I heard you were on the run from the police," Charles said.

"Monsieur Cromb!" David's voice had become a wail. "The Countess!"

He was now very close, and for the first time Charles realised there was something draped across the saddle of the second horse. "The Countess!" He slid from the saddle and ran forward to raise the head which drooped against the horse's flank. "Oh, my God!" At the same time knowing an unspeakable surge of relief that it was not, as he had feared, Anna.

He dragged his wife from the saddle, and laid her on the ground. The other men had all dismounted, and now stood around. But no one was going to bring Alexandra back to life: the entire lower half of her habit was soaked in blood. "What happened?" Charles asked in a low voice.

"She was helping me escape," David said, "The police tried to stop us, so she shot two of them. Then one of them fired at us. I did not know she was hit. She did not say anything. She just fell from the saddle. They did not follow. I do not know why."

Silas knelt beside the dead woman. "She sure looks like a countess," he said reverently.

"She was my wife, Silas," Charles said. Silas gulped. "Put her back across the saddle," Charles said. "And tie her there securely."

"You are going on, Your Excellency?" Anatole asked.

"Of course I am going on, Anatole. If I cannot save, I can at least avenge. You, David, what of the Countess Anna?"

"I do not know, Your Excellency. I believe she is locked up somewhere in the mansion."

"And the Princess Dagmar?"

David licked his lips and hastily drew his sleeve across them to prevent the saliva from freezing. "We left her tied up in the cellar."

"You did, by God. Well, we had better get down there before she frees herself."

"You mean to go back to the house?" David asked.

"That's right."

"There is nothing but death down there."

"And I aim to do a little more in that line," Charles said. "You don't have to come."

David hesitated, then turned his horse beside Charles's. "I loved her, Mr Cromb. I wish the bullet could have struck me, instead."

"I believe you, David," Charles said. "Let's get the fellow who fired it."

Igor Bondarevski looked up from his cup of tea in irritation. He was not on duty until six, and it was only four. "What are you saying?" he demanded.

"It is simply this, Igor. The Countess Alexandra and the man Fine have left the house," said Paul, the footman.

"Eh? You mean the Princess has sent them away?"

"That is what I do not understand," Paul repeated. "The Princess went down to see the man Fine at three o'clock. I was on duty in the hall then, and she spoke to me. But the Countess Alexandra was with her." Igor frowned. "Then she came up alone," Paul explained.

"The Princess?"

"No, the Countess. She told me the Princess was not to be disturbed. She sent me away."

"Why did you not tell me this then?" Igor demanded.

"I wished to discover what was happening. So I waited, and watched. And the Countess went back into the cellar, with clothes and bags, and a few minutes later she returned, with the man Fine, and they left the house."

"When was this?"

"Not five minutes ago."

Igor scratched his head, and wondered where his wife was: he felt sadly in need of advice. He had, indeed, been in a state of constant confusion ever since the return of Dagmar. Then he heard shouts, and shots.

"Quickly!"

They ran outside, while servants appeared from everywhere. "The Countess!" Olaf bellowed from the stable. "She has gone mad! She has shot the sergeant!"

"She has shot me too," the constable protested. He was lying on the ground. "But I think I shot her back."

"You did *what*?" Igor's mind was reeling.

The other two policemen had also appeared. "We must go after her."

"Yes," Igor said. "No . . ." he chewed his lip in indecision. If she had shot the sergeant, it was a criminal business, and no amount of foreign nationality was going to save her from the gallows. His Alexandra! He had always considered her so. But if she had been hit . . . on the other hand, he had only this lout's word for it. "I must speak with the Princess," he decided.

The policemen exchanged glances; they had been in Bolugayen long enough, even if it had been less than a fortnight, to understand how afraid of the Princess woman the servants were. "Then make haste," one of them said.

The other bent over his stricken comrade. "Are you all right, Feodor?"

"I am hit," Feodor said. "I am bleeding."

"Bring him into the house," Igor said, and led the way.

In the porch he met the female servants, led by Madame Rospowa. "What is happening?" Eudoxia Bondarevska demanded.

"I wish I knew," Igor grumbled. "But the Countess Alexandra is in bad trouble."

"And the Countess Anna is upstairs, ringing her bell and calling to be let out."

"Where is the Princess?" Madame Rospowa inquired.

"I will find her," Igor decided. "Where is Dr Fine?"

"Do you not remember? He went over to the Jewish village."

Igor had forgotten. "Then may God have mercy on his soul," he muttered. "Send to the town. Get Monsieur Smyslov, and Father Alexei. We have big trouble on our hands."

He went to the head of the cellar stairs, and hesitated.

318

He could hear the thumps of Anna attempting to summon attention, but as long as Dagmar lived, she was the one to fear. He lit a candle from one of the wall sconces, went down the steps, and opened the door to the meat cellar. He held the candle above his head to peer at his mistress. Dagmar stamped on the floor. Her eyes were bloodshot with rage. "Mmmmmm!" she shrilled at him from behind the gag, pulling on her arms; her wrists were chafed from her desperate attempts to get free.

Igor stared at her. He had it in his power to end it now. He could cut her throat, or drive a knife deep into her belly and watch her die. And then . . . *but* then! Alexandra was gone, a fugitive murderess. And that devil Dubaclov was coming back. There would only be Anna. She might have sworn to kill her sister herself – but would she be able to forgive a servant who had done it for her . . . and this particular servant?

Better the devil he knew than the devil he feared. He reached up and released the gag, put his fingers into Dagmar's mouth to pull out the rolled silk. "Water," Dagmar gasped. "For the love of God, water." Igor went to the butt and held the ladle to her lips. She gulped at it. "Now get me down."

He licked his lips. "It will be necessary to lift you from the floor, Your Highness."

"Then do it, fool."

Igor took a deep breath, and stood against her. He put his arms round her waist, hugged her and lifted. Her cheek was against his. "The cord is only looped over the hook. If you could move your arms upwards, Your Highness," he gasped.

"Then lift me higher, fool," Dagmar snapped.

Igor clasped his arms under Dagmar's buttocks; his chin scraped her breasts as her silk-clad body seemed to slide up his. She gave a convulsive jerk, and her hands came free. Igor overbalanced, but as he fell back he retained his grip on her so that he was underneath to break the

319

force of her fall. Dagmar rolled over and sat up. "Free my hands," she commanded. Igor obeyed.

"When I catch hold of that little bitch . . ."

"She has gone, Your Highness."

"Gone? Did not the policemen stop her?"

"They tried, Your Highness, and the Countess shot two of them. Sergeant Bogatyrchuk is dead, and one of the constables wounded. Then she and the man Fine rode off." He decided against telling her that Alexandra might have been hit.

Dagmar was staring at him. "Alix did that?" she asked.

"I am afraid so, Your Highness. The policeman and Olaf both saw her."

Dagmar tried to get up, and overbalanced. Hastily Igor caught her and held her up. "It is all going round and round," she muttered. "Why did you not send after her?"

Igor had considered his reply to that question. "I did not know where she had gone in the dark. Besides, Your Highness, I considered it more important to find you."

"You are a faithful fellow, Igor," she said. "Help me up the stairs." Igor put his arm round her waist and assisted the Princess up the steps. "What is that banging?" she asked.

"It is the Countess Anna. She will have heard the shots. She wishes to be let out."

"I will see to her later," Dagmar said.

"I have sent for Monsieur Smyslov," Igor said brightly. "And Father Alexei."

Dagmar snorted. She wasn't sure she wanted outsiders, and especially the priest, in the house until she had decided what to do about Alexandra. She strode into the hall and gazed at the policeman Feodor, and the anxious faces about him. "He is very badly hurt, Your Highness," Eudoxia Bondarevska said, her expression registering her amazement at the sight of her mistress: never had she seen Dagmar Bolugayevska so dishevelled.

"Have you stopped the bleeding?"

"We have bandaged him up, Your Highness. But the bullet is still in there, and he is still bleeding. He needs a doctor, but Dr Fine is not here."

"Dr Fine will never be here again," Dagmar told her. "This man will have to manage for tonight. Tomorrow we will send into Poltava for a doctor. And more police."

"I hit her," Feodor muttered. "I know I hit her."

"What did he say?" Dagmar looked at Igor.

He bit his lip. "He thinks one of his bullets struck the Countess Alexandra, Your Highness."

"My sister?!" Dagmar's voice rose an octave. "And you did not send after her?"

"The Countess Alexandra is guilty of the death of a policeman, Your Highness. I felt the decision should be yours."

They gazed at each other. Then Dagmar's face hardened. "I wish a search commenced, tomorrow morning at first light," she said.

"Your Highness, that is twelve hours away. If the Countess is wounded, in the snow, with temperatures below freezing . . ."

"Yes," Dagmar said.

Dagmar had a leisurely dinner. Dubaclov should be back tomorrow. She smiled into her brandy as she sat by the fire after the meal. She looked forward to Dubaclov being back. He was, as Anna had said, out of the gutter – but he was such an earthy man. "Your Highness." The footman Paul stood by her chair. "There are horsemen approaching."

"Dubaclov and Vorontsov! They are back early. Thank God!" Dagmar ran into the porch, and the doors were opened for her. "Constantine!" she shouted. "Thank heavens you have come back!"

"Not Constantine, Princess," Charles Cromb said. "Nemesis."

*   *   *

321

Dagmar peered into the darkness, for a moment not recognising the voice. Then memory returned to her, and she uttered one of her shrieks before turning and running back into the house. "The police!" she shouted. "Where are the police? Bring your guns!"

The policemen came hurrying out, but Charles and his companions had already dismounted and were in the porch. The policemen, armed only with revolvers, faced four rifles. "Shoot them down!" Dagmar screamed, from the stairs.

"Drop your guns, or you are dead men," Charles said.

The policemen unbuckled their gunbelts. "You are cowards!" Dagmar shouted. "You have betrayed me. Be sure Colonel Vorontsov will know of this. Igor, summon the servants . . ." She began to pant, because just about all the servants were already assembled, and none of them was moving to her support.

"Igor," Charles said. "The body of Madame Cromb is outside. Will you have your people bring it in, please?"

Igor hesitated only long enough to work out to whom he was referring, then gave the instructions. Dagmar came slowly back down the steps. "Alexandra? She is dead?"

"Shot by one of your goons, Princess. Now, where is Anna?" Dagmar tossed her head. "Well," Charles said. "I can figure it out for myself."

He watched Alexandra's body being brought in, her face so pure and beautiful in death. "Have you no tears for your wife?" Dagmar sneered.

"Have you no tears for your sister, Princess?"

Dagmar glared at him, then looked at David Fine, who was unashamedly weeping. "You have brought that *thing* back here?"

"Careful, Princess. I've told him he can have a go at you, if he wants."

Dagmar took a step backwards. "You would not dare."

"Sure I would. Trouble is, he doesn't even want to touch you."

Charles faced Igor. "Igor, old friend, I don't want to cause any trouble. I came here for the two countesses. Seems I can't take Alix anywhere. But I sure mean to take Anna. Now, you just don't interfere, and nobody's gonna get hurt. Start something, and you're gonna have a lot of burying to do when I leave. Savvy?"

Igor looked at Anatole, and received a quick nod. "You, I am going to boil in oil," Dagmar told Anatole.

"You'll have to do a bit of travelling first," Charles said. "Well, Igor."

"We will not try to stop you, Your Excellency," Igor said. "But I must warn you that Monsieur Smyslov and Father Alexei are on their way here now."

"Thanks. Silas, you and Anatole stay here and arrest them as they come in. David, you may not like to touch the Princess, but I'm putting you in charge of her. Go stand behind her, put your gun muzzle in the small of her back, and if anyone, anyone at all, makes a move you don't like, blow her in two. Right?"

David thrust the gun at her. "Do as the Captain says, Your Highness. Because I will willingly do as he says." Her body jerked, and her face twisted, but she made no sound.

Charles ran up the stairs and along the gallery. The key was in Anna's lock, and he turned it and threw the door inwards. She was naked and there were bruises on her body, and her hair, far from being in a neat chignon, was a tangled mass on her shoulders. "Charles?" she whispered.

"Oh, my dearest girl!" He took her in his arms. "There is no need to speak."

"Do you know anything?"

"I know everything, my darling."

She pulled her head back to gaze at him. "But, Alix . . ."

323

"Alix is dead. Shot by one of Dagmar's policemen."

"Alix? Oh, poor darling Alix! But Charles . . ."

"I hope you will forgive me for uttering a prayer of thanks that it wasn't you."

"You came for *me*?"

"I came for you both. But I will take you, certainly. If you will come."

She looked up at him. "You have heard about Colin?"

"Some."

"We cannot desert him, Charles. I cannot desert him."

"Come with me, and once you are safe, I will do all I can to help him. You have my word."

Slowly she freed herself. "And your reward?"

"I'm not looking for a reward." He forced a grin. "You're family now. By helping Colin, I'll be helping Jennie. If she can still be helped. If not, well . . . there is nothing for me here, save you."

Anna sat down. "What about the children? We cannot leave them here, to Dagmar."

"Okay. We'll take them with us. The two boys, anyway."

"To America?"

"They'll like America," Charles said. "So will you."

She shot him a glance. "Where is Dagmar?"

"Downstairs."

"I wish to kill her. And Dubaclov!"

"Yeah. Well, you might have to join the queue. Listen." He knelt beside her. "I know what she had done to you. I know how much you must hate her. But you'd hate yourself more, in the end, if you killed your own sister. As for what happened, I don't give a damn, save for what you suffered. I only want to see you yourself again, to see you smile." He squeezed her hand.

She gave him another glance. Then she said, "I must get dressed."

He nodded. "Warmly. And pack a satchel of clothes for changes. We're gonna have to travel pretty far, pretty fast, to be safe. No time for shopping, eh?" He squeezed her hand again, then put his arm round her shoulders to hug her as she stood up.

She gave a faint smile. "The tables are turned, are they not? You are in command, now."

"I wish I were just a little more in command. Now hurry." He stepped outside, closing the door behind him, and saw Silas coming up the stairs.

"Sorry to interrupt you, skipper. But there's a lot of people coming up the drive."

"People? From the town, you mean?"

"These are mounted."

Charles ran along the gallery to the corridor leading to the balcony above the porch, and saw the Cossacks riding into the front yard of the palace, together with the police. "Holy shit!" he muttered. "What about the priest and Smyslov?"

"They never showed up. I guess they're with that lot."

"Right. The doors must be closed and bolted. And the shutters."

"We did that," Silas said. "But say, there's about fifty of them, and they have carbines."

"And there are only five of us. But maybe we can raise a few more. And we have shelter." He ran down the stairs.

"Well," Dagmar remarked. "Now you are going to hang." She looked around her at the servants. "All of you."

"You heard the lady," Charles said. "But the Countess Anna is in charge again now. She'll be down in a moment. Who'd you guys rather fight for?"

Dagmar snorted. "That isn't going to work, Captain Cromb. My prerogatives were restored by order of the Tsar. My people know that. To disobey me means to disobey the Tsar. They all know the consequences of that."

Charles looked over the faces in front of him, saw the indecision there. They would fight for him, or at least for Anna, if they could. But they were too afraid. He sighed. "Okay. Everyone into the cellars. Everyone. Take the wounded man with you."

They hurried to obey, happy to be relieved of all responsibility. There came a bang on the door. "What's happening in there? It is I, Dubaclov. Open up."

Anatole and Yevrentko, standing by the door, looked at Charles. "Constantine!" Dagmar shouted. "They have me a prisoner. Storm the place!"

"You do that, Colonel, and the Princess dies," Charles called.

"By God, but who is that?" Dubaclov cried.

"We've never met," Charles said. "But Vorontsov knows me. I am Captain Charles Cromb, and I am the husband of the Countess Alexandra. Now clear off, and take your men with you."

They listened to a muffled conversation outside. "Do you think you can get away with this?" Dagmar demanded.

"I reckon it's worth a try. Come on, you guys, down you go." He herded the staff to the cellar stairs, watched them go down, and frowned; there was no sign of Igor. If that little bastard was up to his tricks . . .

"You know there is no hope for you, Cromb," Vorontsov called. "Lay down your arms, free the Princess, and I will have you deported. Fail to do so and you will be hanged."

Charles looked up the stairs, at the head of which Anna was standing. She had dressed herself very carefully, wore a heavy fur over her habit, and had even managed to control her hair, which she had tucked out of sight beneath her fur hat. "Ha!" Dagmar remarked. "Where do you suppose you are going?"

"Seems we have a choice, Your Excellency, between fighting or surrendering," Charles explained.

"I will not surrender again," Anna said. "Even if I am hanged beside Colin."

"Right." Charles looked around him. "David, I am

326

going to need every man. Help the Countess Anna secure the Princess."

"Where?" Anna asked.

"To the bannisters. We want to keep her in the centre of things. Now, Silas, will you take the window beside the door."

"Aye-aye, skipper."

"Yevrentko, the right hand drawing room."

Yevrentko, face pale but determined, nodded.

"Anatole, are all the doors at the back secured? Check them out, and then take up a position there. Where is Igor, by the way?"

"I do not know, Your Excellency."

"Well, make sure he's up to no treachery." He stood above Dagmar. David had made her sit on the floor and bound her wrists behind her and to the lowest upright of the staircase.

"You are mad," Dagmar said. "Do you really suppose you can hold this house against fifty professional soldiers?"

"We'll have a go. Upstairs, David. You and I are going to pick them off."

"I can shoot," Anna said.

"I know." He gave her a revolver. "But I want you here, with her."

Anna looked at her sister. "Oh, yes," she said. "If they break in, she will be the first to go."

"What is happening?" Olga had appeared, wearing a nightgown, her hair in plaits.

"Where are the children?" Charles asked.

"They are in bed. But . . ."

"Go and stay with them. No matter what you hear, stay with them."

Olga looked at Anna, and then at Dagmar. "Do as he says," both sisters said together. Whatever their personal differences, neither wished to have the children in the middle of a gun battle.

Olga hurried off. Charles ran up the stairs behind her, David at his heels. As they reached the gallery, Dubaclov called out. "You have had time enough, Monsieur Cromb. If you do not surrender, now, my men will storm the house. Should anything happen to the Princess, everyone inside will hang."

Charles went to the windows overlooking the porch, waved David to one side, and checked the priming on his rifle. It was now past midnight, and the night was utterly dark. Yet the horsemen were still grouped on the drive, the two colonels having obviously not yet made up their minds how best to carry out their attack. Beyond the drive and the trees he thought he could see lights. Those had to be in the town, which would have been awakened by the return of the Cossacks. Although . . . as he remembered it, the town was further off than that. It really was a quite desperate situation, he knew. Especially if Dubaclov used all his assets. As he was now doing, for there came the clip-clop of hooves, and straining his eyes in the darkness Charles could see a group of about a dozen horsemen making their way round to the rear of the building. "If they attack from the back as well as the front . . ." David muttered.

"We could well be overrun. You'd better get down there and help Anatole."

David stood up, and hesitated. "Are we going to die, Mr Cromb?"

"Seems a possibility," Charles agreed. "But we should take a few with us."

"This is your last chance, Mr Cromb," Dubaclov called . . . and was arrested by the sound of more hooves.

"Who is that?" Vorontsov shoutd in Russian. "Stop those men."

They were clearly not Cossacks. "Open fire!" Charles shouted, and squeezed his trigger. There was a scream and the man fell from his saddle. From the lower floor there came three shots, and another man fell. The Cossacks were looking both ways, while the hoof-beats grew louder, and now three horsemen burst through them, firing fowling pieces loaded with scatter-shot as they did so. Horses neighed and reared, men fell, and there was general pandemonium. "Silas!" Charles bellowed. "Let those fellows in."

The front doors crashed open as the men hurled themselves from their saddles, and then crashed shut again as they entered. But by now the Cossacks had recovered sufficiently to return fire, and Charles, running back to the gallery, saw that one of the new arrivals was on his hands and knees, blood running down his legs on to the parquet. Anna was already at his side, while Charles recognised another of the men. "Dr Fine!" he shouted. "By all that is holy, but it is good to see you. How many men do you muster?"

"What you see, Mr Cromb. Those devils," Fine panted. "They have destroyed my people."

"Arm yourself," Charles told him. "And you, sir."

"Shem Cohen, Your Excellency. They killed my wife."

Charles nodded. "We'll avenge her." He looked at the man on the floor, who had now fallen flat. Rolled over by Anna, careless of the blood staining her fur coat, he could be seen to be dead.

"Abner Stein," Fine said. "Your Excellency . . ." Then he looked up, as David ran into the hall.

"Father!" Father and son embraced.

Charles looked at Dagmar. "You sent the Cossacks against that village?"

"I was empowered to do so by the Tsar!"

"May the Lord have mercy, both on you and your Tsar."

"That woman?" Cohen asked, and stood above her, hands opening and shutting.

He was distracted by a fusillade of shots. "Quick, douse all the candles," Charles commanded. "Dr Fine, you and your son join Anatole at the rear." He himself went to the front windows to be with Silas and Yevrentko. Bullets were splattering against the walls, some getting through the windows to shatter the glass, but he understood that Dubaclov, as a professional soldier, would know better than to imagine he could gain a victory by shooting. And as he took up his position, he saw the Cossacks again surging forward.

"Fire!" he shouted, and the four rifles exploded together. Two men fell, but some thirty threw themselves from their saddles and came running up the steps, sabres drawn. There was no time to reload, but Yevrentko, Silas and Charles each had a revolver, and these they fired into the mass of men hurling themselves at the door. To do this, however, they had to throw up the shattered windows, and now they themselves came under fire, and Silas fell with a shout of agony, while bullets whined into the hall. "Lie down!" Charles bawled at Anna, and she dropped to her knees, while Dagmar began to scream very loudly as lead whistled past her and thudded into the stairs.

But the concentrated fire had its effect, and the Cossacks tumbled back down the steps, now leaving seven of their number lying on the verandah. "They'll be back," Charles panted. "Reload." He knelt beside Silas. "How bad, buddy?"

"God, I dunno," Silas grunted. "But I can still breathe, eh! Gimme back my gun."

Charles reached for it, and was alerted by a sudden light coming out of the pantry. He reared back on his heels, desperately pushing bullets into the chambers of his revolver, and saw Mordecai Fine and David, together with Anatole, being forced into the hall by Vorontsov and his policemen, who carried candles as well as guns. "Drop your weapons, Mr Cromb, or these men die, and you with them," Vorontsov said.

"I am sorry, Mr Cromb," Fine said. "They were too many for us. But we are prepared to die."

Charles bit his lip. But there *were* too many policemen. He would die, and so would Anna. He looked
left and right. Yevrentko was trembling; he had never
supposed they would succeed. Cohen was silent, his face
closed, like that of a statue. Only his eyes gleamed
hate. But he too knew that they had lost. "Charles!"
Anna said.

He did not know if she was commanding him or
imploring him. But the revolver was drooping from her
own fingers. Then it came up again, and she turned to
her sister, fiercely. "No!" Charles shouted. She hesitated, and Vorontsov ran forward and wrenched the
gun from her hand. "Not your own sister," Charles
said.

"You do not *know*!" Anna said. Her knees gave way,
and she sat on the step.

"Vorontsov!" Dagmar shouted. "Cut me free. And have
those doors opened."

Vorontsov signalled one of his men to open the front
doors, and himself released the Princess. She stood
up, seeming to ripple from head to toe, as Dubaclov
stamped into the hall. "Four of my men are dead," he
snapped. "And five more are wounded, two seriously.
These dogs . . ."

"Do not fear, Constantine, you shall have the hanging
of them," Dagmar said. "Line them up. Her too. How
lovingly he holds her," she sneered. "But you saw,
Vorontsov! She was armed with a pistol. That is open
rebellion against me, the Princess Bolugayevska, and thus
against the Tsar in whose name I exercise my authority.
Do you not agree?"

"I would say that you are absolutely correct, Princess,"
Vorontsov said.

"Well, then, much as I regret having to condemn my
own flesh and blood, she shall hang beside these other
criminals. Dubaclov, bring your dead and wounded inside.
The wounded must be tended to. The dead will have to

331

be buried in the morning. Now . . . what is that dreadful noise?"

All their heads turned to look out of the front doors, through which the Cossacks were bringing their stricken comrades.

"There are a great many people coming up the drive, Your Excellency," said the Cossack sergeant. "From the town, I think."

"They have been aroused by the shooting," Dagmar said. "Well, that is not surprising. I shall speak to them."

She went towards the porch, and Dubaclov nodded to half a dozen of his men to follow her, as he did himself. Vorontsov followed. Charles felt Anna move against him, and looked down. "If they could but be given the lead . . ." she whispered.

But the same thought had occurred to Dagmar, who checked in the doorway. "If any of the prisoners attempts to make a noise," she said. "Hit him." She looked at her sister. "Or, her. Very hard." Anna swallowed, and Dagmar stepped outside. It seemed nearly all the town was there, a vast mob gathered on the forecourt, trampling down the flower bushes, surging across the lawns. "What is the meaning of this?" Dagmar demanded. "Smyslov? Have you gone mad? Father Alexei? I am surprised at you, associating with such riotous behaviour. Send these people home immediately."

"We seek justice, Your Highness," Igor said.

Dagmar peered into the darkness. "Igor? By God! You are going to hang, Igor, and your wife and children beside you. Colonel Vorontsov, arrest that man." Vorontsov signalled four of his policemen forward, and the crowd moved, a ripple through the ranks. Vorontsov hesitated, and looked at the Princess. "This is rebellion," Dagmar said, loudly. "Very well, Colonel Dubaclov, do your duty."

Dubaclov summoned his Cossacks in turn, and they filed on to the verandah, carbines thrust forward. "Igor

Bondarevski is under arrest," Dubaclov said. "If anyone attempts to interfere with the police, my men will fire into you. Colonel Vorontsov, do your duty."

The Police Colonel led his men down the steps. Again the crowd rippled. "If you let them take me, you are less than men!" Igor shouted. "They are perhaps sixty; we are more than two thousand. How many of us can they kill? Rush them."

The crowd hesitated. It was the age-old fear of authority, of the omnipotent power of these people who represented the Tsar, the most omnipotent of them all. To hasten their decision there came a series of clicks as the Cossacks cocked their pieces. "Igor Bondarevski, you are under arrest," Vorontsov said. "For sedition and incitement to rebellion against your legally constituted Lord, and for being a member of the outlawed organisation known as the Will of the People."

Those standing to either side of Igor shrank away from him. Igor's shoulders slumped. "Cowards," he muttered.

Charles looked down at Anna. Her face was as stoic as ever, but a tear had escaped her right eye and was trickling down her cheek, something he had never expected to see. "He had sworn to save me," she muttered. There was nothing he could say, as Igor was dragged forward and up the steps.

"Now," Dubaclov called. "You people will disperse back to your homes, and pray that your lady Princess does not seek to punish you for your ill behaviour."

"Not Smyslov," Dagmar said. "I want him in here. With his wife."

"Monsieur Smyslov," Dubaclov called. "You'll come into the house. With madame."

He checked at the sound of a bugle call. Every head turned to the drive.

Dagmar went to the top of the steps to peer through the darkness at the troop of mounted men which was coming down the drive. Then she uttered a shriek. "No! It cannot be! Dubaclov, arrest that man. No, shoot him down! He is a wanted criminal!"

Dubaclov also peered into the gloom, slowly making out the big man who led the horsemen, the woman riding at his side, and then, to his greater consternation, the man riding immediately behind him. "Taimanov?" he muttered.

"Are you just going to stand there?" Dagmar demanded. "That man is . . ."

"The Prince Bolugayevski," Colin said. "Despite your machinations, my dear." He gave Jennie a hand down.

"You . . ."

"I have a warrant for your arrest," Colin said. "And yours, Dubaclov. Vorontsov, I assume you were hood-winked into this. You will have to answer charges, but for the time being I command you to withdraw your men and leave my property." Vorontsov look at Dubaclov. "If you do not comply," Colin said, "immediately, Colonel Taimanov's regiment of Okhrana will forcibly disarm you. That goes for your Cossacks as well, Dubaclov. Command them to lay down their weapons."

Dubaclov drew a deep breath. There was no one in Russia, not even a Cossack, who was not terrified of the Okhrana. "You'll not desert me, Constantine," Dagmar begged.

"I have no choice, Princess."

"You wretched bastard!"

"Lay down your arms," Dubaclov commanded. With a clatter, the Cossacks laid their rifles on the verandah floor.

Anna freed herself from Charles' arms and went on to the verandah herself. "Well, big sister," she said. "How are the tables turned, yet again. You and I have much to discuss. But first . . ." She stooped, picked up one of the discarded revolvers, and before anyone could grasp what she intended, levelled it at Dubaclov's groin and fired. Dubaclov gave a scream of agony, and then fell to the floor, clutching at his blood-stained crotch. Anna fired a second time, into his chest.

For a moment no one moved, then Dagmar uttered one of her great shrieks, and leapt over the verandah rail to the ground beyond, ran past the men nearest her, and swung herself into the saddle of Colin's horse, riding astride.

Everyone gaped at her in consternation as she kicked the horse and sent it galloping down the drive. Anna raised her gun again, but Charles caught her wrist. "After her!" Taimanov shouted, and several of his men wheeled their mounts.

"Wait!" Colin snapped. The men checked. "She is my wife," Colin said. "I'll trouble you for your horse, sergeant." The sergeant looked at Taimanov, received a nod, and dismounted. "No one is to follow," Colin said, and rode down the drive.

"I will have a horse as well," Charles said, running down the steps.

"His Highness commanded . . ."

"But I am not subject to His Highness's commands," Charles retorted, vaulting into an empty saddle.

"Charles!" Anna called. "Be careful!"

He gave her a wave as he followed the Prince down the drive, drawing rein at the gate, where Colin had also halted, listening.

"What the devil . . . ?" Colin demanded.

"She caused the death of my wife," Charles said. "Not to mention what she had done to Anna."

Colin shot him a glance, then pointed. "That way."

Dagmar had taken the road towards the town rather than that to Poltava, on which she knew they would overtake her readily enough. Once past the town she would have all of Bolugayen on which to hide, although what she hoped to achieve, out in the snow and the freezing air, without food or weapons or even a heavy coat, was difficult to determine.

In any event, she had first to reach the town, and to do that she must pass through the mass of her people, trailing back to their homes. These parted for her, instinctively, as they heard her hoof-falls on the snow. Colin and Charles, topping the rise behind her, saw her gallop between them without a sideways glance. But then her horse stumbled in a pothole beneath the white blanket, and went down. Dagmar came out of the saddle on her feet, still holding the reins, and turned with an exclamation of anger, tugging at the bridle. The horse did not respond, and now she was surrounded by people. "Help me!" she shouted.

"It's the Princess," someone said. There was a moment of silence, then a great moan rose from the people, and there were more and more of them now, hurrying to swell the crowd around her.

Charles would have urged his forse forward, and Colin reached across to grasp his bridle. "By Christ, man," Charles said. "They hate her."

"They have hated her for a long time," Colin said.

Charles stared at him in consternation, then looked along the road. "Bastards!" Dagmar was shouting, and now she swung her riding whip. The crowd around her moved back, like a molten body, and then moved forward again. "Bastards!" Dagmar screamed again. "Let me pass!" There was another moan, and the people closed around her. Again Charles would have urged his horse forward, but Colin's hand remained fast on his rein.

"My God, man," Charles shouted. "She is your wife!"

"She is a devil from hell," Colin said. "And we cannot help her now, anyway."

Charles gazed into the darkness. He heard Dagmar scream, again and again and again. But then she fell silent, carried off to whatever fate the people she had terrorised for so long had in mind for her. He had to cough, to clear his throat of saliva. "What will you do?" he asked.

Prince Bolugayevski wheeled his horse. "Reverse her destruction, if I can."

"A tragic business," the Tsar said. "A princess, torn to

pieces by a mob . . . and such a beautiful woman. My God, my blood runs cold at the thought of it. And you were unable to discover even the ringleaders, Prince?"

"Would you have had me execute every man in Bolugayen, sire? Every child and every dog? The priest?"

"You are sure they were not inspired by the Will of the People? Vorontsov has indicated that it was their doing, in his report."

"I do not believe it was a conspiracy, at least on the part of the people of Bolugayen, sire," Colin said carefully.

"And yet, they must have hated her, so much. As they hate me, Prince."

"I am sure that is not so, sire. They wish to love you. But . . ."

"Say it."

"They still feel there is much injustice. That a woman like my wife, or the police, can do so much harm in such a short space of time."

"How may I rule without the authority of my *boyars*, of my police? What would they have me do?"

Colin took a deep breath. "Perhaps, if it were possible to give the people, some of the people, the *tzemstvo*, for instance, some semblance of power . . ."

"A parliament, you mean, as you have in England?"

"Well . . . some form of assembly, of representation, so that they could make their views known . . ."

"Hm. Something will have to be done. I mean, Madame Cromb . . . that really is tragic." Alexander raised his head. "You say this American fellow is marrying her sister?"

"I think he is being very gallant, sire. You will understand, that after what my sister-in-law had to suffer at the hands of my wife, she no longer felt it practical to remain on Bolugayen."

"Still, a Russian countess, off to a place like America . . . and what of you, Prince? Your wife dead . . . Of course, I suppose she would have faced the death penalty

337

anyway. Like Dubaclov. But really, to be shot in . . . well . . ."

"As you have said, my sister-in-law merely anticipated the death sentence, Your Majesty. You have the report of what she suffered at that man's hands."

"Yes. And as she is leaving the country anyway . . . what of your Jewish people?"

"I intend to rebuild that community, sire, with the aid of Dr Fine and his son and Mr Cohen. And this time guarantee their safety."

"You will do that, Prince? But your entire family is destroyed."

"Not so, sire. I still have my sons and my daughter. And, with your permission, I would like to marry again."

The Tsar raised his eyebrows. "Do you require my permission to marry, Prince?"

"The lady is, or was, shall I say, sire, of some importance to each of us."

Alexander gazed at him, for several seconds, then laughed. "By God! You swore she had never been your mistress."

"She never was my mistress, Your Majesty, until after you had discarded her. Now I would make her my wife. With your permission."

"You have it, by God. You have it. Take her, Prince." He winked. "I wonder what Vorontsov will make of that?"

Charles was nervous. As Anna could tell. "I shall be a good wife to you," she promised, as they stood at the rail of the ship, Charles' ship, watching the rooftops of Sevastopol fall astern.

"I want you to know that I understand what a turnabout it will be, from being mistress of Bolugayen to plain Mrs Charles Cromb," he said.

She smiled. "You promised I could break a champagne glass every day."

"And so you shall. But . . ."

"No bathing naked in rivers, and no fucking whoever takes my fancy, and no shooting men in the balls. I shall be content, sir, to obey your every wish."

He could never tell when she was mocking him. He held her hands. "And have you no regrets? The boys? Colin? Bolugayen?"

She took them in reverse order. "Bolugayen is a place of horror, for me, now. Colin? We both wanted things, desperately, and we could both only achieve what we wanted by acting in total unison. He has what he truly wanted, now. In every way. Jennie will make him a much better wife than I ever could, simply because she is a much better person than I could ever be." She looked up at him. "Does that frighten you?"

"It excites me. And the third?"

"I wanted Colin to give me a son. He did not manage to. But you will, I know."

He hugged her. "He will only be plain Charles Cromb junior. Not the Prince, or the Count, Bolugayevski."

"Will he not be the happier for that?" she asked. "Besides, I am sure he will meet his cousins, one day. Now let us go below and see how Silas and Anatole are getting on."

EPILOGUE

Catherina Dolgoruka remained Tsar Alexander's mistress for the rest of his life; when, in 1880, the Tsarina died, Alexander married her in a secret ceremony.

Two years later, influenced by the more liberal of his *boyars*, the Tsar gave permission for a constituent assembly for all the Russians. On the same day, 13 March 1882, he was assassinated by a bomb tossed into his lap as he drove through the streets of St Petersburg. The Will of the People claimed responsibility.

When the Tsar's personal effects were sorted, there were found a huge collection of female nudes, drawn by himself.